A Glimpse

of Freedom

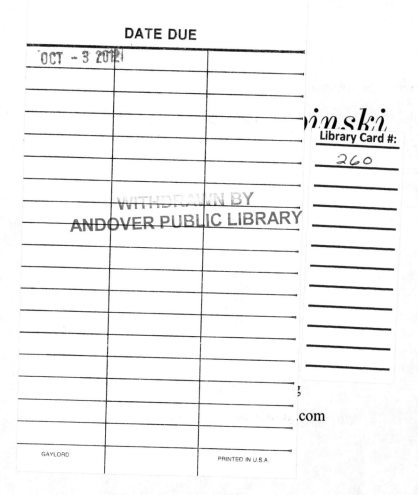

inski

Library Card #:

260

.com

The final approval for this literary material is granted by the author.

First printing

This is a work of historical fiction. Apart from the well known actual people, events, and locales that figure in the narrative, all names, characters, places, and incidents are the products of the author's imagination or are used fictitiously. Any resemblance to current events or locales, or to living persons, is entirely coincidental.

ISBN: 978-1-61296-030-2

PUBLISHED BY BLACK ROSE WRITING

www.blackrosewriting.com

Printed in the United States of America

A Glimpse of Freedom is printed in Times New Roman

Acknowledgments

It is virtually impossible to write a book without having countless individuals in your corner, all of whom simply cannot be named. However, there are a few that deserve my special thanks. First, Ray and Dawn Iram and Dan Horne, whose suggested edits – and over 20 years of friendship – are amazingly appreciated. To my Mother, who for nearly 50 years now has insisted that I was capable of absolutely anything. To my three children, Matt, Alex, and Nick, who have provided the motivation to make them as proud of me as I will always be of them. And finally, to my beautiful wife, Wendy, who has never wavered from her support and encouragement to follow my passion. You have taught me more about myself and the world than I can ever hope to repay.

This book is dedicated to the memory of my Father, Raymond Shupinski. While you may not be here to see this final result, your spirit echoes throughout the pages. I love you, Dad.

PROLOGUE

July, 1777. It has been over two years since the American Colonies and Great Britain have been at war, and just over a year since the Americans have officially declared their independence.

During that time, there has been a series of increasingly bitter and bloody battles, most of which have taken place in either the Boston area, or in and around New York City. Until recently, the Americans have demonstrated their almost complete lack of preparedness to fight an experienced and powerful army and, as a result, have lost virtually every battle they have fought.

General George Washington has been named the Commanding General of the newly formed Continental Army, and has been tasked with the overwhelming responsibility of creating a cohesive and effective fighting force out of a group of citizen soldiers. It is a job that has proven to be more difficult than he could have ever imagined, and on more than one occasion his army has nearly disintegrated due to battle losses and desertions.

But as 1776 has come to a close and 1777 has dawned, two amazing victories at Trenton and Princeton, New Jersey have provided the Americans with a brief but significant flush of success. George Washington has been presented with an opportunity to actually establish an army.

But this opportunity may be fleeting. General William Howe has decided to take his army of British and Hessian soldiers on the attack. He has determined that it is time to once and for all crush the rebellion that has been festering throughout the colonies.

THE SPY
JULY 6, 1777
NEW YORK CITY, NEW YORK

General George Washington had approached several of the young officers in his army, asking them to consider volunteering for a sensitive assignment. He had explained to each of them that they would be responsible for gathering information from the British army located in nearby New York City using "alternative" methods, as compared to more traditional observation and scouting parties.

General Washington had gone on to admit that the Americans were in critical need of knowing the next move of the British army under General Howe. Some of the American generals speculated that they would move south to Charleston, South Carolina, while others believed the move would be north to link up with another British army located in upstate New York.

Lieutenant Samuel Colburn had never even stopped to consider the dangerous nature of his choice as he had almost immediately raised his hand to volunteer. Perhaps if Washington had uttered the term "spy", Samuel might have analyzed his decision in a different light – however, most likely not. Like many young men, he was supremely confident in his abilities, and had complete dedication to the importance of the Cause.

Samuel had been born and raised in New York City, and knew the back streets and alleys as well as anyone. He knew the various establishments throughout the city that were most likely to attract the likes of British "gentlemen", as well as many of the less respectable areas that would serve the carnal needs of these same individuals. It would be these areas that Samuel would prowl in search of information on the enemy.

—

It had been nearly six weeks since Samuel had received his assignment, and until last night it had been an exercise in futility. Night after night spent in pubs and taverns throughout the city, secretly listening in on conversations among the British soldiers and sailors that frequented these establishments on a regular basis, had yielded nothing but an insight into the dissatisfaction these men had for their leadership and their overall lot in life. But grumblings and complaints were of no value to a man looking for clues about the future plans of the British army.

But the night before had yielded something different. Two British officers had been sitting in a back room of Cheevely's Pub, secure in the confidentiality of their conversation. They had no idea that the seedy looking character at a nearby table was anything other than what he appeared to be – just another drunk killing his pain with cheap alcohol.

"So, it looks like we'll be leaving the city soon, eh?" the first officer had commented. "I must say, I'm going to miss the hospitality of some of the residents!"

The two men laughed at the joke, and took another pull from their mugs of beer as they settled more deeply into the cushioned chairs at the table. Most of the pub had only hard wooden benches, but the officers had wasted no time in demanding more luxurious accommodations upon their arrival. The owner, afraid of any retribution for not complying with their wishes, had chased two regulars from their seats and provided them to the Brits.

"Ay, that's a fact," said the second officer. "I may have missed the Wench back home, but these here are much more agreeable – not to mention cheaper in the long run!"

The two men laughed, and Samuel was sickened by the callous nature of their comments. Samuel had been married just over two years, and he and his wife were expecting their first child in just a few weeks. The fact that these men were referring to their respective wives as little more than liabilities made him sick to his stomach, and it further reinforced his decision to join the American army and fight for the Cause.

"I'm told in two days time we'll be setting sail for the Chesapeake Bay. Admiral Howe has all of his sailor boys ready to go, and it should be a fairly quick trip down south. Have you heard anything on where we'll be dropped off?"

"Nah, the Old Boys at General Howe's headquarters have their lips sealed tighter than a duck's arse. Even some of the inner staff members have been kept out of the know," said the second officer. "I'm wondering if the whole thing might be some kind of a trick to head up north and meet up with Gentleman Johnny Burgoyne."

"I think not," responded the first officer. "Some of the other officers were talking about Burgoyne and how much General Howe can't stand the bastard. Even if that was the right thing to do, Howe would rather lose the war than help out the likes of that man. Either way, we best have our boys ready to go by tomorrow, or there will be hell to pay. Howe may take forever to make a decision, but when he does, he wants it to happen right away. I'm heading back to camp and getting a decent night's sleep before all Hell breaks loose in the morning."

As the two men stood up to leave, one of them glanced in the direction of the "drunk" sitting in the corner. Samuel realized too late that he had been staring at the men, his mind focused on hearing and remembering what was being said.

"What're you looking at, you filthy bastard?" asked the first officer, addressing Samuel. "Don't you have enough manners to avert your eyes from two of Her Majesty's finest officers?"

"Beggin' yer pardon, sir," Samuel stuttered, suddenly uncomfortable with the situation. "I was merely admiring the fine quality of your uniforms. I meant no harm, sir."

"I'll bet not," snapped the second officer, "but a lesson in proper etiquette is clearly in order."

Alcohol and arrogance were a bad combination, and the two officers quickly descended on Samuel, one of them kicking the chair out from under him. As Samuel fell heavily to the floor, a small metal object slipped out of one of his pockets and rolled out into the middle of the room.

"Well, what have we here?" said the first officer, retrieving the item and giving it a quick examination. It took the man all of five seconds to recognize it as a small, retractable telescope. "Well now, my good fellow, why would a disgusting ingrate such as yourself carry a telescope? What possible use could you have for such a peculiar item?"

"Please sir," Samuel pleaded, thinking quickly, "I swear I didn't steal that! I found it down by the docks! I thought I might be able to make myself a bit of money by pawning it tomorrow. Please don't take it from me, sir!"

To the misfortune of Samuel, the two officers were neither completely drunk nor completely ignorant. They looked at one another briefly, and then back at the man lying on the floor in front of them.

"What do you think, Dick?" the first officer said, addressing his partner. "I believe this wretch is a bit too good of an eavesdropper, and a bit too bad of a liar."

"Agreed, Reggie," replied the second officer. "It might be best to have some of the boys back at camp talk some more with this lad. Have that sorry excuse for an innkeeper get us a length of rope to insure this maggot behaves himself."

—

Samuel was awakened rudely as two British soldiers entered the tent armed with muskets and roughly grabbed him, shoving him unceremoniously through the flap and into the blinding sunlight. He was marched a short distance through the British camp until he and the two soldiers had reached a structure that was set off a short distance from the main encampment.

As they had walked through the encampment Samuel had surveyed his surroundings, carefully noting the numbers of cannon, horses, and supplies that populated the area as far as he could see in every direction. This, along with what he had learned from the conversation between the two British officers, would be invaluable information to General Washington.

Samuel had not only been amazed by the sheer size of the British camp, but the conditions he observed had been impressive to say the least. While the status of the Continental Army's camp could only be described as disorganized, primitive and, in some places downright filthy, the British camp appeared to be a model of efficiency. The cannon were lined up in precise rows, with all of the necessary support gear carefully bundled beside each gun. Weapons were stacked neatly outside of every tent, each of which had been erected in rows as precise as those of the cannon. Dozens of small structures had been built throughout the camp, and Samuel guessed that these housed the other supplies and ammunition, keeping them safe from the elements. The horses were housed in small, fenced in areas that were, embarrassingly, somewhat cleaner than the troop quarters of the Continental Army.

Samuel pondered the fact that, up to this point, his captors had made no attempt to shield him from observing everything around him. If the British had any clue about secrecy, they obviously wouldn't allow just anyone to gather such significant visual intelligence, and then simply release him for all the world to hear his story. As Samuel reflected on these facts and their implications to his situation, for the first time he felt the cold chill of fear.

Samuel guessed that he was currently facing the living quarters of some higher-ranking officer. His guess was quickly confirmed as a British officer wearing the rank of colonel emerged, almost elegantly, from the structure.

"Ah, I see that I have the pleasure of being in the company of our American spy," said the colonel with a sneer.

"Oh now Colonel, sir, you've got me all wrong," Samuel said in his best British accent. "Like I was tellin' those gentlemen last night, I'm a bit flattered that you would consider me a spy I must say, but I'm afraid I'm no more than a man who likes his drink a bit too much, and his labor a bit too little..."

"Silence!" commanded the colonel. His countenance had changed quickly from one of derision to one of anger. "I'll hear none of your insubordinate babbling! Are you not aware that you are addressing a colonel in His Majesty's army? You will speak when commanded to do so, and at no other time. If you find yourself incapable of holding your tongue, I shall gladly have one of these men drive his bayonet from one side of your throat through to the other. That should solve any talkative tendencies, eh?"

"Ay, sir," was all Samuel could respond, as his fear had changed from a cold chill to an almost paralyzing weight on his body.

"Now, then, let's take this pig to the tribunal for judgment and sentencing."

Judgment and sentencing? Already? Samuel was certain that he would at least have a few days to create a reasonably believable story. They were going to try him for any number of offenses, and he might very well find himself getting flogged within an inch of his life. He had no delusions that any beating he might receive would be anything short of brutal, and he started to physically shake at the prospect of what his near future might hold. Suddenly, Samuel realized that his willingness for gathering information might not have been the best idea of his life.

—

The tribunal, held in a roped off area located a short distance from the British camp, consisted of three British officers made up of two majors and a captain. They asked a few simple questions of Samuel that bordered on being trivial. Where was he from? Where did he live currently? What was he doing in the pub last evening? Samuel had carefully devised answers to these questions that were straightforward and totally believable. He began to relax, thinking that perhaps this was nothing more than a display to scare him and bring some cheap thrills to the British.

"Now, you Rebel slime," one of the British majors addressed him, "we have just one final question before we reach a verdict and pass sentencing on you. Are you, by any chance, acquainted with this gentleman?"

From behind him, a man slowly walked in front of Samuel and faced him. Standing before him, dressed in a British officer's uniform, was Lieutenant Corby Wallingford of the American Continental Army! Not only did Samuel know this man, but at times they had actually shared a tent while in camp!

Samuel could feel his face turn a deep red, and was barely able to stutter, "Why, no sir, I don't believe I've had the pleasure."

"Haven't had the pleasure?" Wallingford said with a wicked smile. "Come now, Lieutenant Colburn, surely our friendship has been more memorable than that. I mean, together we've shared the hardships of life as a Rebel soldier! Please don't tell me you've chosen to block such – 'noble endeavors' - from your mind completely!"

Wallingford's voice was virtually dripping with sarcasm and disdain as he spit the words at the young American officer.

The other British officers of the tribunal laughed loudly, and even the British soldiers serving as guards smiled at the obvious predicament in which Samuel now found himself.

Lieutenant Corby Wallingford had served as an officer in the Continental Army almost from the very start of the war. He had fought adequately at several of the early skirmishes against the British, but Samuel had personally noted that his attitude toward the American cause had slowly begun to deteriorate. The other junior officers had noticed as well, and they began to speculate that Wallingford wouldn't be around for long.

Finally one morning about four months ago, the other officers had awakened to find Wallingford gone along with his personal belongings and his horse. Everyone had assumed that he had simply had enough of army life, and was returning to his home outside of Philadelphia. No one had even briefly considered the possibility that he would join the British army, in the capacity of an officer, no less!

Samuel was speechless, any possible response being clearly ridiculous in the face of his situation. As this fact slowly dawned on him, Samuel began to feel a strange calm born of defiance and pride.

"Noble endeavors, indeed," he said quietly. "To spend time in the service of my country has truly been the greatest honor of my life. And I feel nothing but pity for you Wallingford, for having had the opportunity to experience something truly significant; yet turn your back to become nothing more than a lap dog for these scoundrels. I will gladly receive any beating you choose to deliver, knowing I have done what is right."

"Beating?" one of the British majors exclaimed. "For God's sake, man, did you think we were going to beat you over this? What kind of brutish beasts do you think we are? We have absolutely no intention of a whip ever touching your back. Why, you treasonous bastard, we're going to hang you!"

—

The drums beat a slow rhythm as Samuel was led blindfolded through the British camp. He could hear the jeers and taunts of several British soldiers as he made his way toward what he now knew to be the end of his short life.

"You there, slimy whore, it seems you'll have nothing for your troubles but the bite of the rope around your neck, eh?' one man called out.

"Well, thank ye, now, for providing us some entertainment on what would have been a rather dull morning," shouted another, followed by his hateful laughter.

But what confused Samuel was what he sensed rather than heard. He could feel the presence of many soldiers – hundreds, perhaps even thousands – that were all around him. And he realized that for every soldier that was shouting a profanity or insult at him, there had to be countless others that were simply watching in silence as he was led past. If forced to explain it, he could not have; yet he felt a heavy shroud of *sorrow* emanating from the large crowd around him. Although he may have predicted many reactions from his enemy in this situation, he would never have believed that this would be the most profound. Samuel was shocked to sense that what he felt was – respect.

After a short walk, Samuel was halted as the drums ceased their beating with a flourish. He could almost taste the fear in his throat like bile, and he fought the urge to retch. He was forced to make an about-face, and several hands pushed and lifted him until he was standing atop some kind of stand or stool, perhaps three feet above the ground. At that point, he felt a noose being placed around his neck, and he knew he had but a few precious seconds left of life. Along with this realization came a resignation to his fate, and his fear slowly dissipated.

"Lieutenant Samuel Colburn," a deep voice stated, "you have been tried and found guilty of treason and espionage against the British Empire. For this crime, you are sentenced to be hanged until dead. Do you have any final words?"

Samuel could hear the chirping of birds in nearby trees in the otherwise thick silence, and felt the breeze blowing across his face. He thought of his young, beautiful wife, and of the child she was carrying that he would never see. But once again, he was surprised that his feelings were not ones of grief, but rather an overwhelming sense of pride for what he had been part of, if only for a short time. He felt a sensation that he was sure no other man could possibly feel; that what he had done was amazingly significant. The realization made him smile.

"Ay, that I do. I die knowing that my family, and the next generation, and the next, will tell my story with a heart bursting with pride. And they will tell that story as citizens of a free country. There is nothing that those of you here can do to stop that from becoming true."

He paused, and took a deep breath. "Noble endeavors, indeed."

With that, the stand beneath him was kicked away, and he fell quickly toward the ground.

Private William Devlin
July 29, 1777
Chesapeake Bay

The creak of timbers continued their steady rhythm in time with the now gentle swells of the bay. Outside of the cramped confines of the troop quarters, the shrill sound of hundreds of seagulls had become nothing more than background noise to the British soldiers who had now spent over five weeks on board the HMS Spitfire.

Five weeks had seemed more like five years to the 256 men jammed into an area no larger than the modest dining hall of their previous accommodations in New York City. The smell generated by so many men in such a small space caused even the hardiest of souls to dread their time below decks, and they looked for every excuse and opportunity to go topside and take advantage of the clean, salty air of the Maryland coast.

For the first few weeks of the meandering voyage, there was the virtually constant sound of men puking. This, combined with the heavy odor of excrement produced by so many men, made life a living hell. However, after this much time on board the ship, the men had either developed a tolerance to the motion, or they no longer ate enough to generate much more than occasional retching.

Private William Devlin, Company B of the 54th British Light Infantry, was lying on his back in one of the many makeshift hammocks, his right arm covering his eyes. Nearby, Private Davis and Private Mann were having yet another of their almost continuous arguments, none of which were based on anything of substance.

"I told you, the next time you touched my equipment, I'd smash 'at ugly thing you call a face wif' the butt of my musket," snarled Davis.

"Speaking of faces, why don't you shut 'at hole in the middle of yours?" responded Mann.

For what seemed like the hundredth time, the two men squared off with one another, and several other soldiers had to intervene to avoid another nasty fight. Davis already sported a nasty cut down the left side of his torso from an earlier brawl that had degenerated into the use of bayonets, a weapon the British soldiers prided themselves on their ability to wield in a dreadful and deadly manner.

It wasn't that these two soldiers were either rotten apples within the army, nor were they in any way atypical to the thousands of others that were currently confined in other ships surrounding them. Men can only endure a certain amount of torturous living before they begin to require a means with which to release their pain and frustration. For Davis, Mann, and hundreds of others, fighting was that release. For others, gambling was a constant presence in the troop quarters, and there were now some relatively wealthy soldiers in the British army. On the other hand, there were far more men who wouldn't have a penny in their pockets for months to come.

For Private William Devlin, his personal freedom came in the form of pen and paper. Devlin spent hour after hour creating a history of his time in the British Army. This history took the form of literally dozens and dozens of letters which he mailed back to his sister in Lancashire, a small town just outside of London. It was this small town that had formed the personality of young William during his first eighteen years of life, at which time he had decided to "see the world." Had he only known then what he knew now – about both the world, as well as his selected method of seeing it – he would have been quite content to follow in his father's footsteps in the furniture making business. Although it may not have been the most exciting way to live his life, he had often reflected that at least a rocking chair would have made him throw up to a lesser degree than would a rocking ship.

—

It was on July the 8th that the British army under General William Howe had begun boarding their ships in New York harbor. Their ultimate destination was one of extreme secrecy, and even the men who somehow "got the gouge" on the upcoming activities of the army were in the dark on this one. Many men marveled at the ability of their senior officers to develop complex, exciting plans, yet keep them away from the prying eyes of both their men, as well as the numerous American spies that constantly lurked around the army. Others, more jaded, had a different explanation: it's not so difficult to keep a plan a secret, when no plan had actually been devised. Such were the differing viewpoints of the men.

Since that date, the men had suffered a wide range of inhuman conditions with respect to crowding, poor hygiene, and terrible food. As a result, putrid fever, dysentery, and a variety of other diseases ran rampant throughout the army, and more than twenty men had already died as a result of disease and conditions. Several of these deaths had tragically occurred before the army had actually left New York Harbor, as the ships had bobbed meaninglessly and unmoving for twelve days before they set sail for open water. This was yet another in a long list of decisions made by General Howe that caused the men to scratch their heads in wonder.

When the fleet finally began moving on July 20th, the occupants of all 260 vessels which comprised the fleet had cheered in unison. After all, in order for something to eventually come to an end, it had to at first begin - so reasoned the approximately 23,000 people whose lives had somehow managed to place them in this most unpleasant situation.

It was, in fact, appropriate to use the rather vague term of "people" in reference to the individuals on board the ships, as not all of them were soldiers and officers of His Majesty's British Army. The fleet carried somewhere in the vicinity of 18,000 enlisted soldiers – of these, 13,000 were members of the British Army, while an additional 5,000 were made up of Hessian troops "contracted" by the British government to fight in America. In addition, there were 5,000 others on board, made up of British and Hessian officers, servants, staff members, camp followers, and wives and children of many of the officers.

The temporary euphoria of finally getting underway was quickly replaced, however, with the grim realization that this was not going to be a brief or direct voyage by any stretch. At least initially, the going was slow as the fleet of sailing ships was severely hampered by extremely light winds. At the outset of the voyage, it took the fleet seven days to travel a distance of only 150 miles.

The lack of progress was all the more maddening, as everyone was able to track their movement by watching the shoreline in the distance move by agonizingly slowly. The fact that this shoreline was so close made matters even more frustrating. The only change in this situation came during the extensive periods of thick fog, at which times the fleet was forced to scatter and spread out to avoid collisions with one another, naturally adding more time onto the already seemingly endless journey.

Meanwhile, there was no lack of severe weather, as dozens of thunderstorms battered the East Coast of the North American continent.

In addition, this particular summer happened to be one of the hottest in recent memory, as temperatures in the sun consistently reached the middle to upper 90's. These storms and temperatures meant that life in the cramped spaces below was draining to everyone.

As horrible as these conditions may have been for the 23,000 people on board, there was one final group of passengers who suffered to a far greater degree than any other. At the start of the voyage, the army quartermasters had loaded approximately 500 horses onto specially built animal transports. Within just a few days of departure, these poor creatures began to succumb from the combination of heat and other deplorable conditions, and not a day went by without several of the horses being thrown overboard into the ocean, having become quite literally and figuratively dead weight. In fact, so many dead horses were being thrown overboard, that the grisly scenes of horse carcasses washing up on the nearby shorelines was becoming commonplace for the citizens who lived near these coastal areas.

—

All of these issues had been addressed at one time or another by Private William Devlin in his letters home, almost always in vivid detail. He wasn't exactly sure how his sister Elizabeth was handling such graphic detail, as she had never mentioned it one way or another in the few letters he had received from her. Although he had already been in America for just over a year, he had only gotten three responses from Elizabeth. The fact that correspondence sometimes took as long as three months to reach its intended recipient in England was well known to the men.

In fact, the senior officers in the army often complained that the inability to get timely information and direction from the government and military was often the cause of confusion and uncertainty here in the Colonies. Whether this reality was truly the cause wasn't quite clear – most of the men believed that the senior officers were quite capable of confusion and uncertainty completely of their own accord, thank you very much.

William, now wide awake as a result of the altercation between the two Privates, pulled out his pen and paper from his knapsack which was resting beneath his head. He had started this most recent letter almost a week ago, but due to a fairly severe bout of diarrhea over the last few days, he hadn't exactly been in the mood to be thoughtful and cheerful. He always attempted to sound upbeat in his letters to Elizabeth, knowing that his attitudes and moods not only might affect his sister, but the rest of his family as well. The officers were always telling the men to be positive about the war when they wrote home. After all, if the British Army were to lose its moral support at home, that might not bode very well for the future conduct of the war. And winning the war, after all, was what it was all about. If this small group of upstart ruffians here in the Americas were to show themselves able to dictate their actions to the Crown, who knew what other parts of the British Empire might begin to get similar ideas.

William picked up with the next paragraph of his letter:

"I believe I have told you about Private Hastings of Company A and his struggle with some kind of illness. He had several episodes of a high fever and almost violent chills, and these episodes started to occur more and more frequently. Finally, on Wednesday of this past week, the poor lad gave in to it and died. I was helping the Surgeon's Mate by pressing a cloth soaked in lukewarm water to his head in a rather pitiful attempt to cool him off. Private Hastings kept talking and talking, but none of us had any idea of what he was saying. One minute he would be looking at us and making a bit of sense, when suddenly he would be calling out to 'Tommy' or 'Robert', whom I suspect were childhood friends. Finally, at about a quarter past four in the morning, he looked at me and said, 'Oh Mum, me hands is covered with dirt! How is we ever goin' to get the dirt off?' And then he died. I never figured out what he meant by it, and now I suppose I never will. Someone told me later that he had just turned seventeen but a fortnight ago."

William found these few moments of thought and reflection he enjoyed while composing his letters to be both relaxing and healing. Although he could never fully convey to anyone the tragedy of having another young man die in his arms, at least it afforded William the chance to share that misery with another person. Without such an outlet, he would have gone crazy, and he often wondered how so many others coped with their own personal agony. It obviously wasn't through the use of letters, as few of the enlisted men were literate to any significant degree.

In point of fact, the average enlisted man currently serving in the

British Army in America was, in a manner of speaking, the bottom of the British cultural barrel. Many of the men had been "recruited" out of the prisons and jails throughout England, by being given the option of either serving in the Army, or remaining incarcerated. Not surprisingly, many chose the former. Still others had been "pressed" into service by groups of British soldiers who had been tasked with roaming the back streets and alleys of the cities in England looking for vagrants. The soldiers would then forcibly kidnap these vagrants and make them, for all intents and purposes, prisoners of the Army.

This isn't to say that some soldiers in the British Army weren't volunteers. But even this distinction between these volunteers and those forced into service was somewhat blurred by the recruiting techniques. Army recruiters often spent a good deal of time in the pubs of England, nicely funded by the Army to buy drinks for any young man who was unfortunate enough to show even the slightest inclination toward military service. After a large number of free drinks, these young men were in no condition to make a rational decision, which was just fine with the recruiters. Many a young man had awakened in an Army barracks the next morning with a monstrous headache, a red uniform, and a contract indicating enlistment into service of the Crown – usually signed with a scribbled, barely legible name at the bottom. The fact that this signature was sometimes written in the hand of the recruiting officer was always completely overlooked.

A small percentage of enlisted men were made up of those like William. These were young men who had simply gotten tired of the monotony of their daily lives, and were looking for excitement and adventure. William, along with others like him, felt some degree of patriotism and pride for their Mother Country, and considered it a responsibility to serve the Crown.

—

Regardless of the manner in which they had found their way into the restricting confines of a British uniform, they were all suffering in the same way at this point. If the strategy of the senior officers was to make the men so miserable that they would be willing to fight anyone just to get off these ships – well, then that strategy had been a resounding success.

In the meantime, William placed his pen and paper back into his knapsack, rolled over onto his side, and attempted to employ the time-honored tactic of slumber as a means to escape his misery.

WILLIAM DUNN
JULY 30, 1777
CAPE MAY, NEW JERSEY

The three men had been riding most of the night, and both they and their horses were in desperate need of a rest. On more than one occasion, they had accidentally ridden into one another, having fallen asleep on their mounts as they traveled through the heavy forests and scrubland of New Jersey.

But William Dunn had no intention of stopping now. He had been given specific instructions from General George Washington himself to locate and report back on the location of the British fleet that many suspected was somewhere off this part of the colonies. Dunn had received his orders seven days ago, and he had driven himself and his men mercilessly to fulfill his mission.

At first, the going had been relatively easy, as they traveled along the open areas of the New Jersey coast just south of New York. Despite the lack of any visual evidence that the fleet was headed in this direction, their spirits had been high, confident of the significance of the task with which they had been charged. But when they entered the Pine Barrens of New Jersey, their enthusiasm received its first test. The Barrens, as it was referred to by the locals, was a despicable area for travelers, especially those who were unfamiliar with its nature. The place looked like something out of a medieval nightmare, as heavy forests and unforgiving, scraggly bushes dominated the terrain. The legs of the men, and the sides of their horses had been scraped and bloodied as they made their way through the treacherous land.

Perhaps worse was the fear of encountering the human element that supposedly populated the Barrens. Dunn and his men had been warned about making contact with those who made their home in this miserable world. Made up mostly of outlaws attempting to remain hidden, as well as reportedly almost sub-human creatures who chose to exist in this God forsaken piece of Hell, encountering anyone along the way would almost certainly lead to a violent conclusion.

Having made it through the Barrens without incident on days three and four, the exuberant patriotism of Dunn's companions began to wane. They began to consider the possibility that they had been sent on some kind of wild goose chase. After all, many members of the Continental Army believed that Howe and his men were heading north to link up with General Burgoyne, currently operating in upstate New York. Still others believed that the British fleet would head back to Boston, pursuing the logical strategy of re-capturing that hotbed of rebellion. Still others believed that down South – specifically the port of Charleston, South Carolina, made the most sense. It was only Washington, for the most part, who believed that the British might attempt to land somewhere south of Philadelphia, and proceed north in order to capture the capital of the newly formed United States of America.

In the mind of William Dunn, these contradictions mattered not. He was a former ship's captain who had been ordered to find a fleet, report its location, and continue to track its progress and provide ongoing intelligence. Horses, Barrens, and outlaws may have put him out of his element, at least temporarily – but a fleet of ships was something he knew, and he would be damned before he would allow them to sail in these waters without detection.

—

The ability to locate and report the location and direction of travel of the British fleet had an importance to George Washington that was underestimated even by Dunn. Currently, Washington had strategically placed his army roughly midway between Philadelphia and New York City, not knowing which direction it might need to move. The situation was the best that Washington could devise, due to the fact that he constantly received conflicting intelligence with respect to the fleet. Some of this information came from individuals who meant well, but reported the location of virtually any strange ship they observed. Still other information was carefully crafted by British Loyalists, and was fed to Washington through a variety of channels.

Regardless of its origin, this vast array of misinformation had resulted in Washington ordering his army to march and countermarch to a variety of locations no fewer than five times. As a result, his men were becoming exhausted, and morale was suffering. Washington appeared, for all the world, as if he had no idea what was happening – and that was exactly the case. Were he to receive definitive information on his adversary, he could put into motion a plan to meet and defeat the enemy. This was truly a case in which any plan was better than no plan at all.

—

Dunn and his men were riding up a gentle slope as the sun began to rise. As they crested the small hill, a grand sight awaited their eyes. There, no more than two miles off of the now visible shoreline, was a vast array of ships heading south. Their persistent pursuit and unwillingness to give in to their frustration had paid off – they had located the British fleet!

Dunn quickly pulled his small telescope from its pouch and scanned the scene in front of him. Good God, he thought, there must be over 200 ships out there! He tried to get a more detailed count of the various types of vessels which comprised the fleet, but as they stretched further into the distance, he lost the ability to make any kind of differentiation.

"Well, gentlemen, it appears we have found our Redcoats," Dunn said to the other two men. "I suppose we should consider relaying this information to General Washington; I would imagine he might have an idea or two on how to put it to good use."

Dunn's easygoing humor and penchant for understatement were stereotypically English, which is exactly where Dunn had originated. His comments caused the men to chuckle, but the significance of their situation made this levity fleeting.

"What now, Mr. Dunn?" asked one of his companions. The question was asked by young Joseph Merkens, the son of a Philadelphia blacksmith. Joseph had been selected for this patrol as a result of his strength and stamina, as well as his outstanding horsemanship.

"I suspect, Mr. Merkens, that a suggestion resides within your question. What might that suggestion be?"

"Well," replied Merkens with a sheepish grin, "I thought I might consider a quick trip back home to Philadelphia, departing immediately and at the greatest possible speed. And along the way, perhaps I could stop off for a chat with the Commanding General of the Continental Army. I believe he might find me to be an interesting conversationalist."

"Always scrambling for center stage, eh young Joseph?" teased Dunn. "However, I believe in this case you're quite correct. Before you go chasing off in pursuit of fame and fortune, let's take a few moments to gather our thoughts, survey the fleet before us, and craft a report that will be of the most value to the good General."

The men proceeded to climb from their horses, situate themselves on the ground, and organize what they felt to be the most relevant information to General Washington. They had no way of knowing that what they were providing to the General would eventually have a significant influence on the outcome of the war.

Jacob Landes
July 31, 1777
Salford Township, Pennsylvania

Jacob Landes unhitched the horse from its harness and led it into one of the four stables of the barn. After nearly seven hours of plowing in the 70 acre field across the road, he was bone-tired, but he wasn't quite ready to call it a day.

For all of his 23 years on this earth, Jacob had lived the life of a farmer, as had his father Jacob before him. He loved everything about that life, to include the often backbreaking labor it required. But the rewards were substantial: a feeling of surviving not only on your own, but of providing subsistence to countless others. The freedom to do things the way you felt they needed to be done. The knowledge that you were existing along with the natural rhythms of the earth.

It was for all of these reasons that everyone had been surprised at Jacob's decision to join the Philadelphia Brigade and become part of the Continental Army. And it was because of this decision that he wasn't ready to end his day of farming just yet. Tomorrow he was scheduled to report for his first day of duty as a lieutenant in the unit and, for all he knew, this might very well be the last time he would have the opportunity to live the only life he had ever known. And it might also be the last time he set foot on this farm, a piece of land that was hallowed ground to Jacob.

—

The Landes Farm had come into existence in 1727, when Jacob Sr. had purchased it from a man living in England who had never even set foot on the American continent, let alone this particular plot of farmland. Located approximately 35 miles north of the young and thriving city of Philadelphia, the property consisted of just under 200 acres, with excellent access to several small creeks that crisscrossed the local geography. The size and nature of the property, along with its close proximity to the prosperous markets in nearby Philadelphia, made it an extremely wise purchase. With these natural advantages, combined with the attribute of the Landes family being hard workers, the family soon enjoyed a modest level of prosperity.

Jacob Jr. was the eldest of five children, and easily shouldered the burden that naturally comes with the territory of holding such a position. He was very much like his father in virtually every respect; people often commented not only on the striking resemblance between the two, but also the same way in which they viewed the world. Life rewarded hard work and honesty, they both believed, and they lived their lives in strict accordance of these beliefs.

There was, however, at least one fundamental difference in their respective outlooks on life. Jacob Sr. viewed society as a means to an end. In other words, the loose structure of communities, cities, and colonies that made up the American continent in the late 1700's was simply a convenience for Jacob Sr. It provided him with a more efficient manner with which to distribute the fruits of his labor. Society, in the eyes of Jacob Sr., owed nothing to him beyond the opportunity to survive and thrive. And in return, Jacob Sr. owed nothing to that society except the responsibility to take care of himself and his family.

On the other hand, Jacob Jr. was enthralled by what this society had demonstrated. It was clearly a case of the whole being greater than the sum of its parts, and the amazing feats accomplished by its members were a firm testament to this fact. Jacob Jr. was often frustrated by conversations during which his father stated that the "world would be a better place if everyone just kept to themselves." Jacob Jr. would argue that it was the collaboration of everyone – the willingness to sometimes submit yourself to the greater good of the community – that made the world a better place.

This obvious split in beliefs had created somewhat of a rift between father and son, and both deeply regretted some of the words that had been spoken during these rather heated discussions. There was no doubt that both loved one another, but there was clearly a lack of common ground on this basic perspective that had created a tension between the two for several years. This tension had come to a point of explosion the previous evening when Jacob Jr. had announced to his father his decision to join the Continental Army under General George Washington.

—

"The Army?" Jacob Sr. had shouted. "Good God, son, have you gone mad? You have a farm to run here! You have responsibilities to your family! You can't just run off on a lark and play soldier simply because it happens to strike your fancy."

"It didn't just 'strike my fancy'. I've been thinking about this for months," Jacob Jr. countered. "And now that the British may be directly threatening us right here in Pennsylvania, I figure it's time to stand up for what's right."

"What's right is for you to tend to your duties as a member of this family. What's right is for you to continue on with what we have here; to insure it stays strong and passes on to the next generation, and the next," his father said. "Besides," he continued, "what the British do is of no concern of yours or mine. Let those rich men in Boston and New York and Philadelphia worry about such nonsense. They're the ones who started all of this with their mindless babble about 'taxation' and 'representation'."

"It's not 'babble', Father. It's men with a lot more to lose than us, showing a willingness to stand up for their rights – and ours. Men like George Washington who are risking everything to make us a free country – an independent nation…"

"I'll have no praising of that scoundrel George Washington in this house!" his father had shouted. "That man is nothing more than a money grubbing, slave-owning rich planter – from Virginia, for God's sake! He's not even one of us!"

"Not one of us? Father, that's the whole point! We're nothing if we constantly focus on those things that separate us, that make us different. Look at all the things that make us the same. We're *Americans*! And the British want to squash that. They want to insure we forever remain nothing more than a source of revenue and growth for the Crown. But we can be more than that – we can be a society that accomplishes things that no other country has accomplished before. We have a chance at building something from the ground up, something that will be better than what we have now."

"Enough!" his father shouted. "I've heard quite enough of your political ramblings and high-minded views on life. Where did all of this come from? Where did you ever concoct such crazy ideas that such a thing was even possible?"

Jacob Jr. remained silent for a few seconds, and reflected on his own life and what this family had achieved through hard work and determination.

"I learned it from you, Father," Jacob replied quietly. "You taught me that anything was possible if you believed in what you were doing, and were willing to sacrifice everything to achieve it."

—

As Jacob finished settling the horse into the stable, he closed both the upper and lower stable half-doors, latching them tightly as he did so. Looking to his left, he saw his father coming out of the side door of their house, carrying a small, wrapped bundle in his right hand. As he came down the slight slope of the back yard, he realized once again that his father wasn't moving with quite the same ease he had always shown. The man was getting older – he had not gotten married until a bit later in life - and his health was a constant concern to everyone. And as the man got closer to him, Jacob was surprised to see that his father was crying.

Last night's argument had left Jacob Jr. feeling frustrated and empty. He knew his father was heartbroken over his decision to leave, but it somehow hadn't changed his mind, and he briefly wondered if he was making a mistake. He pushed this doubt aside, and turned to face the man slowly approaching him in the waning light of that late summer day.

—

"Finished for the day, are you son?" Jacob Sr. asked.

For the day; for the season; maybe for his life. The implied finality of the question was not lost on either of the men.

"I am, Father. The horses are all bedded down for the night, fed, watered, and ready for a good night's rest. Perhaps something you should consider as well."

Jacob Jr. knew his father was an incredibly proud man, and Jacob Sr. chaffed at any suggestion that he was slowing down in his later years. Still, Jacob Jr. couldn't resist the need to show concern for the man who had taught and given him so much.

"Well, your Mother has certainly seen to me being fed and watered," Jacob Sr. joked mildly. Myra Landes, the uncontested matriarch of the family was famous for her near obsession with insuring her family never wanted for a good meal, and life on a farm guaranteed that quantity of food was never an issue. "But I don't think I'm quite ready to be put out to pasture, so to speak."

Once again, his father's comments carried implications far beyond the immediate nature intended by Jacob Jr.

"Look, Son, I know you'll be leaving bright and early tomorrow, and all of us will be right there to send you off – you know that. But it may be a while before you and I have a chance to have a private conversation. I didn't want to miss this opportunity."

Jacob Jr. could see that his father was struggling, his tired eyes glistening in the failing light. He shifted his weight uncomfortably from one leg to the other, looking down at the ground. Slowly, he raised his eyes to meet those of his son.

"We both know we've had our differences of late," he began. "Some of those were natural; a young boy becoming a man, and wanting to think and act for himself. Others, of course, were because of your decision to become... to do what you're about to do. You and I will always have a difference of opinion about that decision."

"Father, if you're going to try and change my mind – "

"Son, I came out here to tell you that I'm at peace with what you're doing. I wanted to tell you, more than any differences that we may have, that I can't imagine a father being more proud of his son than I am of you. You've grown into a man that commands respect from those around you. A man that people *trust*. You've become everything that I could ever..." With that, his Father's voice broke down, and he began to sob quietly as he stepped forward to embrace his son.

Jacob Jr. found himself unable to control his own emotions, and he wept openly in his father's arms. The two stayed like that for a short time, as they struggled with the significance of the moment. Finally, Jacob Sr. broke his embrace and extended his hand holding the small wrapped package.

"This is something I want you to take with you when you leave tomorrow. Your Grandfather gave me this the night he died. He told me it had been a source of strength for him throughout his life, and wanted me to have that same strength. I don't want to wait until I'm on my deathbed to pass this on to you. I figure you just might be finding yourself in some situations where you could use a little help."

Jacob Jr. took the package from his father's hand, and carefully unwrapped it. Inside the cloth was a small Bible. Jacob Jr. looked again at his father, and this time saw a look of almost fierce determination on his face.

"That Bible *will* give you strength and keep you safe from harm. Do you hear me? Now, let's go inside so this tired old horse can get some rest."

Jacob Sr. placed his arm around his son's shoulders, and they walked slowly together to the house.

GENERAL GEORGE WASHINGTON
JULY 31, 1777
PHILADELPHIA, PENNSYLVANIA

General George Washington was resting quietly in the dining room of the small house he had selected as his Headquarters. He was reflecting, for the hundredth time, on the fact that he was extremely uncomfortable with his lack of discomfort. Specifically, while he lived in relative ease here in the city, most of his army was encamped somewhere between Bucks County in Pennsylvania, and various counties throughout New Jersey.

Never mind the fact that this arrangement made the most sense from both a strategic and tactical perspective. Washington had been frustrated by these last few weeks as he and his staff attempted to determine the ultimate destination of the British fleet. While that riddle was being studied, Washington needed to stay in Philadelphia where he had access to the Continental Congress, as well as the ability to coordinate communications to his men from a central location. Meanwhile, the Continental Army remained in their current location because it afforded them the ability to move either north to help General Horatio Gates located in upstate New York with an army of approximately 7000 troops, or south to deal with a British army intent on potentially capturing Philadelphia.

General Howe was proving to be his typical confusing self, just as he had been earlier that same year. At that time, Howe had marched his army out of New York City at a pace that could only be described as nonchalant. He had then proceeded to make camp at several locations in northern and central New Jersey, without so much as making a single threatening move in the direction of Washington's nearby troops. Finally, having apparently satisfied himself with a tour of the surrounding countryside, Howe's troops had returned to their original positions in and around New York City. To the current day no one - British or American - could ascertain any logical reason for Howe's movements.

Now in the fall, Howe had apparently decided to take a similar tour of the area, this time using his brother's ships. When the fleet had departed from New York harbor at the beginning of July it had originally headed north, possibly to reinforce British General John Burgoyne operating in New England. However, Washington's spies had lost track of the fleet soon thereafter, and when it was finally spotted again a week later, it had apparently turned south. Following this second sighting, the games began. Washington had dispatched dozens of riders up and down the east coast in an attempt to locate the British fleet. All he had to show for his troubles were tired horses, tired riders, and literally dozens of sightings from supposedly well-meaning citizens placing the fleet anywhere between Boston and Charleston.

Washington was nearing the end of his patience, and the actions of the members of the Continental Congress weren't making the situation any better. Multiple times each day he would receive messages and personal visits from the politicians asking him for updates and advice on what they should do about the location of the American government.

"I'm sure you can appreciate, General, that were the Continental Congress members to be captured by the British, the blow to the morale of the army – not to mention the country as a whole – would be absolutely devastating," he had been told in various ways on numerous occasions. Washington had been initially sympathetic to the plight of these men, and had exhibited more than due diligence in listening and responding to their questions and concerns. But as time had worn on, their constant whining and obnoxious intrusions had begun to tax even Washington's seemingly limitless patience, and he had begun to consider the possibility that the capture of these men might be just what this new country needed.

—

Washington was reviewing the most recent reports he had received concerning his troop strength and supply issues when he was startled by a sharp rap on the door.

"Enter," he said, as the door was opened almost simultaneously with his order.

Major Jarvis, one of the members of Washington's staff, entered the room flushed and out of breath. "General Washington, I beg your pardon, sir. But there is a gentleman here to see you who claims to have important information regarding the location of the British fleet."

In spite of his many recent disappointments around the validity of such information, Washington couldn't help but feel a brief rush of adrenaline from the Major's statement.

"Well, by all means, Major, let's see what this man has to say. Show him in, if you please."

Major Jarvis looked back and held the door wide open, and a man stepped hesitantly into the room. Washington found himself in the company of a man who looked as if he had not seen a bed, a bath, or a meal in a month. His clothes were so filthy that it was no longer possible to determine their color or original make up. The same could be said of the man's face, although the filth was unable to cover the absolute exhaustion displayed there. Washington could not have guessed the man's age accurately within 20 years.

"Good God, man!" Washington exclaimed, "have a seat here before you collapse!"

"Begging the General's pardon, but I've been sittin' quite enough to last me a while, sir. I'm not so sure that certain parts of my body would respond well to a wooden bench, if you know what I mean," the man stated.

Washington chuckled. "Of course. Can I at least offer you something to eat and drink? It appears as if you're in quite a need of such things."

"I'd be most appreciative if the General could see his way to scaring up some food and water - it's been a while since I've had the chance to stop and eat. I've been in the saddle almost 24 hours, sir. Also, if it's not too much to ask, I wonder if someone might see to my horse just outside. I already rode one to death, and I'd just as soon not have to do the same thing again."

"Yes, yes, immediately. Major Jarvis, could you please see to this gentleman's requests? In the meantime, sir, I apologize for my impatience, but I'm told you are in the possession of some information?"

For the first time since their unceremonious introduction, the man broke into a wide grin. "Sir, I'm part of a group of three riders that were sent out just over a week ago, led by a fine gentleman named William Dunn. And that fine gentleman, General, pushed us until I thought I was about ready to knock him out of his saddle and head back home, I'm ashamed to admit. But yesterday at about this very time of day, we were riding down the coast of New Jersey, near an area known as Cape May, when we come up over a small hill and were treated to the sight of the entire British fleet."

"Sir, I apologize for my skepticism – excuse me, but with whom do I have the honor of conversing?" asked Washington.

"Sir, my name is Joseph Merkens from right here in Philadelphia. My father is a blacksmith not but two miles or so from where we are. And I stand ready to assist in our fight against the British in whatever way my talents may serve."

Washington was briefly overcome by a swell of pride, the likes of which he had experienced countless times since beginning his role as the Commanding General of this army. The deep and unquestioning commitment of these men who were willing to abandon their everyday life and fight for – well, for an idea, really – never ceased to amaze him.

"Mr. Merkens, you have clearly gone to great lengths to get here, but I must be blunt with you. I have received many reports from individuals who claim to have sighted the British fleet, and I would only be exaggerating slightly were I to tell you that some of these locations were over 100 miles from the nearest body of water!"

"Oh, General," Merkens began, "I can assure you that this is no false report. I saw with my own eyes over 200 ships, each of which was proudly flying the British flag. And although I'm no expert in the ways of the sea, the Mr. Dunn I have just referred to, most certainly is. In fact, we've taken the liberty of putting our observations down on paper, and it is this report that I proudly offer you now."

With that, Merkens pulled a dirty, crumpled paper from inside of his coat, and proudly extended it in the direction of Washington. "I think you'll find, sir, that Mr. Dunn is no stranger to details. We've recorded a pretty accurate count of the number of ships we could see, along with a description of those that were most visible. I'll draw your attention, sir, to the listing of at least seven men of war vessels, including the approximate number of guns on each. Now, I don't mean to tell you your business, General, but if this here report doesn't convince you of the accuracy of what we saw – well then, I guess I'm at a loss as to what you might be lookin' for, sir."

Merkens blushed slightly, getting the uncomfortable feeling that he may have overstepped his bounds in speaking his mind. But his discomfort quickly disappeared as he watched Washington's face as he read the report. Although considered to be a fairly sober man in terms of his countenance and demeanor, it would have taken quite an effort to wipe the smile off of Washington's face just now.

"Mr. Merkens, I believe I am truly in debt to you, your Mr. Dunn, and the third member of your patrol. I have been waiting many days for a report that contains exactly this kind of information. I am not normally a man of embellishment, but I am confident in saying that you have provided a service to your country the significance of which cannot be overstated. Please accept my immeasurable gratitude for the service you have done. And I should very much like to make the acquaintance of this Mr. Dunn of which you have spoken so highly. For now, I beg of you, get something to eat and drink, and get some sleep. I suspect we will be in great need of men of your character in the coming weeks."

Having received that compliment, Joseph Merkens smiled, nodded respectfully to Washington, and took his leave from the room.

CONTINENTAL ARMY PATROL
BUCKS COUNTY, PENNSYLVANIA
AUGUST 1, 1777

The sun was gradually setting on yet another blistering hot summer day in Pennsylvania. Although the temperature had grudgingly retreated by a few degrees, this fact was lost on the six soldiers riding along the Delaware River near Tinicum Township. The fact that they had been on a cavalry patrol for nearly the entire day insured that they were tired, miserable, and lackadaisical in their actions. Earlier, they had carefully taken note of their surroundings, looking for indications of enemy movement that would put them at risk. At this point, they were simply looking forward to the end of the day at their encampment located just over two miles from their present location. Some hot food, cold water, and a reasonably comfortable bed made from hay and rags would make a relatively pleasant end to what had turned out to be a physically grueling day.

These six men were one of many patrols constantly being conducted by members of the American Continental Army throughout Pennsylvania and New Jersey. Although the British army was not thought to be anywhere near their present location, they had been told to be watchful for local Tories, men loyal to the British Crown. Although Pennsylvania, and in particular Bucks County, tended to be friendly to the Rebel cause, there were still a fair number of individuals located in the surrounding area who vehemently opposed the American plan to break away from the British Empire. Although most of this opposition took the form of indifference to the Continental Army, or perhaps an unwillingness to cooperate in any way, there had been incidents of open and active hostility. Most recently, the previous week a patrol in nearby Montgomery County had come under fire from several men posted in a barn, and although the soldiers had suffered no casualties, the engagement had heightened tensions among the soldiers.

—

"Hey, Sergeant Mason, what's our chances of picking up the pace a bit? My stomach's been grumbling for the last ten miles, and my tongue is so thick I can hardly swallow," griped one of the soldiers in the column.

Sergeant Robert Mason, a man all of 23 years old who had grown up in the surrounding area, was just as anxious to get back to camp as the rest of the men. But he took his responsibilities as a non-commissioned officer very seriously, and refused to show any weakness in front of the other men. It was also due to this sense of duty that he tended to ride at the front of the column most of the time, as opposed to rotating that role among the men evenly, as they had been taught to do.

"We'll get to camp when we get to camp," he responded. "It ain't gonna do anyone any good to go rushin' home before we complete the patrol like we's supposed to, and you know that as good as me. Now pipe down and watch your ground."

At that moment, a shot rang out just to the right of the column, and the men were suddenly alert as they jumped from their horses and scrambled for cover. Two more shots were fired from the brush to their right, and there was commotion from the same area as the ambushers made an apparent hasty retreat from their hiding places.

"It can't be no more than just three of 'em, or they would've unloaded more of a volley," yelled the former griping soldier. "I say we spread out and try to cut 'em off from behind before they get away! Sergeant Mason, you figure we should split up and take 'em from both sides?"

But Robert Mason was in no condition to respond to the question. The first shot, a heavy four ounce ball fired from a smoothbore musket, had struck him in his right side and passed through his chest, coming to rest less than an inch from his heart. When two of the men got to his position, Mason was struggling to breathe while he fumbled for a handkerchief in his pocket to place over the wound.

"Don't... don't sit here with me, you cowards," he whispered fiercely to the other men. "Go and get those bastards. Circle around and..." He coughed violently, and a stream of bright red blood poured from his mouth onto the front of his uniform.

The other men, suddenly devoid of their exhaustion, moved with an immediate sense of purpose and urgency toward the direction of the shots that had wounded one of their own. Two of the men moved quickly to the right, while two others moved off to the left in an attempt to encircle the bushwhackers. The fifth man stayed with Mason, and tried to hold a now blood-soaked rag against the horrible wound.

As the soldiers raced toward their attackers, they could clearly hear their prey moving through the brush. Instinctively, they began to converge on the sounds closest to them, while still other movement was further in the distance. The men who had ambushed them had apparently become separated, with some making greater speed than others. An unspoken decision was unanimously made to pursue what was possibly within their grasp, while allowing the others to escape.

After just a few minutes, the four American soldiers had surrounded their target, a classic example of focusing on the weakest member of the herd. As they moved cautiously forward, they soon came upon a single man lying motionless on the ground, his eyes wild with fear. In point of fact, it wasn't really a man, but a heavyset boy no more than 14 or 15 years old. His empty musket was lying a short distance away from him, having been abandoned in his frantic attempt to escape.

"Well, what have we here," one of the soldiers snidely remarked, as they circled the young boy lying face up on the ground.

"Looks to me like a piece of dung who likes to sit in the bushes and take pot shots at anyone passing by that he don't take a liking to," said another of the soldiers. "What do you suppose we oughta do with somebody who sets out to kill someone without the courage to face 'em down like a real fightin' man?"

"Please, please, I didn't mean nothin' by it!" the boy pleaded. "My Daddy just told me to come along so we could mess with you Rebel soldiers! He said you boys were causing all kinds of trouble around these parts, and we needed to teach you a lesson. I don't care one way or another about what you all are doin' around here!"

"I say we take him back to Sergeant Mason, and let him decide," one of the soldiers said, completely ignoring the boy. "After all, the Sergeant's the one that's taken the worst of what this boy's set out to do."

They all nodded in agreement, and two of the soldiers lifted the boy off his feet and pushed him roughly back in the direction from which they had come. As they moved through the forest, each man took every opportunity to shove the boy, or hit him with one of their muskets in the head and body. With each blow, the boy cried out pitifully as blood and bruises began to appear, and by the time they had reached their starting point, the boy was openly crying.

"Hey fellas, look what we found," one of the soldiers called out as they approached Sergeant Mason and his caregiver. "Sergeant Mason, we'll give you first shot at beatin' this boy within an inch of his life. We figure he deserves to feel at least as much pain as that scrape is gonna cause you in the next few days!"

But Sergeant Robert Mason was no longer capable of inflicting anything on anyone. He was lying in the arms of the soldier that had remained at his side, the front of his uniform covered in the blood he had painfully coughed up. The fact that the bullet had missed his heart had not been a lucky break, but a curse that had resulted in his final minutes on this earth being difficult and painful. He had labored mightily to continue breathing, but in the end, the massive damage the bullet had wreaked on his insides was simply too much for any man to survive.

The soldier cradling Sergeant Mason, a boy of no more than 18, was weeping openly. "Why?" he asked in a confused voice. "Why did this happen to Robert? He was the best of all of us. He was doin' nothin' but riding on a patrol! He was… my friend." The boy's head slumped down, as his tears mixed with the blood on the front of Mason's uniform.

The others slowly turned to glare at the boy they had captured, and they all knew what had to be done. The sadness that they had felt just a few seconds before was replaced with a deep, pure hatred, and never was there a greater desire for revenge by any group of men.

"Stand that scum on his feet and tie him to that there tree," one of the men said. The order, given by someone in no official capacity to do so, was quickly obeyed by the others, and the boy was soon lashed to a large oak tree.

The boy was almost out of his mind with fear as he screamed and begged to his captors to release him, to forgive him, to understand that he had not killed their Sergeant. He screamed mindlessly, incoherently, yelling anything that might change what he knew to be his fate, eventually calling out pathetically for his mother. But nothing could be said or done to change the minds of these men who felt a need to make things right.

"All right, lads," their new commander ordered, "stand here with me and make sure your muskets are loaded and primed."

The men took up positions shoulder to shoulder ten paces or so from the babbling boy, putting their weapons at order arms.

"We, the friends and comrades of Sergeant Robert Mason of the

American Continental Army, find you guilty of the cold-blooded murder of the man now lying on the ground in front of you. Detail, take aim!"

The boy continued to scream, if possible louder than he had before. "Mama, please, tell them! Tell them it wasn't me! For the love of God, I was going out for a ride in the woods! Please tell them!"

"Take aim! Fire!"

Four muskets rang out sharply through the quiet of the forest, sending four heavy musket balls into the chest of the boy tied to the tree. Immediately, his screams ceased, and were replaced by quiet sobbing and muttering.

"Please, Mama, please…tell them. It wasn't me. It wasn't…"

And with that, a heavyset little boy died in the woods, another victim to a cruel civil war that was raging throughout the land.

Jacob Landes
August 1, 1777
Philadelphia, Pennsylvania

Jacob had awakened at dawn that day, anxious to get an early start on his ride to Philadelphia. To say he had awakened was somewhat inaccurate, as he had never really fallen asleep. His nerves had bothered him more than he had expected, as the enormity of what he was about to do began to sink in.

His family had accompanied him to the barn as he saddled his horse, Jackson, for the nearly 40 mile ride. His mother had given him sausages and a large piece of beef wrapped in a handkerchief, which Jacob carefully placed in one of his saddlebags. He had also packed some clothes, but not many, as he anticipated spending most of his time in the uniform of a lieutenant in the American Continental Army. His possessions were rounded out by a few personal items: books, mostly, including the small Bible his father had given him the night before.

Jacob had purposely made his departure quickly, as he knew dragging it out would only make it more difficult on his family. They had exchanged the normal platitudes: wishes to be well, expressions of sorrow and love, promises to write: all surrounded by feelings of fear borne out of the unknown. It was an extremely difficult experience for all, and Jacob had breathed a deep sigh of relief as he turned his horse onto the Sumneytown Pike leading south toward the city. As he rode on, he had time to reflect on the reasons he had made the decision that was leading him away from his home and into a potentially dangerous future. This caused him to relive that fateful trip to Philadelphia, at which time he had first been presented with the idea of making this dramatic move.

—

Several weeks ago, he and his father had made one of their periodic trips into Philadelphia for the purpose of selling their farm products, in this case a sizable load of watercress. The Landes farm grew this rather lucrative crop using an ingenious system of viaducts that channeled water from a branch of the Perkiomen Creek that flowed through their property. Having successfully sold their entire lot to one of the many merchants along Market Street, Jacob's father had gone off in search of a future buyer for some of the iron products that he had decided to begin making on their property. Jacob Sr. had just recently finished building a small blacksmith shop immediately behind the main house, complete with working space, storage space in a loft above the work area, and a fairly sizable brick oven just outside the door of the shop.

Jacob had always loved the opportunities he had to wander around the city on his own, gazing wide-eyed at the variety and strangeness of the products and people that seemed to be everywhere. It was a far cry from the relative calm and solitude to which he was otherwise accustomed, and he had always been drawn by the potential for excitement and adventure that he felt lurked just beneath the surface.

Jacob had been walking by Tun Tavern, a small establishment with a big reputation. It had been here, just short of two years ago, that Captain Samuel Nicholas had begun recruiting a small group of men for special service on board the pitifully few ships that made up the American Continental Navy. These men were not to be used as sailors, but rather would serve the roles of boarding parties for hand to hand fighting on enemy ships, marksmen in the rigging of their own ships, and landing parties to go ashore and fight. Captain Nicholas had accepted only the hardiest and toughest – and some claimed most arrogant – of the men who arrived interested in joining. He had selected only a few of those who presented themselves, and Nicholas' attitude and selectivity had immediately created an esprit de corps among those who were chosen to become part of this new organization: the American Continental Marines.

"You there!" a man called to Jacob as he walked by the tavern. "Excuse me, my good man, but may I speak with you a moment?"

Jacob found himself being addressed by a somewhat rugged looking man in his early to mid-thirties, wearing the uniform of an officer in the Continental Army. "Of course, sir," Jacob had responded. "How can I help you?" Jacob's mother had instilled a sense of politeness in her children, developed through the liberal use of swats to the back of the head for any violations of her strict code.

"Sir," the officer began, "you look like a man of good manners and education – would that be a correct statement?"

"Well sir, I would like to consider myself in possession of good manners, but I'm hardly well educated."

"Ay, but can you read and write by any chance?" asked the officer.

"If reading and writing is your gauge of education, sir, then I am, in fact, an educated man," Jacob responded. "My mother taught me these skills at a very young age, and I've found them to be quite valuable in both my personal and business endeavors. Why do you ask?"

"Well sir, we're looking for young men who are well spoken, literate, and in good physical condition to serve in the role of officers in the American Continental Army. It seems we're finding the right sort we need to be soldiers, but we need men of a – shall we say, higher caliber? – to be their leaders. You sir, strike me as such a person."

"But, I know nothing of military matters, nor have I ever been a leader of anyone but myself," Jacob had protested weakly. The fact was, he was flattered at being regarded as being – what was the phrase the officer had used? – a higher caliber. And in spite of himself, he found himself experiencing a certain amount of interest and excitement as he allowed himself to be drawn into the conversation.

"Military matters can be taught – character cannot," stated the officer. "We have a good number of experienced officers who would be only too happy to assist you in your development into what I'm certain would be a fine military professional. What's your name, young man, and where are you from?"

"My name is Jacob Landes, and I come from Salford Township in Montgomery County – perhaps 35 miles north of here."

"Ah well, then, you would have the very significant honor of serving in Lieutenant Colonel William Butler's regiment. He hails from Allentown, and is responsible for those members of our Army that come from your area. A finer officer you'll never find, other than General Washington, of course."

The mention of Washington's name sent a ripple of excitement through Jacob, which was exactly the effect the officer had intended. Jacob caught a brief glimpse in his mind's eye of what it must be like to serve as one of General George Washington's officers, and he liked very much what he saw.

"Look here, Jacob, why don't we sit for a few minutes and have us a pint while we discuss what your future will look like as a member of the American Continental Army? I think you'll soon realize that you, sir, have the rare opportunity to be a part of history! You have the opportunity to join a group of men that are going to be responsible for creating a new and better world. You, sir, have a destiny!"

The officer's features had become flushed and animated, and he exuded a strength of conviction that was unmistakably genuine. This display, when combined with the fact that he was using words and ideas strikingly similar to those Jacob had shared with his father, made for an irresistibly compelling argument. Jacob strode purposefully into the tavern, his first steps as a soon-to-be soldier.

—

Rousing himself back to the present, Jacob realized he had traveled quite a distance while deep in thought. In addition, he had developed quite a thirst, and was happy to see a small tavern just ahead, set slightly back off the road. As he rode closer, he saw the sign advertising The Wild Rooster, which was clearly not an establishment designed for the gentry. In short, The Wild Rooster looked to be just above the level of a pig sty; but Jacob was parched, and this place was directly in front of him. It was a match made in heaven.

Jacob stepped inside the tavern, allowing his eyes to gradually adjust to the dim light of the interior. His gaze took in his surroundings, confirming his earlier suspicions regarding the condition of the place. However, it also revealed a scene consisting of perhaps 15 to 20 men of all ages, a fairly sizable crowd for a pub at only eleven o'clock in the morning. Furthermore, the men appeared to be a decent lot of working men, judging by their clothes and the fact that none of them seemed to be drunk at this early hour.

Jacob settled himself at a table near the back of the tavern, and sat patiently waiting for someone to take his order. As he was waiting, he began to understand the reason for the crowd: there was some kind of farewell being staged for one of the men up at the bar. People were constantly coming up to the man and shaking his hand, along with offering some congratulatory comment and wishes for good health. The man – not much more than a boy, really – was obviously comfortable with being the center of attention, as he made comments to many of his fans which launched them into fits of laughter. Jacob could only guess that, based on the frequency and enthusiasm with which he was pounded on the back by the others, this young man must be in a great deal of pain.

An older gentleman, his face split by a grin caused by something the young man had just said, soon appeared at Jacob's table to take his order.

"Sir, if I could kindly have a bowl of that stew I see the others enjoying, along with a pint of ale, I would be most appreciative," Jacob said.

"Certainly, lad," the old man responded politely, "I'll have that right up for you. I apologize for the delay just now, but we have a bit of a celebration going on here at The Rooster this morning."

"That much is certain," said Jacob. "At the risk of being impolite, may I inquire as to the nature of the celebration?"

"Oh, that's not impolite at all, son. One of our more popular patrons, Michael Sweeney, is departing this very morning to join General Washington's army in Philadelphia. I swear that boy could make a rock chuckle with his sense of humor. He has the rest of the boys in stitches talking about how the British will be paddling canoes back to England in fear, now that he's going to be part of the fight! Paddling canoes back to England! Can you just picture what that would look like, now?"

Jacob found himself smiling broadly at the image, and judged that the young Mr. Sweeney was most likely well deserving of his humorous reputation.

"That's quite a coincidence, sir," Jacob shared with the old man, "as I too am on my way this morning to join the very same organization."

The man's eyes lit up with delight, and he banged sharply on the table as he turned to face the front of the tavern.

"Listen here, lads, I have somethin' you need to know. This young man is apparently going to be serving with our very own Michael Sweeney! He's on his way to join up with General George Washington and the rest of the boys! Shall we bring him up front and show him a real Rooster welcome?"

The tavern roared its approval, and Jacob was suddenly surrounded by a number of men who literally lifted him to his feet and propelled him to the front of the room. In a matter of seconds, he was standing right next to a grinning Michael Sweeney, with a pint of ale in each of his hands. The man Jacob faced was even younger than he had appeared from the back of the tavern; in addition, he was almost certainly as popular with the ladies as he was with his friends, as he was strikingly handsome. The smiling boy extended his hand to Jacob.

"Michael Sweeney, soon to be Lieutenant Michael Sweeney, of the American Continental Army. With whom am I pleased to make the acquaintance?"

"Jacob Landes, also soon to be a lieutenant in the American Continental Army," Jacob offered quietly, but with a feeling of pride that took him slightly by surprise.

"Well look what we have here, lads," one of the rougher looking men shouted, a smile of amusement on his face. "We have us a couple of officers and gentleman! This may well be a first for The Wild Rooster!" he roared.

The tavern erupted in laughter as another man responded, "Ay, Seamus, and with men like you in here, it'll probably be the last!" The laughter was repeated after the last remark.

"Well Jacob," Michael said to his new friend, "I don't know you from Adam, but you strike me as being as fine a man as I'll meet anywhere within the Army. Therefore, I've decided that you are officially my newest and best friend in the world! Now what say you to that, Lieutenant Landes?"

The room got quiet, and all eyes were on Jacob. He felt as if a member of the Royal Family had just extended their hand to be kissed, and everyone was waiting to see how he would handle it. But it wasn't the pressure from the other men in the room that caused him to choose his response: it was the feeling of genuine warmth that he felt immediately toward this young man standing in front of him with his outstretched hand thrust deliberately at Jacob's chest.

"I suppose I would be honored to call you my best friend as well," responded Jacob, as he firmly grasped Michael's hand with his own.

The men in the tavern roared even louder than before, if that was even possible, and the party continued on with a new member at its center.

PRIVATE WILLIAM DEVLIN
AUGUST 25, 1777
HEAD OF ELK, MARYLAND

William never realized that the simple act of setting foot on dry land could elicit such a wonderful feeling. He, like many of his fellow British soldiers, literally got down on their hands and knees to kiss the ground. Disgusted sergeants and officers kicked the soldiers as they lay prostrate on the ground, physically willing them to their feet to continue the reconnaissance of the unfamiliar area.

"Sweet Mother of God, it's finally over," said Private Willis, one of William's better friends in the regiment. Prior to leaving for America, Willis had literally never been on a ship, and he had repeatedly stated that, given the option, his return to England would be his final seafaring adventure. "I swear, another day on that floating Hell and I would've thrown meself overboard, never mind that I can't swim."

William chuckled at the good-natured humor Willis was capable of displaying, in spite of the awful conditions they had all endured.

And awful they had truly been. By the final two weeks of the journey, most of the decent food and water had run out. The men were reduced to eating zwieback, a type of brutally hard biscuit that was inedible under the best of circumstances. In this case, the biscuits had become infested with a variety of vermin, and the men were forced to deal with them in two ways. Either they would drop the biscuits into a cup of rancid water and wait for the little creatures to drown and rise to the surface, or they could repeatedly beat them on the deck until most of the insects had fled for their lives. Their other alternative to food was small pieces of pork heavily salted to avoid spoiling. Not only was the meat tough and tasteless, but the amount of salt also made the men ravenously thirsty.

The vicious cycle from horrid food to rancid water had quickly taken its toll on the men, and at last count 27 British and Hessian soldiers had died during the journey. The sound of bodies being unceremoniously cast overboard during the final week had become disturbingly routine.

—

The area in which the fleet had landed was overgrown and inhospitable, to say the least. Even the landing itself had been a harrowing experience, as the mighty ships had traveled up a dangerously narrow and shallow section of the Chesapeake Bay. Lord Howe, the Admiral of the Fleet and the brother of William Howe, the General of the Army, had himself taken to a longboat that preceded the lead vessel. Rumor had it that the old boy himself had leaned out of the bow of the boat and taken soundings to insure the safe passage of his precious ships. This was just one of many reasons that Admiral Howe was admired and respected by his sailors, a luxury that was not always consistent with the soldiers' opinion of Brother William.

The soldiers of Devlin's regiment moved slowly through the brush, careful to keep a sharp eye open for a possible ambush. Although the likelihood of such an event occurring was small, the men had long developed a grudging respect for the Rebels' ability to use the local terrain to their own advantage. The men had moved approximately five or six hundred yards inland when the officers gave the order to halt and establish defensive positions.

"All right, men," their lieutenant called out, "pair up and spread out! The general wants a front of half a mile established and secured. The rest of the army will be coming ashore in the next few hours. Come on, now, step lively! I'll have no man lying down or going off in search of anything."

No man grumbled at the officer's directions. Every soldier knew the severity of the punishment for such an infraction. Assignment to weeks of hard labor, whippings, and even hangings were known to be handed out to those stupid enough to commit such a sin.

William and Private Willis selected a spot located on a slight rise that provided a view of the surrounding area for several hundred yards. They quickly dropped their knapsacks and settled into their position, amazingly content to be sitting on a piece of property that didn't constantly rise and fall. Looking behind them, they were treated to a view that displayed the awesome power of the British Empire. As far as they could see, there were hundreds of ships patiently waiting their turn to offload their contents of men, animals, and material.

"Damn, Willis, I'd sure hate to be a Rebel catching sight of this!"

William remarked. "I'd probably piss my pants and hightail it back to Philadelphia! What could possibly be in the heads of these idiots around here, thinking they could stand up to this?"

Willis sat thoughtfully for a few moments, clearly contemplating a response to William's simple rhetorical question.

"I don't know, Devlin. But, I have to figure there's more to it than meets the eye, if you know what I mean."

William, a bit surprised by the remark, looked at Willis. "No, I don't know what you mean. These people have lived under our protection for years, and have had all of the advantages of being members of the Crown. They're well fed, well taken care of, and all they have to do is abide by a few basic rules. Pay their taxes, just like everyone else, follow the guidance given by the government, and for God's sake, don't start thinking they own the place by shooting at British soldiers!"

"Well then, is that it? They're well fed, that's true. But who gets them their food? Not the Crown. They get plenty of that themselves, from the sweat off their backs. These colonists can be accused of a lot of things, but being lazy surely isn't one of them. Take care of themselves? Seems like they have things pretty well in hand in that category, without the need for the likes of you and me. And all they have to do is pay their taxes, you say? And what, exactly, do they get for that? I've heard stories about the lifestyles of the British government officials living here. Mansions and fancy dances, wine and women, and more money than you and I could ever hope to see in our wildest dreams. This may sound a bit odd, but I sometimes think that people like you and me have more in common with these Rebels than we do with our own government we've been sent here to fight for."

William was amazed. These were the type of comments that could get a man thrown in the brig for insubordination; or worse, get him hanged for treasonous statements against the Crown. Still, the man had some valid points that William found difficult to dismiss, much to his dismay. Perhaps selecting Willis as his sentry partner wasn't the best decision he had ever made.

"For God's sake, Willis, keep your voice down. If one of the officers hears you talking like that, you're liable to get us both in a heap of trouble. I'm happy about the fact that my back hasn't had an unfortunate introduction to a whip, and I'd like to keep it that way."

"Whatever you say, Devlin. I'll be careful of what I say, especially if it has the possibility of getting my good friends into trouble. But you might want to consider being careful of seeing everything from the view of an Englishman. We may be the most powerful country in the world, but we still haven't figured out a way to control everything – like the will and thoughts of other people."

The two men settled back into their position, trading glances back and forth between the power of the Fleet that floated behind them, and the unknowns that lay in front of them.

SERGEANT ALEXANDER BICKELL
AUGUST 29, 1777
HEAD OF ELK, MARYLAND

The company of Hessian soldiers moved silently through the woods, their green uniforms blending perfectly with the surrounding terrain. Sergeant Alexander Wilhelm Bickell stayed several yards behind his men, watching them closely for any sign of carelessness. Were he to witness such a sign, he was prepared to deal with it quickly and brutally. After all, those were the underlying principles by which these Hessians conducted themselves in battle – with speed and brutality.

Bickell was a member of the 1st Battalion Grenadiers von Linsinge, some of the most feared and respected soldiers currently serving in North America. The term "Grenadiers" was a throwback to the day when some soldiers actually carried crude grenades as their primary weapon. Due to the weight of these grenades, the men who served in this capacity had traditionally been the largest and strongest available. Although the grenades were no longer used, two things had remained the same: these men were still known as Grenadiers, and they were still the largest and strongest men in the Hessian army. As a result, the Hessian Grenadiers were often used as the "shock troops" of the British Army, in many cases forming the point of the attack against an enemy.

Sergeant Bickell and his men had been part of the second wave of troops to come ashore at this God-forsaken location. They had been given the order to move ashore through the existing defensive perimeter that had been established by the first wave of British troops, and engage in reconnaissance as far as a mile or so inland. In addition to providing a defensive buffer for the army, they were also instructed to find any local inhabitants that might have information on the whereabouts of enemy troops, and "entice" them to return to the army's Headquarters. Neither the British officers issuing these orders, nor the Hessians themselves had any delusions regarding the lengths to which they were permitted to go in order to coax the desired behaviors of the citizenry. Once again, the tenants of speed and brutality would be brought to bear.

The men had been moving inland for the better part of an hour, when one of the Hessian soldiers in advance of the main body came trotting back to Sergeant Bickell.

"Sergeant," the man huffed, "up ahead is a clearing in the woods that appears a bit dangerous to move across without first bringing up some support. I respectfully suggest you come up and take a look for yourself."

The soldier was a good man, and Bickell was already certain that his advice was sound. Nevertheless, one never leads from the rear, at least not if you choose to maintain the respect of your men. Sergeant Bickell moved quickly behind the man for about 100 yards, coming to the aforementioned clearing.

"Ja, you are correct," Bickell confirmed to the soldier. "Bring up Corporal Stein's men and have them posted in pairs along the edge of the woods. I want them covering a front of 200 yards. And tell them to be quiet and still – we don't yet know what might be just ahead of us."

The soldier nodded, and moved away to find Corporal Stein. Bickell noted with approval that the soldier had not saluted him, a courtesy never given when in the possible presence of these Rebels. Such an act only served to alert any sharp-eyed enemy snipers as to who the senior enlisted and officers might be, making them a preferred target. Bickell snorted in disgust at the lack of military honor these Rebels displayed. In the three previous wars in which Sergeant Bickell had fought as a hired soldier, there had always been a sense of courtesy and respect that one side had extended to the other. This took the form in such ways as confronting your enemy face to face without hiding behind rocks and trees, a tactic employed with regular frequency and galling effectiveness by these Continental soldiers. Also, it was considered rude to target officers or senior enlisted troops during a battle – they were to be afforded the same opportunity to be killed as any other men; nothing more or less. Again, this tactic of shooting the leaders of the British Army during an engagement had sometimes had a demoralizing effect on the fighting spirit of these troops, as they often found themselves confused and leaderless at critical times.

Within just a few minutes, Hessian soldiers had spread themselves out in pairs all along the frontage of the clearing, exactly as Bickell had instructed. As he was turning back to bring the remainder of his troops forward, a movement on the other side of the field caught his eye. To his surprise, Bickell could see several Continental Army soldiers standing on a slight rise about 150 yards in front of him. And even more amazing was the fact that at least one of them appeared to be an officer! Under other circumstances, Bickell would have obeyed the rules of civilized warfare, and simply fired a warning shot so the enemy would remove themselves from their observation position. But this was truly an opportunity to provide these barbaric Rebels with a taste of their own medicine.

Bickell moved to the pair of Hessian soldiers situated closest to him, and pointed to the group of men across the way.

"You two, take careful aim and take your best shot at the enemy over there," he said, pointing across the clearing. The two men gave a brief look of surprise at their normally reserved sergeant, but they weren't about to pass up the opportunity to do that for which they were getting paid. They both raised their muskets, centered their sights slightly above their intended target to allow for the drop of the bullet, and fired almost simultaneously.

The range of a musket, even in the hands of an excellent marksman, was just about the distance between Bickell and the Americans. As a result, it was impossible to tell where these first shots had landed.

Bickell called to another pair of Hessians stationed close by, giving them similar instructions to fire at the enemy troops. In addition, he had the first two men reload and take a second shot. As the four soldiers fired the second volley, Bickell could clearly see several leaves in the trees around the enemy soldiers get ripped from their branches.

Like a hunter seized by the moment of stalking his prey, Bickell could feel his excitement rise as he ordered the four soldiers to reload and prepare for their next volley. The only thing wrong with this situation was the fact that the enemy had shown absolutely no indication of taking the rather direct hint to abandon their current position and return to the woods behind them. Even more maddening was the fact that the officer, a man who clearly towered over the others by nearly a head, stood facing Bickell and his men in a posture that could only be interpreted as defiance. Well, *sir*, Bickell thought with contempt, we'll see that you pay dearly for your personal vice of pride. With that, Bickell raised his own musket and aimed carefully at the tall American officer.

"Aim carefully, men, aim carefully. This one will be our shot," Bickell ordered to the four soldiers with their weapons raised into firing position. "On my command – fire!"

The five muskets fired in almost perfect unison, and Bickell noted with satisfaction that one of the enemy had obviously been struck by a musketball as he staggered backwards. However, he was disappointed to see that it was one of the soldiers standing next to the officer, and not the arrogant man for whom he had intended his shot.

As the five Hessians lowered their muskets, the enemy soldiers slowly and deliberately turned to the rear and disappeared behind the rise upon which they had been standing. All except the tall American who smartly came to attention, briskly adjusted his uniform coat, and performed an about face before following the others.

GENERAL GEORGE WASHINGTON
AUGUST 29, 1777
NINE MILES NORTH OF HEAD OF ELK

The six Continental Army soldiers rode along the rutted road at a brisk gallop, a sense of urgency to their pace. They needed to move as quickly as possible toward the landing site of the British in order to determine both the size of the force, as well as the speed with which they were moving inland.

This group of soldiers was not the typical scouting party that would normally have been sent on this mission. Against the strenuous objections of his staff, General George Washington had determined that he needed to see for himself exactly what was happening to the south of Philadelphia. He had received too much conflicting information recently to trust what the local population reported, and even his own soldiers had proven inconsistent with respect to the accuracy of their scouting reports. For these reasons, Washington had opted for the rather unconventional and very dangerous action, of serving as his own forward scout.

Traveling with him was Major Jarvis and a contingent of four bodyguards. These four men, hand selected due to their level of discipline and demonstrated military skills, were the only concession Washington had made to his own personal safety. He had initially argued that this larger group would make him potentially more visible, and therefore more vulnerable to capture, and he advocated for traveling with just Major Jarvis. However, when the remainder of his staff had virtually threatened to physically prevent him from departing in such a manner, he had given in to their demands for the additional men.

"General, we should be about ten miles from where Merkens had reported the landing of the British fleet," one of the soldiers reported. "If we leave the road and head in that direction, "he continued, pointing southwest, "we should run right into it."

"Sir," Major Jarvis cautioned, "if we leave the road and enter into the forest, we won't be able to see if there are any British soldiers which might have been deployed forward. We'll risk being ambushed, sir."

"Perhaps, Major, but we will be as invisible to them as they are to us," said Washington. "It should make for an interesting game of cat and mouse, don't you think?"

Major Jarvis nodded slightly, as the color drained from his face. Prior to the start of the war, Matthew Jarvis had been a banker, and his idea of excitement had been attending the theater with his wife followed by a pint or two of ale. To now be placed in this rather stressful situation was almost more than his frail personality could handle.

Washington, on the other hand, was a career army officer, having served for years in a variety of capacities. His reputation for bravery was well known and, although often embellished, was nevertheless well deserved. Washington had spent many years serving alongside of the British Army, most notably during the Seven Years War that had seen England and France fighting over huge sections of North America. Washington had been a member of General James Braddock's doomed expedition that had been all but wiped out in May of 1768, and the fact that he was one of the extremely few survivors of that massacre had formed the foundation of his larger than life image.

Washington's previous experience serving with the British Army not only provided him with a knowledge of military strategies and tactics, but also gave him an excellent understanding of specifically how his current enemy operated. This insight had already proved to be invaluable on a number of occasions, and would no doubt continue to do so.

—

One of Washington's bodyguards who had ridden a short distance in advance of the party quietly returned to the group. The fact that Major Jarvis had not even noted the man's presence until he had been less than ten yards away did little to settle the Major's nervous condition. The soldier rode close to Washington and spoke in a whisper.

"Sir, the woods come to a clearing about a hundred yards ahead. There's a gradual slope just before you get to the clearing that gives you a good view of the surrounding area. I think you might be interested in what there is to see, General."

Washington turned sharply, his attention suddenly gained by the man's comments.

"Lead on, Sergeant Barclay," Washington commanded. He then turned to face the others. "Gentlemen, follow me if you please."

"Sir," Major Jarvis said urgently, "perhaps it would be best to have two of the men scout the forward position, and return with a full report. I'm concerned about the prospect of having you so close and exposed to the enemy."

"Concerned about *me* being so close and exposed, eh Major?" Washington chided gently. "Come now – we'll be fine as long as we keep our eyes open and our wits about us. Move out, Sergeant!"

The group covered the distance to the clearing carefully but quickly, the ground rising over the last few yards just as the Sergeant had reported. The group dismounted before they had reached the crest of the rise and, leaving the horses to be tended by one of the men, the remaining five men moved forward on foot. As they came to the top of the rise, Sergeant Barclay pointed across on open field to the edge of a woods approximately 150 yards away.

"There, sir, on the edge of that tree line, you can see several Hessians posted just inside the woods. It's a bit difficult to see them at times because of their green uniforms, but every once in a while you can see them move slightly."

Washington could, indeed, see them when they moved, and once he knew where to look, their positions became very apparent. They were spread out in pairs, almost exactly 40 yards apart from what he could tell, and they were exercising excellent noise and movement discipline. Then again, for the Hessians this was no surprise. Although Washington had a great distaste for some of the rather brutish behaviors displayed by these men, he had no choice but to extend a grudging respect for their ability to operate in a militarily efficient manner.

Washington removed a small telescope from his jacket pocket, and slowly and deliberately scanned the positions of the enemy troops in front of him. As he did so, he realized that the Hessians were able to see him as well, and there was a sudden rush of movement as several of them moved back into the woods, probably looking to summon an officer to their position. Meanwhile, several of the remaining Hessians were taking careful aim with their muskets in the direction of Washington and his party. Washington saw a puff of white smoke escape from one of the Hessian muskets, and this was followed a split second later by the loud report of the weapon.

"Sir," a nervous Major Jarvis stated, "perhaps we should retreat back to the road and head back to Headquarters. I believe we've seen what we came to see, have we not, sir?"

"Major, while I will always appreciate your caution, it's not yet time to 'retreat', as you put it. You must understand, our purpose here is two-fold. First, we are here to observe the enemy; his strength, his movement, his disposition. But just as importantly, we are here for the enemy to observe *us*. It is my fervent desire that General Howe knows that we are aware of *his* presence. This may convince the good General to abandon any need for stealth and slow movement, and get him moving with alacrity."

As Washington finished his statement, there were several additional reports of muskets firing which, this time were followed by the sound of musketballs whizzing through the air. The Hessians were apparently starting to improve their aim.

"But sir," Jarvis asked, "why in the world would we want the British moving with alacrity? Wouldn't we rather they stay bogged down here in this God forsaken territory?"

A third round of muskets was fired in the distance, one of the rounds slightly grazing the arm of one of the men causing him to recoil in pain. Washington remained nearly oblivious to the fact that his current situation had suddenly become a dangerous one.

"Quite the contrary: until the British begin moving, I cannot know where they are headed. And until I know where they are headed, I cannot concentrate my Army." With this, Washington slowly turned to face Major Jarvis, a strange, dangerous smile on his face. "And until I can concentrate my Army, I cannot defeat the British."

Coming to attention and adjusting his uniform, Washington calmly turned and walked back down the slope of the rise and into the forest. He was preceded slowly by his three bodyguards, and a bit more speedily and sheepishly by Major Jarvis.

GENERAL WILLIAM HOWE
SEPTEMBER 2, 1777
ELKTON, DELAWARE

General William Howe, Commanding General of all British forces in North America, was leaning over a table carefully examining a map of the local territory when he heard a sharp rapping on the door.

"Enter!" he ordered, and his command was immediately followed by the appearance of Major General Charles Cornwallis, Howe's second-in-command. Cornwallis presented quite the grand sight as he entered the cramped dining room of the house Howe had established as his headquarters for the time being. As in almost all cases when Cornwallis reported to Howe in an official capacity, he was wearing his full dress uniform, complete with sword and sash. Howe had often considered telling Cornwallis that there was no need for such pomp and circumstance, especially when the army was on the move, but he strongly suspected that such a statement would have little effect on Cornwallis' dress code, and might even insult the man. Cornwallis was notoriously vain when it came to his appearance.

"Sir, General Cornwallis reporting as ordered!" the general stated, as he came to sharp attention.

"General, please stand at ease. I wonder if I might have your assistance in reviewing the available intelligence we have regarding our current position, as well as the roads leading north between here and Philadelphia. I must admit, I'm having some difficulty in making any sense of the combination of half-drawn maps, spotty scouting reports, and conflicting information from the locals."

In point of fact, Howe found himself facing a scenario that was significantly different from the one he had anticipated. First and foremost, he had been led to believe that there was a sizable portion of the population in the area was that still loyal to the British Crown. Howe had been told that these Loyalists would be more than willing to provide a wealth of assistance in the form of maps, directions, and intelligence. The reality of the situation was that the Army had encountered no more than a handful of Loyalists, and these individuals had been almost no help at all. Second, Howe had underestimated the amount of time that the Army would be at sea. As a result, he had almost no food remaining on board the ships to feed his troops, and the horses they had brought along had either died during the voyage, or they were so weak as to be virtually useless.

As a means of dealing with the shortage of food, Howe had been forced to send foraging parties out into the surrounding countryside. This was always a risky proposition, as the men sometimes had the tendency to become overzealous. What was intended to be an act of gathering food and paying the local population for anything taken often became nothing more than wandering bands of thieves wearing British or Hessian uniforms. Dear God! Howe suddenly realized that he had authorized those troops who were furthest inland to conduct the foraging, and those troops happened to be Hessians! Those heartless bastards were capable of anything, and he had set them loose on the unsuspecting countryside. Well, at least there was one thing that these Hessians understood, and that was iron-fisted discipline. If any of them were caught plundering, he would have them whipped, or perhaps even hanged depending on the severity of their crime.

Cornwallis laid his hat on a nearby chair, and moved over to the table. Once Howe could get Cornwallis to relax, he found him to be brilliant in terms of his ability to quickly and effectively assess a military situation, and recommend a course of action. As Cornwallis peered intently at the map, Howe could see that his subordinate was already at work putting his thoughts together.

"Sir, I assume these markings on the map are the current locations of our troops, is that correct?" Cornwallis asked.

"That is correct, General. Almost all of our troops have disembarked from the ships, and I have asked my brother to take his Fleet back down the Chesapeake Bay, and to then proceed up the Delaware Bay and into the Delaware River toward Philadelphia. My plan is for our Army to meet his Fleet somewhere south of the city, at which time we can combine our forces and make the final assault necessary to drive off the Rebels and take control of the city."

Cornwallis listened carefully, and nodded. "Yes sir, an excellent plan indeed. However, if I may suggest, we have a more immediate issue at hand, that being the lack of food and supplies for our men. With your permission, sir, I have a suggestion to deal with this potential crisis."

"Please, General, continue."

"Well sir, if we were to divide our Army into two columns which would then proceed northward on parallel courses, we would accomplish several objectives. First, two smaller columns versus one large one would allow us to move more quickly, especially considering the conditions of the surrounding geography. Second, the separation would provide us with the opportunity to forage for food over a larger area, giving greater assurance that our men would be well fed. We may even be able to begin building up our foodstuffs. And finally, when we get into close proximity of the enemy, it would provide us with the option of either regrouping - in the unlikely event of an attack - or have us already in position to flank and envelop any force we come upon."

As Howe listened to Cornwallis speak, he was reminded once again of how much he detested the man. Cornwallis was condescending, arrogant, and ambitious, and rumors had it that he was constantly looking for opportunities to discredit Howe. It was no secret that Major General Charles Cornwallis had every intention of eventually becoming the highest ranking British officer in North America, and that road led directly through Howe. However, if Howe was able to control these personality flaws, he could use Cornwallis' intellect and strategic genius to make himself look good. It was a tricky game, but Howe was good at the game, and the prize was worth it. The only thing that bothered Howe about the plan was that Cornwallis clearly downplayed the possibility of the Americans launching a serious attack. Although it wasn't enough of a weakness to scrap the plan, he had noticed the chronic tendency that Cornwallis had for underestimating the Americans. Howe worried that it would someday prove to be a potentially fatal flaw.

Howe, having almost immediately deciding to do exactly as Cornwallis was suggesting, stepped away from the table as if deep in thought, and allowed the silence to hang in the air.

"Yes, I see your points, General," Howe said slowly. "However, I do not relish the idea of dividing our army in the face of the enemy. I feel we may be inviting disaster if the entire Rebel Army was able to concentrate on one of our wings or the other."

"Sir, if I may be blunt, I don't believe the Rebel Army – or their pompous commander for that matter – is capable of concentrating on anything. I believe the risks we would be taking to be absolutely minimal, and the potential benefits to be significant."

Again Howe pretended to ponder the plan before finally stating,

"Yes, then that shall be our course of action. General Cornwallis, if you would please summon Major Pritchard, I'll have him gather our commanders to inform them of my plan."

Cornwallis, already making his way out of the room, couldn't prevent himself from pausing slightly at Howe's order. Howe, of course, had purposely referred to the plan as being his own for two reasons: the first was to let Cornwallis know that when they held their meeting with the other British commanders, that Cornwallis was expected to act as if Howe had devised the strategy. The second reason was to insure that Cornwallis knew who was still in charge. Howe didn't give a damn who was smarter or more skilled in the arts of military strategy – General William Howe was the man in charge, and he intended it to stay that way. No enemy, without or within, was going to change that.

Brigadier General William Maxwell
4:00 AM - September 5, 1777
Red Clay Creek, Delaware

No man in the Continental Army doubted that Daniel Morgan's Pennsylvania riflemen were some of the best marksmen in the Colonies. They had demonstrated their usefulness to this army time and time again, and they could always be counted on to hold up their end of the fight, and then some.

But Daniel Morgan and his incredible men with their Pennsylvania Long Rifles had been sent north to assist in the fight going on between the American General Thomas Gage and the British General John Burgoyne in upstate New York. Almost immediately, the effects could be felt throughout the army, if only from a morale perspective. Morgan's men had been larger than life, and louder than life, and the absence of their personalities left a gap that was as real as any gap in a battle line.

General Washington had made the decision to send Daniel Morgan north, being aware of the effect it would have on his main army. Therefore, he had also developed a plan to replace these missing men, understanding that the substitute might not fully measure up to its predecessor. Washington had selected Brigadier General William Maxwell, one of the most highly respected officers in his Army, to recruit and train a unit of 700 sharpshooters to be used as scouts and skirmishers. Washington had ordered that 100 men out of seven different battalions would be hand picked to form this new unit, and that the criteria would be experience, demonstrated bravery and, above all, marksmanship. If Morgan's men weren't capable of being in two places at one time then, by God, there would at least be a substitute worthy of comparison.

General Maxwell had jumped at the opportunity to create this new elite unit within the Army, and he had quickly selected his men and initiated their training. While other units sat idly passing the time, Maxwell's men had trained long and hard at infantry tactics, cover and concealment, and marksmanship. Although he had only been given a few weeks to prepare his men, this new battalion was sharp and motivated by the time of their first assignment.

—

In addition to his rather dangerous reconnaissance a few days earlier, Washington had also conducted several additional trips intended to ascertain the intentions of the British. These trips, in addition to the dozens of other patrols conducted by his men, had convinced Washington that the British were moving north in the direction of the Brandywine Creek. Washington had recalled the remainder of his army that had been scattered throughout southern New Jersey and Pennsylvania, and was now concentrated several miles south of Philadelphia. Washington had plans of deploying his army along the creek, but not before he made life miserable for the advancing British.

It was exactly for this purpose that Washington had created Maxwell's Brigade. His plan was to slow the advance of the enemy through a series of carefully placed ambushes along their path, taking advantage of the hit and run tactics employed by his men along with their knowledge of the surrounding area. If successful, this strategy had the potential to not only bleed British manpower as it moved north, but would also demoralize his opponent with continuous casualties and a constant need to be vigilant.

Cooch's Bridge was a logical crossing point for the British as they moved across the Christiana River. Washington ordered Maxwell's men to move south across the bridge and establish an ambush along the road that led north. The topography was perfect for this tactic, with the surrounding woods pressing up closely on the narrow road. A relatively small group of men would be capable of placing themselves just inside the tree line making them nearly undetectable, yet would put them only a few yards away from their intended target. Washington had ordered Maxwell to engage the enemy approximately two miles south of the bridge with instructions to fire upon the British, inflict whatever casualties possible, and then retreat northward to establish a similar position closer to the bridge. The plan was extremely simple, which is exactly what made it so potentially deadly.

—

William Maxwell sat astride his horse, watching as his men filed past him in the moonlight across the Christiana Bridge. He was pleased with what he saw. Although this group of approximately 700 men was far from perfect, they were definitely the best that the Continental Army had to offer. They moved with a speed and efficiency that only comes from a military unit that has confidence in their ability to meet the enemy and emerge the victor. Such a belief isn't something you *tell* an army – it's something you *build* in them. And Maxwell had built such a belief.

It was, unfortunately, a belief that was not held by the rest of the Continental Army, which still feared the British as being bigger, more capable, and more disciplined than they. The fact that this was true wasn't the point – the point was that the Americans *believed* it to be true. Maxwell made a mental note to speak with General Washington on some ideas he had to change the perception the Continental Army had of itself. But for right now, he needed to focus on the situation at hand.

The situation was this: approximately 9000 British and Hessian soldiers were approaching his position along this narrow road to his front. He had briefed his officers to order their men to fire no more than five or six rounds before they were to retreat northward to a second predetermined position along the road. Maxwell knew his men were solid, but he also knew that given time and opportunity, the British troops would rally and attack any position that the Americans chose to defend. Therefore, Maxwell's plan was simple: don't defend a position. His men would hit and retreat, using the concealment tactics many of them had learned from fighting against the American Indians in a hundred small brush wars.

As Maxwell's men moved south across Cooch's Bridge, he noted with satisfaction that they were dividing themselves into two equal columns, one moving to the left of the road, the other to the right. His plan called for approximately three hundred men to position themselves on either side of the road, with the remaining 100 or so men forming a position to provide cover for the retreating forces as they moved north back over Cooch's Bridge. Once again, simplicity was the order of the day.

Maxwell had placed Major Kearney in charge of the left column, while Major Harris would command the right. Maxwell himself would remain at the bridge with the covering force, a position he felt would afford him the greatest ability to manage the entire battle. A year ago he would have placed himself at the very head of one of the columns; however, experience and maturity had taught him that his role needed to be one of commander, not that of a forward scout. Despite this knowledge, it still stung him to see his men move into combat without having himself in the lead.

Maxwell settled himself in his saddle, and continued to offer words of encouragement to his passing troops. Each responded in their own way: some with an enthusiastic wave of a hat, some with comments of confidence and bravado, and still others with a grim nod of their head. How strange to find men of such different backgrounds and personalities; different heritages and social standing; some even with different religions, languages, and races; united together in this one cause. What motivated such men to answer this call to duty? Maxwell realized that he had never really examined his own motivations to answer such a call, and made a second mental note to do so sometime in the future. But not now. Now was the time for action, not reflection.

MAJOR NICHOLAS KEARNEY
8:50 AM - SEPTEMBER 5, 1777
TWO MILES SOUTH OF COOCH'S BRIDGE ·

Major Nicholas Kearney continued to move as quietly through the forest as possible. Although he had sent three scouts forward to alert the main column of the approach of the enemy, he was also aware of the fact that the enemy might have sent their own scouts forward. And those forward scouts would most likely be experienced Hessians who would just as soon slit the throat of any enemy soldier they encountered. As a result, Kearney trusted only his own ability to remain aware of his surroundings.

All around him, men were playing the same game of cat and mouse. The need to remain quiet and undetected was paramount: if the British were alerted to their presence before they had set their ambush, the results could be disastrous. His men would find themselves disorganized and quickly outnumbered, and there could easily be wholesale slaughter and capitulation of his force. At the very least, the Americans would miss the opportunity to draw first blood against an enemy moving to attack their capital.

Kearney saw one of his forward scouts approaching him through the forest. The man came up close and whispered to Kearney.

"Sir, this here's the position we picked out for the ambush. Major Harris is just there on the other side of the road," he said, pointing to his left. Upon looking across the road, Kearney was unable to detect any movement, and realized that either Harris' men were extremely stealthy, or they hadn't yet reached their position. He truly hoped it was the former. "Private Noles just reported in from his position down the road that the British are about a mile away and moving like turtles. He said they was pulling along some cannon that looked big enough to knock down a house, but that it was really slowing them down. He also said that their forward scouts are damn near right with their column! He said they was no more than 100 or so feet in front of the main column! I sure ain't no General, but I can't figure that one out."

Neither could Kearney, but he had long since given up any attempt to understand his enemy. Kearney had grown up on the Pennsylvania frontier, learning at a very early age that when facing an enemy you needed to "spread out and look out," as his father would say. He had since lost count of the number of times that this sound advice had possibly saved his life when facing the Indians. Well, the British may be looking out, but they sure weren't spreading out. The Americans would make them pay for this tactical error.

"All right Private Nash, good job," Kearney whispered. "Now go get Noles and the other scout, and move yourselves back in with the main force. We'll be establishing our position right here. Once you've done that, I need you to carefully and quickly cross the road – *carefully*, Private – and establish contact with Major Harris. Inform him of our position, and insure that his men don't establish themselves any further forward than this spot. When you've done that come back across the road – even more carefully this time, as the enemy will be closer to our position – and report to me. Do you understand my orders, Private?"

"Yes, sir," said the Private, giving Kearney a broad grin as he departed as quickly as he had arrived. Kearney trusted the young scout completely. Not only had the boy proven himself to be steady and competent in the face of the enemy, he was also Kearney's cousin who had come east with him to join the Continental Army just over a year ago. He had promised his aunt, his mother's sister, that he would watch out for his younger cousin and keep him out of harm's way. Kearney realized with discomfort that he had violated this promise more times than he cared to recall.

—

The men had settled into their positions quickly, taking advantage of the cover provided by Mother Nature. Kearney noted with satisfaction that, although he could see his men surrounding him, it was only because he knew where to look. Anyone coming down the road would be oblivious to the presence of his men until they were just a few yards away; and at that point, it would be too late.

As he surveyed his position for the hundredth time, he stopped the movement of his head and focused his attention on something he thought he heard. There it was! The faint sound of jostling equipment! Once again, Kearney was surprised at the carelessness of his enemy when it came to stealth. His men had been instructed to leave any equipment behind that might move about and give away their position. Clearly, the British soldiers had not been issued similar orders, as the sound of clanking bayonets, canteens, and uniform buckles carried clearly through the early morning air.

Kearney prayed that his men would follow the strict orders they had been given. The plan was for Major Harris and his men to open fire first from their side of the road, followed 20 seconds later by a volley from the soldiers on this side of the road. The idea was to not have the entire force fire a volley at once, thereby causing a natural pause while the Americans reloaded. This might allow the British to quickly organize and respond to the ambush. By staggering the volleys, the Americans had the chance to keep their enemy under constant fire, thereby making it more difficult to react. Once each man had fired five or six rounds, their orders were to move quickly to their second pre-selected position about a half a mile back up the road, and greet the British with yet another warm reception. This tactic was to be used a total of three times, at which time the Americans had been ordered to retreat in good order back to the main body located at Red Clay Creek.

Kearney was confident that this first action would be successful, assuming the Americans were able to maintain the element of surprise. It was the second and third actions that concerned him. At that point, the element of surprise would be gone, and they would be facing an alert and angry enemy, intent on revenge for the perceived cowardly tactics of the Rebels. Although he was unhappy to admit it, Kearney knew that his men simply couldn't stand toe to toe with the British in a battle and expect to have any chance of success. Perhaps that sad fact would change someday, but for now it was the reality with which they were faced.

But once again, now was not the time to fret over the conduct of the Continental Army in the future – now was the time to fret about the conduct of his men today. And that question was about to be answered as the first enemy troops appeared on the road.

PRIVATE WILLIAM DEVLIN
9:00 AM - SEPTEMBER 5, 1777
TWO MILES SOUTH OF COOCH'S BRIDGE

The British soldiers moved carefully along the road, casting cautious and fearful glances to the foliage that very nearly enveloped them on their left and right. It didn't take a military genius to realize that they were moving through perfect ambush terrain, and their officers had sharply ordered them to stay alert or risk being shot at point-blank range. The specific use of such a term had had the desired effect, and not a single man in the column could be accused of shirking their military responsibilities at this moment.

Private William Devlin, still a relative novice at the art of war, had nevertheless proven himself to be steady and reliable under stressful conditions. As a result, he was looked up to by the other men in his unit, and was grudgingly respected by some of the more senior corporals and sergeants. Unfortunately, along with this grudging respect often came the assignment of some less than desirable duties – in this case, walking at the front of the column, tasked with being the forward eyes of the British Army. Although the Colonel had deployed some of the Hessians forward as skirmishers, the heavy foliage dictated that they could only move a few yards in advance of the main column. This left William feeling uncomfortably exposed to whatever might lie ahead.

William sensed, more than saw, the two Hessians just to his front and left, suddenly freeze. They moved closer to one another, and appeared to be anxiously conversing in whispers as they pointed forward. One of the two men turned and began trotting back to the main column when the entire world around William seemed to suddenly explode. The Hessian soldier running in his direction was hurled forward, struck from behind by some unseen force. His body landed with a dull thud perhaps ten feet from where William was standing.

The air around William was suddenly alive with whirring, whining projectiles, and he quickly dove to one side of the road scrambling desperately for some protection from the hellish storm. Other men behind him, not so quick to take similar actions, found themselves in a veritable killing zone with nowhere to run. Sickening, dull thuds rang out, as the heavy musket balls flying through the air found their marks in the bodies of the unprotected British soldiers.

William, now lying prone just inside the tree line on the side of the road, looked behind him and was treated to a scene directly out of one of his worst nightmares. Some men scattered about in fear and confusion, literally running into one another. Others more disciplined began retreating quickly back down the road in the direction they had come. Still others used tactics similar to William, as they desperately searched for some protection in the nearby tree line.

As musket balls continued to find their intended targets, the effects were horrendous. One soldier screamed out in pain as his leg was literally shattered just above the knee. Another man dropped his musket and clutched at his chest in horror, as blood gushed from a gaping wound. Still another cried out as he was struck by a bullet in the arm, but his cries were cut brutally short as a second round struck him just above the forehead and cleanly removed the top part of his head. Everywhere men were yelling in agony, in fear, in frustration.

A young private from William's battalion was lying several yards away from him, having been shot in the stomach. The musketball had entered him from the right and slightly behind, and had exited through the front of his torso. Although the musketball was traveling at a relatively slow speed, the fact that it was so large and heavy when combined with how close the marksmen had been from his target, the result was devastating. The boy was lying on his back with his hands pressed against his stomach where the musketball had left his body. William could see that the soldier was holding something close to his body, but he couldn't quite see what it was. The Private spied William hugging the ground just a short distance away, and called out to him in a weak, pitiful voice.

"Hey mate, can you give me a hand here? I need a hand here."

The air continued to be alive with the sound of musket balls, and William didn't even dare raise his head off the ground, let alone move over to the wounded soldier.

"I – I can't come over there. It's too dangerous!" William said to the man. "Hang on just a minute, there will be reinforcements here straight away. They'll help you when they get here."

"But I need your help now!" said the Private more insistently. "I can't hold on to these much longer by myself – they're getting too big!"

With horror, William realized the soldier was referring to his own intestines, which were protruding grossly from the wound in his stomach. The Private was attempting to keep them inside his body with his hands, but the gaping wound was allowing them to gradually escape from the location in which Nature had intended. When the soldier referred to needing a hand, he meant it literally. William was overcome with disgust at what he saw, and he rolled over on his side and threw up into the weeds along the side of the road.

The Private called out with less energy now, as his life continued to slip through his bloody fingers and stain the ground around him. "Please, Mate, just crawl over here. Just crawl over and help me. *Please!*"

"I...can't... come...over!" William hissed. "I'll be shot if I move! Just wait for the reinforcements! They'll be here in a minute, damn it."

"But I don't have a minute, Mate. I need your help *now*! Please don't let me die. You cowardly bastard, please don't let me die!"

—

But even amidst this chaos, there were others yelling orders and attempting to gain some control of the situation. William watched in amazement as Sergeant Myers, his own sergeant, moved recklessly along the road, screaming at men to get on their feet and face the enemy, wherever they might be. William was sure that, with all of the lead in the air, it would only be a matter of seconds before Myers would find himself on the receiving end of a Rebel musketball. But Myers continued to function unscathed, as he gathered up some of the men, got them on their feet, and began to restore some semblance of order. His actions gave many of the men confidence, and they soon formed a ragged yet steady firing line and began to return fire in the direction of the hidden enemy.

William, almost unconsciously, found himself rising to his feet and moving to join his comrades. As he passed the wounded Private, he briefly peered into the lifeless eyes of the man. The soldier's hands had fallen to his sides, giving a gruesome view to a part of his body that had never been intended to see the light of day.

As he reached the firing line, he suddenly felt a searing pain on the side of his neck, on the exposed flesh just above the collar of his coat. He instinctively reached up and placed his hand at the point of the pain, and it came away covered in blood. William staggered and almost fell to the ground as he felt a rush of nausea rumble his stomach, but he was held up by the firm grasp of someone standing by his side. Glancing to his right, William found himself looking at Private Willis, his friend with whom he had shared his position just after the landing at Head of Elk. Instead of the mischievous glint of humor that was usually there, William was surprised to see an almost eerie calmness in the eyes of Willis.

"Come on lad, steady now," Willis said. "Put your arm around me shoulder and let's move slowly back down the road. It won't do for them Rebels to see us running away, now will it?"

Although the term was often tossed about, William realized that he was truly witnessing a quintessential example of courage under fire. He allowed himself to be guided away from the killing zone, which had started to decrease in intensity. And then, almost as suddenly as it had started, the firing ended with the exception of a few scattered shots fired by the stubborn British soldiers still holding their firing line in the middle of the road.

—

Men continued to shout, as reinforcements began to move up from their positions further back in the column. The fact that it had taken this long for additional support to arrive at the point of attack was testimony to the wisdom of the selected ambush site. The road, no more than fifteen feet wide, simply didn't allow for a rapid movement of troops from one point to another. As a result, the Rebels had been able to bring superior firepower to a single spot, and negate the overall strength of the British force. Although this tactic had been used by the Rebels on many occasions in the past, the British still found themselves woefully deficient in their ability to respond effectively. It was something that had continued to be a thorn in the side of the British Army in America, and no one had any delusions that this thorn would be removed any time soon.

Major Nicholas Kearney
9:15 AM - September 5, 1777
Just south of Cooch's Bridge

Major Kearney watched with satisfaction as the volleys of his soldiers wreaked havoc on the ranks of the British. He counted at least 30 British soldiers lying on the road, while dozens of others retreated hastily back in the direction from which they had come. It took all of his self-discipline as a commander to refrain from giving the order to attack the enemy column of troops. They had been surprised and hit hard, and were now retreating in disarray – the opportunity seemed almost too good to pass up.

However, Kearney knew that this action was just a part of a larger plan, and he reluctantly gave the order to pull back to their second position along the road. As many of his men fired a final defiant shot and began to retreat, Kearney stayed a few more seconds to observe the enemy. He quickly realized that his decision to follow orders was not only the strategically correct move, but it appeared to be turning into the tactically prudent maneuver. Despite their initial confused retreat, the British were beginning to form stable lines of defense. Even more significantly, hundreds of reinforcements were beginning to appear, and they quickly spread out with military precision along the road and deep into the woods on either side of the road. Had Kearney opted to remain and fight, he would have quickly found himself facing a much larger and well organized enemy. If the Americans had learned anything in the first two years of this war, it was that numbers and discipline were rarely on their side.

Kearney turned and followed the last few remaining members of his unit as the British reinforcements loosed a coordinated, albeit randomly aimed volley into the surrounding woods. Although none of the Americans were hit, it did serve to encourage them with respect to the speed of their withdrawal.

The ambush had gone extremely well for the Americans. The troops on either side of the road had deployed themselves in almost perfect alignment, thanks in no small part to the brave actions of Private Nash, Kearney's nephew. The boy had personally placed the head of Major Harris' column in position, much to the chagrin of a few of the American officers who had chafed at the idea of a Private acting in a leadership capacity. But combat tends to reveal the character of a man, and Nash had shown himself to be a respectful but forceful individual, finally convincing the perturbed officers that only he had the knowledge necessary to accurately position the head of their column. These officers would later give a grudging acknowledgement of the keen instincts of the boy, and he would be the recipient of many free rounds of drinks while recounting the story of this day over the long and prosperous life he was destined to lead.

But the British were now fully alerted to the presence of the Americans, who would need to be considerably more proficient in their attacks and retreats. Any hesitation on the part of the Americans; any poorly selected escape route; could turn this hit and run battle into a stand and fight battle that held little chance of success for the Rebels.

Major Kearney nearly stumbled upon his men hidden in the thick forest as he continued to move northward to Cooch's Bridge. That's good, he thought, I wasn't able to see them before I was literally on top of them. They had spread themselves out in a manner similar to the first ambush, however this time they had selected a spot that was just beyond a bend in the road. This provided the obvious benefit of not being in the line of sight of the carefully advancing British until the last minute. However, it also carried the drawback of having fewer enemy soldiers in the ambush site at the time of the attack. Colonel Maxwell had decided that this was a fair trade off in that, although there would almost certainly be fewer casualties for the British, there was also less potential for the Americans to suffer significant casualties themselves.

—

As Kearney and his men waited anxiously for the arrival of the British, he reflected on his brief military career that had brought him to this lonely stretch of road in Delaware. Nicholas Kearney had become an officer in his unit by virtue of the fact that he had brought a small amount of combat experience with him from western Pennsylvania. At first he had protested that such limited experience in no way qualified him to be an officer, but after discovering the shameful lack of any military experience at all on the part of most of the other officers, Kearney had reluctantly agreed to the position.

He soon proved himself to be worthy of the title of officer, and became virtually universally respected by the men not only of his own outfit, but of many of the men throughout the small Continental Army. Washington, always on the lookout for promising talent, had quickly promoted Nicholas to his current rank of Major, and had personally recommended to Colonel Maxwell that he choose Kearney as one of his two principal subordinates along with Major Harris when creating his elite unit.

However, Nicholas had quickly learned that having the respect of your men doesn't always translate into getting them to do what you need them to do, especially under the horrifying conditions of the battlefield. During numerous minor and major battles that had been fought between the British and the Americans over the last year, Kearney had been constantly frustrated by the unwillingness and inability of the average American soldier to conduct himself with any degree of discipline when placed in a combat situation. Time after time, Kearney had ordered his men to advance, only to see them frozen in place or worse, retreat as if the Devil himself was chasing after them.

Someday these men are going to have to learn to stand up and fight the British if we're going to have any chance of winning this war, Kearney thought to himself. Despite his genuine belief that this change was possible – even destined – Kearney also believed that things would continue to get worse before they began to get better.

—

Major Kearney roused himself back to the present and took stock of his current situation. He had had an opportunity to speak briefly with Major Harris commanding the column on the other side of the road, and both had agreed that they should conduct only one additional ambush as opposed to the total of three ambushes that had been originally planned. Based on the observation of the enemy's ability to deploy quickly and effectively while under fire, this seemed to the two officers as a wiser course of action.

Kearney, always mindful of the chain of command, had sent a messenger back to Colonel Maxwell at Cooch's Bridge, proposing the change of plans. The Colonel, after being briefed on the situation and the subsequent speedy reaction of the British, had given his agreement to the modified ambush plans.

His men were clearly on edge, judging by the strained looks on their sweat-streaked faces. He considered moving among them and providing some encouragement, but he didn't know how long it would be before the British appeared around the bend in the road. Private Nash had yet to return with a report on the position of the enemy, but Kearney had ordered Nash to advance no more than a hundred yards or so beyond the forward edge of their position. This limited distance would give the Americans precious little time to prepare for the next action.

Almost as if he had been reading Kearney's mind, Private Nash appeared just ahead in the woods, moving quickly in his direction. Unlike the last encounter, this time Nash had lost his almost cocky demeanor, which had been replaced with a definite sense of urgency.

"Major," Nash whispered to Kearney as he came up beside him, "the British are moving at a right frightful pace this time! They've left the cannon they were toting behind them, dropped most of their gear, and put them Hessians out in front – a lot of 'em, too! I don't think it's gonna be as much fun this time!"

Kearney smiled at the innocence of his young nephew, having himself never actually considered the use of the word "fun" when describing combat.

"What else did you see, Marcus," Kearney asked. Kearney rarely addressed his nephew by his first name, wanting to avoid any show of familiarity, as well as maintain some level of military protocol that was so often lacking in the Continental Army. Even after two years of war, the Americans continued to find it difficult to respect the formalities of rank. In this case, Kearney felt as if a brief display of kinship might have the effect of calming down the excited young man.

"I guess them Lobsterbacks figured they ain't too keen on being shot at from the woods," Nash stated, using a newly coined derogatory term for the British soldiers. "Now they're moving down the road with their skirmishers spread out further ahead and some of 'em out on each side into the woods. They sure were actin' stupid the first go round, but I guess they learn pretty quickly."

Maxwell had anticipated this being the case, and as a result had instructed his two subordinates to keep any attacks following the first ambush brief. Maxwell had been explicit in his orders that the purpose of these encounters was to inflict some casualties and demoralize the enemy. There was no intention of this turning into a general engagement until General Washington determined it was the right time and place to do so.

"Very well, Private. Take a position with the rest of the men, and prepare for action. And Private…"

Nash had turned to move to the rear, and quickly stopped and faced his uncle. "Yes, Major?" Nash asked.

"Perhaps this is a story that would be best left untold to your mother and your Aunt Betsy, eh?"

Private Nash smiled broadly, the confidence returning. "Yes sir, perhaps that might be best."

As Nash moved off, the quiet of the woods was replaced by the clear sound of hundreds of men moving closer. Turning to his rear and looking into the faces of the men around him, Kearney could see that he wasn't the only one who was aware of the approach of the enemy.

SERGEANT ALEXANDER BICKELL
9:40 AM - SEPTEMBER 5, 1777
JUST SOUTH OF COOCH'S BRIDGE

Although the British and Hessian soldiers had taken a pounding, they were anything but demoralized or frightened of what lay ahead of them. Quite the contrary – they were now bent on avenging their losses, especially at the hands of a cowardly enemy that hid in the bushes and took cheap shots at a professional army. These Americans could never win this war, or any war for that matter, so long as they lacked honor and appreciation for the true art of war.

These were the thoughts of Sergeant Alexander Wilhelm Bickell, as he moved cautiously but confidently at the head of the column of Hessian soldiers. Bickell had been a hundred yards or so behind the head of the column when they had first been attacked by the enemy, and he quietly scolded himself for not being out front where he knew he belonged. The officers had insisted that the senior enlisted men not recklessly expose themselves by walking ahead of the army, but Bickell knew that in order to have the maximum control of his men, and therefore exert the greatest influence on the fighting, that was exactly where he needed to be. Therefore, he now ignored the orders given to him, and placed himself not a hundred yards behind the lead elements, but 50 yards ahead of it.

Bickell hated to admit it, but the attack had been surprisingly well coordinated, and the marksmanship had been nothing short of excellent. These two factors had combined to make that initial skirmish deadly for the British and Hessians. Bickell had personally supervised the loading of no fewer than 30 soldiers onto the empty wagons that had been brought along for the specific purpose of removing dead and wounded men from the battlefield. He had steeled himself to the pathetic cries and moans that had come from these wretched wagons, as he had always been able to do. Most men avoided the duty of dealing with the wounded as if they were avoiding the plague, and those that were reluctantly drafted into helping in this capacity almost always showed the signs of overwhelming distress. Some threw up at the sight of the wounds that had been inflicted on their friends and comrades, while others cried openly at having to witness things that no person should ever have to see.

But Bickell had developed a sense of detachment that allowed him to function efficiently in the face of overwhelming pain and suffering. He had developed this skill of callousness at an early age, having been raised in an affectionless household by an emotionally distant mother and a father who had apparently derived great pleasure from beating his four children. As the oldest, Alexander had often absorbed the punishment for his younger siblings, sometimes by default, and sometimes because he had willingly taken the blame for the perceived transgressions of the others. The ability to physically and emotionally detach himself from his environment had quickly become both an effective coping mechanism as well as a means for survival.

It had also insured that Alexander would take the first opportunity he had to leave home, which had come in the form of the army when he was 16 years old. His father had learned that the Principality in which they lived, Alsace-Lorrain, was looking for soldiers to be used as mercenaries in the many wars being fought throughout Europe, as well as the rest of the world. The Prince of their territory, always looking for ways to make additional money to line his pockets, had offered a small enlistment bonus to any man who was willing to serve. When Alexander's father had heard this, he had promptly marched his oldest son to the nearest enlistment location, and announced that Alexander had a desire to join the army, serve his Prince, and see the world. Alexander had uttered no such desire to his father or anyone else for that matter, but the chance to get away from his abusive life was more than he could resist. So, he had kept his mouth shut and calmly signed the necessary papers. His father had proceeded to accept the money for his enlistment, and walk away without so much as a glance back in the direction of his own flesh and blood.

That had been almost nine years ago, and Bickell had never once regretted his decision. He had found a level of stability and discipline that had become almost comfortable for him. Alexander's father had beaten him arbitrarily, and had never shown any recognition for positive behavior or achievement on the part of his son. Conversely, Alexander had been beaten only twice during his time in the military, and he had arguably deserved it on both occasions. In addition, as he had demonstrated the natural skills of both being a soldier as well as leading soldiers, he had been rewarded with promotions, culminating in the significant rank of Sergeant that he currently held. He had no delusions about the harshness of the life he had chosen, but it was a harshness with rules and predictability.

—

Sergeant Bickell had been moving briskly for short distances, then stopping and listening to his surroundings. This allowed him to maintain his distance in front of the column, while also affording him the opportunity to stay aware of what may lie ahead. He had been moving in this manner for 20 minutes or so, and was beginning to entertain the possibility that the attack by the Americans may have been a once and done affair. Just ahead of him was a bend in the road, and a sense for danger developed over countless battles and skirmishes told him to be cautious. It was nothing more than a feeling, but he had long since learned to listen carefully when it made itself known.

Bickell motioned to the two men just behind him to stop moving, then slowly instructed them with hand signals to come abreast of him and move silently into the woods on either side of the road. The two Hessians, hand picked by Bickell, did exactly as they were ordered, and the three began to move slowly forward. As they reached the bend in the road, Bickell once again silently ordered his flanking guards to halt and listen.

There! Bickell had detected a slight movement in the trees just to their right front. To the untrained eye, the movement could have been caused by anything from a small animal to the slight breeze moving the hundreds of branches in the surrounding woods. But the warning signals in his brain were flashing much louder than before, and he slowly faced to the rear, and gave hand signals to the troops 50 yards behind him to come to a halt. With a precision borne of hundreds of hours of training, the Hessians behind him quickly fanned out in a skirmish line, and patiently awaited further directions from their Sergeant.

Bickell now faced an important decision. He could attack immediately with this relatively small detachment of Hessians, thereby disrupting the second ambush that was clearly being planned by the Rebels. Although this would certainly ruin any plans by the Americans of surprising the British a second time, it offered little potential for any significant engagement with the enemy. The Americans would simply retreat in the face of an attack, not being willing to risk a general engagement. Or, he could take the time to deploy additional troops on either side of the road and move them farther into the woods. These additional troops, along with the expansion of the flanks, presented the possibility of enveloping the Rebel battle lines and catching them in a trap. But if the Americans became aware of this maneuver, they would be able to escape without any fighting whatsoever.

Bickell chose the option of immediate attack, not being willing to spook the Rebels into a clean retreat. Better to do a little damage, Bickell thought, than to allow these cowards to retreat unscathed. Besides, Bickell had never had the reputation of being conservative in his actions in combat, and he had no desire to alter that reputation.

"Detachment!" he bellowed to his men, "come on line and prepare to engage the enemy!"

The 50 or so Hessians that made up the skirmish line immediately came abreast of one another, and prepared to fire a volley upon the orders of their Sergeant. There was no wasted movement among the men, certainly no confusion, not even a real sense of urgency. The men completed the necessary maneuvers with a calm professionalism that never ceased to amaze Bickell. Many of these Hessians were still teenagers, and virtually none of them had any passion regarding who won or lost this particular war. Yet, they performed as well as any army that had ever fought in the defense of its homeland. Perhaps it was this almost apathetic detachment that allowed them to focus on the task at hand, without becoming entangled in the web of who was wrong or right.

"Detachment, take aim – fire!" Bickell roared, and 50 muskets erupted as a single shot into the woods. The response from the unseen enemy was a ragged return fire with no coordination, as the Rebels had not been prepared for being discovered and fired upon. The sporadic firing from the woods continued for several seconds, as the Americans made individual decisions as to if and when to fire their weapons. The result was a poorly aimed, poorly coordinated volley being unleashed upon the Hessians, and Sergeant Bickell quickly took advantage of the situation.

"Detachment, fix bayonets and prepare to charge!" he shouted, as the skirmish line quickly re-loaded their weapons and locked their bayonets in place in anticipation of continuing the attack. Meanwhile, reinforcements in the form of a battalion of British troops had conveniently arrived to take their place beside the Hessian skirmish line, and Bickell waited for several seconds while these new troops prepared themselves for the bayonet charge about to occur. Although not quite as experienced as their Hessian counterparts, these British soldiers were well disciplined and, more importantly, eager to fight. The addition of these men alongside the original line made for a formidable force, and the men were virtually chomping at the bit to be ordered forward into the face of their enemy.

Ordinarily, an officer would take over command of a unit of this size at this point in time, but none had yet to appear on the scene. Sergeant Bickell realized that he had already far exceeded his role as a senior enlisted man, but had no intention of denying these troops the opportunity to even the score with the enemy. Right or wrong, Bickell was about to make his second momentous decision in the last two minutes.

"Detachment, on my order at the double time – charge!" Bickell shouted, and the entire line of British and Hessian troops moved forward with a roar of approval and revenge. The sight of hundreds of men attacking on his command sent a chill down his spine, and he was reminded once again of why he chose to remain in this profession. It was a life that was barbaric and unforgiving by its very nature, but Bickell couldn't imagine feeling any more alive than he did at this very moment.

Apparently, the sight of a bold attack being made by disciplined troops had a similar effect of sending chills down the spines of the Rebels. A few paused briefly to fire final shots at their enemy, but most had already turned and headed in the opposite direction. By fear, by design, or more likely by a combination of both, the Americans were resorting to their standard tactic of "shoot and scoot", a strategy which had not produced any victories for their army, but had at least insured on many occasions that they would survive to fight another day.

Three or four of the Rebels, however, had been unlucky enough to get hit by the initial volley fired by the Hessians, and their comrades had been unable to remove them from the woods in their hasty retreat. These unfortunate souls were soon set upon by the British and Hessians as they advanced into the woods. The heat of battle was high, and compassion was nowhere to be found in the hearts of the attacking troops as they brutally and repeatedly drove their bayonets into the bodies of the wounded Americans. The high-pitched screams of the slaughtered men could be heard above the din of the battle, and there was no doubt in the minds of anyone within earshot of what fate had befallen these men.

Sergeant Bickell disapproved of this treatment of the enemy; not because he believed in any quarter being given, but because he believed it caused the enemy to retaliate with similar atrocities of their own. It also tended to sway the sympathies of the local population away from the British, thereby making their occupation of the surrounding area that much more dangerous and difficult. But he had arrived too late to take any action to stop it – what was done could not be undone. Bickell angrily addressed the men who had murdered the wounded Americans.

"Damn you for this!" he shouted at them. "Have you no understanding of your actions? Every time you kill a wounded Rebel, you place the life of one of your own comrades at risk!"

"But Sergeant," one of the men stated, "these men were cowards who ambushed us from the safety of the woods. They don't deserve to be treated as soldiers, but rather as common criminals."

Sergeant Bickell glowered dangerously at the soldier who had had the temerity to question his Sergeant. The soldier backed away as Bickell approached him and placed his face inches from the man.

"Let me be clear," he growled slowly. "I have no concern for the welfare of these Rebels. But I do care about the lives of our own men, as should you. Killing wounded Americans does two things: it causes our enemy to take similar action against wounded Hessian and British soldiers. And it motivates every farmer and shopkeeper in the surrounding area to pick up a musket and take shots at what they believe to be the heartless invader – you! Are you not satisfied with fighting the Rebel army that you feel the need to battle their civilians as well?"

The offending soldier had wilted under the dark stare of Bickell, and the other soldiers looked away so as to avoid the wrath of their Sergeant. Bickell cast his gaze around the group of men that surrounded him and spoke with a menacing tone.

"Any man who sees fit to murder a wounded enemy soldier will feel the steel of my blade as surely as these men lying dead in front of you have felt the ignorance of your bayonets. If you don't have enough sense to fear the retributions of your enemy, then you had damned well better fear me!"

Sergeant Alexander Bickell stormed away from the scene of frightened Hessians and murdered Americans, leaving each of the shaken soldiers to image his wrath in their own way.

MAJOR NICHOLAS KEARNEY
10:00 AM - SEPTEMBER 5, 1777
JUST SOUTH OF COOCH'S BRIDGE

The bayonet charge by the British had been a frightful experience for the Americans, even those that had been fighting since the beginning of the war. It was one thing to be struck by a musketball, but quite another prospect to entertain the thought of a long blade of steel being driven into your body. Something so violent and personal was almost impossible for any man to stand up against, so the Americans chose not to do so.

Major Kearney watched helplessly as the men around him turned and headed in the direction of Cooch's Bridge, less than a mile away. He had attempted repeatedly to rally the men, but the fear on their faces was apparent. In fact, if Kearney was to be totally honest with himself, he wasn't exactly keen on the idea of staying in his current position either. Perhaps it would be better to retreat to the safety of the bridge, where the British would be forced to channel their forces in order to cross the small structure that spanned Christiana Creek. Yes, that was certainly the best strategy he rationalized, and followed the last of his men north.

—

The British and Hessian soldiers continued to pursue their attackers, and there were constant shots being fired in the surrounding woods. In addition, the sound of hundreds of enemy soldiers moving quickly through the woods could be clearly heard whenever Kearney stopped briefly to take stock of his situation.

Although the men had retreated, Kearney was pleased to note that the withdrawal was deliberate and orderly. The men had kept their muskets and other equipment as opposed to abandoning everything in a panic, as he had unfortunately witnessed on earlier occasions. But these soldiers were different, he reminded himself, both in their skills as well as their experience. Kearney was surprised and pleased to see that every so often a small group of Americans would stop their retreat, form a quick skirmish line, and deliver a volley in the direction of their pursuing enemy. This not only had the effect of slowing the enemy's advance, but it also maintained the pride and spirit of the Americans who continued to defy their foes.

The heavy woods began to thin out as the Americans got closer to the bridge, and Kearney eventually saw the small wooden structure about 150 yards away. The men were quickly streaming across and fanning out on either side of the small creek. Some of Maxwell's men, who had established a fall back position here earlier that morning, had dug shallow trenches just deep enough to provide some cover while lying prone along the banks of the creek. Majors Kearney and Harris, whose men were now coming back together, filled in any available spaces along the creek, as well as kneeling to form a second line behind the first. The sight was reassuring to the retreating men, and the calm self-assurance they had displayed earlier in the day began to return.

Just to the left of the bridge, Major Kearney observed a rather large flag being held aloft by one of the unit's color bearers. Obviously, this was not an uncommon sight, except for the fact that Kearney had never before seen this particular flag. It consisted of a number of rows of red and white stripes with a blue field in the upper corner. Within the blue field was a circle of white stars, the number of which he couldn't yet determine. Probably a new flag for General Maxwell's unit, he thought, as he crossed the bridge and took up a position approximately ten yards from the flag.

Kearney decided to use the opportunity to raise the spirits of the soldiers around him. "You there," he called out to the man holding the new flag aloft, "those are some fine unit colors for us to have. General Maxwell's men should feel privileged to fight beneath them. Isn't that right, gentlemen?" A somewhat ragged but spirited cheer rose up from the men within earshot.

"Beggin' your pardon, sir," replied the color bearer, "but this flag ain't the new colors of the unit. This here flag is what General Washington is calling the 'Stars and Stripes', and I'm told it's the new colors for the entire Continental Army! Word has it that this particular flag arrived fresh from Philadelphia yesterday afternoon, and General Washington himself ordered it sent out here with us."

"Well then," said Major Kearney, "it appears as if we have the honor of being the first Americans to fight under the banner of the 'Stars and Stripes'. And apparently," he said pointing across the creek at some Hessian soldiers beginning to appear out of the woods, "we won't have to wait long for that honor!"

No sooner had the words been uttered than a volley of musket fire was sent in the direction of the approaching Hessians. Meanwhile, British troops in their bright red coats began to appear on either side of the Hessians, and the entire force moved deliberately forward toward the creek. It was apparent that the plan was for the British troops on the flanks to provide covering fire while the Hessians would attempt to cross the bridge. As usual, the dirtiest and most dangerous assignment was being given to the hired help.

Sure enough, the British soldiers began to form compact lines on either side of the bridge, extending out about 100 yards in both directions. No sooner had these lines been formed when their officers began shouting out orders to load weapons and prepare for volley fire. Meanwhile, the Hessians in the center of the line were quickly dropping their knapsacks and other unnecessary gear in preparation for their frontal assault.

When the assault came, it was direct and violent. Hundreds of British muskets delivered accurate volleys into the American positions, while 250 Hessians simultaneously made a mad dash for the bridge, yelling in German at the tops of their lungs. The result to the Americans was both shocking and deadly, as a number of the soldiers without the benefit of the cover provided by the shallow trenches were hit by the mass of musket balls coming at them.

The Americans were able to get off volleys of their own, but these were uncoordinated and sporadic. The result was that several of the leading Hessians crossing the bridge fell wounded, but the crush of humanity immediately behind them was able to make it across and quickly establish a solid foothold on the opposite bank of the creek.

General Maxwell had returned just in time for the start of the battle at the bridge, having been ordered to General Washington's headquarters located just outside of Wilmington in order to provide the General with an update on the day's actions. Maxwell was furious at being ordered to the rear at a critical time, the result being that he didn't have the time necessary to organize a better defensive position. He rode up and down the American lines on a beautiful white stallion recklessly exposing himself to enemy fire, while alternating between encouraging his men to stand firm and cursing at the attacking enemy.

But the Americans had had their fill of fighting for the day, and even the rantings of their General were not enough to keep them in place against a determined and organized enemy assault. Several of the unit commanders ordered a withdrawal, while still others ordered their men to remain in place in order to cover the retreat of their comrades. Roughly half of the Americans began a slow retreat to the next defensible position, a low ridge approximately a half a mile from the creek. Once there, these men formed a relatively strong line just below the crest of the ridge, and began firing volleys just over the heads of the remaining Americans who were just now retreating from their positions along the creek. All in all, it was a disciplined, organized retreat – but it was a retreat nonetheless.

Major Kearney had remained at the creek as long as he dared, a small pocket of his men around him. Upon surveying his situation, he realized that he and the 30 or so men to his left and right were the absolute last remaining Americans at this now forward position. Realizing that they were within a few minutes of being surrounded and captured, Kearney ordered a hasty withdrawal, which his men only too gladly obeyed.

As Kearney and his men approached the low ridge to their rear, they were surprised and pleased to hear a loud cheer come from the Americans now heavily fortifying the ridge. These were not the actions of beaten men, but rather the enthusiasm and pride that comes from a group of soldiers who knew that they had done their duty on this day. They had been given the mission of slowing the advance of the British army and inflicting casualties where possible, and this mission had been fulfilled in a magnificent fashion.

—

The low ridge was not to be the final point of withdrawal for General Maxwell and his 650 or so remaining soldiers. The Hessian and British troops would continue to press the Americans for several miles, not satisfied with abandoning the chase until they had come within a few miles of the position of the entire Continental army located south of Wilmington.

The running battle had been more than a little frustrating to the Hessians and British, who were never able to gain any significant momentum in their quest to overtake and destroy their enemy. Every time they would begin to make speedy progress and start to close in on the Americans, they would come up against yet another line of determined defense. This would inevitably force them to halt their pursuit, come on line, and engage the Americans in their latest organized position.

Finally, upon seeing the relative strength of the American army now fully deployed and awaiting an assault at the main encampment, the pursuing enemy made the rather judicious choice of abandoning their attack and returning to the main column now several miles to the rear. As the Hessians and British turned and began their own withdrawal to their starting positions at the Christiana Creek, few if any of these soldiers felt as if they had adequately avenged the ferocity and effectiveness of the initial ambush that had been conducted by the Americans. In their minds, there was still work to be done.

—

Meanwhile, a similar thought preoccupied the mind of Major Nicholas Kearney, as he and his exhausted men moved to the rear of the Continental Army's encampment looking for food, water, and a place to relax for a few hours after their rather eventful day. Neither Kearney nor his men had any delusions that there would be a lengthy break between this action and the next. Both Washington and Howe's armies were in close proximity to one another, and both generals were determined to fight. That meant that men like Major Kearney would find themselves busy once again in the very near future with the grisly business of closing with and destroying their enemy on the field of battle. Just where this battle would occur was anyone's guess, with the possible exception of General George Washington.

LIEUTENANT JACOB LANDES
SEPTEMBER 6, 1777
MAIN CONTINENTAL ARMY ENCAMPMENT

It had been over a month since Jacob had reported for duty as an officer in the Continental Army, and he still hadn't adjusted to the difference between this life and the life he had left behind in Salford Township. He was just beginning to realize what an insular life he had led on his farm, as he was constantly being faced with dealing with men from every part of the Colonies. These men were different in so many ways that his mind reeled at his attempts to understand the way they saw the world.

Just this morning, a group of men from southern Virginia had returned to camp in amazingly high spirits, having hunted and killed what they referred to as "good eats". Jacob had curiously gone over to see what the source of happiness might be, only to learn that these men had begun skinning and roasting several large rats that had been wandering about the army's refuse piles! Jacob had lasted only long enough to be offered the first taste of the meat off of the spit, composing himself sufficiently to respectfully decline their generous offer.

This incident did, however, provide yet another indication of something very positive for Lieutenant Jacob Landes. The men not only in his own unit, the 4th Pennsylvania Regiment, but other units as well, had taken a liking to him. But even more importantly, he reluctantly sensed that there was almost a certain level of respect that he was being accorded by the enlisted men. Jacob wasn't exactly sure why he was being extended this honor, but he liked the way it made him feel, and he made a commitment to continue to earn the trust of the men. Although Jacob had yet to see any action against the enemy, he instinctively knew that this type of relationship with the troops was the key to being successful as an officer in battle.

As Jacob walked through the encampment, he was struck by the diversity that existed within the ranks of the American army. There were boys as young as 12 or 13 wandering about, usually serving in the capacity of a drummer boy, but not always. Some of these children –

which is exactly what they were – carried muskets, and a significant number had actually faced the enemy. On the other hand, there were grandfathers in their late 50's, and even a few in their early 60's. The fact that these men were often older than his own father was a source of no small discomfort when Jacob found himself in the position of giving them orders or assigning them their daily responsibilities.

In Salford Township, almost every man was a farmer of some kind, with a few men running the sawmills that populated the local creeks and tributaries. Here, there were men with almost every background imaginable from teachers to merchants to lumberjacks. There were blacksmiths who were tasked with a wide range of tasks needed to outfit an army, and carpenters who constructed the numerous outbuildings that were used to house the supplies. Virtually every occupation that existed in the Colonies was represented to some degree in the army, to include those who had no occupation or skills whatsoever. These unskilled men had come, for the most part, from the jails and debtors' prisons that existed throughout the Colonies, or men who had come from living on the streets of cities as vagrants scratching out a living through odd jobs and begging for food.

The quality of the men enlisted into the Continental Army was of little concern to the recruiters charged with filling out the ranks. The use of "stand-in's" was a commonplace practice in the colonies, a situation which occurred when a man of means was drafted into service. This policy allowed any man who could afford it to pay someone else to take their place in the army. Not surprisingly, many well to do men opted for this alternative by paying anyone off the street a few dollars to enlist in their place. Some of these "stand-in's" were wanted criminals eager to get out of town, men with gambling debts, or other undesirable members of the community. The result was an influx of men who had achieved absolutely no standing in society, and were merely waiting out their time in the army before they could return to their former lives of idleness and non-productivity. To say that the Continental Army was made up, to a large degree, of low quality citizens was an understatement to say the least.

But the group of men that were the greatest riddle to Jacob were the negroes that made up a surprisingly significant percentage of the Continental Army. These men, who hailed from almost every colony in America, had such a varied history among them that it was almost impossible to draw any conclusions or patterns from their behaviors and beliefs. Some were Freedmen who had existed in relative harmony with their white neighbors for years, and viewed themselves no differently from the rest of the army. Many were former slaves who had escaped from farms and plantations throughout the colonies, and were enjoying their first taste of anything that even approached equality. Regardless of their past, their striking difference in physical appearance set these men apart from the others, and Jacob had become increasingly disturbed by the treatment they received from many of their white counterparts. When dirty or strenuous details were selected, the negroes tended to be selected much more frequently than the others. When uniform items and supplies were passed out, they were often forced to the back of the lines, if they were allowed to get in line at all. Most disturbing of all was the fact that the officers, supposedly charged with insuring fair and equal treatment among the enlisted men, tended to look the other way at best, and at worst contributed to the injustice by participating in the discrimination. Jacob had already made more than one enemy among his officer peers when he had attempted to intervene.

—

Jacob couldn't help himself from breaking into a broad smile when he saw Thomas Sweeney approaching him in his typical leisurely stride. Regardless of the situation, Thomas never seemed rushed at anything he did, which was regarded as either a sign of self confidence, or a demonstration of laziness, depending on whom you asked. Either way, it had taken Thomas about two weeks to become one of the most sought after companions in camp, as his jokes and stories eased the tedium of daily life in the army.

"Jacob, I've been looking all over camp for you. Where have you been hiding?" Thomas asked, as he arrived at Jacob's side. There was a look of genuine concern on his face, which was very unusual for Thomas. If Thomas wasn't laughing or smiling, his expression was almost always one of calm and contentedness.

"Why Thomas, you sound like my Mother. Why the seriousness? Are you in trouble with Colonel Humpton again?"

It was true that Thomas was well-liked by both the men and his fellow officers, but that popularity certainly didn't extend to Colonel Richard Humpton, the Commanding Officer of the 2nd Pennsylvania Brigade. Colonel Humpton, a former officer in the British Army prior to adopting America as his new homeland, was a hard man who believed that success in every endeavor was based on hard work, a serious approach, and constant repetition of basic skills. In short, he was tailor made to be a commanding officer in the army, especially in an organization with the somewhat relaxed standards of the Continental Army. Considering the informal approach to life taken by Lieutenant Thomas Sweeney, there was no surprise on anyone's part that Thomas had quickly become Humpton's favorite target of wrath.

"No, no, I haven't been in the Colonel's doghouse since the day before yesterday when he found out I had been sneaking out of camp at night to visit that farmer's daughter. I mean, how was I supposed to know she was only 16? She told me she was 19," pleaded Thomas.

"She told you what you wanted to hear, and you listened. Also, it probably wouldn't have gone so poorly for you if you hadn't brought one of her father's pigs back to the camp and eaten it with the rest of your men," Jacob scolded. "You told the Colonel that the pig had wandered into the camp on its own, but apparently the farmer gave Colonel Humpton a slightly different version of what happened."

"That's not fair," Thomas replied with a feigned wounded expression. "That pig walked in on its own two feet, just like I said. I just chose to leave out the part about the rope around my wrist that just happened to be connected to the pig's neck." Thomas smiled broadly at the story, one which he had undoubtedly already told a dozen times to anyone who would listen.

"But that's not what has me worried," Thomas continued. "Word has it that we're moving the army to a place called Red Clay Creek. Some of the senior officers were saying that the creek is smack between the British and Philadelphia, such that there's no way the British can get to the city without going through us! Everyone seems to think that this could be one of the biggest battles of the war!"

Jacob pondered the information he had just received, trying to determine its validity. One tended to hear a fair amount of gossip and rumors in the army, but this sounded logical. The Continental Congress would be clamoring for Washington to protect the city, despite the fact that this same group of brave men had already evacuated Philadelphia and moved its operations to York, Pennsylvania, approximately 80 miles to the west. The effect on the morale of the country should Philadelphia be captured would be potentially devastating.

Meanwhile, Washington had always been transparent about his

opinions regarding the protection of key locations. He had always maintained that the war would be won or lost based on the ability of the American armies to defeat the British armies in the field, not on their ability to defend a location that was perceived as being valuable. But in this case, taking up a position to defend Philadelphia and keep Congress happy dovetailed quite nicely with Washington's desire to get the British army out into the open. Furthermore, Washington had the advantage of waging the battle on ground of his own choosing in a prepared defensive position.

As Jacob processed all of this in his mind, he came to the conclusion that Thomas' information was most likely accurate. "Well then, Thomas, there is much to be done. You can bet your last penny that the Colonel is going to have the men drilling and conducting target practice even more than usual, so we had better start making the necessary arrangements."

GENERAL WILLIAM HOWE
SEPTEMBER 8, 1777
IRON HILL

"General Howe, your orders regarding the soldier arrested for looting two days past have been carried out," reported the Captain of the Guard. "The guilty party received forty lashes as delivered by the Sergeant of the Guard, sir."

"Very good, Captain. You are dismissed," Howe stated shortly, not looking up from reading his reports. The Captain, however, remained at the door of the small dining room that was serving as Howe's war room.

"Is there something else, Captain?" Howe asked in an annoyed tone, finally looking up and making eye contact with the man.

The officer, clearly uncomfortable with the news he was about to deliver, hesitated for just a second before responding. "Yes sir, as a matter of fact I have the need to report that two additional men were arrested for looting just last night, sir. They were apprehended by the sentries as they attempted to return to camp with a large quantity of food, as well as several household and personal items including silverware and jewelry. I'm afraid the items which were found on them matched perfectly with the items that were reported stolen yesterday by members of the Cartwright family in Willowdale."

Howe breathed a deep sigh and closed his eyes as if in pain. The British simply couldn't afford to anger the locals, for a variety of reasons. First, the local population had quickly become a source of not only much needed supplies, but also of information. Second, Howe had no desire to assist in the expansion of the Continental Army by angering civilians to the point that they joined General Washington as either regular soldiers or militia. And finally, contented, unmolested people tended not to serve actively as spies on behalf of the Americans; however, victims of vandalism, theft, and rape often were motivated to do so.

"To which unit do these men belong?"

"Sir, they are members of Colonel Reichstag's 3rd Jaeger Corps, most of who are deployed forward on scouting duties," replied the

Captain.

Damn! Howe knew it would only been a matter of time before the Hessians showed their true colors. He felt his face turning red with anger, and it took all of his self-control not to fly into a rage in front of this junior officer. Such displays of emotion were not in the best interest of maintaining the perception among the troops that their Commanding General was in absolute and supreme control of his faculties. When Howe spoke next, it was with a measured firmness which belied his true feelings.

"Captain, inform General Knyphausen that I wish him to order a formation of his entire division. You will then proceed to take those two men and have them hanged in front of that formation. Is that clear?"

The Captain's face clearly expressed his shock at the severity of the punishment being ordered by his General. Involuntarily, he asked weakly, "Hanged, sir?"

"Yes, Captain, hanged!" Howe stated loudly. "Hanged until there is no life remaining in their pathetic bodies! Hanged until Death! Hanged until the others realize that there is no tolerance in this army for the violation of direct orders! Are you in need of any further direction on this matter, Captain?"

"No sir," stammered the clearly unsettled man. "I shall see to it immediately, sir. Very good, sir."

The officer quickly removed himself from the headquarters of his Commanding General and set off to complete his dreadful task.

—

Howe returned to reading the volume of reports which had been coming into his Headquarters over the past few days from a variety of sources. Some of the information was from patrols that Howe had ordered sent out to scout the surrounding countryside. Some of Howe's intelligence came from the rather extensive network of spies that he had commissioned immediately upon landing at Head of Elk, if not before. Much of Howe's knowledge and understanding of the current situation, however, came from the local populace. It was not uncommon to have three or four farmers, shopkeepers, or tradesmen wander into the British camp each day eager to provide updates on the whereabouts and activities of the Continental Army.

It was the group of locals that tended to provide the most detailed information to Howe. Unfortunately, it was also this same group that had the tendency to provide information that was inaccurate, either intentionally or due to the fact that they simply weren't trained in the art of observation and reporting.

Ironically, the most recent intelligence had come from six American dragoons, or mounted scouts. These men had apparently been alerted to the fact that the British Army was dreadfully short of healthy horses and were paying a handsome sum for any mounts that could be made available to them. These six Continental soldiers had decided that the money was simply too good to pass up, especially in light of the fact that their own pay in the American army was extremely low. In fact, pay often wasn't provided at all depending on the status of the fledgling government.

When taken into custody by the British, these men had quickly struck a deal that was beneficial to both parties involved. The Americans would provide their six horses to the British, along with a detailed report of where the Continental Army was located. They had also been willing to provide the most recent rumors regarding the most likely direction of movement of their army. In exchange, the British would pay each man the rather princely sum of 100 British guineas. Finally, these six men would return to their original units at the time of the next prisoner exchange, using the story that they had been captured and their horses had been confiscated by the enemy. This was certainly not the first instance of this particular arrangement being made, but it never ceased to amaze General Howe that these supposed soldiers were so willing to betray their own army so blatantly.

In any case, a preponderance of the reports Howe was receiving indicated that Washington and his army apparently intended to defend Philadelphia, most likely at a place called Red Clay Creek. Howe's patrols had taken the liberty of observing the position from a distance, noting that the enemy had begun erecting a formidable defensive position. Although Howe didn't fear the prospect of attacking the Americans regardless of their disposition, it was not in his character to needlessly expend the lives of his men on ill-considered frontal assaults. General Howe had been present at the Battle of Breed's Hill the previous year, and he had observed first hand the effects of a massed assault on entrenched American troops. Although the British had eventually pushed the Americans out of their position and prevailed on the field of battle, it had taken five assaults and over 1,000 British casualties in order to do so.

Many British officers had remarked that it would only take a few more of these types of "victories" to effectively lose the war for England.

After consulting with General Cornwallis as well as several other members of his staff, Howe had decided to move northwest around the Americans, thereby forcing them to abandon their defensive position at Red Clay Creek. In order to better facilitate this maneuver Howe had ordered several units to stage a demonstration on the right flank of the Americans. While the enemy was preoccupied with determining the intent of this attack, Howe would move around the Americans. He could then either move directly into Philadelphia if the opportunity presented itself, or at the very least force an engagement on more equitable terms.

Having made this decision, Howe called out to his Chief of Staff located in the next room. "Colonel Wilson!"

The Colonel appeared immediately, almost magically, at the bidding of his General. "Yes sir?"

"Inform my Staff that movement of this army is imminent, and that they are to assemble here at my Headquarters with all possible speed."

As Wilson disappeared as quickly as he had arrived, General Howe began writing the orders that would send his men into their next confrontation with the Americans. But that confrontation would not occur at Red Clay Creek, as was the hope of General Washington. Howe was not a man who responded well to being told what to do with his army.

GENERAL GEORGE WASHINGTON
SEPTEMBER 8, 1777
RED CLAY CREEK

In the opinion of most people who knew George Washington personally, he was a relatively quiet, unassuming man who rarely showed his emotions. In fact, many of his closest friends would admit to having never seen Washington lose his temper in a public setting.

But Washington's headquarters was not a public setting, and General Washington was ranting and raving in a manner that none of his staff had ever seen before.

"He was just a few miles in front of us, for God's sake!" Washington nearly shouted. "I ordered patrols to constantly scout his lines and report any movement immediately to this headquarters! How can an entire army simply march away without being detected? We're talking about thousands of men, horses, and wagons picking up and heading off. Were these scouts deaf and blind?"

General William Howe had stolen away in the middle of the night, leaving nothing behind but a small force which had staged a demonstration on the right flank of the Americans. This demonstration, much to the embarrassment of the Americans, had caused the entire Continental Army to jump to arms at 3:00 AM and prepare for what everyone thought was an attack by the enemy. The Americans had been rowdy and enthusiastic as they had formed their ranks, fully prepared for what they believed to be a long overdue opportunity to settle an old score with their British enemies.

But the morning had given way to early afternoon, with still no attack by the British. Washington had ordered a body of men to advance in the direction of the enemy for the purpose of luring them out of their inactivity, but this had failed to elicit a response. Still the Americans waited, and the afternoon became early evening with the men still holding their positions in anticipation. Finally, as the probing attacks by the Americans became bolder and bolder, it was discovered that the opponent they faced was a distressingly small group of a few hundred men, who immediately made their retreat upon the discovery of their ruse.

In the meantime, the bulk of the British army had made their way north with the clear intention of avoiding a confrontation at Red Clay Creek. This would effectively force the Americans to move to an alternate location if they had any plans of defending Philadelphia from British occupation. To make matters even worse, it had taken the entire day for Washington to realize what the British had done, and it was now nightfall. It was difficult enough to get his rather undisciplined men organized for a tactical movement, let alone attempting to do so in the darkness. Washington would be forced to wait until morning to begin any countering maneuvers, and that fact would provide the British with even more time to place the Americans at a tactical disadvantage.

Although Washington's outburst was loud and passionate, it was also brief. With visible effort, he composed himself and took a seat at the desk from which he had recently been penning a letter to one of the members of the Continental Congress.

"Gentlemen," Washington addressed his staff in a now calm and controlled voice, "you are dismissed for now."

The rattled staff moved quickly out of the room, happy to place some distance between themselves and their perturbed commander. After the room had emptied, Washington addressed the one man remaining.

"Colonel Harrison, if you please, I believe it would be prudent at this time to write the necessary orders to get our army on the road at the earliest possible opportunity," Washington said to Lieutenant Colonel Robert Hanson Harrison, his military secretary.

"Certainly, sir," responded Harrison, as he took a seat at a nearby table and prepared himself to capture the orders of his Commanding General. "Please begin at your convenience, General."

Washington quickly stated his orders for sending out immediate patrols to locate the current position and direction of movement of the enemy. Once that information was ascertained, a defensive position could be selected that would once again place the Continental Army between the British and Philadelphia. No one could be sure that Philadelphia was the true objective of the British. Perhaps they were attempting to move towards York and capture the members of the Continental Congress. Perhaps they were intending to move toward Reading, Pennsylvania, where Washington had located his primary supply depot. But Washington had more than a hunch that the British were aiming to capture the Colonies' largest city. After all, these were Europeans who had waged wars for hundreds of years under the rules that occupation of your opponents' largest population centers was tantamount to victory. And Washington had spent enough time serving with these men to understand the way they approached the art of war.

"Finally, Colonel, this army will be prepared to move at first light. We must make every possible effort to regain control of our tactical situation if we are to have any chance of dealing a serious blow to the British. After what this army has been through over the past two years..."

Washington's voice trailed off without finishing his thought. It had, indeed, been a difficult and demoralizing time for the Continental Army. After the euphoria of forcing the British to abandon Boston, what followed had been a series of disasters. Long Island, Harlem Heights, White Plains – these were places that would forever be burned into the memory of George Washington. In every case the Continental Army had been both outfought and outmaneuvered by the British, and there were many people throughout the Colonies that had come to the conclusion that the Americans were simply no match for the better trained, better equipped, and better led British Army.

Then had come the almost miraculous victories for the Americans at Trenton and Princeton, and morale had been dramatically elevated. These battles had proven that American soldiers had both the will and the ability to fight effectively in the face of almost overwhelming adversity, and the impact had been immeasurable.

However, the situation that Washington was currently facing was vastly different from these two previous victories, in that the Americans were now facing a sizable force equivalent to their own. Between the Continental Army and the British Army, there were approximately 30,000 troops on the verge of facing off against one another – numbers of this magnitude had simply never before been present on the field of battle during this war. In addition, Trenton - for all its glory - had been a surprise attack against a force of unprepared Hessian troops, rousted rudely from their drunken slumber the day after Christmas. The enemy that Washington faced now was made up of disciplined and experienced regular British troops, with the Hessians in a supporting role. And this wasn't an army that would be either drunk or surprised by anything the Americans did.

—

General Washington had other issues with which to contend as well. As was almost always the case, the army was suffering from a large number of desertions. And due to the fact that it was coming up on the harvest time, this number was even greater than usual. Washington loathed the fact that his soldiers often chose to sneak away at night, and whenever a man was caught attempting to do so, the punishment was swift and severe. But Washington understood their motivation and, in many ways, he couldn't fault them for their actions. After all, these were citizen soldiers to a large degree – many of these men had walked away from a life of domestic responsibilities to fight for an ideal that they believed in very strongly. Many of these same men had families back home whose very survival relied on the men's ability to provide food and shelter. For these families, an abundant harvest equated to the ability to survive for the following year.

Just last week, Washington had watched as a man had received forty lashes with a whip for attempting to return home before the end of his enlistment. It had taken every ounce of self discipline for Washington to observe the flesh being ripped from the man's back as he cried out in pain for the General to show mercy. But to show mercy was to risk being seen as weak, and weakness was an emotion that this army could ill afford to display.

Another reason that many men chose to desert from the ranks was that the promises that had been made to them simply weren't being kept. Specifically, they had been told that they would be paid for their service, which was almost never the case. But most importantly, they rightfully expected to at least be fed for their trouble, which occurred sporadically and in varying degrees of quality. For example, the typical days' rations for a soldier in the Continental Army was supposed to consist of the following: ¾ to one pound of beef, a pint of milk, one ounce of butter, and a pound of bread or flour. However, this quantity of food, which had a price tag of approximately 11 cents a day per soldier, rarely made it to the men. Oftentimes spoilage was the culprit, while other times the speed of movement of the army made it difficult for the supplies to keep pace. But more often than not, the food was simply unavailable due to a grossly underfunded budget, and an even more grossly inefficient supply system.

Washington had spent countless hours writing letters to the Continental Congress, using every form of persuasion that he could devise. He had begged, he had reasoned – he had even threatened the Congress with the disintegration of the army if they were unable or unwilling to take the necessary actions to preserve this fragile conglomeration of men. Although he had a few allies in the government, Washington was painfully aware of the fact that there were many members of Congress who were actively or passively opposed to providing significant support to his army. And he knew why.

The very nature of this Revolution was the result of a fundamental distrust of a strong central government, in this case King George and his government in England. The perceived tyrannies that had been heaped upon the Colonies were sufficient evidence to demonstrate that governments existed to propagate their own power and glory. Therefore, anything that increased or solidified governmental power was viewed with suspicion by many Americans.

Washington knew that there were quite a few members of the Continental Congress who had openly opposed the creation of a standing army, believing instead that the fighting should be accomplished by a loose grouping of militias commanded and supplied by the individual colonies. This arrangement would insure that there was little chance of organized collusion amongst these military units. A standing army, it was feared, could be used to overthrow the government and place power in the hands of one man. And many individuals feared that this one man would be General George Washington.

But Washington knew that this same insurance against collusion would result in disorganized chaos, and there would be no ability to effectively oppose the armies sent to the Colonies by the English government. This had been apparent very early in the war, when many of the Colonies had refused to allow their militias to fight anywhere other than within their own boundaries. Even when these militias did venture beyond their own borders, there was a reluctance or even refusal to abide by any orders other than those coming from their own officers.

Finally, wiser minds had prevailed in the controversy, and the Continental Army had been created and placed under the command of Washington. However, the resistance to this strategy had not completely disappeared. It had simply gone underground and resulted in the consistent sabotage of creating a well prepared, well supplied military organization.

—

Washington refocused his mind on the situation in front of him. He realized that a defeat of Howe's army would have an amazing impact on his problems of desertion, lack of supplies, and troublesome politicians. In order to accomplish this, he needed to find another strong defensive position between the enemy and Philadelphia, and place his army at that location.

As Washington moved to a nearby table to study a map of the surrounding region, his staff officers and generals began to arrive at his headquarters. The first to enter the room was Major General Nathanael Greene, a man whom Washington would be forced to admit was probably the general he favored most in the army. Greene, who had been born in Rhode Island just 35 years earlier, had started the war as a private in the Rhode Island militia. He was quickly recognized as a man who possessed intelligence, a knack for military topics, and most importantly, unquestionable integrity. His subsequent rise to the rank of Major General had been predictable and speedy.

"General Greene, if you please, come join me."

"Of course, sir, how may I assist you?" Greene asked.

"Our army needs to be placed in such a location as to provide both the strategic advantage of protecting Philadelphia, while at the same time providing a strong tactical defensive position," Washington explained.

General Greene moved to the table opposite Washington and briefly studied the map. After several moments, Greene placed his finger on the map, indicating a spot just south and west of Philadelphia.

"I am familiar with this area, General," Greene stated. My division has passed directly through here on more than one occasion, and I have actually noted that it would provide a defensive force with quite the formidable position. It's called Chadds Ford, and is located along the Brandywine Creek."

"Ah, yes," Washington said, nodding his head in agreement. "The rather narrow ford located there could be protected quite nicely from the bluffs located on the east bank of the creek. Also, if the British intend to march on Philadelphia, they will have to pass somewhere very near to that location. General Howe may be many things, but a coward he is not. If he is aware of our presence there blocking his move on the city, he may be lured into an attack."

As Washington and Greene continued their conversation, they were joined by several of the other division commanders to include Major Generals Adam Stephen, John Sullivan, William Alexander and John Armstrong, as well as Brigadier Generals Anthony Wayne and Henry Knox.

The discussion continued for the better part of an hour, during which various individuals advocated either for or against the decision to place a stake in the ground at Chadds Ford. The debate was lively and, at times heated, which is exactly what Washington encouraged from his generals. After all was said and done and Washington had heard arguments from both sides, it was time to make a decision.

"Gentlemen," Washington began, "as always I value your keen judgment and opinions, and I continue to be humbled by the intelligence that surrounds me. I have come to the conclusion that there is no time like the present to confront our enemy, and I suspect that we will find no location better than Chadds Ford on the Brandywine Creek. So it shall be. I would suggest that you rejoin your units and begin making preparations for movement to that location."

The men nodded their assent, all being firmly committed to the task at hand now that the decision had been made, regardless of their original position in the discussion. Each moved quickly from the room without so much as a word to one another, their minds becoming quickly preoccupied with the myriad of orders and details that needed to be addressed over the next few hours.

MAJOR NICHOLAS KEARNEY
9:15 AM - SEPTEMBER 11, 1777
CHADDS FORD

There was to be, apparently, no rest for General Maxwell's light infantry of the Continental Army. Having inflicted numerous casualties on the approaching British army as a result of several skirmishes, many of Maxwell's men had made the assumption that they would be given time to rest and prepare for any upcoming engagements. But that had been an incorrect assumption, as Maxwell's Brigade found themselves forming for yet another movement in preparation to face the enemy.

Major Nicholas Kearney had heard the initial grumbling from the men, and had even been tempted to join in on the complaining himself. But then it had occurred to him that the reason he and his men were being tasked with their current assignment was that General Washington felt that they were the only unit he could trust. After all, everyone knew that the next few hours would most likely witness the largest battle of the war to date, and Washington needed every possible advantage at the outset. This realization on the part of Kearney caused him to swell with pride, and he shared his epiphany with the men of his unit.

"Gentlemen," he asked the troops, "has it not occurred to you the reason for which we are being overburdened? General Washington is desperate to put the British on their heels before they can fully engage our army."

"That may be so, sir, but haven't we done our part in slowing down the enemy?" asked one of the soldiers in his unit. "There must be dozens of other units that can cross the Brandywine Creek alone and try to draw the British into a battle. Ain't that what we just done a couple of days ago?"

"That's exactly what we did a couple of days ago, and we did it well. The fact is, we did it so well that General Washington himself ordered us forward again. Gentlemen, we're about to face the greatest challenge in the brief history of our country, and the Commanding General picked *us* to lead the charge!" Kearney stated. "I swear, if I live to be a hundred –

and I pray to God that I do – I can't imagine a greater honor being given to me than the one that has been offered to us this day. Our country requires the best; our country deserves the best; and gentlemen…that happens to be us!"

The men, captivated by the impromptu speech given by Major Kearney, erupted in a cheer that surprised Nicholas. Although he had always been a man of few words, on this occasion those words had apparently hit the mark. And they had done so because they had been sincere and come from the heart.

Within minutes, Maxwell's Light Infantry was on the road which led across the Brandywine Creek and into harm's way once again.

—

Washington had placed his roughly 15,000 troops at several positions along the east bank of the Brandywine Creek. These positions began a mile or so below Chadds Ford, and extended approximately six miles north of that location. Most of the Continental Army had been placed within a mile or two of the Chadds Ford crossing, as Washington was convinced that the British would make their main assault at that point. The remainder of his army was broken into smaller detachments that had been assigned to guard the various fords along the creek, most of which were north of the main American position. Although Washington believed the British attack would come at Chadds Ford, he was not about to leave his flanks unguarded – a hard lesson he had learned in previous battles of this war.

The final aspect of the army's positioning called for Maxwell's men to deploy to the west bank of the Brandywine Creek and harass the enemy as they approached the main American position.

—

As dawn broke on the morning of September 11th, Major Kearney began moving along the position his men had taken on a slight elevation overlooking a fork in the road. His actions were in no way random, and he had many purposes for the brief conversations he had with the men. For those who were more experienced, he requested their steadiness and support during the upcoming battle. For those who were relatively new to the business of war, he expressed his confidence in their abilities, and ordered them to stand firm until given the direction to withdraw to their secondary position. To many, he simply offered encouragement and best wishes, and reminded them to check their weapons and ammunition.

The plan called for Kearney and his men to fire an initial volley at the approaching enemy column and then retreat to their secondary position which would be commanded by Major Charles Simms. From this position, they would again attempt to inflict casualties on the enemy with a brief encounter, and then withdraw to the third position commanded by Colonel Josiah Parker. Once again, the plan was to engage briefly and withdraw, this time to the final position along the Brandywine Creek under the command of General Maxwell himself. It was a plan that was eerily similar to the tactics used at Cooch's Bridge a few days earlier, however this time the entire Continental Army would be waiting for the enemy at the end of the road.

No sooner had Kearney completed his inspection of the men and his position when he was greeted by his nephew, Private Nash.

"Sir, the enemy's coming down that road, no more than a few hundred yards. They'll be right below us in a few minutes!"

"Very good, Private. Now take your post and prepare to engage the enemy."

True to the report given by Private Nash, the enemy appeared within five minutes. Kearney noted with grim satisfaction that the enemy column was being led by the Queen's Rangers, a group of American colonists who had remained loyal to England. Well, thought Kearney, they'll pay for that misplaced loyalty today.

The men had been instructed that there would be no verbal order given to initiate the attack. Rather, the convenient feature of the fork in the road would be used as the signal to fire. Once the lead man in the column had reached that juncture, the attack would begin.

Kearney realized he was holding his breath as he watched the column approaching. They were no more than thirty yards from the fork in the road. No more than twenty yards…no more than ten…

The surrounding woods erupted in a sheet of flame as the one hundred or so men of his unit unleashed a deadly volley on the column. Almost instantly, Kearney saw a number of the enemy soldiers collapse onto the ground, the most recent victims of the marksmanship of Maxwell's Light Infantry.

As quickly as the men had fired, they began their planned withdraw to the second position. Kearney waited just a few seconds to observe the reaction of the enemy, and was both impressed and pleased by what he saw. The Queen's Rangers, taken completely by surprise, had not retreated or buckled under the ferocity of the ambush. Rather, they had quickly gathered themselves and set off in an almost headlong pursuit of the Americans. This reaction was admirable, but also exactly what Washington had predicted.

Kearney's men retreated approximately a half mile at a dead run, with the Queen's Rangers in hot pursuit. As they approached their secondary position, Kearney ordered his men to place themselves behind a farmer's fence at the edge of a field. To the right of the fence, Major Simms had concealed his men just inside a wood line that extended north from the position of Kearney's men.

As the Queen's Rangers moved toward Kearney and his men, they saw that the Americans had stopped their retreat and taken a stand. The commander of the Rangers ordered his men to halt, and formed them into a disciplined line of battle in preparation for an assault. Having done so, the officer ordered his men forward, and they began to quickly close the distance between themselves and the men who had just ambushed them. It was apparent in the speed and attitude of their attack that they were bent on revenge.

Kearney watched as the enemy came within 100 yards of his position along the fence line, and he was suddenly startled by a vicious volley being poured into the flank of the attacking Rangers. Their line seemed to shudder, as dozens and dozens of heavy musket balls thudded into the bodies of the unsuspecting men. Kearney watched as many of the enemy soldiers bent down to provide assistance to one of their fallen comrades, only to have many of their own lives cut brutally short by the volley that Kearney had just ordered.

Simms' troops fired a second volley into the reeling ranks of the Rangers, and Kearney felt almost embarrassed at himself as he ordered a second volley to be fired by his men. He quickly chastised himself for this inappropriate emotion, reminding himself that his enemy wouldn't hesitate to afford him the same treatment were the circumstances to be reversed.

—

The action for Maxwell's men was far from over for the day. Simms and Kearney withdrew their men to a third and eventually fourth position, effectively engaging the enemy in both locations. However, the British were not to be surprised again this day, and the main portion of their column was brought on line and advanced on the Americans.

Finally, after General Maxwell had assumed command of his entire brigade just to the west of the Brandywine Creek, the British nearly succeeded in swinging a brigade around behind Maxwell, threatening his line of retreat across the creek. Maxwell made the decision that at this time discretion was the better part of valor, and he withdrew his force across the Brandywine and took up a position on the left flank of the Continental Army.

Likewise, the British determined that their pursuit of the Americans had become somewhat unorganized and General Knyphausen, commander of the British forces at this point in time, took up a position on the west bank of the Brandywine and coordinated his army.

At this point, it was only 10:00 AM. Unbeknownst to Major Nicholas Kearney and his men, the events of this September day were just beginning.

PRIVATE WILLIAM DEVLIN
11:45 AM - SEPTEMBER 11, 1777
NORTH OF CHADDS FORD

The army had been marching since 5:00 AM, and it was now almost noon. The sun had been brutal, and the temperatures were high as was usually the case at this time of year. For the hundredth time, Private William Devlin cursed his decision to become a foot soldier, as opposed to the more glorious and apparently more comfortable job of being a dragoon. That must be the life, he thought. Riding around the countryside, scouting for the enemy, getting off of your horse only long enough to grab a quick drink at a tavern or chat with some of the local ladies who always seemed more than willing to engage in conversation with these dashing young lads.

William was also aware that being a dragoon presented its downsides as well. Over the last two weeks of maneuvering and brushes with the enemy, these horsemen had been in the saddle almost constantly. In addition, virtually all of the day to day casualties that occurred when the army wasn't fighting an actual battle were incurred by the dragoons. A day failed to pass without some young man disappearing from a cavalry patrol, or one of the scouting parties returning with the lifeless body of one of their comrades draped across his saddle.

Furthermore, as the clashes with the Americans had become more and more bitter, the dragoons most often suffered the wrath of the enemy. As a result of the almost constant plundering that was committed by the British - despite the direct orders given by General Howe to the contrary - the Americans had begun meting out their own style of revenge. Just yesterday, two British dragoons had been found by an advance infantry column hanging from a tree alongside of the road. The men had been stripped of their clothes, had their hands bound behind their backs, and been strung up by their necks. At the feet of each man was the carcass of a dead chicken, these presumably being at least part of what had been stolen by these looters. Both chickens had been decapitated, and the head of each chicken had been forced into the mouths of the dead soldiers. If the orders and threats of General Howe were not enough to dissuade the British and Hessian soldiers from looting, this vivid example of the potential consequences would almost certainly make any man take pause before engaging in pillaging.

William had made a full recovery from his wound, which had turned out to be nothing more than the graze from a Yankee musketball. It had been so slight, in fact, that William had been receiving good-natured ribbing from the other men in his unit about having had the wound attended to at all. First in line to do so, of course, was Private Willis.

"So 'ow's our wounded hero making out over there, eh?" Willis asked with a smile on his face. "If you'd like, Devlin, I can have the surgeon come on up and spend a few more hours making you better."

The men nearby laughed heartily at Willis' ever-present humor, and even William was forced to grin at the comment. After all, he considered, he would much rather be the healthy butt of the jokes than the wounded recipient of pity. Also, William figured that Private Willis was entitled to a few snipes at the very least, as Willis had been the first one to come to William's aid in the middle of the violent confusion. As long as he lived, William would never forget that moment of quiet heroism displayed by a most unlikely character.

"I'll be just fine, you filthy rogue," Devlin replied good naturedly. "I'm no worse for wear, and I'll march you into the dirt as usual. This here soldier is as healthy as a horse – thanks to a friend," William said, shooting a glance in the direction of Private Willis.

"That's enough yapping, you men. Save your breath for what's up ahead," ordered Sergeant Myers, the most senior enlisted man in the regiment.

"Can you let us in on what that might be, Sergeant Myers?" asked one of the men in the column.

Sergeant Myers, at the grizzled old age of 33, looked sharply at the man. "What makes you think I'd know anything about what's going on, eh? I'm just another poor foot soldier like all of you."

"Ah, come on now Sergeant Myers, you always know what the story is," another man prodded. "You knew when we was sailin' out to sea, and you knew when we was headin' into shore. Some says you knew even before the General had made up his mind to do either one!"

Once again the men laughed, and even the serious Sergeant Myers allowed a small grin to grudgingly form on the side of his mouth.

"Well now," began the Sergeant, "I don't know nothin, for sure, of course. All I hear is rumors, ya see." Before continuing, the Sergeant gave a wary look around for the presence of an officer. "Do any of you men remember the battle we fought at Long Island last year?"

"Ay, that we do, Sergeant. 'Twas a fine day to serve in the King's army, as I recall," said one of the men.

"Indeed it was. As you may recall, General Howe sent some of us right at Washington's main force, and the rest of us he sent on a march up and around Hell's half acre. Now, I'll be the first to admit, I did my share of cursing about having to make that trek. I couldn't understand why the enemy was right in front of us, and we was marching away! But when we came up over that rise and saw the beautiful sight of the Americans – looking the other way, mind you! Ah, now that was a sight for sore feet."

The men laughed at the memory of that day, as well as Sergeant Myers' re-telling of it.

"Now Sergeant Myers," asked one of the men, "you wouldn't be tellin' us stories of the past as a way of gettin' out of telling us stories of the present, now would you?"

"Boys, there's one thing you have to learn about officers, and that is that they're predictable. If they find somethin' that works, they stick with it. Hell, sometimes they stick with somethin' that doesn't work, just 'cuz it makes 'em feel all safe and comfortable inside," joked Myers. "Well, that plan of marching around the flank of the Americans must be somethin' that makes Howe feel safe and comfortable, 'cuz word has it that we're doin' it again."

"But Sergeant, we're marching straight ahead, followin' right behind the rest of the army. We'd need to be splittin' up if we was to be doin' what you say," reasoned one of the soldiers.

Sergeant Myers gazed slowly around at the men in the column. "You wouldn't be doubtin' old Sergeant Myers, now would you? Did any of ya happen to notice that our dust cloud ain't as big today as it was yesterday? That means we ain't got the whole army in line with us right now. If I was a bettin' man – which of course I am – I'd say we had about half of our army in this here column."

The soldiers in the column, to a man, gazed around them as if seeing their surroundings for the first time. Some of the men began shaking their heads in agreement and understanding, while others remained unsure of their Sergeant's assessment of the situation.

"But Sergeant," one of the brighter soldiers offered, "if what you're saying is true, then that means that General Howe has split us in half.

Why would he do such a thing when we're about to fight a battle?"

"Ah, the same thoughts were had by our friend George Washington at Long Island and Brooklyn. He was sure that General Howe would do no such thing, because it's not what generals are taught to do. But, my lads, that's exactly why it worked! What you need to do is hope that old General Washington is dumb enough to fall for the same trick yet again."

"Hell, Sergeant Myers, Private Willis here knows more about leading an army than Washington! Why, that man wouldn't know a good plan if it jumped up and bit 'im in the leg!"

The laughter that followed from the men was not shared by Sergeant Myers, who turned and stared menacingly at the soldier who had made the comment.

"Just remember, gentlemen, there are two kinds of idiots in the army; the idiot who's afraid of everything about his enemy; and the idiot who's afraid of nothing about his enemy. I'd suggest you men refrain from being either one."

William had realized many months ago that Sergeant Myers, while not being exactly what one would describe as "book smart", was quite possibly one of the most intelligent men he had ever met. Many men owed their lives either to the direct actions of this man in battle, or indirectly as a result of the training and advice he had passed on to the men on countless occasions. William decided that this was yet another one of those occasions, and made specific note to keep the advice from Sergeant Myers in the very forefront of his mind.

GENERAL WILLIAM HOWE
12:15 PM - SEPTEMBER 11, 1777
JEFFRIES FORD

The soldiers had been marching at a brutal pace for most of the day, and General Howe could see the effect it was having on his men. Earlier in the day there had been almost a lightness to their steps, as they anticipated the opportunity to defeat their American adversaries yet again. But as the day wore on, their enthusiasm began to wane as the fatigue worked its way into every bone and muscle of their bodies. Howe decided to cross the Brandywine Creek, and then call a halt for the men in order to dry their clothes, regroup and reorganize, and get a well deserved rest.

This respite, however, was to be brief. Howe knew that in order for his flanking maneuver to be effective, it needed to contain the element of surprise, much as it had at Long Island the previous year. Howe couldn't prevent a smile from crossing his face as he recalled the events that day – a day that had certainly added to his already blossoming military reputation. This day, as well, would be another chapter to add to his rather lengthy book of successes.

Howe's current masterpiece called for General Knyphausen with approximately 7,000 men to advance on the American position at Chadds Ford. Howe was counting on Washington buying into the belief that this force would be launching the main attack across the Brandywine Creek, and would therefore hold the bulk of his army in place there. Meanwhile, Howe and Cornwallis had taken just over 8,000 soldiers and marched north along the Brandywine Creek to their current location at a place called Jeffries Ford. Howe had originally planned to march his men a relatively short distance in order to flank the Americans, but Washington had not seen fit to cooperate. British and Hessian scouting parties had confirmed the existence of American soldiers at each of the possible fording locations along the creek for several miles to the north, and Howe had been compelled to take his column almost twelve miles before they had found a location both suitable for a crossing as well as unguarded by the enemy.

The ability of the British to locate this crossing was a bit ironic. Soon after they had landed at the Head of Elk, a colonist named Curtis Lewis had presented himself at the tent of General Howe. Lewis claimed to be "loyal to the death" to King and Country, but more importantly he claimed to have a familiarity of the local geography that was unrivaled by any man in the county. Howe had seen no harm in allowing the man to prove both his loyalty and his geographical knowledge, and this decision had paid off handsomely for the British. The irony was that Washington, operating in his own countryside, was about to be defeated due to a relative lack of intelligence of his own land, while the British were privy to a wealth of intelligence on that same topic.

In addition to this fortunate recruit, Mother Nature had seen fit to shine upon the British, as the morning had been cloaked since sunrise with a thick fog. This had served to conceal the movement of such a large force from the prying eyes of the enemy patrols, several of which had been heard on the other side of the creek as the British had marched north. On virtually any other day, Howe and his army would have been spotted by any number of these patrols, but the fog had hidden their movements just as surely as a curtain being drawn on a window.

It appeared as if everything was going in favor of the British and to the detriment of the Americans. When would these Rebels realize, Howe wondered, that they literally had no chance of winning this war?

—

Howe watched as his men spread out along the eastern bank of the creek, taking advantage of these few precious minutes to rest and tend to a variety of housekeeping items. He was soon joined by General Cornwallis who rode up with his typical flourish of gaudy horsemanship, trailed close behind by his staff and bodyguard. Cornwallis dismounted and approached Howe, stopping at attention with a crisp salute.

"Sir, I beg to report that the entire column has crossed the creek and is preparing to continue the march upon your orders. In addition, several scouting parties comprised of Captain Ewald and his mounted jaegers have been sent in the direction of the enemy in order to screen our movements and ascertain the exact location of the Americans. As I'm sure the General can see, our fog is beginning to dissipate."

"Very good, General. Have any of our scouts reported making any contact with the enemy?" Howe asked.

"Sir, several of our patrols have reported that they were almost certainly observed by enemy scouts. However, all of these patrols have been comprised of only a few men, and would most likely be mistaken as simply protecting the flanks of our main force further south," Cornwallis stated.

"Yes, perhaps so – I hope you are correct on that. Have you received any initial reports back from Captain Ewald on what lies ahead?"

Cornwallis nodded grimly, and Howe got the impression that he had been waiting for just that question to be asked.

"As a matter of fact, sir, Captain Ewald located a very narrow defile through which we will have to pass in order to continue south toward the enemy. At first, Ewald was quite concerned, and asked that I personally observe the situation he was facing. Upon arrival at the location, it became immediately apparent to me that a very small force of the enemy would be capable of holding up this entire column almost indefinitely."

Howe, becoming annoyed at the almost theatrical manner in which Cornwallis was relating his story, asked brusquely "yes, yes, so what did you do? What's the situation?"

Cornwallis, oblivious to the edge in his Commanding General's tone, continued. "Well sir, I ordered Ewald to take a small detachment of men and make his way through the defile to determine if the enemy had taken advantage of this terrain feature. Of course, I was prepared to make the reconnaissance myself, but the men were too concerned for my safety. I decided the morale of the men should come first."

"General Cornwallis, if you could please come to the conclusion of your report. We do, after all, have a war to fight."

"Of course, sir. Much to my relief – but I must admit, not to my surprise – I ascertained that the enemy had not placed any men to defend the defile. These Rebels are not exactly – how would you say, sir? – skilled at the nuances of war. I proceeded to order a larger unit of men to traverse the defile and establish a strong position on the far side. This will insure that the enemy doesn't come to their senses at some point and attempt to take advantage of the tactical situation there."

Howe, almost exhausted at having to endure the self-aggrandizement displayed by Cornwallis, had to admit that it had been handled with absolute perfection by his second in command.

"General Cornwallis, you have once again demonstrated your keen tactical awareness. I thank you for your actions and your report. Now, please return to your men and prepare to continue our advance within the half hour."

Cornwallis beamed like a young child being patted on the head by an admiring schoolmaster. "The General is too kind," he stated with a bow. "I shall see to your orders immediately."

Cornwallis mounted his horse, saluted General Howe, and disappeared with his staff in the direction of his men.

Howe knew that Cornwallis was a brave and capable officer, and much of the success of this army was due to his judgments and actions. However, those talents came with the rather steep price of having to endure his arrogance and grandstanding. Perhaps, Howe thought with just the hint of a smile, the Americans will dispose of the good General Cornwallis in battle. Otherwise, Howe may be tempted at some point to kill Cornwallis himself.

Douglas Shupinski

GENERAL GEORGE WASHINGTON
12:35 PM - SEPTEMBER 11, 1777
CHADDS FORD

Reports had been coming in from a variety of sources beginning early that morning and continuing to the present. Several of these reports, coming from extremely competent and reliable officers and scouts, assured Washington that there was absolutely no sign of British troops anywhere to the north. However, still others reported the existence of enemy units of varying strengths in this same area. At least two messages, in fact, had been received indicating that a very large component of the British army was north of Washington's current position, preparing to threaten the right flank of the Americans.

Washington tended to discount these reports of a large enemy force on his flank. After all, if these reports were accurate, it would first mean that dozens of scouts had completely missed the presence of a sizable enemy force operating in the exact area that they were supposed to be observing. Although this was always a possibility, it was extremely unlikely. After all, many of the men serving as scouts were extremely familiar with this area, and had grown up within just a few miles of their present location. Secondly, it would mean that Howe had split his army into two or more smaller units, and was risking being attacked and annihilated in a piecemeal fashion by Washington's army. Surely, a general of Howe's capabilities and conservative tendencies wouldn't consider such a tactic. True, he had done so on an earlier occasion, but that was when the Continental Army was small and disorganized. Surely, General Howe would not attempt such a tactic at this point. Not again.

—

The day had become almost unbearably hot, and Washington resisted the temptation to remove his coat as a means of getting some relief. This was no time to display behaviors that might be perceived by his men as lackadaisical or undisciplined. He did, however, allow himself the luxury of removing his hat and wiping the sweat from his forehead with a handkerchief.

A flurry of activity was occurring a short distance from the main command post, and Washington was compelled to give this distraction his attention. Moving quickly toward him was Colonel Thomas Pickering, the Adjutant General of the Continental Army, followed closely behind by Colonel Theodorick Bland, the commanding officer of one of the cavalry regiments that had been conducting patrols in the area north of Chadds Ford since yesterday evening. The appearance of Colonel Bland caused an immediate alarm to sound in Washington's head, as he realized the potential significance of the appearance of this officer in the obvious agitated state in which he appeared to be. Regardless, Washington made every effort to maintain his composure as Colonel Pickering presented the cavalry officer.

"Colonel Bland," Washington began in a relaxed, friendly tone, "it is always a pleasure. To what do I owe the honor of your visit to our Headquarters?"

"Sir, I felt it necessary to come personally to you to report the existence of a large enemy force to the north of this position. I would estimate this force to consist of between 8,000 and 10,000 soldiers, and as of twenty minutes ago this force was located approximately ten miles north of our present location."

Washington was now faced with a dilemma. This report being delivered by Bland was in direct conflict with other reports that he had received earlier. To make matters even more convoluted, it would be somewhat of an overstatement to suggest that Colonel Bland was one of the more experienced officers in the Continental Army.

Theodorick Bland was, by profession, a doctor. Having been sent to England as a young man to study, Bland graduated from the University of Edinburgh in 1763 as a physician. Bland had returned to America to practice medicine, which he had done until just a few years earlier. The fact that Bland had risen to the rank of colonel was as much a factor of his formal education and former occupation as it was a result of his demonstration of proficiency in combat. Although Bland's observance of enemy soldiers was obviously very real, it was also completely possible that his estimation of its size was somewhat exaggerated.

Nevertheless, even if there was a chance that this information was accurate, Washington could ill afford to ignore it. The consequences of a major enemy assault on his right flank without warning was simply too grave of a risk to take. Washington made his decision at that moment to respond to this possible threat with the assumption that the enemy to his north was a diversion consisting of only a fraction of Bland's estimate.

But as Washington continued to ponder this new information, he suddenly realized that he was being faced with both a threat as well as an opportunity. If there *was* a force of British troops to the north, that meant that the force opposing him at Chadds Ford must be somewhat depleted and vulnerable to an attack. Washington decided to respond to the current situation in two ways. First, he would order General Stirling and General Stephen's divisions to move north and east and establish a defensive line at a right angle to their current position. And second – Washington smiled involuntarily at the audacity of the move – he would order General Wayne and General Greene's divisions at Chadds Ford to launch an immediate attack on the enemy they faced across the Brandywine Creek. General Sullivan, commanding Washington's fifth and final division, would remain in his current position just north of Chadds Ford. This would allow Sullivan to provide reinforcements to either the Chadds Ford position, or the northern position that was about to be established in response to the threat being reported by Bland.

"Colonel Harrison!" Washington shouted, summoning his Military Secretary who appeared as quickly as usual. "I wish to send orders to each of my division commanders."

Washington quickly dictated his orders to Harrison, who proceeded to personally write the necessary orders to the five division commanders. Once that task was completed, they were given to five riders who were dispatched to the respective commanders and their divisions.

—

Washington was rousted from his thoughts by the appearance of Colonel Pickering at his side. "Sir," Pickering asked with a salute, "shall I prepare your headquarters for relocation?" As Adjutant General, one of Pickering's responsibilities was coordinating the movement and security of Washington and his staff. Washington realized with a start that with the commotion of receiving reports and issuing orders over the last thirty minutes, he had failed to consider where he would physically place himself during the upcoming battle. After brief consideration, Washington made his decision.

"No Colonel, that won't be necessary. Although I believe this threat to the north to be very real, I also believe it to be very much a diversion.

This is General Howe's way of distracting us from his true intention to launch his major attack directly across the Brandywine Creek at Chadds Ford. We'll see how the good general reacts to being attacked himself before he can launch his own."

Major Nicholas Kearney
1:15 PM - September 11, 1777
Chadds Ford

Several of the men of Major Kearney's company watched quietly with mixed emotions as the soldiers of various other units assembled for their assault across the Brandywine Creek. On one hand, Kearney's men were thankful that they were finally getting a well deserved rest from their hours of playing hit and run with the British. On the other hand, no soldier worth his salt is happy about sitting on the sidelines while his comrades confront the enemy.

"I gotta admit, sir, I thought we'd never get a break from that fightin' today," said Private Nash to Major Kearney. "I mean, it got mighty hot a few times. When them Hessians tried workin' their way behind us, I thought we was goners."

"Come now, Private Nash, surely you don't doubt the leadership abilities of your officers," Kearney said with a smile, mildly taunting his young nephew. "Why, our escape route back across the bridge was never in danger – well, not *really* in danger."

Both men laughed, able to joke about the precarious situation now that it was a thing of the past. In reality, had the Americans waited another ten minutes to make their withdrawal to the eastern side of the creek, they might very well have become either casualties or prisoners of war. In most cases, the men would have preferred being casualties rather than risk the embarrassment – and possible agony – of being taken prisoner by the British.

—

Becoming a prisoner of war was an extremely risky proposition for American soldiers, in that the British government had refused to recognize the Continental Army as a legitimate military foe. As a result, Americans taken into custody by the British by any means were considered traitors and not officially prisoners of war. The subsequent treatment of these men varied greatly. The lucky ones were eventually either returned to the Continental Army in exchange for the return of British troops, while others were "paroled" by their captors. Under the agreement of a parole, the captured soldier was allowed to return to his home after he had made the promise that he would never again participate in armed conflict against the Crown.

Those prisoners that weren't fortunate enough to be either exchanged or paroled were placed in some form of captivity, the most common being the prison ships used by the British in New York City harbor. Those that had spent any time onboard these ships told frightening tales of the conditions in which they had been held. Starvation, sickness, rats, and cruelty by the guards, all contributed to a nightmare existence for the thousands of men that were held in this way.

One man in the 7th Maryland Regiment had spent just over eight months on board the HMS Jersey, having been captured during the final charge at Breed's Hill. He had talked about going days without so much as a scrap of food, or a drink of anything other than a small amount of rancid water that caused a man to gag. As prisoners had gotten ill, they were placed in a separate area of the ship and were completely neglected by their captors until they died. When that happened, their corpses were thrown unceremoniously overboard, only to wash up on the nearby shores. Finally, the Maryland man had been exchanged for a group of British soldiers that had been taken captive by the Americans during the Battle of Princeton.

One final option existed for Americans taken prisoner: they could agree to serve in the British army. Although most men refused to even consider the possibility, there were a number of others who saw it as a survival technique. Besides, many of the men in the Continental Army had considered themselves Englishmen until just a short time ago, and many had just recently arrived in the Colonies from England. The transition from American soldier to British soldier was not quite the long journey that one might imagine, and at times involved simply changing the color of one's uniform.

—

The artillery fire had intensified in the last few minutes, indicating an impending attack. As Major Kearney and the other men watched from the heights on the eastern side of the creek, hundreds of American soldiers entered the shallow waters of the Brandywine and began wading across toward the enemy on the opposite shore. In addition to most of the rest of Maxwell's Brigade, there was also the 3rd Maryland Regiment commanded by Lieutenant Colonel Nathaniel Ramsey.

Almost immediately, the British artillery switched from solid shot to canister, shells which exploded as they left the muzzle of the cannon sending hundreds of sharp pieces of metal toward their target. The effects of this weapon were appalling, as men were cut down in small groups by the blasts. Major Kearney watched as three men coming out of the water on the far side of the creek were hit by a canister shot just off to their right. All three men – or at least what was left of them - were hurled back into the creek, creating bloody swirls in the water as they began floating downstream.

Musket balls could be seen throwing up small splashes all around the men in the creek, as well as peppering the eastern side of the shoreline as still other soldiers moved forward to enter the water. Although the firing by the enemy was galling, it was fortunately not particularly heavy, as the British had not been fully prepared for an assault. The Americans were able to make excellent headway in the initial minutes of the attack, and it appeared as if it would only be a few more minutes before they had successfully established a position on the western side of the creek.

Suddenly, orders were being shouted by several officers on the American side of the creek to the men in the water and those coming out on the far shoreline.

"Withdraw! Withdraw! You men in the water, on the double! Return to your previous positions, quickly!"

The entire assault came to an immediate standstill, as men looked about at each other confused and disoriented by the strange orders being shouted at them. The officers continued their urgent commands to the men to cease the attack and withdraw. The confusion on the part of the soldiers quickly turned to anger, as they began to realize that their efforts in the face of the enemy were about to be nullified most likely due to the incompetence of their leaders. Men cursed and shouted insults at the officers giving the orders to retreat, as they thrashed urgently back across the creek to their starting point. Several men pitched forward as they withdrew, suffering the ultimate insult of being shot in the back by the enemy.

Finally after several minutes, the men had begun to file into their original defensive positions, and the cannon and musket fire on both sides of the creek began to decrease.

"What the hell was that all about?" asked Private Nash, an expression of anger and confusion on his face. "That attack was goin' just fine! Why, them men would've been set up on the other side of that creek in another five minutes, and we coulda all followed them over right after that!"

Kearney was confused as well by the chain of events he had just witnessed, but he wasn't quite yet willing to believe that there had been no good reason for the orders. After several combat experiences, Kearney had begun to appreciate that the men fighting the battles didn't always have the luxury of seeing and understanding the Big Picture, and that there was an absolute necessity on the part of the foot soldiers to trust that their higher ups were doing what was best for the army as a whole. Of course, this didn't always turn out to be the case; Washington and the other senior members of the Continental Army had certainly made their share of poor decisions. But to immediately jump to the conclusion that the generals were incompetent was an infection that would quickly spread throughout the army and lead to its ultimate death, just as sure as an infected limb would eventually kill a man.

Almost as if by magic, General Maxwell appeared on his horse in front of Major Kearney and his men. Many of them began calling out to him.

"General Maxwell, what's goin' on, sir?"

"Why'd we stop the attack, General?"

"What should we do now, sir? Do we keep retreating or stay where we are?"

The questions came fast and furious as Maxwell brought his horse to a halt in the middle of a gathering of his men.

"No, no further retreat, for God's sake!" Maxwell ordered. "Return to your positions and make preparations for a major attack by the enemy."

"But sir, we was told that *we* were making the attack, not the enemy! You saw it yourself, General – some of the men had already made it across the creek! All we needed was to – ."

"Gentlemen, enough about the attack," Maxwell interrupted. "We have just received word that the British have a force of over 8,000 men coming down on our right flank on *this* side of the Brandywine Creek. If we were to conduct an attack across the creek and establish a position over there, we would be splitting our army when it was about to be attacked on both flanks. We would have no way of reinforcing one flank or the other, should a need arise to do so. We must stay together as a fighting force if we are to defeat the British on two fronts."

The men looked at one another, the light of comprehension dawning on their faces as they processed this new information. Thankfully, Major Kearney had been right – Washington did have a method to the apparent madness that had just taken place, and the men realized that the right decision had most likely been made.

The curses and insults by the men ceased, replaced with the orders of their officers as they began to restore some semblance of discipline and control. The threat of an impending attack by the British provided a sense of urgency to the task, and the men were soon back in strong defensive positions awaiting the next move of the crafty General Howe.

LIEUTENANT JACOB LANDES
3:45 PM - SEPTEMBER 11, 1777
BIRMINGHAM HILL

The 4th Pennsylvania Regiment, commanded by Lieutenant Colonel William Butler, had been detached from their main unit and assigned to the 3rd Pennsylvania brigade. The 3rd Pennsylvania was the smallest brigade in the entire 5th Division, and due to the fact that they were currently being dispatched to a potentially critical location, it was determined that a few reinforcements would be in order. The brigade had finally completed an amazingly fast paced march of approximately four miles, and had moved into position on the crest of an eminence known to the locals as Birmingham Hill. During the march, word had filtered through the unit that they were moving to face the advance of a British column coming down from the north in an attempt to flank the American position at Chadds Ford. The fact that this maneuver by the enemy had been detected and countered by their commanding general put the men in very high spirits indeed. Clearly, this was not going to be another Battle of Brooklyn.

Lieutenant Jacob Landes had marched at the head of his men for the duration of the movement, occasionally moving back among them to check on their condition. Only when he was satisfied that all was well would he then return to the head of the column and continue moving toward their objective. The recruiting officer Jacob had spoken with those several weeks ago had been absolutely correct: military skills could be taught *to* a man, but leadership was a quality that came *with* the man. Jacob still had a great deal of learning to do with respect to military matters, but it was clear to his men that he was a natural leader.

General Stirling's Division, to which Jacob and his men had been attached, occupied the very center of Birmingham Hill, while General Stephens' Division had moved in on their right. Meanwhile, General Sullivan's Division had originally been posted to the west of Birmingham Hill, but Sullivan had decided that the half mile gap that existed between his division and the divisions on Birmingham Hill was not the best tactical position for him or his men. Therefore, Sullivan had taken it upon himself to move his division around behind Birmingham Hill and then up to the crest where he was currently in the process of moving in on the left of Stirling's Division.

There had been sporadic musket fire in the fields and woods just in front of Birmingham Hill for about the last hour or so, so the men knew that the British were close. Predictably, the shots they heard were the clashes between the various pickets and dragoons that had been sent out by both sides, attempts by each commander to ascertain the positions and relative strength of the various enemy units. In the last few minutes, the volume of these clashes had begun to increase, and the men waiting on the hill were becoming visibly anxious in anticipation of battle.

Jacob was dismayed to discover that he was far more nervous than he had anticipated he would be just prior to his first battle, and he chastised himself to remain calm. He reminded himself that he needed to always serve as an example to his men, and what kind of an example would he be if he showed his nervousness? He took a quick drink from his canteen and drew several deep breaths which served to calm him down to some degree.

However, if Jacob was nervous, Lieutenant Thomas Sweeney was downright terrified. As Jacob glanced over at his best friend to his left, he saw that Thomas' face was almost completely white, and his hands were visibly shaking. Jacob decided a brief chat might do them both some good, so he moved in the direction of his friend.

"Well Thomas, it appears your opportunity to win the war is close at hand, eh? Are you sure we need all of these other men, or were you planning to whip the British all by yourself?" Jacob joked lightly.

But Thomas was apparently in no mood for jokes, as he turned and stared at Jacob with wide, empty eyes.

"What are we doing here, Jacob?" Thomas asked. "I don't have the first damn clue what I should be doing when the shooting starts! These men around us know what they're doing. The British that are coming toward us know what they're doing. I have no idea! Jacob – this is *serious*!"

Jacob was disturbed by Thomas' demeanor, and realized he had to do something to calm him down or else he might well get himself and others around him killed.

"Thomas, you know your men like you. There's a reason for that – they trust you. They'll do what you order them to do because they trust you."

"Trust me!" Thomas almost shouted. "I tell you that I don't know what I'm doing, and you tell me that they'll do what I order them to do! Are you making fun of me, Jacob?"

Jacob suddenly realized that he had made a mistake, and tried to change tactics. Humor hadn't worked; consolation hadn't worked. Perhaps what Thomas needed was what Jacob's father had given him on many occasions – a good kick in the seat of the pants.

"Well if they don't follow your orders, Thomas, whose orders are they going to follow? Well? You're an officer in the Continental Army, and it's your responsibility to lead these men to the best of your ability! Without officers - without orders – these men are a shapeless mass that will operate as a confused, disjointed group. And they will die. But with proper leadership, they at least have a chance to survive as a single unit working together. Thomas, you owe them that at the very least! Now stop your damn whining, and prepare your men for battle!"

Thomas seemed to snap suddenly out of his trance-like state, shocked at the tongue lashing he had just received from his friend. Jacob had never spoken a cross word to anyone before, especially to Thomas. And Jacob had cursed! Thomas' face turned a deep red, and his anger rose to the boiling point. Who was this farmer's boy to tell Thomas Sweeney about his responsibilities? This holier-than-thou character who still had cow manure on his boots from working in the fields…

With sudden clarity, almost as if the proverbial clouds had parted, Thomas realized what his friend was trying to do. Jacob realized that survival in this situation was contingent on Thomas' ability to function in his capacity as an officer; and Jacob was willing to resort to whatever tactics were necessary to facilitate that result. Thomas' anger immediately dissipated and was replaced with a profound feeling of affection toward Jacob.

"Well, well" Thomas said softly with a smile on his face, "I guess the farmer's boy isn't as naïve and innocent as I thought he was. You've only known me a couple of weeks, and already you know how to tick me off."

"That wasn't my intention, Thomas, honestly."

"Oh yes it was. I was so scared a minute ago that I was about to let go with a load in my trousers! But you got me angry, and it cleared the cobwebs in my head. Don't get me wrong – I'm still scared. But now I can manage my fear, thanks to you. Why Jacob – you may have just saved my life and the lives of some of these men."

"Please, let's not exaggerate things," Jacob protested. "I just knew if I let you carry on like you were, I was probably going to be the one who had to wash your trousers after the battle!"

Thomas laughed heartily, and the last of the fear and tension drained from his body. Thomas extended his hand in the direction of his friend.

"Now, Lieutenant Landes, let's make these Redcoats pay for their arrogance, eh?"

With that, the two men shook hands and returned to their respective units.

SERGEANT ALEXANDER BICKELL
4:15 PM - SEPTEMBER 11, 1777
BIRMINGHAM HILL

The Hessians hunched lower as the musket balls peppered the air around them as they continued their advance in the direction of the Americans on Birmingham Hill. Although casualties were still relatively light at this point, several of Sergeant Bickell's men had already gone down with the typically awful wounds inflicted by the large round balls of metal coming at them. Between the sound of the cannon and muskets being fired both behind and in front of them, the shouted orders of officers and senior enlisted men, and the pitiful cries of the wounded, a man could barely hear himself think.

But thinking wasn't what Bickell wanted his men doing right now. His experience in combat had taught him that the most critical time during an assault was when contact was first made with the enemy. If you were able to press the attack and keep the enemy off balance, you would almost always take the position you were after.

It was during those engagements when the attacking force began to get bogged down that it became most dangerous. The troops defending a position held a natural advantage, in that they were stationary and usually behind some kind of cover. Meanwhile, the troops making the attack had to advance primarily in the open and maintain momentum in the direction of the enemy. This also tended to be completely against the natural instincts of a man. Virtually any sane person - given the opportunity to stop and contemplate his actions at a time like this - would most likely turn around and retreat, or at least seek the safety of the ground or behind some object. It was for this reason that Bickell needed his men to respond to orders right now and not think.

And respond to orders they did. Even after years of combat experience, Bickell continued to be amazed at the bravery of the men with which he served. Even as the intensity of the incoming fire increased, they rarely faltered from their objective, moving forward with grim faces and fixed bayonets.

The Hessians had reached the base of the hill, and Bickell paused his men briefly in order to reorganize them. In their current position, they were somewhat shielded from the firing of the Americans on the crest of the hill, and the men took the opportunity to take a quick swig of water from their canteens, reload their weapons, and prepare themselves for the final assault.

"All right men, it's time to earn your pay," Bickell shouted to the men around him. "Follow me up the hill, but don't get too bunched together. We don't want to make ourselves easy targets for the American muskets and cannon, not that they could hit the broad side of a barn."

Bickell's attempt at humor was rewarded with smiles and light chuckles from the men. They appreciated Bickell's calm under pressure, and if given the opportunity to be led by any man on earth, these soldiers would choose Sergeant Alexander Bickell. Time and time again he had proven his bravery, his skill, and his intelligence in combat, and these men had no doubt that today would be no different.

"Look there," Bickell commanded his men, pointing to the top of the hill. "You can see those troops starting to come on line into their position. If we can hit them before they get themselves settled in, they'll run like jackrabbits. But we must move now, and move fast. Who's with me?" he shouted.

A deep roar from the men provided all the answer Bickell needed, as he straightened the tall cap on his head, hefted his musket, and surveyed the troops around him.

"All right then, you German bastards!" Bickell shouted, "it's time to show these Rebels what it means to be a soldier!"

On that order, Sergeant Bickell and his men charged up the hill toward the enemy with shouts of approval.

—

Sergeant Bickell and the Hessian Grenadiers apparently weren't the only ones to recognize the opportunity being presented by the unprepared troops at the top of the hill. Several other nearby units that were part of the British Grenadiers to the left of the Hessians had been ordered to attack at the same time, and the result was a wave of British and Hessian troops assaulting the hill simultaneously.

The Americans had begun firing canister from their cannon, and the resulting blasts occasionally tore great holes in the lines of the attacking units. As Bickell looked to his left at the advancing British, he could see men being hurled backwards like ragdolls, their bloodied remains falling unceremoniously to the ground, or hurled against a tree or rock with a sickening thud.

Fortunately, Lieutenant Colonel Linsing, the commanding officer of Bickell's unit, had made note of the fact that the artillery fire was less intense toward the right of the attacking force. This was due to the fact that the slope of the hill, as well as the surrounding vegetation, provided some cover from the enemy's fire on that side. Linsing ordered the Hessians to veer to their right in order to take full advantage of this situation.

Bickell and his men, no longer getting punished as badly by the enemy fire, moved with greater speed to the top of the hill, intent on closing the distance between themselves and the enemy as quickly as possible. As they came to the crest of the hill, they were presented with the sight of an entire enemy regiment moving toward them down a narrow country lane a short distance away. The lane was lined on both sides by heavy woods, and the result was that the enemy unit was forced to bunch themselves into a tight column in order to make their way forward.

The Hessians immediately recognized the opportunity, and officers began shouting orders to deploy into a firing line. Their advance up the hill had caused many units to become separated and disorganized, but the combat experienced Hessians knew how to handle confusion and uncertainty on the battlefield. Within just a minute or two, the officers had successfully coordinated the movements of their men to create a firing line consisting of over two hundred soldiers.

Bickell had been able to rally many of his men into this firing line, and he stood immediately behind them prepared to echo the necessary commands to fire that would be given by an officer to his left. As he heard these commands being given, he shouted to his men.

"Present! Take aim! Fire!" he shouted, and over two hundred muskets erupted simultaneously. The Americans had noticed the massing Hessians almost immediately but, to their credit, had continued to advance down the lane in the direction of their enemy. For the second time in the last few days, Sergeant Bickell had to acknowledge a grudging respect for these farmer-soldiers who really had no business being on the same battlefield with some of the best soldiers in the world.

The effect on the advancing Americans was immediate and

predictable. At once, thirty or forty of those closest to the firing line collapsed to the ground, dead or wounded. Some of those who weren't struck by the first volley attempted to form their own line, but the confined space in which they found themselves prevented this from happening to any significant degree. Still others, splattered by the blood and brains of their comrades, panicked immediately, dropping their weapons and fleeing back down the lane.

Additional Hessian troops had continued to make their way to the crest of the hill, adding to the size of the firing line facing the Americans. The officers and senior enlisted men, including Sergeant Bickell, calmly ordered the men to reload their muskets and prepare to deliver the next volley, even as they began to receive sporadic but accurate return fire from the enemy.

One of Bickell's men, Private Heimbach, dropped his weapon and pitched backwards, throwing both of his hands over his face. He landed on his back no more than three feet in front of Bickell, his eyes staring blankly at the sky. A ragged hole was visible just above the Private's right eyebrow, with just a small trickle of blood coming from the wound. Bickell knew, however, what the back of Heimbach's head would look like when he was eventually lifted from the ground by the burial details. Bickell was the unfortunate veteran of having seen dozens of similar exit wounds, and he quickly blocked the images from his mind.

The Hessian officers ordered the firing of the second volley, and then a third, striking down more and more of the Americans trapped in the natural killing zone of the narrow country lane. Although they tried to maintain their position and return fire, the coordinated attack of the Hessians was simply too much for the outmatched and out positioned Americans to counter. The final straw came when an American on horseback, most likely the commanding officer based on his direction of the men around him, was thrown from his mount and landed heavily on the ground. The ensuing lack of direction caused additional confusion and panic in the American ranks, and within minutes they had ceased firing and begun a somewhat organized but speedy retreat back down the lane.

With a loud roar, the ranks of Hessian soldiers moved forward in the direction of the retreating Americans, intent on pressing the attack and taking advantage of the situation. By this time, Lieutenant Colonel Linsing had recognized the fact that he was attacking the left flank of the enemy, and had the opportunity to jeopardize the entire position of the enemy atop Birmingham Hill. With that thought in mind, Linsing urged his men forward before the enemy could organize an effective defense.

For Sergeant Bickell, these were always the moments of supreme clarity. It was almost as if the world was moving in slow motion, as he made note of every detail around him. The sight of the enemy retreating in confusion and disarray; the shouts of his men as they surged forward; the pungent smell of gun powder that almost choked a man – all of his senses were as sharp as the bayonets on the ends of the Hessian muskets. Every scene similar to this one that he had ever experienced had been recorded in perfect detail in Bickell's mind, and he knew that this day would be added to that history.

Bickell knew that he should be appalled by what he was experiencing right now, yet he also knew that he would forever consider these to be the greatest moments of his life. The fact that this life of his might last for just a few more precious minutes only added to the intensity of his emotions, and he screamed long and loud as he rushed ahead with his men. The combination of adrenaline and the sheer joy of being alive at this exact moment gave Bickell a feeling of invincibility, and he almost – not quite, but almost – felt sorry for the enemy that had the unenviable task of facing his power.

LIEUTENANT JACOB LANDES
4:20 PM - SEPTEMBER 11, 1777
BIRMINGHAM HILL

It hadn't taken long for the fighting to become hot and heavy in the area immediately in front of Lieutenant Jacob Landes and the 4th Pennsylvania Regiment located atop Birmingham Hill. The American artillery was pouring a murderous fire down on the attacking British, and Jacob could see the canister having its intended terrible effect on the enemy. The result was that the British soldiers were staying very close to the ground, rarely even risking the act of raising their heads to scope out their enemy just above them.

Jacob moved back and forth among his men, encouraging them to stay low but to continue taking carefully aimed shots at the British. He was encouraged by their spirit and discipline, as almost all of them were remaining calm amidst the relative chaos going on around them. As he moved along the line, many of the men gave him a brief smile or a thumbs up to indicate that they were holding on just fine.

Unfortunately, things didn't appear to be going quite as well to the left of the 4th Pennsylvania. Jacob noted with deep concern that a steady stream of Americans could be seen moving down the backside of Birmingham Hill where General Sullivan's division had been attempting to move into position. Although Jacob had never had any military training and this was his first combat experience, his gut told him that the left flank of their brigade should be reinforced just in case. Just as this thought was crossing his mind, Lieutenant Thomas Sweeney came into view, moving from his position on the extreme left of the brigade's position. As he arrived at Jacob's side, he had to shout over the sound of the battle to be heard, despite the fact that he was no more than an arm's length away.

"Jacob, I can see Sullivan's men collapsing on my left. There's a unit of Hessians pushing them back, and I'm concerned we'll be taken on the flank by the enemy if we don't do something."

Jacob was somewhat surprised to see that Thomas was completely calm and objective in his assessment of the situation, and there was absolutely no hint of fear in his voice.

"Has Captain Browning ordered any movement of the unit?" Jacob asked, referring to their Company Commander.

"Browning's dead," Thomas said in a tone completely devoid of any emotion. "He was shot through both legs about 15 minutes ago and bled to death. I guess that puts you in charge of the company, since you were commissioned about ten minutes before me" Thomas said with a slight smile.

"You'll do anything to get out of responsibility, won't you?" Jacob joked, returning the smile of his friend. "We'll need to shift our lines and bend the extreme left back to protect our flank. If Sullivan's men collapse completely, we'll be on our own."

But even as Jacob and Thomas spoke, the ground immediately to their front erupted in musket fire. The two men were shocked to see an entire regiment of British soldiers assaulting their position, even as their left flank continued to deteriorate.

"Thomas, return to your men and concentrate their firing to our immediate front. If we don't halt that attack, it won't much matter what happens on our flank" Jacob shouted.

As Thomas returned to his unit, Jacob moved forward to the firing positions of his men, offering constant encouragement and direction to them. They were taking many more casualties than before, as the enemy moved closer and was able to concentrate their fire on the American positions. Some of the men made attempts to retreat to the rear, but Jacob and several of the non-commissioned officers forced them back into the firing line.

The situation was quickly going from bad to worse as Jacob could see General Stephen's division to his right taking heavy casualties from the advancing British. Similar to the left flank, some of the men on the right had begun moving off the firing line and retreating down the hill in ever increasing numbers. The way Jacob saw it, they were about to have both of their flanks exposed, and they would be receiving fire from their left, their right, and to their front.

"Sergeant Winston!" Jacob shouted to one of the non-commissioned officers. Winston had been the owner of a tavern before joining the Continental Army just over a year ago, and he knew how to handle men who got out of control. He had risen quickly from Private to Sergeant as a result of this skill, and Jacob had heard stories of him breaking a man's jaw for failing to comply quickly enough with a given order. Although not a particularly large man, his demeanor gave him a presence that demanded respect. Winston moved quickly toward Jacob from his position on the firing line.

"Lieutenant," Winston acknowledged simply.

"I'm sure you can see that we're about to be flanked on both sides," Jacob shouted above the noise of the battle. "Sullivan's men to our left have already abandoned their positions, and Stephen's men on our right are about to do the same. I need you to gather about thirty of our men and move down the back of this hill about 100 yards and set up a position to cover our retreat."

Sergeant Winston looked closely at Jacob, but his expression revealed nothing of his feelings about the order he had just been given. Winston leaned to his right and spit a stream of tobacco juice onto the ground before he responded.

"You think of this yourself, did you Lieutenant?" Winston asked, never taking his eyes of off Jacob even for a second.

Jacob began to feel uncomfortable under the heavy stare of the man, and realized he was giving orders to someone who had an infinite amount more experience in combat than he did. What if Winston refused to carry out the order? That thought had never occurred to Jacob, and he realized he had no idea how he would handle such a situation. He tried to appear calm and confident in front of the Sergeant.

"If you're asking me if I've been ordered by someone to do this, the answer is no. But I believe we will need to retreat in the next few minutes, and a covering force to our rear will allow us to do so in good order and discipline."

"Well, I'll tell you what I believe, Lieutenant," Winston replied, slowly chewing on his wad of tobacco. "I believe you're right. I just don't understand why a youngster like yourself was smart enough to figure that out, when no one else thought enough to give us that order," Sergeant Winston said with a slight smile. "No disrespect intended – sir."

Jacob silently exhaled a huge sigh of relief, as Sergeant Winston moved off to gather the necessary men and move to his new position closer to the base of Birmingham Hill. Jacob decided he had better check on the status of Thomas and the left flank of the 4th Pennsylvania, being that he was now the acting Company Commander.

The fighting had gotten noticeably closer on both flanks as Jacob began moving to the left. He saw dozens of men lying in various positions on the ground, some moving painfully and holding their wounds, others motionless in death. Jacob fought to keep his fear under control as he could feel and hear musket balls ripping the air around him. One man stood up abruptly and turned to run from his position, but stopped suddenly in mid stride. His eyes looked at Jacob in confusion as he stumbled forward, his mouth working unsuccessfully to speak. As he collapsed on the ground, a gaping wound in the man's back became visible, gushing blood at a terrifying rate. Jacob tried to push the scene from his mind and focus on his mission.

Before he had covered much ground, General Conway, the Commanding General of the 3rd Pennsylvania Brigade of which the 4th Pennsylvania Regiment was a part, rode up on horseback, followed closely by his staff of four aides.

"Lieutenant Landes, how are your men holding up," Conway asked. Jacob realized with a start that Conway actually knew who he was, a fact which boosted his confidence for some unknown reason.

"Sir, I don't believe we can hold our position for much longer. Our flanks are collapsing, and my men are beginning to take severe casualties," Jacob replied, the image of the dying man shot in the back returning involuntarily to his mind's eye.

"Very well, prepare to retreat. Some units have already dispatched small covering forces further down the hill, and we're trying to gather some of the men retreating from the flanks to shore up our positions there. Begin pulling your men back in about fifteen minutes – that should allow us sufficient time to bolster our defense down below."

—

The 4th Pennsylvania Regiment was fighting well, as was the rest of General Thomas Conway's 3rd Pennsylvania Brigade, and Jacob began preparations for the orderly withdraw of his men. But at that moment, the British Grenadiers to their front and right, and the Hessian Grenadiers on their left gave a loud shout, and rose up from the ground almost as one, brandishing their muskets with their fixed bayonets. They began to quickly close the distance between themselves and the fighting positions of the Americans, and the effect was immediate.

The Americans had marched for miles that day to get to their current positions. They had then waited for several stressful hours in anticipation of an enemy attack. Finally, they had been fighting and dying for the last two hours or so, all on a day whose temperatures had climbed into the 90's. These men were exhausted, and they had had enough for one day, especially when faced with the prospect of having to deal with the bayonets of the British and Hessians. Although a few men stayed and fired a final defiant shot at the attacking enemy, most of the men began moving back down the hill. The retreat was not a rout in any sense of the word, which was partially due to some semblance of discipline still remaining, and partially due to their utter fatigue. The men simply picked themselves up and followed their officers and non-commissioned officers down the back of Birmingham Hill.

GENERAL WILLIAM HOWE
5:00 PM - SEPTEMBER 11, 1777
BIRMINGHAM HILL

Despite the surprising tenacity displayed by the Americans, the battle was going exactly as General Howe had planned. The flanking march conducted by the British had nearly been a complete success, marred only by the fact that Washington had reacted just quickly enough to place an organized force in the way of the British on Birmingham Hill. But that force was now retreating in the face of the superior numbers of British and Hessian troops bearing down on them from all sides. If Howe were to be fully honest with himself, he would have preferred to see the Americans routed by his attack, as opposed to the rather orderly retreat he was currently observing. But one rarely gets everything they desire on the battlefield, so an enemy retreat would have to do for now.

Howe quickly gathered his senior officers on the battlefield, giving them orders to press their attacks and take full advantage of the opportunity that presented itself. Although the men had been through a great deal already this day and were almost completely exhausted, Howe knew that to ease up now would eliminate the possibility of a complete victory.

As the colonels and generals returned to their respective units, Howe's Chief of Staff, Colonel Wilson, approached him with obvious trepidation.

"What is it, Colonel?" Howe made every attempt to keep the normal edge out of his voice, although the stress of the situation made that difficult. Wilson was one of the best staff officers he had ever seen, and the man's loyalty to Howe was complete and unquestionable.

"Sir," Wilson said haltingly, "with all due respect, may I suggest that your ability to coordinate the actions of your commanders would be best served by operating from a headquarters position that was – how shall I say it sir? – more strategically located?"

In spite of himself, Howe was quickly becoming annoyed by the rather vague comments of the Colonel.

"What are you trying to say, Colonel? Out with it, man, I haven't the entire day to play word games!"

Wilson remained undeterred in his determination to make his point to Howe.

"Well sir," Wilson began, "it's simply that the Staff is concerned by the fact that you are constantly placing yourself at the point of heaviest fighting on the battlefield. We have already seen evidence that these Americans, although not being the most disciplined soldiers in the world, certainly seem to have a knack for hitting a particular target once they set their sights on it, if you'll forgive the unintended pun, sir."

Howe's annoyance softened somewhat, as he realized that Colonel Wilson was exercising his role of Protector over his Commanding General.

"Colonel, I truly appreciate your concern over my personal welfare, and I assure you that I have no particular desire to receive the greetings of a musketball from the enemy, any more than you do. But a General must be present where the greatest need exists, and unfortunately for my survival, the greatest need tends to correlate almost directly with the greatest danger."

"Yes, sir," Wilson responded weakly.

"That being said," Howe continued, "your point is well taken. Were I to meet an unfortunate demise at the hands of the Americans, I would hardly be able to do my duty, now would I? Therefore, I will make every effort to remain *near* the front, as opposed to remaining *on* the front. Will that satisfy you and your group of cackling hens?"

Wilson brightened a bit, his suggestions having had their desired effect.

"Quite, sir. The cackling hens and I are most grateful" Wilson responded with just a hint of a smile.

—

Although Howe's commanders continued to press their attacks exactly as they had been ordered, the desired rout of the Americans was slow in coming. In fact, not only had the American retreat not turned into a mad rush for the open fields, but they had actually begun organizing a secondary defensive line a mile or so southeast of Birmingham Hill. Had General Howe not seen it with his own eyes, he would have never believed this group of rabble was capable of gathering themselves after the thrashing they had already taken.

But they were. The Rebels had selected a location that afforded an elevation above the surrounding ground that Howe judged to be at least 400 feet, providing their few cannon a greater range, and their muskets a field of fire that was somewhat disturbing.

"Colonel Wilson, if you please," Howe called out to his Chief of Staff. As always, Wilson appeared immediately at his side.

"Colonel, dispatch riders immediately to my Regimental commanders with the following instructions. Under no circumstances can we allow the enemy to organize a strong defensive line on that elevation. They will not stop to reorganize their men, nor will they stop to allow their men to rest even for a moment. Tell them that every second that they delay will be paid for in blood. Do you understand, Colonel?"

"No stopping, no reorganizing, but press the attacks on the hill. Every second of delay will be paid for in blood," Wilson repeated. "Yes, sir, I understand."

"And one other thing, Colonel – tell the men to drive them with the bayonet," Howe said in a cold tone.

Wilson spurred his horse, and bolted in the direction of his messengers located several hundred yards to the rear. Within minutes, five riders had been dispatched to the various commanders with Howe's orders.

Within just a few minutes, the effect on the British advance was visibly evident. The British lines, which had begun to grind slowly to a halt in some places, were suddenly revived, and the men moved forward with a new sense of purpose. These men were veteran soldiers, and they had needed only a slight reminder that the faster they were able to drive the enemy from the field, the sooner they would have the chance to rest and recover. The promise of an end to this long day created new fire in them, and the roar of the battle became audibly louder.

Howe watched as the red lines moved up the slope of the hill, the second such obstacle his men had dealt with on this day, and was pleased to see that there was no delay in the advance as there had been on Birmingham Hill. He was further pleased to clearly see the glint of sunlight off the bayonets of their muskets, and knew that the enemy was being treated to a display of strength. Although Howe had to admit that the Americans had performed better than he might have predicted, there was no way that they had the fortitude to make a stand against this latest attack.

Being the pragmatist that he was, Howe realized that the speed of the advance was not truly a result of his motivational orders. It was due in large part to the fact that the Americans were fairly disorganized, and they lacked the artillery support they had enjoyed earlier in the day. Regardless, the fact of the matter was that his men were moving forward, and the enemy appeared incapable of stopping the inevitable result.

LIEUTENANT JACOB LANDES
5:45 PM - SEPTEMBER 11, 1777
DILWORTH

The Americans had selected an excellent position for their rallying point against the British attack. The hill upon which they stood provided a commanding view of the approaching enemy, and the American commanders had done a good job of dispersing their troops in such a manner as to provide support between the various units.

However, it was a classic case of too little, too late. Had they been able to muster a significant number of men along with appropriate artillery support, the result might have been different. As it was, virtually every man that had combat experience knew that they were simply buying time for the rest of the army to place some distance between themselves and the advancing British.

General Conway had personally placed Jacob and the remnants of his unit in a key position at the center of the American defensive line. Due to the disorganized nature of the retreat, Jacob found himself in command of quite a few men whom he had never seen before, and realized quickly that his current unit was no more than a conglomeration of dozens and dozens of men whose actual units had simply ceased to exist.

This was of no consequence to Jacob, who had been ordered to hold this position as long as possible. Whether he had Pennsylvanians under his command, or a loose grouping of men from New Jersey, Virginia, Maryland, and God knows where else, these were members of the Continental Army. Jacob was pleased, and slightly surprised, to see that these men who had no idea who he was were responding to his orders as quickly as if they had fought together for months. It was yet one more indication that this army was slowly but surely maturing into a cohesive unit, as opposed to a gathering of men from different colonies.

There had been no time to construct any type of breastworks, so the Americans simply hid behind whatever meager cover they could find. Many of Jacob's men had placed themselves behind a fence that ran the length of the front of their lines, reasoning that the narrow rails might stop an occasional musketball. Besides, it provided them with somewhere to prop their muskets as they took aim at the enemy.

No sooner had the Americans settled into their position when the enemy appeared at the base of the hill. Many of the men had hoped that the British and Hessians would be simply too exhausted to continue their attack, but this was clearly not to be the case. If anything, their opponent seemed filled with a renewed source of energy. There wasn't even a hint of sluggishness or hesitation in their step, and they moved forward, bayonets at the ready, appearing for all the world like the Devil himself couldn't stop them.

Jacob ordered the men around him to prepare for volley fire on his command, as did several other officers on either side of him. As these orders were given, two American cannon which had been successfully removed from Birmingham Hill fired the first shots of this most recent chapter of the battle. Men cheered along the line as one of the two solid shots fired from the cannon found their mark, ploughing through the ranks of the advancing British and Hessians. The screams of the wounded men could be heard even at this distance, but none of the Americans felt anything but satisfaction at the sound.

The two cannon fired again a minute later, with both shots finding their mark this time. But the enemy was moving briskly, and the distance between them and the Americans was decreasing rather quickly.

When the British and Hessians were within 100 yards, officers began giving the order to their men to fire their muskets. Jacob waited just a few more seconds, and gave the same order to his men. Almost immediately after Jacob's men had fired their volley, the two cannon let loose with canister shot, muzzle loads of small pieces of metal that acted like a giant shotgun blast. The combination of musket balls and canister took a terrible toll on the advancing enemy, as dozens of men collapsed on the ground with horrible wounds to every part of the body imaginable. But the enemy continued to advance, and after the second volley fired by Jacob's men, the battle had become hand to hand as the two battle lines merged into one.

Although the Americans had given a good accounting of themselves thus far, this was clearly not the type of fighting that favored the relative inexperience of the Continental Army. While the British and Hessians maintained their ranks and their discipline while bringing the terrible might of their bayonets to bear, the Americans resorted to using their muskets as clubs in little more than a back alley brawl.

The fighting became savage and desperate, men screaming and cursing at one another, at themselves, as they fought for nothing more than survival from one moment to the next. Some men panicked immediately and fled from the field, while others lost all semblance of being civilized beings, consumed by the brutality of the battle.

Jacob was trying mightily to maintain the position of his men, but the overwhelming power of the enemy assault was nearly impossible for his men to bear. At one point, a young officer on a white horse wearing a French uniform rode into the midst of the American line, urging them to stand firm and fight the enemy. But the confusion of the battle nearly drowned out the pleadings of the young man, and he was soon wounded in the leg by a British musketball and was compelled to remove himself from the field, albeit with a dignity and grace unique to the French. Later, Jacob would learn that he had witnessed the bravery of a French officer volunteering in America by the name of Marquis de Lafayette. Jacob guessed that this would not be the last time that this young man would distinguish himself on the field of battle.

Meanwhile, to the right of Jacob's men, Brigadier General Muhlenberg's Virginia brigade was attempting to hold on with the assistance of another foreign volunteer. Count Casimir Pulaski, a former Polish cavalry officer, was serving as a member of Washington's staff, ostensibly to provide advice on the employment of the American cavalry. As Jacob watched from the center of the line, Pulaski rallied a small group of thirty or forty American cavalry, and attacked directly into the enemy assault. Although the shock of the charge initially halted the advance of the British and Hessian troops, there were simply too many, and Pulaski was soon obliged to retreat from the scene or risk certain capture or death.

Five times the enemy had assaulted the American positions, and five times they had been repelled by the stubborn Continental Army. With each British and Hessian attack, the Americans had stood their ground and fired volley after volley. But every man has his breaking point, and the appearance of several hundred British troops previously lost in the surrounding woods was the final straw. Although both sides were completely exhausted at this point in the battle, these relatively fresh troops threw themselves into the fighting with the ferocity borne of their frustration at having missed the rest of the battle up to this point.

When it became apparent that there was no hope of holding their position, Jacob ordered his men to conduct an orderly retreat. Initially, the men attempted to do so, but this most recent wave of British troops soon turned a controlled situation into one of fear and panic. As men saw their comrades impaled on the ends of the enemy bayonets, a complete rout ensued.

The ultimate result was, for all intents and purposes, a foregone conclusion. The British and Hessian troops had been trained for exactly this type of engagement, while the Americans relied primarily on their skills of cover and concealment along with their outstanding marksmanship. Within minutes, the Americans had abandoned their positions and were streaming back through the fields and forests in the direction of nearby Chester.

GENERAL GEORGE WASHINGTON
6:00 PM - SEPTEMBER 11, 1777
DILWORTH

Washington and his staff had ridden hard and fast through the Pennsylvania fields in order to get to the fighting around Dilworth. Washington was furious with himself for waiting so long before leaving Chadds Ford and tending to the right flank of his army, but he had simply refused to believe that the action on his right was anything other than a diversion. Despite the ever increasing sounds coming from the direction of Birmingham Hill, as well as reports from several of his scouts, Washington had continued to hold on to his theory that the main British attack would be coming across the Brandywine Creek. This belief had been reinforced by the fact that the action along the creek had begun to heat up by the time he had reluctantly placed General Anthony Wayne in charge of the troops at Chadds Ford and hurried off to tend to his struggling flank.

By the time Washington reached the area of most intense fighting, the Americans had retreated from Birmingham Hill completely, and were exhausting their final attempt at making a stand at Dilworth. Although his mere presence was enough to make some soldiers return to the firing line, most continued their movement away from the battlefield. Finally, his frustration at yet another defeat, coupled with his own inability to adequately understand the battle, boiled over into a fury that startled his staff.

"For God's sake, men, turn yourselves around and fight!" Washington shouted at his retreating army. "Never turn your back to the enemy! You are soldiers, and by damned, you will *fight*!"

Washington continued to ride forward into the mass of retreating men, getting closer and closer to the point of the enemy assault. Soon, musket balls were whizzing through the air all around him, and his staff responded by urgently insisting that he return to the rear.

"General Washington, I beg of you," Colonel Harrison implored. "You must move back from the front line, sir. If you are captured or killed, this army could not stand the loss!"

"This army cannot stand *this* loss, Colonel," Washington shouted above the noise of the battle. "We must do everything in our power to halt the advance of the enemy, and if that requires us to place ourselves in harm's way, then so be it."

As Washington spoke, one of the young captains on his staff was struck in the side by a musketball. The man fell from his horse and landed hard on the ground, holding his side and screaming in agony. The location of the wound was such that it would almost certainly be mortal.

The violence of this event caused Washington to take pause, and allowed him to get his anger under control. He realized that this army did, in fact, look to him for its ultimate leadership, and that nothing positive would come from him throwing his life away in frustration. Although the fact didn't quite sit right with him, Washington had to remind himself once again that he was no longer the young officer responsible for leading his men into the teeth of the enemy assault. He was now the commander of an army, whose responsibilities went beyond the immediacy of the moment and extended to the strategies of the future.

Washington knew that the Americans didn't have to win this war. He realized that if he were able to keep this army together – if he were able to keep its spirit alive long enough – the British would eventually tire of the cost of continuing this conflict. It had already cost Great Britain dearly in both lives as well as money, and there was a small but vocal group within the British government insisting that negotiations be initiated with the Colonies. The longer the Continental Army was able to continue to fight, the larger and more vocal that group would become.

All of these thoughts passed quickly through Washington's mind as he continued to see men dying around him. The young captain wounded in the side had been lifted onto the horse of another member of Washington's staff, and his aides looked anxiously at him awaiting his direction.

"Let us move to a position from which we can organize a covering force, and see to the safe withdrawal of the remainder of the men," Washington said calmly. "We must see to the health as well as the spirit of this army."

—

Meanwhile, Washington's predicted British attack across the Brandywine Creek at Chadds Ford had finally started. General Knyphausen, in charge of the approximately 7,000 British and Hessian troops remaining at that location, had launched his assault across the Brandywine after waiting to hear the battle to his north reach a crescendo. Satisfied that the Americans would be unable to move reinforcements from their right flank back to the approximately 5,000 men currently holding the original position at Chadds Ford, Knyphausen had ordered his artillery to begin a barrage of the American lines, which he followed with an assault by several regiments.

Although these attacking regiments initially suffered heavily, they continued to push stubbornly across the creek. Eventually, the numerical superiority of the British and Hessians, combined with their artillery support, began to weaken the American defenses.

Meanwhile, the British assaults on Birmingham Hill and Dilworth had caused the Continental Army to retreat on that flank, and British and Hessian forces began pushing down on Wayne's men from the north. The Americans quickly realized that they were in an untenable situation, and the forces along the Brandywine Creek withdrew.

—

Although the Continental Army had suffered yet another defeat at the hands of the British, this one somehow felt different to Washington, even at this seemingly low point of the day. Although the men were retreating, they were doing so with defiance, and only after they had stood their ground and inflicted heavy losses on the enemy. It was a situation not unlike a young boy on the brink of becoming a man who recognizes that he's becoming something different – something more confident and powerful – but hasn't quite understood how to fully realize that new potential.

Washington had seen this happen with men in his past military experience. His army had ceased to be a group of civilians, and were quickly losing their transitional label of being "citizen soldiers". Slowly, painfully, these men were becoming simply "soldiers".

PRIVATE WILLIAM DEVLIN
DAWN - SEPTEMBER 12, 1777
DILWORTH

The pitiful cries of the wounded could be heard in every direction as many of the exhausted British and Hessians attempted to get some sleep on what had been massive killing fields just a few hours before. To make matters worse, the smell of the already decomposing dead was enough to make a man gag, and many of the men had tied handkerchiefs around their faces in a vain attempt to stave off the stench of war.

But for all of the unpleasantness these slumbering troops were forced to endure, their situation was dramatically better than those men who had been assigned to burial details. These poor unfortunate souls were tasked with the responsibility of picking through the bodies on the battlefield, sorting out those that were actually alive but in various stages of unconsciousness, and those that had truly departed from this earth. Needless to say, the severity and graphic nature of the wounds with which they were confronted was enough to rattle even the heartiest of souls.

—

Private Devlin was one of those unlucky enough to have been assigned to a burial detail, and he had long since lost count of the number of bodies he had carried to what was soon to be their final resting place. Although he continued to retch at the sight of many of the bodies, he had already vomited up everything that was in his stomach.

"I can tell you one thing, Willy," said Private Miles Parker, another man in his company, "that's definitely the last time I tell the Sergeant to go to hell under me breath. I swear that man could hear a mouse pissin' on a bale of cotton."

Although William was in no mood to carry on a conversation, he found that a bit of chatter at least took his mind briefly off of the disgusting task in which he was engaged.

"At least you did something to deserve what you got," William complained. "I was just standing around minding my own business when Sergeant Myers points at me and says, 'You there, Devlin, you get to tendin' to the stiffs.' I mean, that's just not right, calling these dead boys 'stiffs.'"

"Maybe not for our boys, Willy, but these here Rebels ain't nothin' more than dead dogs in my eyes. Why, if it was up to me, we'd be leavin' 'em for the animals to root out instead of puttin' 'em in that there ditch."

The ditch to which Private Parker was referring was a long, wide trench that had been dug at the base of the hill on which the Americans had made their final stand. Whereas the British and Hessian dead were being buried in individual graves, the dead Americans were simply being placed into this long trench like rows of cordwood. There was no dignity in this treatment, and William was disturbed by what he was being ordered to do.

"C'mon Miles, these men may be our enemy, but they gave a good accounting of themselves today. If you don't believe that, try taking a look around at the number of graves we've dug for our own men, and the number still waiting to be buried. No, these men are soldiers like you and me, and when we dishonor them, we dishonor ourselves."

William and Miles paused their conversation long enough to examine the body of a British soldier that was propped up against a tree about halfway up the hill. The man had been shot through both thighs, and the loss of blood had been enormous. Hundreds of flies were buzzing around a wide, deep pool of the man's congealed blood that had collected at the base of the tree. The expression on the face of the dead soldier was one of peace, and William said a quick prayer that his last few minutes of life had not been painful.

"That there's Corporal Abernathy," said Miles quietly. "Good man, was Abernathy. He never did throw his rank around like some of these other self-important oafs do. Figures, he'd be one to get killed, eh?"

William snorted in grim amusement. "I don't believe an enemy musketball knows the difference between a good man and a pompous ass, do you? I mean, it's pretty much the luck of the draw the way I see it. One minute you're here, the next minute you're pushing up the daisies."

Private Parker looked at William sadly. "Ay, that it is, Willy, that it is. But try explainin' that to Abernathy's young wife and that little daughter they had last summer. I gotta figure they'd want more reason for the loss of their man besides 'the luck of the draw', don't you?"

William immediately regretted the casual tone of his previous comment, and he bowed his head quietly in shame at the insensitivity of his words. He made a promise to himself to never again trivialize the death of another human being.

"Let's get him over with the others," William said in an attempt to move past his indiscretion. The two men lifted the dead soldier, carrying him to the next open grave that had been dug earlier, and laid him almost gently into the rather shallow hole. The two men looked silently down at their fallen comrade, each saying his own version of a prayer that the man's soul might find some peace in the next world.

"You ever get scared of dyin', Willy?" Parker asked, not looking up from the grave. "You know, when you're in the middle of one of these here battles, and things ain't lookin' too good. You can hear them musket balls just a-zippin by you, and you see some of the other lads getting' hit, and you just wonder if the next one's gonna get you. Are you ever scared then? Cause I gotta tell you, I'm almost scared out of me pants sometimes."

William realized that Parker wasn't really looking for an answer from him, but that the man was confessing his fears at a time when he felt most vulnerable. Burying thirty or forty men, some of whom had been your friends just a few hours before, tended to have that effect.

"Of course, Miles, everybody feels that way sometimes. I mean, even the bravest man knows it may be his time at any point – at least any man with a brain in his head."

"Maybe, Willy, maybe," Parker mused. "But I'll tell you one man that ain't afraid to die, and that's General William Howe. Did you see that man during the battle, Willy? Wherever there was the worst fightin', that's where the General was. And he had himself sittin' up on a horse, for God's sake! Sittin' on a horse! Talk about makin' yourself a target for the Rebs! No, not every man is afraid to die, Willy."

It occurred to William that he had just made reference to the fact that a man required a brain in order to be scared, and that General Howe apparently lacked fear. He smiled privately upon the realization that General Howe must then, at least by William's definition, lack a brain.

The two men eventually pulled themselves away from the grave of Corporal Abernathy, and continued their grisly task of moving on to the next body. They didn't need to go far, as this part of the battlefield was literally carpeted with the dead and dying from both sides.

"Here, Miles, let's take care of this one," William said, pointing at the body of an American soldier lying face down on the ground. Parker hesitated, his previous feelings toward the enemy clearly apparent, but he finally moved over beside William as he turned the body over.

William and Parker found themselves looking at the body of a man – actually no more than a boy – of perhaps sixteen or seventeen judging by his youthful appearance. His features had become almost wax-like, but it was still possible to see that he had been a handsome young man. The bullet that had killed the soldier had clearly struck him just below the heart, as both of his hands were covering a hole there that had, until recently, been bleeding profusely.

"What's he got there?" Parker asked, pointing to something that the young man was clutching to his bloody chest. William reached down and carefully removed a piece of paper from the grasp of the soldier and examined it.

"It looks like a letter to his Mum," William observed. He felt uncomfortable reading the letter, almost as if he were looking secretly into the life of another human being. He knew he had no business knowing what was in the letter, but his natural curiosity got the best of him. William took a few seconds to read over the first paragraph or two, and a profound sadness overcame him.

"It seems this boy had just joined the Continental Army a few months ago, and it sounds like his Mum wasn't too happy about it," William explained to his friend, as he continued to read. "He says, 'I know you was worried about me bein' in some fightin' Mother, but it don't look like we're gonna get us a chance to do that. And even if we do, you know I can take care of myself, just like I been takin' care of things for you and the others since Father died.' Hell, Miles, this lad wasn't much more than a boy, and he was the head of a family!"

Parker stared quietly at the ground, unwilling to meet William's eyes.

"He goes on to say, 'I know you was mad at me when I left you all, but if I ain't willing to fight for what I believe in, then I ain't fit to be the man of the family. I hope you can understand that, and forgive me someday. I miss you and the others terribly, but I'm hoping to see you in a few weeks when the winter sets in and we get a chance to take some leave. You can bake me one of those apple pies I love so much and...'"

William's voice trailed off as he got to the end of the letter.

"That's all I can read," William said, looking up at Parker. "There's a few more lines at the end, but they're so covered with blood that I can't make out what they say."

Private Parker reached over and removed the letter from William's hand. Leaning down over the soldier's body, he replaced the letter into the hands of the boy.

"Get his feet, Willy, and I'll get his head," instructed Parker. "And we ain't takin' this one to that trench at the base of the hill. This boy's at least gettin' himself the decency of having his own grave."

William looked at his friend in surprise, worried that they might get into trouble for placing an enemy soldier into a grave that had been dug for their own dead. But the grim expression on the face of Miles Parker indicated that there was no room for discussion on the matter.

As they placed the body of the young American into a grave, William breathed a huge sigh of relief, wiping the sweat from his face. As he looked over at Parker, William could see that sweat wasn't the only moisture the man was wiping from his face.

—

The British remained on the battlefield for an additional four days, during which time they continued to bury the dead and tend to the wounded. To that end, the British soon realized that their medical resources were simply not sufficient to handle the huge number of casualties that had been suffered, many of which were wounded enemy soldiers that had been left on the battlefield when the Continental Army had retreated. General Howe, combining humanity with simple practicality, sent a messenger to General Washington, requesting that Washington send some of his own surgeons to tend to the wounded Americans that remained under British control. Several doctors and medical assistants soon arrived at the British camp, and did what they could to save their wounded, and make those they could not at least a bit more comfortable.

GENERAL GEORGE WASHINGTON
SEPTEMBER 15, 1777
CHESTER COUNTY

The Continental Army had spent the last few days rounding up their scattered troops and licking their wounds. Thousands of men who had hidden in woods and fields throughout the Pennsylvania countryside gradually found their way back to the American camp. Some returned of their own volition, while others were returned at the rather insistent urgings of the many patrols that had been dispatched for miles around for this express purpose. Soon after the battle, an entire regiment made an appearance at the camp, having hidden in the woods for almost two days in order to avoid detection and capture by the roving British patrols.

General Washington was pleasantly surprised to discover that his final losses, once thought to be almost catastrophic, were only about ten percent of his total force. This, combined with the fact that his army had stood toe to toe with the enemy and inflicted significant losses of their own, eased the pain of having retired from the fight leaving the British in command of the battlefield.

Lieutenant Colonel Harrison approached Washington, carrying several dispatches in his hand. A Commanding General rarely received these types of messages with enthusiasm following a battle, certainly a battle that would have to be categorized at the very least as a tactical defeat. Such messages tended to be either reports of the dead, wounded, or captured soldiers, or rebukes from the government delivered from a suitably safe distance. Although he understood that it was the responsibility of the Continental Congress to insure accountability, it never failed to irritate him that this accountability was being demanded by some men who had no interest in or appreciation for what his men had endured.

"General Washington, I have several messages from members of the Continental Congress who have marked them 'urgent', and request immediate responses from you," Colonel Harrison stated. Well, Washington thought with grim amusement, better to receive notice regarding dead weight rather than dead men.

"Very well, Colonel, thank you. I shall read them and respond presently. If you please, what is the general gist of these messages," Washington asked his Chief of Staff. Washington and Harrison enjoyed an absolute trust between them that was critical to their collective ability to manage the administrative burdens required of any large organization, and Harrison had complete latitude to read all messages that were addressed to the Commanding General.

Colonel Harrison shuffled his feet and gazed uncomfortably at the ground in front of him. Washington took note of the uncharacteristic behavior of Harrison, who was normally direct and to the point.

"Come now, Colonel," Washington jibed, "the distinguished members of our government can't be that agitated, can they? Are they so disgusted with the performance of this army that they are demanding my resignation?"

"Not *your* resignation, sir," Harrison responded. "They are demanding the immediate removal and court martial of General Sullivan."

Washington was shocked by the revelation. He looked at Colonel Harrison for several seconds, while he struggled to understand.

"General Sullivan?" Washington almost sputtered in disbelief. "General Sullivan was at the heart of this battle, and his actions were completely appropriate in light of the situations he was forced to deal with! He redeployed his men in the face of an enemy attack, he held the line against repeated assaults by superior numbers, and he was instrumental in organizing a defense that allowed hundreds of our men to retreat safely in the face of potential capture!"

Colonel Harrison continued to look at the ground, and Washington realized he was defending one of his generals to a man who was more aware of the true nature of the situation than almost anyone else. In effect, Washington was preaching to the choir, and he immediately regretted the insinuation that Harrison was not acutely aware of everything he had just said.

"My apologies, Colonel," Washington said quietly. "I did not mean to lash out at you – I know you are aware of that."

"Of course, sir, there is no need for an apology," Harrison said. "I share your indignation with respect to General Sullivan. My concern is regarding the potential for this accusation to gain momentum. If General Sullivan is forced to be relieved of his command, this army would be without his presence at a most critical time."

Washington slowly smiled at the man who had become the most important person in his life on a day to day basis. As was always the case, Harrison had succeeded in cutting through the clutter and emotion of a situation, and reducing it to the most important and urgent elements.

"You are, as always, perceptive in your assessment, Colonel Harrison. The immediate need is to place a buffer of time between General Sullivan and his detractors. I will respond immediately with my decision to keep General Sullivan in his current role, with my assurance that these charges against him will be satisfactorily addressed at the earliest opportunity. How does that sound to you, Colonel?"

Harrison was visibly embarrassed by the fact that the Commanding General was clearly seeking approval on how he was planning to handle the situation. Still, Harrison couldn't help but feel a certain pride in the confidence Washington was displaying in his judgment.

"Of course, His Excellency has no need to seek my agreement," Harrison began. "If that is the course of action determined…"

"Damn it, Colonel!" Washington interrupted. "How many times have I told you not to refer to me using that term? I am a soldier, and a general in this army! I'm not some royal personage that requires the flattery afforded by some ridiculous title of self-importance!"

Harrison smiled mischievously, having used the title for the express purpose of diffusing his own uncomfortable situation. Washington quickly realized he had been the victim of the Colonel's keen ability to exert upward influence, and he let out a quiet laugh.

"Very well, my clever friend," Washington said. "I'll deal with the General Sullivan issue immediately. And I shall deal with your petulance later," he concluded, unable to hide a smile. "What other matters are there requiring my attention? If possible, can we speak of something pleasant for a change?"

Harrison searched through the many papers that he had brought with him, his face set in deep concentration as he quickly perused their contents. Finally, he appeared to locate the object of his search, and presented it to Washington.

"Sir, your request to create the position of 'Commander of the Horse' has been approved by the Congress. In addition, they have also approved your request to appoint Count Pulaski to the position, and promote him to the rank of Brigadier General."

Washington was both surprised and thrilled at the fact that he not only had been given permission to organize his cavalry into a more useful structure, but that he was able to place an experienced cavalry commander at its head.

Prior to coming to America earlier in 1777, Pulaski had fought for many years for his mother country of Poland, primarily against the invading forces of Russia. The young French nobleman, the Marquis de Lafayette, had recruited Pulaski to come with him to America in order to take part in the revolution that had burst upon the world stage. Upon his arrival, Pulaski had written an impassioned letter to General Washington, offering his services to the Continental Army. In the letter, Pulaski had stated, "I came here, where freedom is being defended, to serve it, and to live or die for it." Washington had been impressed by the letter, as well as the military reputation that preceded the Polish Count. In dire need of experienced military professionals, Washington had immediately taken Pulaski up on his offer to assist the Americans.

One of the first recommendations that Pulaski had made to Washington was that the cavalry forces be completely reorganized. Currently, each of the divisions commanded their own units of cavalry, a carryover from the days when the units had been staunchly independent from the overall army structure. Although this allowed each division commander to use these units as he saw fit, it failed to establish the cavalry as a truly strategic component of the army. Pulaski immediately recognized that if the Americans were going to stand up successfully to the British, they would need a centrally controlled cavalry organization to carry out the critical tasks of scouting and reconnaissance, screening of the main body, communication between units, and executing probes and quick strikes during a battle.

"Well," Washington replied to his aide, "I must say that my surprise at the request being granted so quickly is only exceeded by the potential of this opportunity. Please ask Count Pulaski to report to me immediately so that we may begin instituting the changes that he and I have been discussing these last few weeks."

"Yes, sir, I shall to it immediately," Harrison replied, turning to depart.

"Oh, and Colonel?" Washington said, interrupting the departure of Harrison. "Please insure that the Count's interpreter accompanies our Polish friend. Being that Pulaski speaks precious little English, and I even less Polish, I would surmise that our meeting might be somewhat unproductive without a translator."

"Of course, sir," Harrison said with a smile. "The two men will be at your disposal in a short time."

—

Washington had two pressing needs as it related to the location of his army. The first was to continue to be in a position to defend Philadelphia. The second was to also be in a position to defend the massive army supply depot that was located in Reading, Pennsylvania. In Washington's opinion, the supplies located in Reading were far more critical to the continued survival of his army than was the defense of any city, to include Philadelphia. However, Washington was a wise enough man to understand the political and economic implications of losing Philadelphia to the British, not to mention the effect on the morale of his army and the rest of the country.

No, Washington needed to place his men in a position to defend both of these locations, and a previous study of the local maps told him that White Horse Tavern was just that position. With that decision quickly made, he sat down at his small field desk and began preparing the orders that would send his men marching yet again.

GENERAL WILLIAM HOWE
7:00 PM - SEPTEMBER 16, 1777
WHITE HORSE TAVERN

The British staff officers had rarely seen their Commanding General as angry as he was right now. He had been stomping back and forth across the floor of the tavern for over ten minutes now, shouting obscenities and blaming everyone from his division commanders to God Himself.

"Do any of you have any idea how rarely such an opportunity presents itself?" Howe shouted at no one in particular. "Washington and those fools he calls officers had practically handed me most of their army! They were right in the palm of my hand, and I had but to close my fist around them! And then what? Rain! Fog! For the love of God, Mother Nature herself has deemed us unworthy of winning this war!"

Howe's staff continued to cower in the corner of the small room, fearing even to make eye contact with the ranting general. Although the officers were no stranger to the quick wrath of Howe, this current tirade was truly something to be remembered.

—

What Howe was referring to was what the men were already calling the "Battle of the Clouds." It had started just after midnight, when Howe had ordered his army to form two columns and depart the Brandywine battlefield. It was an order that was gratefully obeyed by the men, who had become sick of the smell of the dead bodies that had begun to re-surface following their hasty burials.

General Cornwallis had departed with half of the army first, and had headed in the direction of White Horse Tavern where Howe's spies had reported the Americans to be located. He had been followed by Knyphausen just after dawn, who had taken the Washington Pike toward Boot Tavern. Howe, who was accompanying Knyphausen, was planning to once again utilize the tactic of flanking his enemy, although this time he would do so on both flanks at once.

General Washington had been alerted to the approach of the British around 9:00 AM, and had immediately moved a significant portion of his army directly at the British. Howe had initially been surprised by the rather bold move, and had assumed that Washington's plan was to attempt to attack the British while they were strung out over several miles. However, Howe became further confused when Washington halted his advance and formed his men along an approximately three mile long line that ran from a place called Three Tuns Tavern on the American left to Boot Tavern on their right.

Howe's men had continued to move toward the American position, consolidating their forces as they arrived. In the early afternoon, two American divisions had moved forward, and run into several Hessian units that had been deployed in advance of Howe's main body. The Hessians had turned the tables on the Americans, fighting "Indian style" and giving the enemy a dose of their own medicine. So effective were the Hessians in their tactics that the larger American units were forced to retreat to some cornfields located on a plot of high ground immediately to their rear.

Howe had seized the opportunity to bring the remainder of his army to bear on the vulnerable position of the American divisions, and had ordered the columns under Cornwallis and Kynphausen to simultaneously attack the exposed flanks of the enemy. Had Howe drawn the scenario out on a piece of paper, it could not have been any better. The two columns had quickly formed, and had begun to move out at a brisk pace with the assurance of an army that was on the verge of soundly defeating their enemy.

It was at that point of the battle that Divine Providence had chosen to turn its back on the British and look squarely down upon the ragged ruffians that called themselves the Continental Army. The skies had literally opened up, unleashing a deluge of rain onto both armies that made it virtually impossible for either side to fire their muskets, soaking each soldier's gunpowder in a matter of seconds. The rain had been so heavy that the British and Hessian soldiers, marching across a grassy plain that separated them from the Americans, had lost sight of other units that were located just a short distance away. Despite the extensive discipline and experience of the army, a degree of confusion quickly appeared, with some units stopping to get their bearings while others continued moving in the direction of where they assumed the enemy to be.

To make matters even worse, a dense, low fog had quickly formed over the surrounding countryside making the two armies located on opposing hills invisible to one another. The attacking British, unable to accurately locate the Americans, and unable to fire on them even if they could see them, recognized a hopeless situation when they saw one. The British division commanders had requested permission to withdraw their attacking units to their original positions, and Howe had angrily agreed.

Had the weather not intervened, it was completely possible that the British and Hessians may have attacked, enveloped, and destroyed two of the five divisions of the American army. Washington, battered and grossly outmanned, would have been forced to put his army on the run, which would have allowed Howe to accomplish two goals. First, he would have taken Philadelphia without so much as a shot being fired at his army. And second, Howe would then have set out to destroy the remainder of the Continental Army at his leisure, operating with the reassurance that there was no way for the small surviving force to launch any type of attack. Howe could have ended the rebellion by Christmas, and been home in time to enjoy the spring of 1778 with his family.

But now, because of bad luck and bad timing, Howe would be forced to continue his pursuit of General Washington and his Rebels, as well as his capture of Philadelphia.

—

Howe's ranting had begun to deplete itself, as he gradually ran out of scapegoats and energy. Although his anger and frustration remained, the professional side of him recognized the need to concentrate on his next move. Howe commanded the various staff officers in his presence to disappear, who did so gratefully. The British general needed time to think, and he did this best when he was alone. Howe sat down at his small field desk, and began making notes on the back of a map of the local area.

Basically, Howe realized that he was facing two distinctly different options. One option was that he could pursue the battered American army under Washington, forcing it to face his own army in yet another major battle, and yet another after that if need be. Howe was confident in his army's ability to successfully defeat the Americans in any scenario in which the accepted rules of civilized warfare applied, meaning a battle in which the opponents faced each other openly and with honor. Although the Americans had proven surprisingly capable of giving a good showing of themselves at Brandywine, that in no way insinuated that they were capable of actually *winning* a battle.

But this strategy of focusing on Washington and his army carried with it some very real risks. First, although Howe had enjoyed excellent intelligence provided by many of the local Loyalists, that situation could change quickly in favor of the Americans. Second, while Howe had no ability to reinforce his army or replace his battle losses, Washington was able to continuously draw new recruits from the surrounding area. And finally, even if the Americans were simply able to *survive* their future engagements against the British, that might be enough to cause the British pacifists back home to gain momentum and convince the British Parliament to sue for peace. The mere thought of the most powerful nation on the face of the earth agreeing to negotiate with this rabble made Howe's stomach churn.

The other option with which Howe was faced was to practice the more European strategy of warfare, specifically taking and controlling the major population centers of the enemy. If Howe was successful at capturing Philadelphia, that might be enough to so damage the morale of these Rebels that the Continental Army might simply dissolve from a lack of will to continue the fight. If nothing else, the occupation of Philadelphia would provide Howe's army with a much needed rest, especially in light of the bitter Pennsylvania winter that was just two or three short months away.

There was one final consideration that Howe dared not write down. When the British had occupied New York City, Howe had become extremely close – friends, so to speak – with the wife of one of his staff officers. The New York winters had not been quite so cold as a result of her company, and Howe genuinely missed this type of female companionship in his life. The fact that there were a large number of British Loyalists in Philadelphia was no secret to anyone. If the British army happened to spend a few months in the warm and hospitable arms of the great city of Philadelphia, perhaps – just perhaps – General Howe might find himself once again the recipient of the type of female companionship for which he so dearly longed.

Howe sat back and reviewed the notes he had made in the last few minutes. Pursue Washington and his army, or occupy the Rebel capital of Philadelphia? The choice seemed clear. Howe really had no right to risk the fate of the war on the daring strategy of pursuing the American army. Clearly, the safe bet was to capture and occupy Philadelphia and, in the process, bring the American Colonies to their knees. And, if a friend or two happened to introduce themselves into Howe's life – well, he would just have to deal with that as best he could.

Howe allowed himself a broad smile, as the details of the plan began to form in his mind.

"Colonel Wilson!" Howe shouted to his Chief of Staff, who appeared immediately at the doorway, "inform my division commanders that they are to report to me immediately. We must make preparations to conduct the necessary steps to win this war."

GENERAL ANTHONY WAYNE
1:30 PM - SEPTEMBER 20, 1777
PAOLI, PENNSYLVANIA

The American Army had marched for almost two straight days, barely stopping to rest. Although the men were bone-tired and complained constantly, they knew what they were being ordered to do was the right thing at the right time.

The battle they had fought at Brandywine, combined with the debacle that had occurred a few days later at White Horse Tavern, had left the army dangerously short of the supplies necessary to fight a war. And although they could always forage from the local countryside in order to replenish food for themselves and their horses, one thing they could not replenish so easily was gunpowder and ammunition, both for the muskets of the soldiers, as well as the voracious appetite of the cannon. At the "Battle of the Clouds" at White Horse Tavern, Washington's army had had over 400,000 musket cartridges ruined by the weather, a loss they could not easily absorb.

As a result of this, General Washington had decided to temporarily move his army to the supply depot that had been established at Reading Furnace, north and west of his previous position he had held during the aborted "Battle of the Clouds." Washington's plan was to rest and resupply his men, and then reposition himself such that he could defend against any British move aimed at capturing Philadelphia. Washington realized that his move away from the city was risky, creating the potential for the British to capture the Colonial capital if they moved quickly and decisively. But Washington was a pragmatist, and knew that if he were forced to face the British in yet another major engagement, he simply didn't have the supplies necessary to effectively meet such a threat. Washington's decision, in effect, had been made for him.

However, not every unit of the Continental Army was being moved to Reading Furnace. General Anthony Wayne and his brigade of approximately 1,500 men had been selected to perform a very different task.

—

Anthony Wayne had been born and raised in Chester County, Pennsylvania. When the war had broken out, Wayne organized the 4th Pennsylvania Militia and had been elected as its Colonel. In 1776, Wayne and his regiment had been ordered to proceed north into Canada and attempt to assist the remnants of a retreating American army under the command of a bold young officer named Benedict Arnold. This army had unsuccessfully attacked the British at Quebec City in December of 1775, and was now being chased southward by a reinforced British force.

Wayne's regiment confronted the British at a place called Trois-Rivieres, or Three Rivers, and was soundly defeated by the better equipped and larger enemy force. However, Wayne had demonstrated the ability to stand firm in a difficult situation, and his actions were instrumental in allowing most of Arnold's army to escape.

—

Wayne had departed from Washington's headquarters having been given orders to confront yet another difficult situation. Wayne was to circle his unit back behind the British Army and harass their supply lines. Washington had also told him to engage the enemy, if favorable opportunities presented themselves. Such opportunities included harassing the numerically inferior rear guard of the enemy, or being presented with a scenario in which the British were strung out in a long column and would therefore be unable to bring a significant number of troops to bear on any single point.

Anthony Wayne was the perfect man for the job. Not only had he already proven himself to be a highly capable combat officer, but the British were quite literally camped in his own backyard. Wayne had, in fact, grown up in southeastern Pennsylvania, and he knew the roads and surrounding terrain as only a boy exploring throughout his youth can come to know an area. On countless occasions, Wayne had played "war" with his young friends, usually fighting mock battles against fierce Indians attacking his house and home. Invariably, Wayne and his friends had emerged exhausted, but victorious.

Suddenly, Anthony Wayne found himself about to face a very different kind of enemy, with the eventual outcome not so predictable.

—

The young officer rode up in a flurry of dust and hooves, his horse coming to an abrupt halt just a few feet from where General Anthony Wayne was standing with several members of his Brigade staff. He quickly dismounted and approached the group, throwing a quick salute in the rough direction of his Brigade Commander.

"What do you have to report, Lieutenant?" Wayne demanded of the young man. Although the men who served under General Wayne generally admired and respected him, he was not particularly known for his patience with subordinates.

"Sir, I wish to report that the British are well settled into their encampment, having established strong picket positions, and dispatched various patrols into the surrounding area. They have apparently decided to spend the night, sir."

"Damn!" Wayne exploded. "We had them where we wanted them just a few hours ago! If only I had more men, I could have attacked and landed a damaging blow on the enemy! And now they've consolidated their forces – I simply cannot attack a numerically superior force in an established position. Damn!"

Wayne paced back and forth in front of the Lieutenant, seemingly lost in thought. The young officer, accustomed to these outbursts from his general, stood calmly and awaited further instructions. After a minute, Wayne turned and addressed his staff.

"Gentlemen, we have been sent here to engage the enemy, and that is exactly what I intend to do. Although the enemy force is clearly larger than our own, we have several things that are in our favor. First, we are operating upon the very fields of our homes. This part of the country belongs to *us*! And we will use this fact to our advantage. Second, we should be receiving reinforcements in the very near future, which will help to minimize the enemy's numerical advantage. But most importantly, we will be attacking first thing tomorrow morning, much to the surprise of the British. We will strike as they are arising for their morning tea and crumpets, and we will crush them with boldness and speed!"

Wayne's fiery oration had the desired effect on the staff officers, as they responded as one in agreement.

Wayne moved to a map of the local geography that was spread out on a nearby table. He briefly studied it, more for confirmation than for information as Wayne had no real need to consult a map of this area. He then motioned for his staff to join him.

"We must first move ourselves such that we are not in such close proximity to the enemy. At present, we can be no more than a mile from the British position. We shall move ourselves here," he stated, pointing to a spot on the map. "It is an open field that will allow us to adequately prepare for tomorrow's battle, but the surrounding woods offer us the seclusion that we require to remain undetected. Colonel, please make the necessary arrangements immediately. I should like to begin moving within the hour."

—

What General Wayne didn't know was that the advantages he had laid out to his staff existed only in the mind of Anthony Wayne. First, although the Americans were, in fact, operating in an area that was very familiar to them, it was also filled with a great number of individuals who had remained loyal to the British Crown. And these individuals had no problem with providing the British with information regarding the whereabouts of any nearby Rebels. Second, there were absolutely no reinforcements forthcoming; General Maxwell's men originally scheduled to come to Wayne's aid had been diverted to a completely different location. And finally, the British – unlike the imaginary Indians Wayne had fought and defeated during his childhood – were not about to be as cooperative.

GENERAL CHARLES GREY
7:45 PM - SEPTEMBER 20, 1777
BRITISH CAMP
PAOLI, PENNSYLVANIA

The sun was just beginning to set on the Pennsylvania countryside, as thousands of British soldiers began the daily ritual of settling in for the evening. Those fortunate enough to have avoided picket or patrol duty were just now tending to the small campfires they had made, preparing to attempt yet another hopeless miracle. That miracle involved turning the small pieces of tough, salted meat they had been issued into something edible, even in the most generous sense of the term.

Others, resigned to eating stale bread or some raw vegetables, had begun the cathartic task of writing letters to friends and family back home. The fact that these letters wouldn't reach their intended recipient for many weeks, sometimes even months, mattered not to these men. These correspondences offered a single thin thread of connection between this foreign land and the familiar surroundings of their homelands.

Finally, there were those that had no time for either eating or writing, as there was money to be made – or lost. A wide variety of games were always taking place throughout the camp, and almost all of them involved the wagering of what little money these men possessed. Most of the games revolved around playing cards or dice, and the army had spawned legends in terms of those who seemed immune to losing at these competitions. Many new recruits had learned the hard way that, when it came to cards and dice, there was no such thing as a "friendly game."

General Charles Grey rode slowly through the camp, making his way from General Howe's headquarters back to where his own men had pitched their tents. He knew that none of his troops would be wrestling with their evening meal, having been fed earlier with the quickly drawn and prepared rations from the Quartermaster's private stock. This rather rare event had been made necessary by the fact that General Grey and approximately 5,000 men would be departing the British camp in just a couple of hours, and therefore would not have the luxury of preparing their own meals in the quickly approaching twilight hours.

General Grey was somewhat of a legend within the British army. He had first joined the military as a young man in 1848, giving him almost 30 years of service in support of King and Country. During that time, he had fought in countless minor and major engagements, having been wounded on more than one occasion. These years of service had aged General Grey like a fine wine, as he had become virtually unflappable in any situation. He was known for his calm demeanor at the most hectic and desperate of times, and had frequently compelled the men around him during a battle to remain steady and reliable simply through his presence.

The orders that General Grey had just received had the potential to either significantly add or detract from the larger than life image he had developed over his many years in the army. As far as Grey was concerned, the jury was still out on which way these next few hours would go. Regardless, he knew that his leadership and experience would be put to the test. Grey also knew that the fate of he and his men was, to a large degree, in the hands of the cocky young lieutenant that was currently riding along beside him. To say that General Grey was made uncomfortable by this fact would be to challenge the British penchant for understatement.

—

General Howe had been receiving reports throughout the day from a variety of local citizens, informing him of a nearby body of Rebel troops. At first, Howe had dismissed the reports as the idle ramblings of people who had long since become afraid of their own shadow. However, after the fourth such report, Howe was forced to concede that the existence of a nearby enemy was something that at the very least needed to be investigated.

Howe made a special selection to investigate the situation. Lieutenant Corby Wallingford, of Her Majesty's 2nd Light Infantry, was a unique figure within the British army. Lieutenant Wallingford had spent the first part of the war as an officer in the fledgling Continental Army, serving under General Washington himself, but had quickly realized that there was no future in such endeavors. As a result, he had decided to offer his services to the British army, who had suspiciously accepted. It wasn't until Wallingford had successfully identified and implicated an American spy who had subsequently been hanged, that the British began to trust that Wallingford had, indeed, switched his allegiances.

Howe saw the current situation as an excellent opportunity to kill two birds with one stone, so to speak. First, Wallingford had been raised in this part of Pennsylvania, and could therefore serve as a guide to any British troops who needed to navigate through the countryside. And second, if Wallingford proved to be honest and accurate in his guidance, it would remove whatever doubt might remain regarding his allegiance to the Crown.

Wallingford had returned from his scouting mission with the report that there was a contingent of well over a thousand Rebel troops setting up camp in a nearby secluded field, no more than a few miles from the current location of the British army. The fact that Wallingford had been successful at locating the position of the enemy was due only to his familiarity of the local area, as almost anyone else could have ridden within a hundred yards of the camp and not been alerted to its presence.

After consulting with the many other patrols that had been dispatched throughout the surrounding countryside, Howe was confident that this group of Rebels was acting independently and wasn't part of a larger plan to outmaneuver the British. Howe had therefore decided to dispatch a sizable portion of his army to surprise and attack this group of brazen Rebels who had the temerity to locate themselves so close to his command, not to mention the fact that they enjoyed no support from the rest of their own army.

In addition, Howe had decided that the only reason such a force would be located so close by would be to launch their own attacks on some portion of the British army, probably the tenuous supply lines that provided the proverbial life's blood to these thousands of British and Hessian troops. Howe could conceive of no other plausible reason for their existence. If this was the case, then it was imperative for Howe to strike at this group of Americans as quickly as possible, before they could do any damage of their own. As a result, Howe had ordered General Grey to make his attack on the enemy that very evening, in the dead of night.

Such an attack was inherently risky, especially for an enemy force operating in unfamiliar territory. But Howe had reasoned that Lieutenant Wallingford would not only minimize such a risk, but would actually provide an edge to his men. Just to make sure, Howe had selected his most experienced and reliable General to make the attack.

—

The soldiers had now been fully informed of their nighttime mission by the junior officers and senior enlisted men, and it was obvious that many of them were uncomfortable with the information they had been given. They were ordered to leave all of their equipment at the campsite, carrying only their weapons. It had been explained to them that many of the items they would typically carry, even when traveling light in preparation for a battle, had the potential to make noise. And when sneaking up on an unsuspecting enemy in the middle of the night, noise was quite possibly the greatest enemy they faced.

However, leaving behind most of the equipment they normally carried was not the most disturbing order the British and Hessian soldiers had been given. General Grey had circulated throughout the groups of men himself, calmly instructing them to remove the flints from their muskets. The order had been quickly taken up by the officers, and soon all 5,000 of the men had removed that small but vital component of their weapons that allowed them to fire.

The flint was a small piece of stone that was placed on the hammer of the firing mechanism of the weapon. When the trigger was pulled, the hammer fell sharply, causing the flint to strike a metal pan which held a small amount of gunpowder. This action resulted in a spark which ignited the gunpowder in the pan, and subsequently the larger amount of gunpowder that had been poured down the barrel of the musket. Finally, this resulted in the musketball placed in the barrel of the weapon to be propelled out of the end of the barrel, theoretically in the direction of the enemy.

As long as there was no flint placed on the hammer of the musket, there was absolutely no way for the weapon to be fired, which was exactly why General Grey had ordered the removal of the flints. Grey explained to his confused men that the firing of their weapons on an attack such as this one would result in nothing positive. First, the accidental discharge of a weapon during the few minutes prior to the attack would alert the Rebels to the presence of an enemy force, and would virtually eliminate the advantage of surprise. And second, there would almost certainly be a great deal of confusion that would ensue as the attack began, due to the darkness. By not loading their weapons, the British and Hessians would know with certainty that anyone firing a musket would be an enemy soldier, and could be safely attacked without fear of killing or wounding one of their own.

The men complied with the order, albeit reluctantly. After all, a soldier without the ability to fire their weapon may be better able to advance unseen and unheard, but was of little danger to the enemy once he got there, was he not?

Slowly, the Master Plan of General Grey became apparent to the men. The one item that had the potential to cause noise that was not being left behind was their bayonet. The British and Hessian soldiers would be stepping back in time this night, fighting their enemy in a manner that had not been used for many years. As opposed to standing a hundred or more yards apart, they would be closing with and destroying their enemy with the terrible sharp devil that each man attached to the barrel of his musket. This was not even waiting until you saw the "whites of the eyes" of your enemy, as had been done to the attacking British at Breed's Hill by the Americans two years earlier. This was getting so close to the other man that you smelled the stench of his breath as you killed him.

And a terrible weapon was The Bayonet. Designed to be attached to the "Brown Bess", the nickname used for the muskets carried by the British and Hessian soldiers, the British bayonet was approximately 18 inches long, and had a triangular shape. The rationale for the shape of the bayonet was both ingenious and horrendous. When plunged into the body of the victim, the wound caused by the triangular bayonet gradually got wider as it entered, from point to hilt. As a result, when it was removed from the victim it tended to leave a gaping hole in its place. The wound to the victim caused massive bleeding, as well as significant internal damage when used on the torso of a human body.

General Grey had considered his plans carefully. He felt confident that the silent approach in the dead of night followed by a bayonet attack would have an extremely damaging effect on the enemy. Such an attack had the potential to rout the Rebels from their position, compelling them to abandon any thought of harassing or attacking any part of the British army, to include the vulnerable supply lines.

However, Grey was also a wise enough man to know that the most devastating impact of tonight's attack wasn't just the potential tactical benefits - it was the psychological impact. Grey's bold actions were about to send a message to the upstart American army that they weren't even safe in their own backyard. The British army still ruled the Americas, and those foolish enough to challenge that fact were in danger of finding themselves on the receiving end of the feared bayonet.

GENERAL ANTHONY WAYNE
10:30 PM - SEPTEMBER 20, 1777
AMERICAN CAMP
PAOLI, PENNSYLVANIA

Despite what he had been led to believe by General Washington, General Anthony Wayne had yet to receive a single additional soldier to reinforce his somewhat precarious position. Although this fact weighed heavily on Wayne, it was nowhere near as concerning as the nature of the reports he had been receiving throughout the evening. One of the locals had wandered into the American camp several hours ago with the revelation that there was an impending British attack being planned on Wayne's position. Apparently, a servant of another local citizen had been apprehended and detained by the British, at which time he was questioned regarding the condition of the various roads in the area; specifically, he had been asked about the viability of utilizing certain roads at night.

After they had finished questioning the servant, the British had sequestered him in the back room of the house they were using as a headquarters, and proceeded to conduct what the servant had referred to as a "council of war". During this council, according to the servant, the British had specifically debated the possibility of "attacking that nearby camp of Rebels", to the point where roads were identified, troops were assigned, and plans were laid.

Initially, this had all sounded like so much contrived drivel from bored people prone to exaggeration and embellishment. After all, it certainly wouldn't be the first time that the army had been the recipient of information that ended up being completely fallacious. In addition, Wayne's own informants operating in the local area had heard from any number of sources that the British army was packing up to begin moving against Philadelphia.

However, since late in the afternoon Wayne's patrols had been reporting the sighting of numerous enemy soldiers moving throughout the surrounding countryside. Although this wasn't altogether unheard of -

any well-run army dispatched patrols to investigate the area around their main body - it was the frequency of these reports that had become troublesome to Wayne.

This conglomeration of events kept nagging at Wayne. Although he couldn't put his finger on it, something kept telling him to be careful of ignoring the story he had heard from the local man, or of dismissing the enemy patrols around his camp. Perhaps it was the conviction with which the story had been related to him. Or maybe it was Wayne's natural inclination to be conscious of everything around him, however minor or insignificant it seemed to be. Either way, Wayne had summoned Colonel Hartley and Colonel Humpton, his two brigade commanders, to meet with him. The two men had just arrived at Wayne's tent.

—

"Gentlemen," Wayne began, "I'm sure you have been made aware of the report I received earlier this evening regarding a possible attack by the enemy. According to this report, the British have gone so far as to select their route of attack, as well as the units that will be participating. In addition, we've also had any number of reports from our scouts stating that there exists a significant amount of activity by the enemy in our general area. Your thoughts?"

Colonel Richard Humpton spoke first. "General, I must admit to a fair amount of skepticism with respect to this story we've been told. I find it very hard to believe that the British army would be so bold as to organize and launch an attack at night, sir. The British army, for all of its strengths and attributes, is not what I would call - how should I say, sir - *creative.*"

Humpton had served as an officer in the British army for a number of years before resigning his commission and coming to America. He had become so attached to his adopted homeland that he, as had many thousands of other members of the Continental Army, chosen to fight for his new country against his former country. The fact that Colonel Humpton found it hard to believe that the British would launch a night attack made Wayne briefly question his caution on the matter - but only briefly.

"Furthermore, General," Humpton continued, "I think it very unlikely that the enemy is even aware of our existence so close to them. And even if they are aware, I'm confident that they would be unable to locate this remote location that you have chosen for us. Why, they would need to know this area like the back of their hand, much like you do, sir."

Wayne turned his gaze to his other brigade commander, Colonel Thomas Hartley. Although Hartley did not possess the depth of military experience of Humpton, Wayne considered both his abilities and his judgment to be outstanding. In point of fact, Wayne valued the opinions of Hartley much more highly than those of Humpton. It was a commonly held perception within the Continental Army that it was only a matter of time before things exploded between Wayne and Humpton. The exact reasons for this predicted confrontation varied widely, depending on who was telling the story.

"With all due respect to Colonel Humpton," Hartley said, somewhat hesitantly, "I am inclined to be more concerned by the reports from our patrols than I am of one old man coming in with a story. Perhaps the man is telling the truth, perhaps not. But we know for certain that our patrols have been encountering the enemy over the last few hours with a frequency that I must say is most disturbing."

What Colonel Hartley chose not to share with Wayne and Humpton was that about 6:00 PM that evening, Hartley had written a letter to a friend in which he had stated his virtual certainty that the Americans at Paoli would be attacked in the next few hours by the British. To Hartley, the evidence was copious and obvious.

"Gentlemen, as always I appreciate your candor and your insights. I understand that one of you feels it extremely improbable that the British have either the capability or the wherewithal to launch an attack on us in our present location. I believe your opinions, Colonel Humpton, to be based on sound judgment and a deep experience and understanding of the tactics and tendencies of our enemy."

Although Humpton was not one of his favorite officers, General Wayne still recognized the need to maintain a civil, if not respectful relationship with the man. His remarks directed toward Humpton had been intended to somewhat lighten the blow he was about to administer in basically dismissing the man's opinions. Unaware of this fact, Colonel Humpton allowed a slight smile to cross his face, which quickly disappeared as Wayne continued to speak.

"However, I believe in the old adage of 'better safe than sorry', especially when dealing with the safety of our men. Therefore, I believe it prudent at this time to take the necessary actions to ensure that our position is well defended, and that all possible precautions have been taken."

Despite the unforeseen turn the conversation had taken, both colonels hid their surprise, managing to portray an expression of being calm and collected. They looked at their Commander in expectation of his orders. General Wayne paced back and forth several times in thought before addressing his subordinates.

"Gentlemen, we will increase the number of pickets that we have placed around the perimeter of our camp. It is my understanding that there are currently four pickets in position - I would like to see that number increased to a total of six. Also, I would ask that these pickets have their locations moved to increase the distance they are placed from our camp. Should we have any unannounced visitors, it would be my desire to have their arrival announced as soon as possible, eh?"

The pickets being ordered by General Wayne actually referred to a picket post, which was generally comprised of one lieutenant, one sergeant, one corporal, and 16 privates. The men in these pickets were spread out over a small area, while being controlled by the lieutenant from a central position.

"Sir," Hartley stated, "might I also suggest that we increase the number of mounted patrols we currently have in place. That would serve to increase our surveillance to an even greater degree."

"Excellent, Colonel, I would agree," Wayne replied. "Gentlemen, please see to it that these steps are taken immediately. No time like the present to make our visitors feel welcome, should we have any company arrive."

The two men smiled slightly, saluted sharply, and strode quickly away from Wayne's tent to make the necessary arrangements.

Alone now with his thoughts, Wayne wondered if he was becoming a careful old woman, scared of his own shadow. Such were the burdens of a Commanding Officer. Show too much caution, and you were labeled a coward. Be too cavalier, and you were accused of thoughtlessly gambling with the lives of your men.

It was difficult enough to carry the weight of commanding a brigade. Wayne wondered how General Washington managed to bear the weight of the entire army – some would say the entire country - on his shoulders. Anthony Wayne made a mental note to show the old man a bit more respect in the future.

LIEUTENANT JACOB LANDES
11:15 PM - SEPTEMBER 20, 1777
AMERICAN CAMP
PAOLI, PENNSYLVANIA

The 4th Pennsylvania Regiment had spent the better part of the last two days marching about the countryside, halting just long enough to catch their breath, shove a bit of food quickly into their mouths or, at one point, grab a few hours of sleep. When combined with the residual stress of having fought a major battle just a few days earlier, the result was a group of soldiers who were tired, irritable, and careless.

Lieutenant Jacob Landes, having returned with his Company to their proper regiment following the previous battle at Brandywine Creek, was no different than the rest of the men in his unit. In fact, while most of the others had at least been given a chance to sleep for three or four hours earlier in the day, Jacob had been assigned to organize several patrols that had been sent out to scout the surrounding area. Finally, it appeared as if he was going to have a few hours of peace and quiet in one of the hastily constructed huts that had been erected along the tree line that formed the back of the American camp. These huts were being used in lieu of the usual accommodations, as orders had been given to leave all tents behind in order to travel lighter and move faster.

Jacob experienced a brief pang of guilt as he laid his blanket out on the floor of the hut, the image of his friend Thomas Sweeney manning some lonely picket post somewhere outside of the camp perimeter intruding itself into his consciousness. Lieutenant Thomas Sweeney, now a combat veteran, had volunteered to take responsibility for one of the several outposts located around the camp, designed to provide an early warning of an enemy's attempt to advance on their position.

Jacob reflected on the change that had taken place in his best friend since the battle at Birmingham Hill just over a week ago. Prior to his baptism under fire, Thomas had been an easygoing young man, viewing the world around him – including the war he had recently joined - as an adventure to be enjoyed to its fullest. However, the unexpected realities and horrors of war had resulted in a marked change to the young man's personality. Whereas Thomas had previously been prone to making light of things and joking with everyone around him, he now exhibited a seriousness that was striking when compared to his former demeanor. His carefree attitude had been replaced by a man who seemed to shoulder a burden that threatened to crush him into the ground. Jacob reflected that this change in Thomas had resulted in the birth of a confident and capable officer, at the expense of causing the death of his innocence. Jacob was fairly certain that the transition had been both necessary - and tragic.

But Jacob had his own demons to battle. He worried that he had failed in his duties as an officer and a leader. His men had retreated at both Birmingham Hill as well as at the final stand at Dilworth, and he constantly criticized himself that there must have been something he could have done on both occasions to change the eventual outcome. Had he adequately prepared his men for the fight? Had he placed them in the best tactical positions to defend the areas they had been assigned? Had he exhibited bravery and leadership when it was needed the most? He was fairly certain that the answer to at least some of these questions was "no." While he didn't fully appreciate it, Jacob was battling with the same doubts that had plagued every man who had ever served in a leadership capacity during a battle.

The sounds of an active camp echoed through the night, as men prepared themselves for launching the impending attack they had been ordered to expect in the morning. Even beyond that, though, there was a degree of anxiety that indicated a more immediate concern. Rumors had been circulating throughout General Wayne's men that the British were moving about in a manner that was indicative of an offensive intention. Patrols had reported running into sizable groups of enemy soldiers, and stories of local citizens wandering into camp with tales of doom had heightened the alertness of even the most slovenly individual. If sleep was to come to anyone in camp tonight, it would be a troubled, restless slumber.

Jacob laid down on the floor of his hut with all of these thoughts swirling in his mind. Although he innately knew that he would never really sleep, he also knew that his body was in desperate need of at least a brief respite from the stress he had been experiencing over the last few days. His father had always told him that an exhausted body was the worst enemy to allowing a man to live up to his responsibilities. Jacob smiled tightly as he reflected on the fact that, while his father was no doubt correct in his lesson, there was no way that he could have ever predicted the seriousness of the consequences of violating this sage advice.

After a few minutes, Jacob drifted into a restless state of half-sleep and half awareness, as he continued to hear the sounds around him. Muted conversations of nearby soldiers, the restless movement of horses tethered to stakes placed in the ground, and the ever-present sounds of the woods at night competed against his natural need to sleep. Finally, Jacob admitted defeat, and roused himself from the ground.

Jacob stepped out of the hut into the night, and was immediately surprised at the brightness of the camp. Everywhere he looked, campfires had been built by the men, and each one was surrounded by dozens of soldiers huddled close to the flames in an attempt to chase off the chill of the late September evening. Jacob was briefly concerned about the lack of any semblance of light discipline, given the nature of the reports that had been thus far received. But he quickly admonished himself for thinking that he might know better about such things, realizing that General Wayne and the other senior officers must certainly have a better understanding of the situation.

Jacob walked toward the closest group of soldiers, recognizing several members of the 4th Pennsylvania in the light being given off by the campfire. Corporal Stanton, a middle-aged man from just outside of Philadelphia, was delivering one of his famous lectures to the younger men surrounding him. These lectures always involved advice on the female species, and they were generally entertaining.

"So boys," Stanton was saying, "the bottom line is you gotta show 'em who's boss. There ain't a woman on the face of this earth that respects a man who lets her walk all over him."

"But Corporal Stanton," one of the younger men noted, "I thought you said last night that you never argued with your wife. You said it was just easier to let her have her way than to try and talk some sense into her."

"Damn it, Boy, that's *my* wife we was talkin' about! God never created a meaner soul than when you cross that woman. I'm just now referrin' to the gentler portion of the gender, if you know what I mean."

The other men seemed to understand Stanton's point, and nodded slowly at the wisdom of this older man. One of the men noticed Jacob, and began to rise from his seat on the ground, followed by several of the others. It was a show of respect that had only recently been demonstrated since the battle at Brandywine Creek, and Jacob still wasn't comfortable with it. He quickly stopped the men with a palm-down motion of his hand.

"Please, gentlemen, keep your seats, I beg you," Jacob said, slightly embarrassed. "I was having trouble sleeping, and thought some interesting conversation might help pass the time. When I saw Corporal Stanton, I knew I was in the right place."

"That you are, young Lieutenant Landes, that you are," Stanton acknowledged with a slight bow of his head. "I was just educating these men on the wiles and trickery of our womenfolk. It appears not every man has the same level of wisdom and insight on the topic as me."

The serious nods of agreement around the circle clearly indicated that the men were aware that they were truly in the presence of greatness as it related to this particular subject.

"Sir, I don't mean to be personal, but some of the men heard that your Father was in poor health," Corporal Stanton said to Jacob. "I hope everything is alright with Mr. Landes."

Jacob was touched by the show of concern, and he was surprised at his inability to answer the man immediately due to the lump in his throat that quickly developed. It was true that in the last few letters he had received from his Mother she had indicated that his Father's health had taken a turn for the worse. It was something his family had worried about for years, and it seemed that their anxiety had increased dramatically in the last few weeks.

"Thank you for asking, and that's not too personal at all. I'm sure my Father will be just fine, the Lord willing. I'll be sure to pass along to him that you were asking about him - that's just the kind of medicine that will raise his spirits."

The men mumbled softly in agreement, pleased that they had struck a positive chord with this young officer that they had quickly come to trust and respect. The unspoken agreement among the soldiers - unspoken at least in the presence of the officers - was that this army could do with more of the likes of Lieutenant Landes in the ranks.

"Lieutenant, why don't you pull up a piece of dirt and settle down with us for a few minutes?" Corporal Stanton offered. "You may not find us to be the most educated lot in the world, but we're a good bunch to help pass the time when you got a lot on your mind."

Educated or not, Jacob had come to realize that these men had become the closest thing he had to a family while he was away from home. He smiled his appreciation at the offer, and sat down gratefully among this amazing group of soldiers.

SERGEANT ALEXANDER BICKELL
12:30 AM - SEPTEMBER 21, 1777
PAOLI, PENNSYLVANIA

The soldiers had been moving quietly along a remote country lane for the better part of an hour, and as far as they could tell had yet to be detected. They had been forced to pass by several houses along their route, but the members of these households had been detained to preclude their ability to inform the Americans of the presence of British troops so close by, should they be so inclined.

Much to his dismay, Sergeant Alexander Bickell had been detached from his Hessian unit and had been assigned as a guide of sorts for the 2nd Battalion of British Light Infantry. Although Bickell obviously had no problem fighting alongside these British soldiers, he felt much more comfortable when he was doing so as a member of his own unit. Not only were there language barriers, but there were also significant cultural differences.

For example, Bickell had sensed immediately that there was a certain amount of dismay on the part of the British regarding the order to only use their bayonets in the upcoming attack. He could tell that these soldiers were more than a bit squeamish about the personal and somewhat barbaric nature associated with this style of warfare. For his part, Bickell considered the bayonet to be just another tool of the trade, that trade being the art of waging war on the enemy. To be uncomfortable with the use of such a weapon was as foreign to him as was the undisciplined conduct of the Americans. To Bickell and the other Hessian soldiers, you received your orders and carried them out to the best of your ability. If these orders involved getting your hands a bit bloody, then so be it.

Bickell, three other Hessian soldiers that he had hand picked from his unit, and two British scouts had been assigned to place themselves approximately fifty yards in advance of the main British column of Light Infantry, which consisted of approximately 500 men. Initially, Bickell had been concerned about the ability of this column of British soldiers to travel quietly along a dark road through unfamiliar territory. Such behavior required a great deal of discipline, and complete confidence in those around you to do their respective jobs. But up to this point Bickell had to admit that the men behind him had been completely undetectable to his ear, and more than once he had been compelled to stop for a minute and listen carefully to insure that the main column was still there.

No doubt, the noise discipline being displayed by the British was influenced by the fact that General Grey had informed his unit that any man who violated the command for absolute silence would be court-martialed and immediately put to death. Such statements, which were by no means idle threats, tended to compel the men to act in the desired manner.

In fact, quite contrary to the stereotypes that were held by the soldiers of the Continental Army, the Americans weren't the only ones who possessed the capability to fight "frontier style", as the term was used. Specifically, many American soldiers held the belief that the British were capable only of massing in densely-packed rows of troops, concentrating their firepower on the enemy and moving forward in an almost automatic, mindless manner. However, these Light Infantry troops currently stalking the American camp were trained to perform in a very different manner. They were the "shock troops" of the British army, capable of moving quickly and silently through any terrain, day or night. They were experts at dispersing themselves in such a manner as to make it difficult to bring firepower to bear on any sizable portion of their unit at any one time. In short, they were absolutely perfect for the mission they had been given on this September evening.

Suddenly out of the darkness just ahead came a challenging voice with an American accent.

"You can just go ahead and stop right there. I got my musket pointed right at your chest, so you best let me know who you are right now."

Bickell was initially startled by the fact that the enemy picket could see them, as their uniforms would be a dead giveaway as to their identities. But he quickly realized that the picket must be bluffing, or he would have opened fire by now.

One of the British scouts standing just to Bickell's left, had been selected for his current duty by virtue of the fact that he had spent most of his life living in the American colonies. As a result, he had no trace of a British accent, and sounded exactly like these Rebels. In fact, rumor had it that he had actually served with the Continental Army in the recent past. To make the situation even more odd, Bickell had overheard one of the British officers referring to this scout as "Lieutenant Wallingford". That meant Bickell was currently entrusting his life not only to an officer – for whom he had a natural distrust, as did most experienced enlisted men – but an officer who had already demonstrated a willingness to betray his comrades. Things just kept getting better for the Hessian.

"Easy there, man," said the British scout calmly. "I'm one of you out on a damn patrol. I guess neither of us will be gettin' much sleep tonight, eh?"

"You'll be gettin' more sleep than you know what to do with, unless you tell me the password for the evening," snarled the American picket.

For the countless time during this campaign, the assistance of the local citizens loyal to the Crown was about to pay yet another dividend. A farmer had obtained the password issued by General Wayne to his pickets and patrols, and this information had been given to the British and Hessian troops moving in advance of the main column for the exact situation that had just presented itself.

"Here we are and there they go," said the British scout. "Now, let us pass, will ya?"

"Yeah, come on through," replied the American picket, his voice clearly indicating his relief. "Ya know I don't mean to be an ass, but apparently the Old Man thinks there might be some of them British bastards somewhere nearby. Can you believe that? Like the British would have the guts to be walking around here in the dead of - "

The soldier had his sentence cut short by the thrust of two bayonets through his chest, one by the British scout, the other by Sergeant Bickell. A slow gurgling sound forced itself from the throat of the stricken American, as he attempted to cry out. Bickell withdrew his bayonet from the soldier's body and quickly moved forward, placing his hand over the soldier's mouth and slowly lowering his body to the ground to avoid any unnecessary commotion.

As much as Bickell hated to admit it, he had to grudgingly acknowledge that this turncoat officer of theirs knew how to handle himself. In the past two minutes he had tricked an obviously alert enemy picket, and then dispatched him with his bayonet in a manner that was as efficient as it was heartless. Nevertheless, Bickell made a note to keep his eye on this one. Bickell's rather stunted sense of honor saw nothing wrong with fighting for someone in order to make a profit. But to change from one side of a war to the other without any obvious reason – well, that just couldn't be trusted.

Immediately, the other four men of Bickell's advance party moved forward and spread out in anticipation of other enemy soldiers being nearby. Initially, it appeared as if the picket they had just killed had been a lone sentry, and their advance could continue unnoticed. However, Bickell soon heard the sound of horses' hooves coming down the road from a short distance away. Obviously, the dead sentry had been part of a larger unit, and other members of that unit were about to arrive on the scene.

The silhouette of two horses, their masters riding atop them, appeared in the faint moonlight of the evening. One of the horsemen called out quietly into the darkness.

"Harry? Harry? Is everything alright up here? The sergeant said he heard something goin' on up here."

The British scout with the American accent replied quietly in an attempt to disguise the distinctiveness of his voice. "Yeah, everything's fine. Just stretching my legs."

The second horseman, immediately alarmed, cried out, "Why, that ain't Harry! You don't sound nuthin' like Harry! Who goes there!"

The horsemen were answered by six soldiers moving forward and quickly closing the distance between themselves and the mounted patrol. Both Americans spurred their mounts and attempted to turn them around to retreat in the opposite direction, but for one of them it was too late. Three British soldiers managed to thrust their bayonets at the looming figure in the darkness. One of the bayonets pierced the side of the horse, which elicited a loud and shrill response from the stricken animal. The other two bayonets found their mark in the horseman, one penetrating completely through the thigh of the soldier, the other driving upward into his midsection. The second bayonet thrust, delivered to the left side of the man, succeeded in piercing his heart and killing him instantly.

The other horseman managed to escape his attackers, galloping off toward his comrades, shouting at the top of his lungs, and firing a shot from his musket as he fled. Although the shot whistled harmlessly into the night, the damage had been done – the British surprise attack was officially no longer a surprise.

Sergeant Bickell and the other five soldiers turned in the direction of the main body of troops to the rear. He knew that time was now on the side of the enemy, every minute that passed allowing the Americans to prepare themselves for an attack. The fact that the British soldiers would be unable to fire at the enemy during their assault made it all the more important to attack quickly before an organized defense could be put together. Bickell shuddered at the image that appeared in his mind of the British coming out of the darkness into the open fields of the enemy camp, only to be confronted by a sturdy line of troops firing volley after volley of devastating fire into their ranks. The only options at that point would be to either continue to advance into the teeth of the enemy, or scurry back into the darkness like a pack of roaches being exposed to the light. Neither choice seemed particularly attractive.

—

Bickell and the others quickly returned to the main body, arriving to find that the other 500 or so men had already deployed into a line of battle. Obviously, the Regimental Commander had come to the same conclusion as Bickell regarding the need for rapid movement. and no sooner had the advance guard formed to the right of the line when the order was given to move out at the quick step.

This first wave made up of British Light Infantry was the first of three waves that prepared to move against the American camp. The second wave consisted of approximately 350 members of the 44th Regiment, and the third wave was made up of nearly 600 men of the Royal Highland Regiment, also known as the "Black Watch". This third wave of Scottish soldiers were some of the most feared members of the British army, their reputation well established for being both fearless as well as brutal.

Sergeant Bickell felt the familiar sensation of adrenaline coursing through his body as the battle line began moving forward into the darkness. Although the pretense of surprise had for all intents and purposes been abandoned, there persisted an eerie silence to the men. They knew that any unnecessary noise would only make it easier for the enemy to pinpoint their location and unleash musket fire on them. Every soldier understood that victory this evening would come from speed, confidence, and the points of their bayonets.

LIEUTENANT JACOB LANDES
12:30 AM - SEPTEMBER 21, 1777
AMERICAN CAMP
PAOLI, PENNSYLVANIA

The casual conversation around the campfire had come to an abrupt end with the sharp, rapid reports of musket fire off to the right of the American camp. Jacob and Corporal Stanton were the first two men on their feet, with Jacob running quickly back to the hut he had occupied to grab his coat and sword. Meanwhile, Stanton was unceremoniously grabbing and shoving the men in the circle toward their appointed stations, cursing up a storm the entire time.

All around the camp men were running about, some with a defined purpose, others in absolute confusion. Officers and senior enlisted men were shouting orders to the soldiers with varying degrees of coherence and effectiveness. It was a scene that appeared to be mass confusion, with men literally running into one another in their haste to get anywhere other than their previous places of relaxation and rest.

In a testament to the previous discipline that had been instilled by General Wayne and his officers, the situation gradually developed into some semblance of order, as units began to form in the main area at the front and center of the American camp. Some of the men who had arrived without their weapons were sent back to their huts to retrieve them, and within fifteen minutes or so, most of the men had arranged themselves in formations ready to receive further instructions.

General Wayne had managed to locate his mount, and was galloping back and forth among the groups of soldiers that were scrambling into formation. He was continuously shouting orders and encouragement to the men, his voice fading in and out of the darkness as his words were sometimes drowned out by the urgency of the moment.

"Come on, boys, stay steady! Find your officers! Find your mates! Stay calm and prepare yourselves for battle!" he shouted. "The enemy has made the mistake of awakening the Americans! Here is our chance to make them pay!"

Jacob had quickly retrieved his necessary equipment and moved to the left side of the camp where the 4th Pennsylvania Regiment had been stationed. Upon arrival, he was pleased to see that many of the men were in ranks with their weapons, and the heat of the moment was giving way to a scene that bordered on being under control. He immediately set about the task of calling out into the night in search of the remaining members of his unit.

"4th Pennsylvania, 4th Pennsylvania!" he shouted. "You are over here, men! Come quickly and form with the regiment!" Unfortunately, he realized that his calls were being drowned out by the similar entreaties being made by dozens of other officers, and Jacob decided quickly that the most effective use of his time would be spent preparing those men that were organized and prepared for the upcoming engagement.

Returning to the head of his unit, Jacob saw that Captain McCavish, one of the company commanders within the regiment, had arrived on the scene. Captain McCavish was a stereotypical large Irishman, with a huge red beard and amazing amounts of red hair flowing out from underneath the hat he had quickly jammed atop his massive head. Whereas the men followed the orders given by Jacob as a result of the respect they had for the young man, the men followed every bidding of Captain McCavish out of abject terror. His imposing physical appearance and deep, bellowing voice carried with them an implied threat that any man unwilling to give immediate obedience would be swiped from the face of the earth. At this critical point in time, many of the men felt it was safer to face the enemy than to face the wrath of this officer.

Jacob approached Captain McCavish, who appeared more a devil than a man in the light of the evening campfires.

"Sir, what are your orders?" Jacob asked the Captain.

McCavish's eyes, wild with the energy of the moment gradually focused on Jacob, and he appeared to gather himself.

"Young man, prepare the regiment to face to the left and begin moving out of the camp. If we can move out of this God forsaken spot, we'll be better able to maneuver," the Captain said.

Casting his eyes about the scene all around him, Jacob quickly realized that the man was correct. If the Americans were caught in this confined space, there would be no chance for them to operate in any effective manner, either offensively or defensively. While Jacob had no idea what might be coming out of the woods to the right of the camp, he knew that they would have a better opportunity to face the threat with the benefit of an area in which to maneuver. With this thought in mind, he faced the regiment and prepared to deliver the necessary orders.

Gradually, the men of the 4th Pennsylvania made their way through a gap in the fence line that marked the left boundary of the American encampment. Their progress was agonizingly slow, as hundreds of men were attempting to push through an opening that was only a few feet wide. Many of the men, after navigating the passage through the fence, simply ran headlong into the night, ignoring the orders of their officers and the curses of their fellow soldiers. Others, possessing more discipline and courage, attempted to form with their respective units to conduct an orderly withdrawal. Fortunately, most of the men of the 4th Pennsylvania belonged to this second group.

Jacob had been one of the first members of his regiment to reach the other side of the fence, and began forming the men with the help of several of the senior enlisted men. Captain McCavish had chosen to remain within the confines of the camp. reasoning that his imposing figure would facilitate the movement of the men. As the unit began taking shape, Jacob formed them into a firing line facing back into the camp. The plan was to use these men as a covering force for the other American soldiers in the event that the enemy appeared out of the night.

—

Suddenly, a loud roar erupted to the right, and Jacob could sense rather than see a large force of soldiers bearing down on the American camp. Hundreds of figures were running in the direction of the 4th Pennsylvania Regiment, but the confusion of the scene and the lack of any significant light made it impossible to determine whether these figures were friend or foe. Many of the Americans facing this onslaught of humanity chose not to take the time for making any distinction, and dozens of shots were fired into the approaching mass.

"Cease fire, men, cease fire!" Captain McCavish shouted, "you may be firing on our own men!"

However, the words had barely escaped his lips when he was run through by the bayonets of two British soldiers who were part of the leading element of the attack. Clearly, the American officer had incorrectly assessed the nature of the situation – these were, in fact, enemy soldiers. McCavish summoned his incredible strength, and turned to face the two men who had delivered the strikes that would have instantly killed almost any other man. He raised his sword and delivered a vicious blow to the head of his closest attacker which nearly split the skull of the man. The second man fared no better, as McCavish drove the point of his blade into the soldier's torso. Both British soldiers staggered backwards, withdrawing their bayonets from the captain as they retreated, and were dead by the time they had fallen to the ground.

But McCavish, while an enormously powerful man, was a man nonetheless, and his time on Earth was quickly ended as three additional British soldiers quickly closed on him and administered three additional thrusts with their bayonets. The last of these pierced the heart of the courageous giant, and he fell to the ground, his eyes staring blankly into the dim light of the night.

Jacob was stunned at the sight of his fallen comrade, and briefly lost his composure. Despite the fact that he was now a veteran of combat, no previous experience could prepare someone for the shock of the scene with which he was now presented. Hundreds of additional enemy soldiers seemed to appear almost magically from the darkness, mingling themselves within the ranks of the Americans attempting to escape from the chaos.

The situation was made worse by the fact that the gap in the fence through which the Americans had been retreating had now become impassable. One of the four cannon that General Wayne had brought with his force had broken from its carriage, and now lay lodged perfectly in the gap, with dozens of men frantically attempting to move it from its position. Their efforts were being made more difficult by the fact that many of the soldiers, oblivious to the situation, continued to try and press their way through the narrow escape route.

Gathering himself, Jacob once again began issuing orders to the men, urging them to prepare themselves to repel the enemy onslaught they were about to face. However, he realized that he was now unable to take any immediate action to assist his comrades on the other side of the fence line, as the American and British soldiers had become so intermingled that a volley fired by his men was just as likely to kill friendly troops as it was to kill the devils in red. Helplessly, he watched as the desperate battle took place before his eyes, literally yards away from where he stood.

The scene that was being played out could have been taken directly from some Faustian vision of Hell, as the struggle took on a personal nature rarely seen in this war. Men from both sides were shouting, crying, screaming, as they lashed out at one another in a frantic attempt to survive. The occasional shot being fired from a musket of an American was soon replaced by the flash of swords and bayonets, with muskets being used as clubs to strike out at an adversary. The battle had been reduced to a level that could just as easily have taken place hundreds of years in the past, when armies faced one another with the brutality of using only simple, primitive instruments of death.

Several British soldiers had surrounded one of the teamsters, a driver of one of the dozens of wagons that carried the equipment and supplies of the army. Despite the fact that this man was a civilian, carried no weapon, and was sitting helplessly in the seat of his wagon, the British began thrusting their bayonets repeatedly into the man's body. The teamster fell from the wagon onto the ground, for all intents and purposes, dead. Nevertheless, the soldiers continued to stab him repeatedly, made insane by the heat of the battle.

Nearby, a group of about a dozen Americans led by a young officer had formed themselves into a cohesive line of battle. The officer raised his sword and shouted a command that was immediately lost in the night air, but was understood by his soldiers. They launched themselves headlong into the attacking enemy, grossly outnumbered at their point of attack. They were quickly surrounded by thirty or forty enemy soldiers, and a desperate sideshow battle took place for several minutes. At the conclusion, all of the Americans lay dead or dying on the blood-soaked ground, but not before they had taken many of the enemy with them. The shock of this attack also had the benefit of temporarily taking the momentum from the British assault, and valuable minutes were gained for other men to make their way through the hole in the fence that had finally been cleared. These nameless men would be lost to history, but their heroics had saved the lives of a countless number of their comrades who would never know that they owed their future to these brave souls.

Several of the men of the 4th Pennsylvania began taking aim at the confusion on the other side of the fence, believing they might be able to pick out specific enemy targets. Jacob recognized the inherent danger in this idea, and quickly interjected.

"You there," Jacob shouted, "lower your muskets, damn it! What are you thinking? You're just as likely to kill one of our own men as you are to hit the enemy!"

The few men taking aim quickly dropped the muzzles of their weapons, partly due to the logic that Jacob had given, and partly due to their shock that the straight-laced, religious young man from the farm had actually *cursed* at them!

Jacob was far beyond caring about such formalities, as he was literally shaking with rage at his inability to effect the course of the struggle from his position. He briefly considered returning his men to the other side of the fence, but realized that it was not only impossible to go back against the tide of men streaming in their direction, but also that he now had the responsibility of protecting the retreat of Wayne's army. Exerting incredible self-discipline, and fighting what every bone in his body wanted to do, he ordered his men to retreat approximately fifty yards to create some additional space with which to operate. If the enemy was going to pursue the Americans through the gap, they would be facing a formidable obstacle of dozens of American muskets prepared to deliver a devastating volley directly into them.

GENERAL CHARLES GREY
12:50 AM - SEPTEMBER 21, 1777
AMERICAN CAMP
PAOLI, PENNSYLVANIA

The night was filled with the screams and shouts of men fighting and dying, all semblance of order and discipline lost by the leaders of both armies. The singular struggle to survive had replaced the thin facade of humanity that both sides had brought to the start of a war that had quickly become a brutal contest of who could kill who with greater speed and efficiency.

General Grey watched in horror as many of his men perpetrated acts of cruelty on the Americans, many of whom were clearly helpless and attempting to surrender. His tactics of a nighttime surprise attack made solely with bayonets had unleashed a level of violence he had never before witnessed in his many years as a professional soldier.

To his credit, General Grey began moving throughout the American camp, shouting orders to cease and desist these heartless actions, urging his officers to take firm command of the situation and return it to some level of control. In some cases, Grey himself physically assaulted his own men who were engaged in these unspeakable acts, and his actions began to have a somewhat calming effect to the situation. Gradually, the British soldiers stopped their slaughter and began to take prisoners, as droves of Americans dropped their weapons and threw up their arms.

Lieutenant Colonel Wellesley, Grey's adjutant, appeared at his side, composed and formal as always.

"General, the reports indicate that Americans are retreating from the other side of their camp and are forming a blocking force to face us. Should we pursue the attack, sir, or begin to organize and re-form the men?"

General Grey, having witnessed this scene of exuberance on the part of a victorious army, knew that taking control of the momentum of the attack and returning it to order was one of the most difficult things to do in battle. The natural inclination of a soldier was to continue to push forward, to add fuel to the fire of adrenaline that had been unleashed. However, Grey also understood that many successful attacks could become disastrous if these unorganized actions were not curtailed. The enemy, if successfully organized in their retreat, could quickly change the fortunes of war that seemed completely in favor of the attacker. Although Grey seriously doubted that these undisciplined Americans were capable of such coordinated actions, he was unwilling to take such a gamble.

"Send our officers forward to the furthest point of attack, and have them recall the men from their pursuit. The darkness and the disorganization of our army puts us in a dangerous situation were we to come in contact with reinforcements being brought upon us by the enemy," Grey ordered quickly. "I wish to have the units re-formed, and the prisoners gathered in a central location as quickly as possible. We will then proceed to return to the main encampment after we have gathered all supplies, weapons and ammunition that has been abandoned. Is that clear, Colonel?"

"Perfectly, sir. I shall see to it immediately," Wellesley replied. The adjutant rushed off into the darkness, his mind swirling around how he was going to carry out these orders. The Colonel was no stranger himself to the confusion of battle, and he realized that the direction given by his commander was the correct one. He knew that the task he had been given was a difficult one indeed, but he was now completely responsible for making it happen.

—

General Grey noted with satisfaction that the grueling training to which his men had been subjected was gradually beginning to pay dividends. They had begun to respond to the orders being given by their officers, and the situation was becoming controlled.

Despite this fact, Grey was appalled at the scene around him. It seemed as though everywhere he looked his gaze was met with the dead bodies of the enemy. Even more disturbing was the condition of these bodies. Although the aftermath of a battlefield was always a gruesome sight, the condition of the casualties that lay about was more than he could fathom. While the wounds inflicted by the penetration of a musketball were horrendous in their own right, the bloody and repeated wounds rendered by the bayonets of his men had created a nightmare of death and suffering upon the Americans.

As he surveyed the carnage, Grey tried to convince himself that this was not what he had intended. He rationalized that his decision to attack in the middle of the night using only the sword and bayonet had been made for the express purpose of protecting his men from the volleys of American musket fire that would have certainly doomed them to defeat.

Yet in spite of these facts, Grey also knew that the outcome had been predictable. He had always known that the superior discipline and experience in close quarters combat possessed by his men had the potential- even the certainty - of resulting in what he now observed. He should have anticipated that the Americans really had no chance of adequately defending themselves against this surprise attack, given their limited training and experience. In the end, given their exposed position and lack of reinforcements, he realized now that it had been a foregone conclusion.

Quickly, Grey chastised himself for this second guessing regarding his decisions. War was war, and a general was sworn to wage it in such a manner as to create every potential for victory. Sometimes this meant putting your own men into a dangerous and risky situation which might well result in their slaughter and defeat. And always it meant carrying out a plan that you hoped would result in fatal consequences for one's enemy. If the opposition was foolhardy enough to place themselves in an untenable position, then the opposing commander had every right and obligation to make them pay for their transgressions. After all, it was these Americans who had started this war in the first place. Had they simply recognized their place in the overall scheme of things and not blatantly challenged the control of the Crown, these men now lying pathetically about would most likely be at home plying their trades and tending to their fields. God knew, their performance on this night demonstrated that this is exactly where they belonged.

If nothing else, General Charles Grey was an intelligent and aware man. He knew that his actions had resulted in the British army delivering a stinging blow to the American cause for independence. Not only was the tactical result significant, but the psychological effect was even greater.

Despite all of these rationalizations, one damning fact continued to nag on the subconscious of the General. Charles Grey also knew that this battle would forever be a part of his legacy as a military commander. He would from here on be known as the man who had ordered a nighttime bayonet attack on a group of unsuspecting and unprepared men that had resulted in a massacre seldom seen in warfare. The evidence of this fact lay before him on the bloody ground lit by the dying campfires of a totally vanquished enemy.

GENERAL ANTHONY WAYNE
1:30 AM - SEPTEMBER 21, 1777
AMERICAN CAMP
PAOLI, PENNSYLVANIA

Anthony Wayne had seen a great deal of combat during the brief time he had been a member of the American Continental Army. His sensitivities related to violence and death had long been replaced by a cool detachment that allowed him to function effectively in the most chaotic of circumstances.

But what he was currently facing challenged any man's ability to remain cool and collected as a soldier, let alone the Commanding General ultimately responsible for the outcome of an engagement. Wayne recognized the obvious - that his army was literally falling apart in the face of a violent and coordinated attack by a clearly better trained and organized force. The real question became, what was his response going to be that might possibly salvage the carnage around him?

Wayne had vainly attempted to rally his men at the point of the British attack, placing several units in the woods just to the right of where the enemy had entered their camp. While these units had briefly met with some success by firing two volleys into the advancing ranks, this success had quickly been eliminated by the speed and ferocity of the advancing army. In the best of circumstances, his soldiers could fire roughly two rounds per minute. However, due to the fact that they were operating in almost complete darkness, combined with the foul weather that made every coordinated movement a chore to accomplish, the rate of fire had been reduced to approximately one round per minute at best.

As a result, the British had been able to absorb the impact of these volleys while quickly closing on the columns of Americans formed just inside the tree line. Once the advantage of firepower had been eliminated, it became a matter of who possessed the greater organization and skill with respect to hand to hand combat. There was no doubt in anyone's mind that this advantage lay with the British.

The first wave of British soldiers had passed through these forward lines of defense, disappearing into the camp that had been swarming with disorganized and terrified American soldiers. Immediately, they were followed by a second wave of men that had proceeded to mop up any resistance from the units placed in the woods, as well as providing additional momentum to the attack that had now moved completely through the encampment to the far fence line.

However, the most devastating attack had come from the third wave of British troops which had been made up of a fearsome unit of oddly dressed soldiers shouting terrifyingly into the darkness as they advanced. These men, members of the Scottish "Black Watch", had exhibited absolutely no mercy on their adversary as they had moved purposefully through the camp. Those American soldiers that still remained in and around the initial point of attack - and there were hundreds - had become so frightened and disoriented that they had ceased to possess the capacity for resistance. In addition, most of these men had long since abandoned their weapons and were simply wandering about in shock or lying helplessly on the ground.

This had made no difference to the Scots, as they began systematically surrounding and slaughtering the helpless Americans. Any number of men had been subjected to these attacks, some men being assaulted by literally dozens of thrusts from enemy bayonets. The result was a grisly spectacle of screaming attackers and the writhing, bloodied bodies of their victims.

—

General Wayne soon realized that any efforts to repel the waves of attacks being launched by the enemy would be futile. There were simply too many enemy soldiers advancing, and too few American soldiers attempting to make any type of organized defense. Wayne's priority quickly shifted to determining the most effective way to extricate his men from this killing ground in such a way as to preserve his army. To that end, he had moved to the gap in the fence line on the left side of his encampment where his men continued to exit with an almost insane sense of urgency.

Throughout his movements, Wayne had been accompanied by several members of his staff who had exhibited commendable calm in the face of the evening's events. He now called upon their assistance in order to carry out his plans.

"Gentlemen," he yelled to his staff officers, "I need you to move to the other side of the fence and assist in the organization of a covering force. We must find a way to slow the attack of the enemy if we are to have any hope of saving this army. As these men continue to move out of the camp, you must halt their retreat and organize them into functioning units - do you understand my orders?"

Captain Langston, the junior member of his staff who was normally quiet and reserved, spoke up immediately.

"General Wayne, with all due respect, I believe you are the one who has the best chance of halting this retreat. If the men see you at the rallying point, they will stop and form on you. The rest of us may not have that same effect."

The other staff officers nodded and mumbled in agreement with Langston. General Wayne realized that the young man was correct, but loathed the fact that he would now have to order these brave men to remain inside the camp and continue to push the soldiers toward the opening and ultimate safety. Anthony Wayne was a proud man, but above all else, he was a pragmatist. If his greatest impact with respect to saving his army could be achieved by moving out of the killing zone, then so be it.

"Very well, gentlemen, I shall reposition myself such that I am able to organize our scattered troops. General Smallwood and his Virginia militia should be moving in our direction even as we speak. If we can successfully rally our men and halt the advance of the enemy, we have an excellent chance of retiring in good order. In fact, if the enemy is so foolhardy as to attempt to continue their pursuit, we may well find ourselves in a position to strike back at them and make them pay for their heinous conduct this night."

Although Wayne realized that a counterattack at this point in the battle was pure folly, he knew there was a need to provide a sense of hope to these men. The very lives of the soldiers in his army relied on that. In fact, Wayne's staff appeared to physically rise up in their saddles as a result of the confident demeanor being displayed by their General.

"All right then," Wayne ordered, "get to your business. Majors Walters and Hannigan, you will come with me in order to assist our efforts in forming a rear guard. The rest of you will make every necessary effort to move our men through the fence line in an orderly manner. Is that clear?"

The staff officers grunted and nodded in understanding, and they immediately moved off to accomplish their assigned duties. Wayne paused briefly before moving toward his own assignment, watching as these incredible soldiers galloped off without hesitation. Everyone realized that the orders given might well be the last of their young lives, yet not one man had displayed even the slightest fear in doing what he had been told. For the countless time, Wayne marveled at the dedication of the men with whom he had the honor to serve.

—

The situation was becoming more desperate with each passing minute. While the American officers had had some measure of success at organizing a defense and compelling the men to retreat in an orderly manner, the center of the camp was still boiling with action.

In their panic, some of the American soldiers had attempted to find protection by hiding in the makeshift huts they had built out of limbs cut from the surrounding forest. The British had quickly determined that the best way to roust these men from their sanctuaries was to simply set fire to these flimsy, flammable structures. In many cases, the Americans quickly fled from hiding, only to be bayoneted immediately as they made

their exit. Others, terrified beyond all reason, chose to remain in the huts and be slowly burned to death. The terrible cries of men having bayonets driven repeatedly through their bodies, mixed with the high-pitched screams of those that were literally burned alive.

Gradually, the situation began to decrease in intensity, as more Americans found their way to freedom on the other side of the fence line, and the number of targets available to the attackers began to diminish. As the night wore on, men on both sides took stock of the situation around them and were universally appalled by what they observed. The remaining Americans were amazed that they had successfully survived the onslaught of the enemy, and the British were amazed that they had been capable of the results that lay before their eyes. More than a few soldiers from both armies broke down in tearful fits of emotional release.

Finally, the nightmare ground to halt, as the few pitiful pockets of American resistance were overwhelmed. Hundreds of prisoners were gathered into the center of the camp, and guards were assigned to move them back to the main British encampment several miles away.

—

To the men on both sides who had been witness to its bloody brutality; to those who experienced its ferocious rage and furor; to those who looked about and were greeted with the disastrous results of what would forever be known as the Paoli Massacre; it was a night that would never again be matched in this war as a display of man's potential for both an abundance of heroism as well as a lack of mercy.

Douglas Shupinski

General William Howe
September 23, 1777
Centreville, Pennsylvania

Things were definitely going well, Howe mused as he sipped on a rather pleasant French wine and reviewed the most recent reports coming in from the many patrols he had dispatched throughout the surrounding area.

First, a sizable force of the Rebels had been routed in the middle of the night, no doubt sending waves of terror throughout the Continental Army. Second, the British appeared to be in a position to outmaneuver the enemy and take control of Philadelphia. And third, this potential occupation of Philadelphia would mean that General Howe would once again have the pleasure of some female companionship in the form of a junior officer's rather young and stunning wife.

With respect to the first matter, Howe had been complimentary to the responsible parties, without being too effusive in his praise. After all, as a Commanding General one must always leave his subordinates with the belief that they hadn't *quite* lived up to his expectations. That would insure their fullest efforts in the future.

General Grey had made the obligatory appearance in front of Howe immediately upon returning from the "nighttime skirmish", as Howe had dubbed it. Grey, ever the professional, had given credit to the efforts of his junior officers and senior enlisted men, informing Howe that they had seized the initiative and acted boldly at every opportunity. Howe was keenly aware of the fact that such an official accounting of what had occurred by General Grey created the opportunity for Grey to have some level of deniability, should the brutality of the affair ever reach the wrong ears within the British government.

There were a significant number of men in the British Parliament who believed that their army needed to exercise restraint, or even respect, while conducting the war. After all, once this whole sordid affair had ended and the British had finally regained complete control of the American Colonies, there would be a need for cooperation between the two previously feuding factions. The economy of the Colonies simply couldn't survive without British support and endorsement and, the truth be told, it would be extremely difficult for the British economy to flourish without the raw materials and markets provided by America.

Howe snorted in disdain at the whole concept. Show restraint and respect to the enemy? That was like trying to win a war with one hand tied behind your back. If everyone would simply stop meddling in his affairs and give him the necessary resources, Howe was certain that he could win this war by Christmas and have the trading floodgates open in time for the spring. If he were given another 20,000 troops and free reign to conduct the war where, when, and how he saw fit, all would be a foregone conclusion.

Instead, Howe constantly begged for reinforcements from England that never arrived, was given "suggestions" on what strategies to use, and – for God's sake – was told to use restraint and respect! If Howe didn't know better, he would swear his country was actually *trying* to lose this war.

—

But General Grey's masterful and brutal defeat of the enemy was water under the bridge. The question currently on General Howe's mind was how to take advantage of the somewhat untenable position in which General Washington had recently placed himself. It was obvious to Howe that Washington was conflicted over whether to guard against an attack on Philadelphia, or whether he should protect the precious supplies that were positioned in the small town of Reading, Pennsylvania. General William Howe, in an effort to be magnanimous to his enemy, was about to make that decision for Washington.

Howe had summoned his Chief of Staff, Lieutenant Colonel Wilson, to his Headquarters. The premise of his summons was to have Wilson draw up and issue the orders necessary to move the army. Although this would be the eventual result of the meeting, Howe would first review his plan with the Colonel and gauge his reaction. It was a practice he had engaged in for many months now, and on more than one occasion Wilson had cautiously and respectfully identified a possible oversight in what Howe was preparing to order. And while neither man would ever acknowledge that this unspoken practice occurred – it smacked too much of equality and collegiality, of all things – it was a subtle dance that had resulted in dramatically better results time and again for the British army.

—

"Colonel Wilson, reporting as ordered, sir."

The Chief of Staff stood stiffly at attention, eyes forward, waiting patiently to be formally invited into the room. By his demeanor, one would have thought that this staff officer had never before been in the presence of the Commanding General, so precise was his military decorum. General Howe, who appreciated professionalism above almost any virtue, demanded nothing less.

"Colonel, come in, please," Howe ordered. "I believe our fine army will once again be on the move in the very near future and, of course, I will require your services to publish my orders to my commanders."

"Of course, sir. I'm ready to begin at your convenience," Wilson replied, removing his note pad from his uniform pocket.

"Before you begin taking notes for the orders, I will require a moment or two to talk through my plans. As you know, I find that things acquire a certain…clarity when I do so." Howe paused briefly, and just a fleeting glance of understanding passed between the two men.

"As you are aware, General Washington is currently attempting to guard both his supplies at Reading, as well as the city of Philadelphia," Howe continued. "It is, of course, a weak attempt at best, as he has too much territory and too few men to accomplish such an ambitious goal. Many of the patrols I have sent out have reported that there is virtually no presence of the enemy in any number of locations, but most specifically at a place called Fatland Ford. In fact, just today I dispatched General Cornwallis to confirm this fact, and he returned and informed me that he was actually able to cross to the other side of the Schuylkill River with absolutely no opposition."

Wilson remained respectfully silent for several moments until it became obvious that Howe was waiting for him to respond in some way.

"Yes, sir" Wilson replied, "General Cornwallis was kind enough to share his observations with me just a short time ago."

"Very well, then, you are apprised of the situation to some degree. In any case, my intentions are to move our army in the direction of Fatland Ford, while maintaining a small but noticeable presence in our current location. In that way, we will deceive the Rebels into believing that we are remaining here while, in fact, the bulk of our army will be on the move."

"Much as you did just a short time ago at the battle along the Brandywine Creek," Wilson observed.

"Precisely, Colonel. I believe we have found that while General Washington graces us all with many flaws as a military commander, perhaps two of the most endearing of his qualities are that he is cautious and gullible. I believe we are faced with yet another opportunity to exploit these weaknesses."

General Howe rose from his chair and crossed the room to a table upon which was laid a map of the surrounding area. He motioned for Wilson to come over to the map, as he continued his thoughts.

"As you can see, Colonel, I have placed our current location here," Howe stated as he pointed to the map, "with Fatland Ford right here," he indicated. "Reports indicate that General Washington has placed the bulk of his troops here and here," he said, continuing to identify each location as he spoke. "As you can see, if we are able to cross successfully and without incident at Fatland Ford, we will effectively place ourselves directly between the Rebel locations and Philadelphia."

Colonel Wilson carefully studied the map as Howe spoke, his mind quickly running through all of the possible scenarios of the General's proposed plan. Wilson was not at all surprised to see that the plan was bold, but sound – both hallmarks of General William Howe. But yet, there was one small aspect of the plan that caused a nagging concern in the back of the staff officer's mind. Wilson knew that he was being asked to offer his opinion, however he also knew that he must do so with the utmost of tact and diplomacy.

"It appears, sir, that your strategy is nearly perfect in order to take advantage of our situation. I shall immediately see to the task of generating the necessary orders, sir."

Howe considered his Chief of Staff carefully, as Wilson continued to stare dutifully at the map. "*Nearly* perfect, Colonel? Do you perhaps have something to say?"

"No, sir, not at all, "Wilson replied matter of factly. "I was just beginning to formulate the exact verbiage of the orders in my mind. I was considering how to best incorporate the information we have received from our various patrols that have been sent out, and it occurred to me that I hadn't had the opportunity to speak with those that had been dispatched to the north of Fatland Ford."

So that was it, Howe realized. This was Colonel Wilson's ever-tactful way of saying that there had been sparingly few patrols sent north. Howe had chosen to focus on what was south of their army where they were headed, and west of the army where the Rebels were believed to be located. If, in fact, there happened to be a sizable force of the enemy located just north of Fatland Ford, the British would be in a vulnerable position to be attacked by that force while they were making their crossing of the river. It was not an overwhelmingly likely scenario, but it was definitely a contingency which Howe had not fully considered.

"Yes, I had actually considered that myself," said Howe. "And it is for that reason that I have also decided to place several blocking units just north of Fatland Ford just prior to our arrival at that location. Such a covering force should insure our safe crossing, as well as discourage any prying eyes that might be sent out by the Rebels. I will assume that such a movement will be clearly indicated in the orders that you develop."

"Absolutely, sir," Wilson said. "I apologize for clearly speaking before the General had concluded the review of his plan."

"No apology necessary, Colonel. While you clearly possess many fine qualities, one of those qualities is obviously not the ability to read my mind and know that I had not finished. Now, if you please, see to the orders immediately. I shall expect to have them for my review within the hour."

Colonel Wilson snapped to attention, and delivered a crisp salute to Howe. As always, the Colonel was the epitome of poise and professionalism as he did so, but Howe couldn't help but notice what appeared to be just the slightest twinkle of satisfaction in the eyes of his Chief of Staff.

Perhaps Colonel Wilson didn't possess the ability to read his General's mind, Howe thought as Wilson departed the room. But he was pretty damn close.

OCCUPATION OF PHILADELPHIA
SEPTEMBER 26, 1777
PHILADELPHIA, PENNSYLVANIA

The morning of September 26th arrived clear and moderately warm – a perfect day for the British and Hessian soldiers marching from their base in Germantown toward the city of Philadelphia. The entire procession appeared to be more of a parade than the actual military maneuver that it was. Bands were playing a variety of uplifting songs along the route, ranging anywhere from the most popular marching songs to a rather flourishing version of "God Save the Queen".

The occupying force was led by General Cornwallis, as General Howe had opted to remain in Germantown with the main British army; there was still the matter of General Washington's army lurking somewhere nearby. Howe would eventually make his way into the city in order to inspect the defenses that were to be established there, but for now he was content to assuage the ego of Cornwallis by allowing him to play the role of Conquering Hero. Cornwallis was accompanied by the British Grenadiers, the Hessian Grenadiers, and several units of cavalry and artillery. The Grenadiers, typically the most physically imposing members of the army, had been specifically selected as a means of providing a particularly impressive display as the army entered the city.

At about 10:00 AM, with bands playing and crowds cheering, the British army entered the city and officially assumed control of the former American capital. Several hundred citizens of the city who had remained loyal to the Crown lined the streets in order to welcome what was to them an army of liberation. General Cornwallis was accompanied at the head of the procession by several Philadelphia Loyalists, who were soon to be installed into positions of power and responsibility in the new city government.

The fact that there were such a significant number of British Loyalists remaining in the city was of little surprise to anyone. Despite the fact that Philadelphia had served as the capital of the fledgling nation since nearly the beginning of the war, the city was well known as a hotbed for Tories who openly supported England, as well as many who were dubious as to the legitimacy of the new American government. This situation, combined with the fact that almost anyone who supported the Rebel cause had chosen to leave the city, made the occupation of Philadelphia more of a logistical and administrative evolution than a military operation.

—

The exodus from Philadelphia of patriots loyal to the cause had begun weeks before, as the approaching British continued to enjoy success after success on the battlefield. The Continental Congress, always a cautious group when it came to their potential capture, had opted to evacuate the city approximately a week earlier, relocating their governing responsibilities west to York, Pennsylvania. Most of the munitions and supplies for the Continental Army had been relocated to Reading, an appreciably safe distance from their previous location. And many of the wounded American soldiers who had been recovering in the city were sent north to the towns of Allentown, Bethlehem, and Easton, Pennsylvania. In addition, many of the symbols of the Revolution such as banners, flags, and numerous bells were removed from the city as a means of preventing the enemy from exploiting their capture for propaganda purposes. One such item was the so-called Liberty Bell.

The Liberty Bell had, ironically, been cast in England and delivered to the Colonies in 1752 for use in the Pennsylvania State House. Upon first being tested several months later, the bell inexplicably cracked simply from the contact of the clapper onto the interior surface of the bell. Despite this rather inauspicious start, the bell had eventually assumed a certain level of honor and significance to the Revolutionary Cause as it was rung in 1774 to announce the opening of the First Continental Congress, in 1775 following the Battle of Lexington and Concord, and on July 8th, 1776, just prior to the first public reading of the Declaration of Independence.

Unfortunately, the impending arrival of the British had required the removal of the Liberty Bell to points north of the city. While enroute to its eventual final hiding place in Bethlehem, the bell had been forced to spend a rather unflattering evening in a barn next to a tavern called the Rising Sun Inn located in Franconia Township. A British patrol had been spotted just a half mile away, and the men charged with the bell's safekeeping had quickly and unceremoniously stashed the bell into the barn. These appointed guardians of the bell saw no need to take any unnecessary chances with the enemy so close by, and chose to remain safely in the tavern for the rest of the evening. The next day the bell continued its journey northward, however for some reason the chaperoning party got a bit of a late start, having opted not to awaken until nearly mid-morning.

—

Meanwhile back in Philadelphia, the occupation of the city continued to progress smoothly and without significant incident over the coming days and weeks. Even those who had been openly supportive of the American cause soon determined it was relatively safe to leave their houses after a number of braver souls of their kind had ventured outside without causing any kind of alarm. Apparently, the British were more interested in controlling the city and keeping the peace than they were of exacting retribution on any suspected Rebels.

In fact, many of the local merchants and businessmen demonstrated that their true allegiance did not lie with either the blue uniforms of the Continental Army or the red uniforms of the British Army, but rather with the color of gold. The Americans had often been unable to pay for goods and services in hard cash, usually resorting to either IOU's or recently issued American money. Both of these items were viewed with a great deal of suspicion, and there was not always the greatest confidence that their value would prove to be permanent.

On the other hand, the British were more likely to pay with hard currency, the value of which was - well, as good as gold. It wasn't long before many of the businesses in and around Philadelphia had shed their dismay for the British invaders, and were openly doing business with what had been only recently the dreaded enemy. Such are the odd partnerships that often develop during a time of war and economic strife.

The British army chose to establish three camps in and around the city. One camp was located north of the city in order to defend against any potential attack that might develop from that direction. A second was established along the city docks. This camp, in conjunction with several vessels of the British Navy, was charged with the defense of the Delaware River and its approaches to the city. And the third and final camp was established within the boundaries of the city itself.

British troops were quickly assigned quarters within many of the homes throughout the city, a practice which was received with mixed emotions by the citizens. Some welcomed the men openly and made every effort to insure their comfort during their stay, a stay which appeared to many as being planned as a lengthy one. Others resented the imposition, and did everything in their power to insure their visitors knew that they were not welcome under any circumstances, despite what General Howe and King George might desire.

The more devious and, some might say, reckless of the citizens true to the Patriot Cause began devising ways to gather information regarding the placements and movements of the British. Their goal was to develop methods to get this information out of the city and eventually to the eager ears of the Continental Army encamped just a short distance north of the city. Their efforts at engaging in what was, for all intents and purposes espionage, ranged from being ingenious and effective, to being stupid and ineffective. Those of the former group enjoyed a certain amount of success at achieving their objectives. Those of the latter group were at best bumbling and useless, almost to the point of being humorous. They often found themselves arrested by the alert British Army and subject to prosecution and incarceration for extended periods of time. It didn't take long for people to realize that the art of spying was neither a game to be taken lightly, nor was it for the faint of heart.

—

So began the occupation of the Rebel capital by the invading British army. As opposed to a bitter fight, the British had simply waltzed into town and taken control. This maneuver would insure that the British had a warm and comfortable winter base from which to operate in the coming months. On the other side of the lines, not only had this occupation denied the Americans a comfortable encampment, but it had also been a serious blow to the morale of the fledgling army. Only time would tell if this blow would prove to be fatal.

LIEUTENANT JACOB LANDES
SEPTEMBER 26, 1777
SALFORD TOWNSHIP, PENNSYLVANIA

This had always been Jacob's favorite time of the year. The Pennsylvania countryside in the fall was truly a sight to behold, as the countless trees had begun to provide a myriad of colors to enjoy. Soon these leaves would begin to make their gentle descent to the ground, causing the world to appear as a carpet of reds, golds, and browns. But for now, the leaves held stubbornly to their branches, determined to take advantage of the summer-like weather for a few more days.

Jacob was just cresting the final ridge that stood between he and his family as he headed southeast from the Continental Army's current location at Pennypacker Mills. He began riding down a road that moved along the top of the ridge just north of his house known by the locals as the Ridge Road – the Pennsylvania Dutch clearly wasted no effort in naming their thoroughfares – and gazed down at his home lying just below him in the valley no more than a mile in the distance. The sight of something he had missed so dearly made his anticipation almost painful, and it took all of his self-discipline to not spur his horse and madly gallop the final leg of his journey. Such an impulsive act, while possibly appropriate for the young man that had left this place just a few months ago, was obviously not befitting an officer of General Washington's Continental Army. Even so, perhaps a brisk trot would surely maintain his dignity.

At this increased pace Jacob arrived in a short time, just a few minutes before 7:00 PM. It was exactly as he had planned. His family would just be sitting down for dinner, and he would catch all of them totally by surprise. There would be shouts of joy, there would be hugs and kisses and slaps on the back – and there would be food. Not the barbaric slop that passed for food when one was part of an army. Spoiled vegetables, rotten meat, and maggot-laden biscuits were pretty much the typical fare endured by the enlisted men and those junior officers without the money to buy something better for themselves. No - what Jacob was about to enjoy was his Mother's cooking. And he would be doing so at a time when the local harvests were just coming in, which meant that she would be serving the freshest, juiciest, tastiest offerings that God had ever seen fit to place on the face of the Earth.

Jacob made his way to the back of the barn and tied his mount to one of the stable gates. He would come out a bit later and bed the animal down properly, insuring that it was treated to the equine equivalent of the food Jacob was about to experience. Jacob reflected on the fact that the last time he had spoken to his father was at this exact spot just a few months ago. It was at that time that his father had given him the Bible that Jacob now carried with him at all times. He absently reached up and patted the outline of the small book which currently rested in the inside pocket of his uniform jacket.

His uniform! Jacob had become so accustomed to wearing it that he had never even thought to change into civilian clothes before making this trip home. He was suddenly afraid that his appearance at the Landes homestead dressed as an officer of the American Continental Army might disturb or even anger his father. He stopped in mid-stride on his way toward the house, momentarily undecided on what to do. But he quickly regained his composure, realizing that while his father may not approve of who he was, Jacob himself was supremely proud of that person.

As Jacob approached the side door that led into the dining room where the family always met for dinner, he sensed that something was different from what he had expected. The normal dull uproar that accompanies a large family preparing to eat was strangely absent. Instead, there was solemn silence inside the house, and Jacob wondered if his family had made a trip somewhere leaving the house temporarily vacant. He was just beginning to feel the initial pangs of disappointment when he detected movement through the window to his right that looked in on the massive living room that dominated the first floor of the house. Looking more closely, Jacob was pleased to see his younger sister, Rebecca, moving about the room and lighting several candles in preparation for the coming evening.

Jacob was unable to suppress a huge grin, and he nearly sprinted to the side door of the house, entering it without the slightest pretense of dignity or restraint. In the huge fireplace to his left there was a fire burning, but there was no indication of a meal being prepared. Where normally a large pot would be hanging in the hearth steaming from the heat beneath, there were only a few small logs barely smoldering. But it made little difference to Jacob - he was home!

Jacob heard the scuffling of many feet coming down the hallway to the dining room, and prepared himself for the onslaught of his family. He had just a moment to straighten his uniform jacket and pull himself up to his full height before the first member of his family came through the door. It was Joshua, his younger brother just over thirteen years old, who was quickly followed by his other brothers and sisters. The look of surprise on all of their faces was priceless and, after a brief pause of recognition, they all flew into Jacob's broad, outstretched arms.

Just as he had anticipated, there were kisses from his sisters, hugs from everyone, and a feeling of peace that only comes from being in the company of those you truly love. But this moment of pure joy was short-lived. He suddenly realized that, much to his dismay, many of his siblings were softly crying as he held them in his arms. But these weren't the tears of joy that Jacob knew his family would shed, and that he hoped he could contain from himself. These were clearly sobs of depression and sorrow that he thought he had left behind, at least for now, on the horrible battlefields of his recent past.

"Everyone, please," Jacob said, "I'm home and I'm safe. Why are you crying so?"

Samuel, the second oldest son in the family who was nineteen years old, took control of the situation by gently moving the many family members away from Jacob. In a moment, it was just the two brothers facing one another. Samuel stepped forward and placed his hands on his older brother's shoulders.

"It's Father," Samuel stated simply, his eyes cast down to the hardwood floors of the room. "He's not..."

Jacob felt a sudden surge of panic, as he jumped to the worst possible conclusion he could imagine.

"He's not what, Samuel? Father isn't what?" Jacob demanded a bit too loudly, and he immediately regretted the force of his words.

"He's not doing well, Jacob," a feminine voice said from the doorway leading into the hallway.

Looking over, Jacob saw his Mother leaning heavily against the doorway, looking to all the world as if she were an old woman despite the fact that she was barely in her forties. He was momentarily shocked by the change that had occurred in her appearance in just the short time since he had last seen her. Jacob moved carefully through the many family members standing between he and his Mother, coming to her and gently taking her in his arms. He had quickly regained his composure, realizing instinctively that this situation called for all of his strength of character.

"Mother," Jacob said quietly, "everything is better now. I'm home, and I'm safe, and we're all together as a family. Now, tell me – how is Father?"

—

Jacob and his Mother walked quietly up the stairs to the second floor where there were four bedrooms, one of which was used by Jacob's parents. The additional two bedrooms on the third floor made for a comfortable living arrangement for the usual seven members of the Landes family. As the oldest child, Jacob had had the honor of having ownership of one of the largest of these bedrooms. It had been his own space, and he had cherished the privacy it had provided him in an otherwise noisy and crowded house.

Jacob's Mother moved to the door of her bedroom, pushing down carefully on the door handle in an obvious attempt to avoid making any noise. She looked back at Jacob, indicating that it was alright for him to enter the room. The silence was so profound that he could literally hear the ticking of the clock that hung on the wall of the dining room downstairs.

As he entered, Jacob took in the familiar surroundings of his parents' room. To his left was the chest of drawers that contained the few articles of clothing owned by his Mother. Immediately next to that, hanging on pegs driven into the stone walls, were his Father's work clothes. A small vanity with a large round mirror – the one luxury his Mother had ever allowed herself – completed the sparse furnishing on that side of the rather large room.

As Jacob turned his gaze in the other direction, he saw the poster bed that dominated the right side of the room. His Mother had taken simple wooden rods, hung them from small pieces of chain fastened into the ceiling, and had hung old draperies from the rods to ingeniously fashion a beautiful scene of elegance that seemed almost – but not quite – out of place in a house that was otherwise designed purely for efficiency.

Lying on the bed, in the quickly diminishing light of the late summer evening, was Jacob Landes Sr. Upon first seeing his Father,

Jacob was immediately taken aback by the sight. Even in the last few years when the family had known that their Father's health was beginning to decline, he had always been a picture of strength and stability. But the man that Jacob now saw had declined in a manner that he would have never thought possible in just a few short months.

Quietly, Jacob moved to the left side of the bed closest to where his Father was laying. Jacob's Mother had obviously placed her husband in a position where he could lay relatively comfortably, propped up on several pillows, and gaze out of the window immediately to his right. Jacob smiled to himself, envisioning the brief argument that must have occurred between his parents, Jacob Sr. complaining about all the fuss that was being made over him. But Mrs. Myra Landes was not someone to be trifled with even by her husband, and Jacob was certain she had quickly gotten her way – as was always the case.

Jacob knelt on the floor next to his Father, not wanting to disturb the man if he was asleep and comfortable, at least for the time being. But Jacob Sr., even in his declining state, was aware of everything around him.

"Well, I see our prodigal son has returned from the war," Jacob Sr. said quietly. "How are you, son?"

"The question, Father, is how are you? It seems there are some members of your family that are concerned about you – and you can add me to that growing list."

"Ah, that's silliness – I'm just a bit under the weather" Jacob Sr. stated, but there was clearly a lack of conviction to his forced statement of confidence. They were the inflated words of a man who knew his time was not long. Jacob Jr. had heard such statements made too many times in the last few months. "Now, let me ask you again – how are you?"

Jacob was touched by the genuine show of concern being exhibited by his Father. Even on what was quite obviously his deathbed, Jacob Sr. wanted to know that his oldest son was doing well.

"I'm fine, Father. I haven't a scratch on me. And to be honest with you, I haven't even once been in any danger. It seems my bold adventure has been nothing more than a lark. I've met some fine men, and the army has seen fit to insure that young Jacob Landes remains far from anything that even resembles..."

"Enough, Jacob," his Father interrupted. "I may be ill, but I'm not an idiot. I know what General Washington's army has been through these last few weeks, and I know that you were at the center of it all. Charles

Rest came to visit me just a few days ago, home from the war with a wounded leg. He gave me quite the recounting of your exploits on the battlefield."

Damn! Jacob had gambled that his Father would have had no direct news of the war, and he had lost. He immediately regretted his pitiful attempt to protect his Father from the realities of what he had experienced, and he now feared he had insulted the man.

"Well Father, Charles could always spin a tale or two, you know that. I'm sure his version of the truth contained more than a shred of embellishment."

"Did it? So would these embellishments have also been a part of the casualty rosters that I saw for the 4th Pennsylvania Regiment? As I recall, that's your unit, eh, Jacob? So tell me, son – " with that, Jacob Sr. turned his head and looked his son dead in the eye – "am I to believe that you were never in the thick of the fighting, as I have been led to believe?"

Jacob knew his ruse was hopeless. His Father knew all there was to know. Or did he? Could he know that his son had held the hand of a sixteen year old boy who had been shot in the gut and cried out for his Mother time and time again until he died? Could he know that Jacob had seen a cannonball tear the insides out of a man as cleanly as a butcher's knife? Could he possibly understand the sight of a young father clutching desperately to a letter from his young daughter; that letter asking him when he would return home; as the man's life slowly drained away into the mud of the Pennsylvania countryside? Thankfully, Jacob was certain that his Father could never – and would never – understand such things.

"Father, my deepest apologies. I was merely trying to spare you the details of what I've been through these last few months. I never intended to insult or offend you in any way. Surely, you understand that."

Jacob Sr.'s eyes softened as he gazed at his oldest son. He slowly reached out and took Jacob's hand in his own, clutching with a firmness that belied his declining physical condition.

"Jacob," his Father said purposefully, a strength coming to his voice, "I have heard many things about the type of officer you are. I have learned many things about the type of man you have become – that you always were. And I can tell you from the deepest part of my heart, that I cannot imagine a Father being any more proud of his son than I am of you at this moment."

With that, Jacob Sr. turned his head away and closed his eyes in rest, a strange slight smile on his lips.

—

Jacob Landes Sr. died sometime later that night. He passed away quietly and without any fanfare, just as he had lived his life. At the moment he took his final breath, he was surrounded by his wife and children.

Jacob had chosen to remain several feet back from the bed, allowing his Mother and younger siblings to have the last physical contact with their Father. Much to his surprise, Jacob did not shed a single tear, despite the fact that he felt a terrible sorrow when he realized that his Father was gone. But men died – he understood that now, as he had never understood it before. And he also understood that, for this man lying here, there was nothing he could have done to stop the natural progression of Death. But with a newfound clarity he knew there were many other men, whose deaths would not be so natural, for whom he could do a great deal.

Although Jacob would remain just long enough to bury his Father, he knew it was time again for him to go back to where he was most needed.

GENERAL GEORGE WASHINGTON
SEPTEMBER 30, 1777
PENNYPACKER MILLS, PENNSYLVANIA

The last few weeks had been difficult for the American Continental Army, to say the least. They had suffered a painful defeat at Brandywine, being driven from the field by a General that had outmaneuvered them, and an army that had outfought them. They had suffered the loss of thousands of soldiers - some from the deaths and wounds that had occurred on the battlefield, even more from the less dramatic causes of desertions and expiring enlistments. They had had a portion of their army surprised and routed most unceremoniously in the dead of night, a fact which had contributed significantly to the current feeling of unrest that ran throughout the men. And they had watched helplessly as the British had marched unopposed into the capital of their young nation.

General George Washington may not have considered himself the smartest man to ever walk the face of the earth, but he recognized a crisis when it was staring him in the face. He also knew that something needed to be done, and done quickly. In effect, he was faced with two basic options. The most logical option was to find a place to rest and replenish his army. Washington could relocate to a place that was a safe distance from any British attack coming out of Philadelphia, and use the opportunity to give his exhausted men a rest. In addition, the army could be resupplied with food, supplies, and ammunition, all of which were available from the Reading, Pennsylvania supply depot. And finally, replacements could be recruited from the surrounding colonies, as well as be called in from some distant units currently operating elsewhere against the British.

Yes, that was certainly the most logical strategy to pursue. And George Washington would be damned before he would use it.

The other option was to completely surprise the enemy by doing something that they least expected the Americans to do. George Washington would attack the British – and he would do so within the next week.

While a seemingly foolhardy and reckless move at first glance, further analysis had convinced Washington that attacking the British at this time was exactly the right thing to do. First, Howe had once again engaged in the practice of separating his army. While the main British force had been stationed at Germantown just on the outskirts of Philadelphia, a significant number of troops had been detached in order to occupy the Rebel capital. In addition, many of these detached troops were the cream of the British army, specifically several of the British and Hessian Grenadier units. All told, Washington's spies had reported that Howe had no more than 8,000 troops in and around Germantown, with the remaining troops at such a distance that would make immediate reinforcement difficult.

Second, in the last few days Washington's force had been bolstered by the arrival of several units. This included General Smallwood's Maryland Brigade, another unit that had previously been detached to upstate New York, and several small groups of militia. All told, Washington could count his men at around 11,000, which would provide him with a numerical superiority for the first time of the war.

Third, the scouts Washington had assigned to constantly monitor the location and disposition of the enemy had reported a mood of uncharacteristic lethargy on the part of the British. Specifically, the size, frequency, and range of the enemy's patrols clearly indicated that the last thing they expected was a full-scale attack by the Americans.

And finally, if the Americans could launch a successful attack, they could regain some momentum and confidence, and possibly retake Philadelphia all in one masterful stroke. Yes, further analysis clearly resulted in a bias for action, not recovery.

The problem was that Washington needed to convince his Commanders that this was the right course of action. Although he could technically order the army to do his bidding, Washington was wise enough to know that he needed commitment from his men, not compliance. This was a plan that required complete coordination from all units involved, and those commanders who were not convinced of its validity might well gum up the works by simply moving too slowly. No, now was not the time to be George Washington the General; now was the time to be George Washington the diplomat.

—

The group of men had been called to a meeting being held in the small living room of the main house at Pennypacker Mills. Pennypacker Mills was a beautiful mansion that had been built somewhere around 1720 by the original landowner, Hans Jost Heijt. In 1747, Peter Pennypacker had purchased it from Heijt, and christened the house and surrounding 170 acres with its current name. While a sizable house overall, still most of the rooms were characteristically small, and the twelve commanders and staff officers quickly created a somewhat cramped situation.

As always, the conversation between the men was lively and boisterous, as opportunities to get together as an entire group were fairly infrequent. Topics of conversation ranged from inquiries regarding the health of a man's family, to the re-telling of stories from previous battles.

Washington had been conferring quietly with General Sullivan in the corner of the room, and many of the officers present assumed it was about the charges that had been brought against Sullivan immediately after the battle that had been fought at the Brandywine Creek three weeks earlier. The result was a constant stream of nervous and uncomfortable glances in the direction of the two conferring generals. Every commander in the room was aware of the old adage of, "There but for the grace of God go I." The opinions and support of the men who made up the Continental Congress were indeed fickle, and any one of the men in the room knew that the slightest error – or perceived error on their part brought with it the potential for public censure and disgrace.

But for some reason, General John Sullivan had a habit of frequently and repeatedly attracting the negative attention of the Continental Congress. This fact was somewhat ironic, as Sullivan had actually been a member of that original body of politicians, but had opted to leave that position when he was appointed as a Brigadier General in the Continental Army. Perhaps it was this display of bravery that annoyed some of the remaining members of Congress, as those qualified for military duty were forced to confront their own unwillingness to face the enemy on the battlefield.

General Sullivan on the other hand, had demonstrated his willingness to face the enemy time and time again. He had been there at the very beginning of the Siege of Boston, had fought in Canada, and participated in the battles that had been fought in and around New York

City. It was during the Battle of Long Island that Sullivan had become a prisoner of war, when he almost single-handedly faced a unit of attacking Hessian soldiers. Even after his release as a result of a prisoner exchange, Sullivan had elected to remain with the army and had fought at the battles which occurred in Trenton and Princeton. And finally, Sullivan had been at the very heart of the fighting, as always, during the most recent battle along the Brandywine Creek. For these reasons, Sullivan was held in extremely high esteem by his fellow soldiers, regardless of the opinions that may have been formed by those who sat at a distance and observed, and then proceeded to feel at liberty to comment on the outcomes.

Finally, Washington and Sullivan appeared to complete their conversation, and Washington moved to the center of the room and waited patiently for the conversation to die down. After just a few moments, all eyes were on the Commanding General.

"Gentlemen, as always I appreciate your willingness to temporarily suspend the important duties that must be completed by all of you," Washington began. "I assure you that I have no intention of taking you away from your men any longer than is absolutely necessary."

The men around the room all nodded in acknowledgement, despite the fact that they knew it was a façade. The Commanding General could take whatever time he damn well pleased, and not one man in the room would have made so much as a peep to the contrary. Nevertheless, the respect being extended by Washington to his commanders and staff was greatly appreciated, even if it was so much window dressing. Washington continued.

"The purpose of today's meeting is for us to make a decision regarding our next move as an army. The way I see it, there is no advantage to be gained by maintaining our current position. Our attempt at guarding both Philadelphia and Reading has been rendered irrelevant by General Howe who is, as we speak, resting comfortably in our capital.

"Meanwhile, we find ourselves in a position of doing one of two things. First, we can retreat to the north and west. This will allow us to guard our supplies at Reading, protect our wounded in Bethlehem, and provide our men with an opportunity for rest and recuperation."

Washington was completely aware of his use of such words as "retreat", "guard", and "protect", all of which carried connotations of defensiveness and submission. He paused purposefully and gazed around the room, literally looking each man in the eye as he let his words sink in.

"Our other option is, quite simply, to attack. To refuse to relinquish the initiative, to refuse to stand idly by while the enemy frolics in our capital. At the risk of being heavy-handed, gentlemen, I personally believe that we face no real choice at all, no legitimate decision. It is time to *act*, and to do so boldly!"

Washington caught himself, aware that he was perhaps selling his idea too hard and risking turning off his commanders with his soapbox diatribes. But as he glanced quickly around the room, he saw that he had done nothing of the sort. From the look in the eyes of each man, they had already come to the same conclusion that he had before ever setting foot in this room. For the countless time, Washington realized that he was dealing with men of action. A man didn't walk away from a guaranteed life of wealth and privilege to become a member of a ragtag army of Rebels fighting for the mercurial cause called Freedom unless you were, at your very core, a gambler. And that is exactly what Washington was asking them all to do right now – gamble.

General Sullivan stepped forward and faced the men in the room.

"Gentlemen," Sullivan said, "I believe we should vote on General Washington's proposition. Do we retreat in the face of the enemy to lick our wounds and recover? Or do we lash out at those that would have us remain as second class citizens to a foreign government? All those in favor of attacking the enemy, say 'Aye'."

The room resounded with a booming chorus of "Aye's", accompanied by men raising their hands in assent, just in case there was any confusion. To a man, they had voted for action.

George Washington, as he had so many times in the past when confronting situations like these, felt a lump form in his throat. He remained quiet for a few seconds, slowly surveying the room in what he hoped passed for a display of thoughtfulness and satisfaction. Finally, after he had regained his composure, he addressed the room.

"So be it, gentlemen. You have all agreed to action. Now, the Devil is in the details. We must develop a plan of attack that insures our victory, and see that every one of our officers and men understands what is expected of them. Let us be clear; the coming battle will be a desperate, bloody struggle. The gravest error we can possibly commit is to underestimate our enemy. But this army has shown the ability to stand up to the British and fight them on their own terms. Now, we shall stand up to them once again, but this time it will be on *our* terms."

At the completion of these remarks, General Washington dismissed his commanders and staff officers with a nod of his head. The men quickly filed from the tiny room, anxious to return to their men and pass on the exciting news.

In a minute, Washington found himself quite alone. And for the first time since his plan had formed in his mind, he felt just the slightest twinge of self-doubt. What if his plan failed? Could this army really withstand yet another defeat, or would it simply disintegrate as men disappeared into the surrounding countryside? To be sure, this army was made up of heroes and patriots, but even heroes have their limits. Would another defeat push them past their limits?

It was time again for George Washington – not the General, not the wealthy Virginia landowner, but George Washington the Man – to exhibit his greatest qualities. And those qualities were perseverance and confidence. One cannot quit, Washington thought, and as long as one does not quit, one cannot lose.

GENERAL WILLIAM HOWE
OCTOBER 2, 1777
PHILADELPHIA, PENNSYLVANIA

The ticking of the large grandfather clock in the far corner of the room was a welcome reminder to William Howe that he was finally living within some semblance of civilization. While he had never hesitated to spend time in the field with his men - living and sleeping in a tent, eating barely cooked food and drinking bad tea – he had always been quick to admit that his preference was a solid house containing a warm bed and well-prepared meals.

General Howe had specifically chosen one of the largest and most opulent houses in the city to serve as his Headquarters. He had rationalized this selection as being necessary to accommodate the rather large meetings he often held with his officers, as well as the fact that the house was located in the center of the city and provided him with the greatest degree of access to his troops stationed in and around Philadelphia. If the luxurious surroundings also contributed to his personal comfort – as well as the personal comfort of a certain lady visitor who frequented the Headquarters – then so be it.

However, at this particular point in time, General Howe had suddenly found his potentially idyllic lifestyle threatened by the most unlikely of causes – the Continental Army. Howe, like every other member of the British army, had made the assumption that the Rebel army bloodied by the battle at Brandywine Creek and embarrassed by the debacle at Paoli would do exactly what they were supposed to do. An army in such a condition needed to retire to a safe and distant location and reorganize. Many had even hoped that the recent thrashings might even lead to the disintegration of the army through desertion and expiring enlistments.

There was only one flaw in this logic being used by the British – someone had apparently neglected to inform the Americans of their expected behavior. As a result, Howe had just received word through his extensive network of spies that it appeared as if General Washington was not only failing to retreat, but that he actually intended to attack the British!

Howe had summoned General Cornwallis to his Headquarters in order to discuss the possible implications of this information. Howe could hear a rush of activity in the next room that served as his Chief of Staff's office, and made the assumption that Cornwallis had finally arrived. Howe had been waiting for his subordinate for the better part of two hours, and had become impatient.

—

"Enter," Howe said, in response to a brisk knock on the door of his office. Immediately, Cornwallis burst through the door with an obvious sense of urgency that he reserved only for the battlefield and when responding to the requests of the man who literally held his future career in the palm of his hand.

"Sir, General Cornwallis reporting as ordered," Cornwallis stated as he came to formal attention in front of his Commanding General.

"I was beginning to think you had opted to decline my invitation, General. It has been nearly a lifetime, I believe, since I requested the pleasure of your company," Howe said coldly, his voice dripping with sarcasm. Cornwallis was a completely competent and professional general, and Howe hated him for that. He always had the distinct impression that Cornwallis was just waiting and biding his time until Howe made some grand mistake that resulted in his removal as head of the army. That would almost certainly result in Cornwallis being promoted to Commanding General. The result was that Howe placed very little trust in Cornwallis, and looked for every opportunity, however infrequent it might come, to chastise the man for incorrect or inappropriate behavior. Making your Commanding General wait was certainly such an occasion.

"Begging the General's pardon, sir, I apologize for the delay in my arrival. I was out at Germantown inspecting the current disposition of our troops there. Your message reached me at a place called Mt. Airy, which is the northernmost point of our army, sir. I had placed a number of pickets at that location in order to insure we would be alerted to the presence of any enemy patrols operating there."

In light of the intelligence that Howe had just received regarding the intentions of the Americans, Howe had to grudgingly admit that

Cornwallis was taking the correct actions. The fact that Cornwallis was not privy to the current update on the Americans made it all the more impressive, and Howe felt some of his anger and impatience subside.

"Very well, General, I have no doubt that your intention was not to deliberately make me wait," Howe conceded. "I am simply agitated by the nature of some information I have just received regarding the enemy."

Howe moved to a large map of Philadelphia and the surrounding area that had been hung on a wall on the opposite side of the large room, motioning for Cornwallis to accompany him. Howe pointed to an area north and slightly west of Philadelphia on the map.

"As you are aware, Washington's army was reported to be located at a place called Pennypacker Mills. We received this information approximately one week ago. I have recently learned that Washington is no longer located there, but has moved his entire command."

Cornwallis nodded knowingly and responded. "Yes, sir, we had anticipated such a movement. It was only a matter of time before he would be compelled to withdraw his army to a location where he would be able to safely rest and refit his men. The most likely locations would be either Bethlehem to the north or Reading to the west."

"Not quite, General Cornwallis. While our assumptions that the Americans would move has proven to be accurate, the direction of that movement was completely incorrect. Our intelligence network has just informed us that Washington's entire army is currently at a place called Methacton Hill, which is located here," Howe said, pointing to a spot on the map that seemed to Cornwallis to be distressingly close to their current location.

"In addition," Howe continued, "I have been told that Washington has ordered the removal of his sick and wounded troops to some point north of his current location. And finally, his troops have apparently been ordered to detach themselves from all but the most basic of weapons and provisions."

Cornwallis glanced quickly at Howe. Both men knew that such actions and orders would only be given in the event of an imminent attack. It was a scenario that was as far fetched as Cornwallis could have ever imagined.

"Sir, may I respectfully inquire as to your confidence regarding this information. After all, sir, it is not inconceivable that this intelligence could have been devised and planted by the Rebels themselves as a means of distracting our efforts to bolster the defense of Philadelphia."

Cornwallis was referring to the fact that it was common practice for an army to engage in providing misinformation to the enemy. Not only did the misinformation have the immediate effect of causing confusion as to one's true intentions, but if done consistently well, it also caused the enemy to begin doubting all intelligence they received. While the Americans were far from being fully proficient in such nefarious tactics – they had only been in existence for just over two years, after all – they had shown themselves to be more than willing to try their hand at such strategies.

"I had considered the possibility that this information has been intentionally allowed to reach me," Howe said, "but I do not believe that this is the case. I have received the information from more than one source, and each of these sources has proven to be reliable in the past."

Cornwallis remained quiet, and gazed thoughtfully at the wall.

"What are you thinking, General?" Howe asked his subordinate.

"Sir, if I may?" Cornwallis asked, nodding toward the map on the wall.

"Of course, General, proceed."

"This information provides a very different perspective on some observations that have been made over the past several days," Cornwallis began. "Beginning approximately three days ago, our patrols have noticed a significant amount of enemy presence in these areas," he stated, sweeping his hand from left to right just above Germantown. "I was not particularly alarmed, as this presence has only taken the form of no more than a half dozen men on horseback, and has never posed a threat to our positions. I also was operating under the assumption that the purpose of these enemy patrols was to insure that *we* were staying in place and not intending to attack."

"When in effect," Howe picked up, "these patrols are scouting our positions in preparation for an attack of their own. I must say, this is not the first time that I have been conflicted over my assessment of General George Washington. He is either a courageous and wily character, or he is a complete blithering idiot."

"Sir, may I respectfully suggest that we move several battalions of our troops from their locations here in the city out to Germantown in order to reinforce that position? After all, Germantown has not proven to be the best defensive position given its relative lack of significant terrain features of which to take advantage. With the exception of the steep banks of the Wissahickon Creek on the extreme left of my position, Germantown offers us no tactical benefits."

General Howe looked at the map for several seconds, then walked slowly back to his desk and sat down. He was clearly contemplating the situation, and secretly wished he had the ability to discuss things as a colleague with Cornwallis. But to do so would suggest a certain amount of both indecision and equality, and the ambitions displayed by his subordinate made such behavior on the part of Howe simply unacceptable to him. He would have to make this decision on his own, and he would have to make it now.

"I do not believe it necessary at this time to bolster our defensive position at Germantown. General Washington can have no more than three or four thousand troops fit for duty at this time, and even those will be tired and demoralized. If the Rebels have the temerity to attack us, we will surely deal them yet another decisive defeat, and that group of rabble simply cannot absorb that. If we were to reinforce now, these enemy patrols of which you speak would observe such activity, and it might cause Washington to change his mind. No, General Cornwallis, attack is exactly what we would like the Americans to do."

Cornwallis was not so sure of the situational assessment that his Commander had just completed, but he knew Howe well enough to understand that there was no room for discussion. On more than one occasion in the past, Howe had nearly exploded when Cornwallis had attempted to offer a differing opinion. Therefore, Cornwallis came to rigid attention and saluted Howe.

"Very well, sir. Will you be accompanying me to Germantown at this time?"

"No, General, I have other – uh, responsibilities here that must be attended to." Howe replied. "See to your men and prepare for this so-called attack by the Americans. Once again, be cautious that you do not over-prepare and alert the enemy to our knowledge of their plans. I will expect a full report of our victory after they come limping toward our defensive positions and are crushed by the finest army on the face of the Earth."

With a noticeable hesitation, General Cornwallis departed. He left leaving Howe to dwell on his Headquarters responsibilities, and Cornwallis to contemplate how to prepare for an impending attack without actually making any preparations.

General George Washington
10:00 AM - October 3, 1777
Worcester, Pennsylvania

The dozens of commanders and staff officers had quickly gathered in the small house that General Washington had been using as his Headquarters. Washington had spent the last few days developing his plan of attack on Germantown, but had opted to wait until the last minute to share the details with his subordinates. Washington suspected that a great deal of information regarding the movement of his army had been getting to the ears of the British, and Washington was unwilling to risk the possibility that these final plans might make that same journey.

Although most meetings of this group of men were often boisterous affairs - something akin to a family reunion of sorts - on this occasion the men were quiet and immediately attentive to their Commanding General. An observer aware of the existing circumstances might well come to the conclusion that the commanders of this army knew that they had reached a crossroads, and that at least one of these roads led to a dead end for the existence of this army. And a dead end for this army most certainly meant a dead end for the United States of America. It was, by all measures, a truly momentous occasion.

"Gentlemen," Washington began, casting his gaze around the room, "I am keenly aware of the sacrifices that you and your men have made in these last few weeks, of the hardships that you have experienced. God knows, no army has ever had their resolve tested in a way that was any more severe than that which you have all endured."

The group nodded in unison, acknowledging the accuracy of the words being spoken by their General.

"It is for this reason that I want you to understand how much I appreciate the magnitude of that which I am about to order. Just a few days ago, you all voiced your desire to attack the enemy. While I was moved by your valor at that time, I must tell you that I have agonized over the wisdom of whether or not to go through with such a bold move. But I believe you will all be pleased to hear that I have chosen to comply with your unanimous wishes – attack it shall be!"

The group, which had been held in suspense for the few seconds prior to the announcement of Washington's intentions, exploded in a deep cheer of celebration. After all, it was the honor and competence of each of these men that was under question, and they were chomping at the bit for the opportunity to prove that they and their men were as fine a group of soldiers as had ever taken to the battlefield.

"If I may draw your attention to the map that Colonel Harrison has posted on the wall behind you, I will outline the details of our plan of attack."

The room turned to the rear while creating an opening for Washington to pass through as he made his way to the back of the room. When he arrived there, he faced the group and began his briefing.

"As you can see by the red markings on the map, the British are currently spread out on a line that runs roughly west to east from the Schuylkill River on their left flank to the York Road on their right flank. The length of this line is approximately five miles. What you may not be able to ascertain from your distance from the map are the markings of some of the individual units that are located along this line. While these identifications are almost certainly not 100% accurate, I am confident that their indication of the strength of the British army is fairly accurate. As you can see, by sending our entire army in an attack on these positions, we will have the rather unfamiliar advantage of numerical superiority."

Brigadier General Francis Nash, standing just to the right of Washington, cleared his throat discreetly as an indication of wishing to speak. Nash was a former lawyer from North Carolina who had quickly risen from the rank of Lieutenant Colonel to his current rank of Brigadier General. Although protocol prohibited open acknowledgement of the fact, it was well known that Washington had a special respect for young Nash. Washington quickly acknowledged his subordinate with a nod of his head.

"Sir, I understand that we will have an advantage with respect to actual numbers of troops," Nash stated. "But what about the ability of the enemy to quickly shift troops from one position to another in order to reinforce the actual point of attack? While I firmly believe in the fighting capabilities of our men, we must also acknowledge the capabilities and professionalism of the army we are about to face yet again."

Washington smiled as Nash concluded his comments.

"General, as always your observations are intelligent and insightful. I also had similar concerns related to the enemy positions and capabilities, but I hope you will see as I review the strategy that I have taken into account exactly what you have just identified."

General Nash blushed slightly at the deference being afforded him by the Commanding General, and he quickly stammered a reply.

"Of course, sir, I have no doubt that you had done so. I was merely..."

"You were merely being a responsible member of my Command Group by insuring all possible contingencies had been addressed," Washington interrupted with a smile, "and I would expect nothing less. Now, allow me to review the plan of attack, and I would request – no, I would *demand* – that you all analyze it severely for all of its potential strengths and weaknesses."

Washington turned back to the map and began pointing to various areas as a way of clarifying and emphasizing his verbal descriptions.

"Our attack will consist of four separate columns, with the two main columns coming down the Limekiln Pike here and the Germantown Pike here," Washington stated, sweeping his hand from north to south on the map.

"General Greene, you will lead the largest of our columns, consisting of nearly 6,000 men, down the Limekiln Pike and strike the right flank of the British line. This column will consist of your own division, along with the divisions of Generals Stephens and Douglas. Meanwhile, I will lead a second column of approximately 3,000 soldiers down the Germantown Pike which will strike at the center of the enemy line. This column will include the commands of Generals Wayne, Sullivan, and Stirling."

If General Washington wanted to insure the greatest potential for success, then placing the main column in the hands of General Nathaniel Greene was exactly the right thing to do. Greene had been a self-made man right from the start, educating himself on a wide variety of topics which included military tactics. Despite the fact that he had been raised a Quaker, a sect known for their pacifism, Greene became heavily involved in military matters when the fervor for independence escalated in the early 1770's. This proclivity toward the military vocation resulted in his eventual expulsion from the Quaker faith, a result for which he had little regret.

Greene had been part of the Continental Army literally from the very beginning, having been named one of the original four Major Generals under General Washington. He had seen action in Boston, New York City, Trenton, Princeton and most recently, Brandywine. General Greene was the consummate military professional, competent in every way. And while Washington may have had a special respect for General Nash, he placed his absolute trust in General Greene. It was for this obvious reason that Washington had entrusted the brunt of the attack on the shoulders of this particular General.

"As was wisely observed by General Nash just a moment ago," Washington continued, "in order to fully capitalize on our numerical superiority at the points of attack by these two columns, we must insure that the enemy is unable to move troops from one section of the line to another, thus nullifying any advantages we will enjoy. We will accomplish this by using an additional two columns of troops that will attack both the left flank of the enemy as well as the extreme right flank. These columns will be composed primarily of militia under General Armstrong on the British left flank and General Smallwood on the British right flank. Each of these columns will consist of approximately 1,500 troops."

At this point, Washington paused and faced his Commanders, indicating his desire for any questions or comments. After waiting several seconds and receiving neither, he continued.

"It is my desire for our army to depart from their current encampments beginning around 6:00 PM this evening, with the units having the farthest distance to travel departing first. We must time the movements of each of the four columns such that they are all in position to attack at dawn tomorrow."

General Nash, apparently emboldened by the acknowledgement of his previous comment, spoke up once again.

"Sir, it appears that this plan relies on a significant amount of coordination between all of the attacking columns. If one column were to attack prior to the others, it might well result in disaster. And the fact that we will be moving in the middle of the night along roads of which we have little knowledge – well sir, I must respectfully submit that this is a point of concern."

Several commanders nodded in agreement, while others wondered at the audacity of this young officer to question the wisdom of the Commanding General. The variety of responses was typical of this group, as they had all traveled dramatically different paths in order to arrive at their current situation. Regardless of their responses, the room became quiet as all eyes were fixed upon Washington in anticipation of his reaction to being challenged by a subordinate. He remained quiet for several seconds, clearly formulating his response.

"Gentlemen," Washington began, "I believe I have taken every possible precaution to insure our success in the upcoming engagement. First, each of you will have someone from the local area assigned to you as a guide. Each of these men has an intimate knowledge of the area roads and countryside, and they have assured me that the ability to successfully shepherd you to your appointed locations – even in the darkness – will in no way be an issue. Second, we have had dozens of scouting parties operating throughout the area for several days, and they themselves have become quite familiar with the road system. They, as well, will be at your disposal to assist in navigating to your attack points. And finally and most importantly – " Washington paused here for effect as he surveyed the room – "I have each of you. I have one of the finest group of commanding officers that has ever donned a uniform and stepped onto the field of battle."

The stillness in the room would have been shattered by even the slightest noise, as each man drew himself up to a height that was several inches taller than just a moment before.

"I do not make this statement lightly, or in a cavalier fashion," General Washington continued. "I make it with a level of conviction that can only be achieved by enduring a trial by fire that we have all endured together. I have absolutely no question in my mind that you will all do your duty in a manner that will result in a victory for this army. A victory that is long overdue and God knows, well deserved.

"Colonel Harrison will meet with each of the commanders of the four columns in order to review the details of the routes and timing of their attacks. I will invite the rest of you to return to your units and prepare for what I'm sure will be a tiring and challenging evening. I trust you will all do what is necessary to insure the morale and preparedness of your men is at its very peak."

General Washington came to a position of crisp attention and saluted the men in the small room. In complete unison, the men snapped to attention and rendered a rigid salute, many of them with a notable glistening in their eyes. This was a group of men that believed in their Cause, their men, and most assuredly, their Commanding General.

MAJOR JAMES AGNEW
6:00 AM - OCTOBER 4, 1777
BRITISH OUTPOST
MT. AIRY, PENNSYLVANIA

The early morning sun was just above the horizon, but it afforded limited light to the surrounding countryside due to a heavy curtain of fog that had descended in the last hour or two. Despite the fact that it was still early, the British soldiers manning their respective posts had long been awake and alert. Just after 3:00 AM, Major James Agnew of the British 2nd Light Infantry had been alerted to the presence of the enemy somewhere to his direct front, and had immediately ordered all men to their assigned positions along the northernmost defensive line of the British army. Almost two miles to their rear was the rest of the British force at Germantown, with the remainder of the army still camped comfortably in Philadelphia. These soldiers here at Mt. Airy were anxiously aware of the fact that they were the advance force of the advance force of the entire army.

Major Agnew, an experienced and competent officer, calmly rode along the entire length of his position, checking to insure all were alert and prepared. To some he offered words of support and encouragement, while others less fortunate were issued a sharp rebuke for even the slightest transgression of military protocols. Agnew had been a soldier for many years, and had seen many battles. One did not develop such a resume without being demanding and observant in the oversight of one's men.

"Lieutenant Milford," Agnew said sharply, summoning one of his aides to his side, "if you please."

"Yes, sir," Milford replied stiffly as he took his place beside his Commanding Officer.

"Ride to our rear and locate Lieutenant Colonel Musgrave of the 40th Regiment and inform him of our situation here. Tell him I will keep him informed if anything develops."

"Begging your pardon, sir," the young officer responded after a brief pause, "but I'm not exactly sure what our situation *is*."

"Damn it, man, must I spell everything out for you!" Agnew exploded his outburst causing several enlisted men within earshot to carefully smile at one another. In almost all walks of life misery loves company, and the troops were always happy to see one of the officers getting treated in a manner that was normally reserved for their own lowly ranks.

"Our situation is as follows," Agnew continued slowly. "We are aware of an enemy presence to our front, and possibly to our right. It is my belief that this presence is merely several small scouting parties attempting to ascertain the disposition and strength of our position. While I perceive no immediate threat of attack, I am informing him of the situation for future intelligence purposes. These scouting parties may be looking to find opportunities to strike the sides or rear of our army in order to either harass us or capture some supplies. Now, unless you are in need of me drawing a small picture to provide further clarification, I trust you will be able to deliver my message."

"Very good, sir, I will do so immediately," Lieutenant Milford stammered, and quickly rode off in the direction of Germantown, eager to distance himself from the sharp-tongued Major.

Major Agnew had little respect for anything short of perfection, and even less respect for the Americans he was facing. As a professional soldier, he resented the fact that these Rebels had the audacity to believe that they belonged on the same field of battle as the British. Agnew's opinions of the Americans had further deteriorated following his participation in the attack that had occurred just a few days ago at Paoli. Even his dismal views had been an overestimation of the Rebels' preparedness that night, and he and his men had personally seen to it that they had suffered for their laxness. More than a few members of the Continental Army had been left for dead after receiving numerous thrusts of the bayonet or slashes of the sword from Agnew and his men.

The appointed messenger had barely disappeared from view when a volley of musket fire erupted directly to the front of the British. A young soldier to the right of Major Agnew screamed and grabbed his face, blood pouring from between his fingers. A second soldier that had been walking between two of the prepared positions collapsed to the ground, a musketball having shattered his left leg just below the knee.

Several seconds after the first volley, two additional volleys were fired on both flanks of the British position. In every direction men scrambled to find cover behind the prepared defensive positions, while those already behind cover burrowed more deeply into place like a tick into the fur of a dog. Officers and senior enlisted men began cursing and yelling at their men, ordering them to prepare to return fire. Those soldiers foolish or cowardly enough to hesitate to do so even briefly were called every vile term that would come to mind, or were physically struck if they were within reach. Within a minute or so, the British had successfully returned several ragged volleys of their own.

Agnew sensed, rather than observed, that the Americans firing at them consisted of a relatively large force, and he also became aware that this force was moving towards them as opposed to staying in their current position. The heavy fog between the British and their attackers made any direct observation virtually impossible, and Agnew realized that most of the less experienced men would not realize that they were about to bear the brunt of a major attack.

"Gentlemen!" Agnew shouted, addressing the small group of staff officers that had been riding with him, "scatter yourselves along the line and inform the platoon and company commanders to prepare for an immediate attack! Move!"

The half dozen or so men departed with a noisy combination of shouts and thundering hooves. Agnew himself began riding amongst the units immediately to his front, giving orders to fix bayonets and prepare to repel an attack.

Once again, Agnew sensed the enemy to his front, this time just a hundred yards or so away, and he realized that they were preparing to deliver yet another volley into his ranks.

"Cover! Find cover!" Agnew shouted desperately, even as the morning was shattered by the discharge of hundreds of muskets just a short distance away. All at once, the air was alive with bullets, some whistling harmlessly overheard, others hitting with a loud thud into the logs and mud that had been erected as protective positions. Finally, there were those that made the most sickening of sounds as they impacted the bodies of British soldiers.

Two young soldiers standing right beside one another were hurled backward almost in perfect unison, as musket balls hit their bodies in several locations. Both men were dead before they hit the ground five feet behind them.

One of Agnew's staff officers, Lieutenant Niles Cavendish, was sitting rigidly astride his horse giving orders to the soldiers around him.

As he opened his mouth wide to shout additional instructions, a musketball struck him in the throat, knocking him to the ground. Several soldiers, as well as Major Agnew, rushed immediately to the Lieutenant's side to render whatever assistance they could. As they all watched in horror, the young man futilely attempted to speak, his mouth working like a gaping fish having just been pulled from the water. Instead of words, streams of bright red arterial blood poured from his mouth, creating thick pools on the ground in front of him. Thankfully, the man's life continued on for but a few more seconds, as the astounding loss of blood resulted in his mercifully quick death.

All along the British line, soldiers were unnerved by the strength and ferocity of the attack they were facing, yet the officers and senior enlisted men still possessed the presence of mind to prepare their men to not only maintain their positions, but attack the enemy. Agnew watched with pride as his company commanders quickly organized their units into cohesive groups in preparation of an order to advance.

Through the fog could be heard the shouts of the Americans taunting and challenging the British, and it became clear that Agnew's men were facing the very enemy soldiers who had been the victims of their night assault at Paoli a few days earlier. Despite himself, Agnew felt a chill go down his spine as one American, probably moving in advance of the main line of attack, shouted toward the British, "all right lads, let's kill us some Bloodhounds! It's our chance to avenge General Wayne – show them the bayonet!" With that, a deep, loud cheer went up from the American lines, and Agnew fully appreciated for the first time the size of the force they were facing.

Earlier, the British had learned that the Americans had successfully identified the exact units that had participated in the Paoli attack, and had taken to calling these British soldiers "Bloodhounds" for their lack of control that night. It was becoming frighteningly clear that the Americans intended to demonstrate the same lack of restraint on this day as the British had in the recent past.

Matching shout for shout, Agnew ordered his company commanders to attack the oncoming Americans. Almost as one, eight companies of British troops rose up and moved forward into the swirling fog of the Pennsylvania morning. Despite the fact that they had no idea of what faced them, there was no hesitation as they pitched headlong into the blinding mass.

The Americans, not expecting this response that bordered on

reckless, were momentarily stunned by the sight and sound of an enemy assault. However, they quickly recovered their composure and fired a volley directly into the face of the oncoming attackers and followed it with a charge of their own.

The previously peaceful morning was suddenly filled with the shouts that can only be ripped from the throats of men desperately engaged in the life and death struggle of direct combat. Some men cursed, others cried, still others laughed almost gleefully as the two forces closed upon one another and engaged in the most brutal form of hand to hand fighting. Muskets were fired when loaded, but most often the bayonet was the weapon of choice. Still others used their muskets as clubs, or resorted to fists and stones.

Despite the impeccable order and discipline of the British, the sheer numbers of the Americans was more than they could withstand. After just ten minutes, the British found themselves retreating back to their original defensive positions, but again only briefly. The enemy's attack had gained momentum, and nothing could hold them back as they rolled over the British line.

Major Agnew, who had been wounded slightly in the side, could do nothing other than order the retreat of his men. Fortunately, other than the unlucky lieutenant who had died so horribly at the outset of the fight, most of the officers and senior enlisted men were unhurt. This allowed the army to maintain control of itself and avoid a most embarrassing rout, although the movement of the soldiers to the rear was accomplished with a significant amount of urgency.

In some cases, this speed was sufficient to insure the ultimate safety of the soldier. But in many cases soldiers chose to make brief, heroic stands, and in these cases the Americans were successful at catching up to their retreating enemy. When this occurred, the Americans showed that they were capable of displaying the same level of callous brutality as the British had shown at Paoli a few weeks before. Even in those rare instances in which a British soldier stopped, dropped his weapon, and raised his hands, these actions had little effect on the Americans hell bent on revenge.

Shouts of, "Remember Paoli!", and "Revenge for General Wayne's men!" could be heard through the fog, usually followed by the awful scream of a man being bayoneted to death. These screams served as significant motivation to those British soldiers who were continuing to retreat, as the possibility of stopping and surrendering ceased to be an option.

—

At one point during the retreat, Lieutenant Colonel Thomas Musgrave arrived with the British 40th Regiment in order to reinforce the retreating men and attempt to make a stand. Despite the fact that they were temporarily successful at setting up a defensive position, this ended up being short lived. A combination of sheer numerical superiority on the part of the Americans, combined with limited ammunition on the part of the British combined to soon make the new line of defense untenable.

With the British force now consisting of the original men at Mt. Airy combined with the 40th Regiment, the retreat continued for a distance of nearly two miles, the Americans in hot pursuit the entire time. The weary British soldiers had no opportunity to stop even briefly to catch their breath, and the appearance of the main defensive line at Germantown was a most welcome sight indeed. Men began streaming through these defensive positions, past their puzzled fellow soldiers, not stopping until they had reached a position that was several hundred yards behind the main line. Only then did the exhausted men stop, drop their muskets which almost every man had gamely retained, and collapse to the ground in their first display of undisciplined behavior.

These surviving British soldiers had escaped the wrath of an army that had just demonstrated a disturbing combination of resiliency and savagery. Not a single one of them would ever again speak scornfully or dismissively about the abilities of this enemy.

BRIGADIER GENERAL FRANCIS NASH
7:30 AM - OCTOBER 4, 1777
MT. AIRY, PENNSYLVANIA

The battle was going better at this point than anyone on the American side had the right to expect. The British were in full retreat from their northernmost defensive line at Mt. Airy, despite the fact that there had been a plethora of mistakes over the last ten hours or so since the Continental Army had broken camp and begun their march from Worcester to their current location.

The plan had been for the four columns of the army to move separately to their appointed attack positions, all arriving at roughly the same time. The problems started when General Greene, leading the largest of the four columns, was accidentally led by a local guide down Morris Road when, in fact, he was supposed to be traveling down Skippack Pike. This resulted in Greene's men becoming separated from the rest of the army to a degree such that it would be virtually impossible for the attacks to be coordinated.

In addition, the heavy morning fog was turning out to be a mixed blessing. While it had provided excellent cover and concealment for the Americans as they had moved into position for their initial attack, it had also created significant challenges in terms of communication and coordination. As a result, General Francis Nash was confident that the attack for which his men were providing support was going well, but could not speak to the success of his counterparts. This caused Nash, as well as the other commanders a great deal of concern. If one of the columns of the four-pronged attack were to encounter less resistance than the others, it would run the risk of moving too far forward in relation to the rest of the army. This could result in a lack of flank support, leaving the column vulnerable to counterattack. Likewise, it could be mistaken by the lagging American columns as being the enemy. Neither of these options appealed to General Nash at all.

For now, all General Nash could do was to continue to encourage the advance of his men in support of the main attack to their front, and manage the couriers that were being sent out in all directions in an attempt to gain some level of understanding regarding the overall progress of the battle.

In spite of the guilt he knew he would feel later, Nash couldn't help but experience the same exhilaration he always felt during a battle. The shouts of men, the confusion that always existed, the scream of the artillery shells as they flew in every direction – Nash greedily soaked in every heightened sensation that it created in him.

In his last letter to his wife that he had written just the previous evening, Nash had shared with her his innermost feelings, as he always did.

"My dearest, please know that I gain no pleasure in the brutality and horrible results that must always accompany war. Yet I must confess that I feel so <u>alive</u> when I am in the midst of a battle, knowing that I am part of something greater than I will ever be by myself! What we are trying to achieve – what we <u>will</u> achieve – is worth more than any single man's life. And that includes my own. While I do not wish to depart this Earth and leave you behind, I do not fear that possibility should it occur."

But right now, General Nash did not have the luxury of considering such deep thoughts, as he and his men found themselves tangling with the ever-tenacious British army yet again. While the Americans continued to advance, it was not without significant effort and loss on their part. The British were giving ground, that much was clear. But they were doing so while giving out at least as much as they were taking.

Reports had begun to arrive indicating the British were continuing to retreat toward their main line of defense, which Nash knew had been posted about two miles to the rear at Market Square. If the Americans could maintain both momentum as well as good order and discipline, they had an excellent chance of overwhelming that position. At that point, the British would be forced to retreat their entire army into the city of Philadelphia, and General Washington and the Continental Army would have gained several advantages.

First, the defeat of the main British army might induce additional men from the surrounding area to join the American army, possibly resulting in an overall numerical advantage for Washington. Second, depriving Howe of his outposts in the areas just outside the city would allow Washington to move to the immediate outskirts of Philadelphia. This would make it possible to constantly harass the British at every opportunity, and deprive them of a steady flow of supplies. The British would be forced to rely on supply via the Delaware River, which could then become the next target of the Americans. And finally, Washington might choose to attack the city itself, were conditions to prove favorable. Expelling the enemy from the capital of the Colonies would provide a boost to the sagging morale of the army that would be worth the same as receiving thousands of reinforcements.

All in all, a great deal of opportunity was riding on the outcome of the battle that was now well underway.

As Nash contemplated the next move of his brigade, he was joined by one of his aides, Major James Witherspoon. Major Witherspoon had been recommended by his father for duty as one of Nash's staff officers, and Nash could hardly refuse the "suggestion". John Witherspoon, the father of Major James Witherspoon, was a prominent man within the colonies, to say the least. As a member of the Continental Congress, John Witherspoon had significant influence over the conduct of the war. In addition, he was also the President of Princeton University, as well as being one of the signers of the Declaration of Independence.

All of this resulted in Nash basically being forced to accept James as one of his aides, and Nash had initially disliked the young man out of resentment. However, within a very short period of time Nash realized that young Major Witherspoon was not only a supremely capable officer due in part to his own education at Princeton, but that he was also completely devoid of pretensions. The fact that his father was one of the most influential men in America seemed lost on James, and he conducted himself with the utmost of humility and respect, especially when in the presence of General Francis Nash. This had ultimately resulted in Nash and Major Witherspoon forming as much of a friendship as can be appropriately developed between a Commanding General and one of his subordinates.

"Sir, I wish to report that General Wayne has requested that you move your brigade forward in order to provide support to his attack on the enemy center," Major Witherspoon stated.

"What is General Wayne's current situation, Major?" Nash inquired.

"Sir, General Wayne is enjoying excellent success in his attack, and is pushing the British back nearly as fast as his men are able to move forward. His main concern, as he shared it with me, was that the speed of the advance would leave his flanks vulnerable to counterattack in the event that the units on either side of him are not able to move ahead with the same speed. If I may be so bold, sir, General Wayne is having one hell of a good time!"

Nash looked quickly at Witherspoon, a bit startled by this uncharacteristic showing of informality, especially in light of the fact that his father was a member of the clergy. Witherspoon's eyes were literally glowing with energy, and Nash immediately realized that the emotions he himself experienced during a battle were being shared by this young man beside him. He could not control just the briefest of smiles at the enthusiasm of his staff officer.

"Very well then Major, I suppose you and I should move forward in order to gain a better understanding of the situation. After all, General Wayne is not the only man on this battlefield today who deserves to enjoy a hell of a good time, eh?"

Major Witherspoon smiled from ear to ear at the realization that his Commanding General was acknowledging and accepting his reaction to the situation, and the two men spurred their horses simultaneously in order to move forward into the swirling morning fog.

Lieutenant Jacob Landes
8:00 AM - October 4, 1777
Mt. Airy, Pennsylvania

The air was literally alive with flying metal, but by now Lieutenant Jacob Landes had become almost immune to the terror that it had previously created in him. His fear now came not from the potential for death or injury, but from the fear that he and his men would not accomplish their assigned objective. In this case, it was to prevent the British from stopping long enough to form an effective defensive line, and Jacob was driving his men without mercy to keep the pressure on the retreating enemy.

"Come on, men, keep moving!" he shouted. "Only stop to fire your muskets when you have a target in your sights! Then drive forward – forward!"

Jacob's men had been the first to encounter the British northernmost units almost three hours earlier, and his men had been fighting almost non-stop since that time. He realized that at some point they would need to rest and regroup if they were to maintain any level of combat effectiveness, but that time was not now. The sense of urgency he attempted to impart on his men had become contagious, and they moved forward with an energy and furor that was almost superhuman.

Private Fowler, a seventeen year old boy from a small town just a few miles from Jacob's home of Salford Township, suddenly pitched backwards, as if he had been struck by some unseen force. Jacob quickly ran to Fowler to check on the boy. When he arrived at his side, he found the young man bleeding profusely from a terrible wound to the chest. Fowler was already struggling to breath, as each exhale resulted in a frothy, red substance oozing from his mouth. Jacob realized immediately that the boy had been shot through the lung, and there was nothing that anyone could do for him at this point.

"Sir, what's happened to me," the boy asked, his eyes wide with fear as he gazed wildly up at Jacob. "I was… just running forward as you…. as you ordered us, Lieutenant. I think I got hit with……. with something, and it's… making it hard….it's making it hard to breath," he gasped in between his labored breathing.

Jacob was surprised to realize that he was praying fervently for the boy to die quickly, as much to relieve the boy's suffering as to relieve his own. In addition, Jacob had many men that were still alive that needed his leadership, and he was anxious to get back into the thick of things. This level of callousness was almost shocking to Jacob, and he felt momentarily embarrassed at his lack of compassion.

"It's alright, Private Fowler," Jacob lied. "Just stay calm and we'll get a stretcher bearer to help you. For now, try and stay quiet in order to conserve your strength."

"But I… can't breathe… I can't… breathe, sir. And I'm so… I'm so cold…"

Jacob was suddenly furious. He was angry at the fact that this young boy was about to die in his arms. He was angry at the fact that there was nothing that he could do about it. And he was angry at the fact that virtually no one would ever know or remember that this soldier had made the supreme sacrifice for his country. How many others, Jacob thought, would be lost to history? How many thousands of others would simply vanish into the mist of the past, and never be mentioned beyond their most immediate families?

Private Fowler was becoming delirious, and had started calling out to his mother. He asked for a blanket to get warm. He asked for his favorite meal of chicken and biscuits. And finally, he made his last request on this earth.

"Dear God," Fowler said, his eyes suddenly shining brightly, yet seeing nothing, "please help me!"

With that, the boy ceased his struggle to breath and with it, his struggle to live. His eyes closed almost peacefully, and his body went limp in Jacob's arms. Jacob gently laid him back onto the ground, just as two men carrying a stretcher arrived at their side.

"You men carry on," Jacob said coldly, his fury refusing to subside. "Go find someone that will benefit from your efforts."

—

As Jacob rejoined the advance, he found himself alongside of his friend, Lieutenant Michael Sweeney. Michael had just recently rejoined the unit after a few days of convalescence leave having received a minor wound during the recent battle at Paoli. Michael's men had been some of the last to depart the battlefield that day, and he had received numerous accolades for his actions in providing excellent cover for a large portion of General Wayne's division during the retreat. His conduct had possibly saved the lives of many soldiers, and he had quickly changed from being just a popular officer in the unit to also being one of the most respected.

Unfortunately for Michael, it was during this covering action that he had briefly faced away from the advancing enemy when he was struck by a musketball in the backside. Although the resulting wound was in no way life threatening, it had been extremely painful both physically as well as in terms of his personal dignity. And while he was known as a master at doling out good natured ribbing to his fellow soldiers, Michael quickly learned what it was like to be on the receiving end of that type of banter. In fact, it had gotten to the point that Michael's return to his home ostensibly to recover from his wound was actually more a means to get a break from the constant abuse he suffered.

Lieutenant Sweeney was shouting at the top of his lungs, exhorting his men to advance in much the same manner in which Jacob had done with his own men. The troops were responding superbly, as the British continued their speedy retreat toward their main line at Market Square, now less than a mile away.

"Michael!" Jacob shouted at his friend, "have you seen any other units on either of your flanks? I'm worried we may have advanced beyond the rest of the army!"

"No worries, Jacob," he replied, "I've seen a number of the Maryland boys to our left, and General Sullivan's men are just slightly behind us on the right. My concern is that large house just ahead of us. If I were in the enemy's shoes, I'd hole up in there and try to ride out the storm as it passed."

The house that Michael was referring to was a massive mansion fashioned from walls that were made of stone three feet thick. It was known locally as Cliveden, named after the owner who had built it seventeen years earlier. The current owner, Benjamin Chew, was a known British sympathizer, and he had been forced to abandon his residence earlier in the war leaving the structure abandoned.

Jacob immediately realized that Michael was absolutely correct. If the British could fortify that house, it could prove to be extremely difficult to drive them from that position. Furthermore, any advance of the Continental Army beyond The Chew House would result in an enemy stronghold remaining in their rear, a situation that no Commanding General would be happy to have. Despite this fact, the mission of Jacob, Michael, and their men was clear – continue to advance and drive the enemy before them. Any hesitation on their part, or on the part of the other units to their right and left would create an opportunity for the British to regroup and form a solid defense. The Americans had already seen that happen one too many times, and they were in no mood to repeat that particular mistake on this battlefield.

"I see your point," Jacob acknowledged to Michael, "but we cannot slow the advance for fear of that house. We must press on and trust that the supporting units to our rear will address whatever situation may develop there."

Michael Sweeney stopped and looked Jacob square in the face, his expression clearly revealing his hesitation. But this lasted for just a few seconds, and was quickly followed by a grin that reminded Jacob of that fateful day just a short time ago when the two had first become friends at the Wild Rooster Tavern. Jacob realized that their initial meeting seemed like a lifetime away, so much had their lives changed in that time. He was briefly saddened by a sense of loss, knowing that neither he nor Michael could ever go back to being the young men they were at that time.

"Well then, my good friend Jacob, let us continue our drubbing of the British, and be damned with what may become of us! Pennsylvanians!" Michael shouted in the direction of his men, "attack the enemy! Let us send them to Hell, where they rightfully belong!"

A loud roar erupted from the soldiers scattered around the two young officers, and all were swept up in a storm of violence and purpose.

Douglas Shupinski

Lieutenant Colonel Thomas Musgrave
8:20 AM - October 4, 1777
The Chew House
Germantown, Pennsylvania

The combination of smoke and morning fog had made it nearly impossible to see anything on the battlefield that was more than a short distance away. This fact, when combined with the incredible volume of noise resulting from shouting men, muskets discharging and cannon firing, made the situation completely chaotic for both the advancing Americans as well as the retreating British.

Lieutenant Colonel Thomas Musgrave had taken the initiative of moving his 40th Regiment forward when he had observed the British outposts at Mt. Airy being driven back in disarray. He had planned on halting the retreat of those British soldiers streaming back from the north, and combining them with his own troops in a fortified line that would stop the advance of the enemy. His plan had encountered two fatal flaws: first, the retreating British soldiers had indicated no appetite for halting and facing the enemy, quickly bypassing his men on their flight south; and second, he had drastically underestimated the size of the enemy force that was now bearing down on he and his men. To make matters significantly worse, Musgrave had come to the realization that his regiment had effectively become cut off from the rest of the British army, and was in danger of being surrounded and annihilated.

Fortunately, the chaos of the situation was actually working in favor of the British colonel. The Americans had become temporarily flushed with success, and their momentum was driving them forward at a speed that caused them to completely overlook the presence of Musgrave's men hidden by the smoke and fog. This was buying Musgrave just a few minutes of valuable time, and he was determined to take advantage of this window of opportunity.

At this point, he was joined by Captain Hains, one of his company commanders. Musgrave noted quickly that Hains appeared hesitant to speak, something that was typically not the case. Musgrave soon realized why when the young man addressed him.

"Colonel, I've taken the liberty of giving the order to the men to cease fire," Captain Hains reported to his commander haltingly. "I beg your pardon for that, sir, but it seemed to me that it might be best to not draw undue attention to ourselves right now."

Captain Hains, a young man of only twenty-seven, had demonstrated himself to be an officer of uncanny talent in many areas. While others may have excelled at promoting themselves, Hains had shown that he was a man who was keenly aware of his surroundings. His assessment of the current situation was yet another indication of this skill. In addition, on several earlier occasions he had displayed a level of cool-headed bravery that had made him a favorite among the troops who innately gravitated to such an officer.

"Captain, as always your assessment of the situation demonstrates a level of leadership and combat experience well beyond that which you should be expected to display. I commend you on your decision."

Hains, visibly relieved at having received the blessing of his commander, pulled his sagging figure to a full upright position in the saddle and addressed Musgrave.

"Sir, what are your orders? I fear we may not have the benefit of our invisibility for very long, sir."

"No, Captain, I believe that is true. The problem is, we cannot retreat, as that will put us directly in the midst of the enemy. Just the same, we cannot advance, as I would imagine even these amateur soldiers will have reserve units following their main advance. That means we must make the best of what is in our grasp. And that – " Musgrave stated, pointing to a large stone mansion just off to their right – "is within our grasp."

Musgrave was indicating the Chew house, also known to the locals as Cliveden. His selection was not completely a matter of chance, as the British had identified The Chew House as a staging location for ammunition and supplies. As a result, Musgrave knew that there would be significant amounts of both for his troops to utilize in what he suspected might be a protracted struggle.

"Organize the men for a movement into that house, Captain," Musgrave ordered. "We must insure that we are prepared to fight our way in, as the Americans may not be so agreeable as to allow us to simply walk in as if making a Sunday visit for tea."

Captain Haines, unaccustomed to his commander demonstrating a sense of humor, stared for a moment in confusion before comprehending his colonel. At that point, he broke into a wide grin, saluted Musgrave, and moved off to carry out his orders.

—

Lt. Colonel Musgrave had approximately 120 men under his command, and he would be damned before he surrendered them to the Americans. However, he was also not a madman willing to sacrifice the precious lives of his men simply to save face. Therefore, barricading himself inside the Chew House offered him the best combination of avoiding capture – at least temporarily – while also giving his soldiers an opportunity to defend themselves in what just might turn out to be a militarily defensible position.

In just a few minutes, Captain Haines returned and reported that the men were prepared to move forward and take possession of the Chew House.

"Very well then, Captain," Musgrave acknowledged. "At the double time!" Musgrave shouted, "March!"

With Lieutenant Colonel Musgrave leading the way, the force of British soldiers moved briskly in a tight formation toward the Chew House and possible safety. However, the group had not gone more than thirty yards when their movement caught the eye of several American units operating close by. The enemy seemed to immediately sense the intentions of Musgrave, and realized that there was an opportunity to destroy an isolated group of British soldiers. The Americans quickly altered their direction of advance to intercept Musgrave and his men before they could reach their intended destination.

Musgrave noted with dismay that the enemy had reacted more quickly than he had anticipated, and that there was no way he and his men were going to get to the Chew House before being overwhelmed by a superior force. In that moment, Musgrave made the decision to confront his adversary in an attempt to buy some time.

"Regiment, halt!" he shouted above the noise of the battle, much to the surprise and dismay of many of his soldiers who had clearly focused on the safe haven now just a mere fifty yards away. "Companies, form and prepare to fire!" he yelled.

On that command, his men understood their commander's intentions, and reacted swiftly to the orders. Within seconds, they had faced the oncoming Rebels and assumed a firing position.

"Companies ready! Aim! Fire!" Musgrave shouted, and a volley of musket fire was discharged directly into the faces of the pursuing enemy. The volley had the immediate effect of staggering the attacking soldiers, and they were momentarily thrown into a state of disarray by the unexpected action of their prey. Their confusion was only brief though, and within a minute or so they were prepared to renew their pursuit. However, a minute was all that was required for Musgrave and his men to enter through the gaping front doors of the large stone mansion, and by the time the Americans had reorganized themselves, the British had slammed the doors behind them.

Musgrave immediately began organizing his men to defend the house, appreciating the fact that they were most vulnerable during the first few minutes following their occupation.

"Captain Hains!" he shouted, the company commander appearing immediately by his side. "Take your company along with Captain Marin's company and prepare to defend the first floor of the house. Close and barricade all of the shutters on the windows, and barricade these front doors!"

Hains ran off in search of his fellow company commander to begin the process of fortifying their position, recognizing immediately that he had been given the task of defending the most vulnerable part of their fortress. In spite of the seriousness of the situation, he couldn't help himself from grinning slightly at the fact that his Commanding Officer had entrusted him with the most difficult task.

Meanwhile, Musgrave moved with the remaining four companies to the second floor, where he posted two companies at the windows of that floor, as well as two companies to the windows on the third and uppermost floor. Upon conducting a quick inspection of these positions, he was satisfied that he had placed his men in the best positions to defend the house. He now moved quickly to the first floor, where he knew there was the greatest potential for his defenses to be breached.

As Musgrave moved through the house, he noticed that an almost eerie silence had settled around his position, and he realized that this probably meant one of two things. Either the Americans were massing their troops for an assault on the Chew House, or the enemy had inadvertently bypassed the house, failing to comprehend the fact that it had been occupied by a sizable force of the enemy.

It was the latter. Looking out several windows which provided an excellent view of the grounds surrounding the house, Musgrave was amused to see that his fortress was being bypassed quite casually by hundreds of enemy troops. Apparently the soldiers that had pursued his men into the mansion had been ordered to move on without alerting anyone else to the fact that there now existed, for all intents and purposes, a fortified castle directly in the middle of their line of advance.

Musgrave could clearly hear the orders of the Rebel officers directing their men to move in one direction or another, close ranks, spread out, or any number of other commands typically given during a battle. Musgrave had to admit that, much to his surprise, the orders being given were almost immediately carried out by the Rebel soldiers with an impressive degree of efficiency. Despite the fact that the situation was hectic, there was absolutely no indication of confusion or hesitation on the part of the army that was passing by.

Musgrave was now faced with a quandary. If they were to remain quiet and hidden from view in the Chew House, the enemy might very well pass them by and offer them the opportunity to escape once the entire army had passed. On the other hand, the fact that they had gone unnoticed offered them a very different option. They could open fire on the passing enemy, thereby disrupting the attack and possibly diverting enemy troops from their advance on the main British defensive line at Market Square.

Lieutenant Colonel Thomas Musgrave was the quintessential officer and gentleman who prided himself in his manners, his adherence to protocol, and his self-discipline. But above all, Thomas Musgrave was a warrior. The option of hiding quietly was never really a serious consideration in the mind of the Colonel, and he therefore set about giving the necessary orders to inflict the greatest damage to the unsuspecting enemy.

"Company commanders!" he shouted, his voice resounding through the massive house. "Front and center at the base of the main stairway!"

GENERAL WILLIAM HOWE
8:45 AM - OCTOBER 4, 1777
MARKET SQUARE
GERMANTOWN, PENNSYLVANIA

Word had arrived at the main British headquarters in Philadelphia several hours ago that the Americans were attacking the positions in Germantown. Everyone, including General Howe, had assumed the reports were simply exaggerated accounts of the enemy's attempts to harass their foe and cause whatever confusion they could. As a result, Howe had taken the liberty of making a deliberate and almost leisurely journey to his northern positions, clearly aggravated that his morning had been disrupted by the inconvenience of having to babysit his skittish commanders.

As Howe drew closer to Germantown, he was forced to acknowledge that the volume of fire consisting of both muskets and artillery was considerably greater than he might have anticipated. Interesting, he thought, that the Americans would mount such a significant display simply to rattle our cages. Try as he might, Howe could simply never understand the motivations of these Rebels.

As he arrived at the fortified positions that had been established at a place called Market Square, Howe was shocked to see hundreds of British troops streaming toward him through the morning fog, clearly retreating from their forward positions in and around Mt. Airy. He suddenly felt his face become hot with anger, appalled that experienced soldiers of the Crown would be so cowardly as to run from what was certainly a pathetic display of aggression on the part of the enemy. To make matters worse, Howe could discern the uniforms of his Light Infantry among those that were appearing before him. These were experienced, battle-tested troops, for God's sake!

"For shame, Light Infantry!" he chastised the retreating men. "I never saw you retreat before. Form! Form! It's only a scouting party."

But even as the words were leaving his lips, Howe observed three enemy artillery pieces being positioned and aimed just a short distance from where he sat astride his horse. With surprising speed and accuracy, the guns were fired directly at his location, and the group of trees underneath which he was sitting were peppered with the small bits of angry metal that comprised a discharge of canister.

"I'll be damned!" Howe muttered to himself, completely surprised by the fact that what he was facing was truly a determined attack by the Americans. Looking about, Howe quickly came to the realization that he was the only one that had doubted the seriousness of the enemy. Several of the officers were practically grinning in satisfaction that their Commanding General had finally appreciated the gravity of the situation – a situation that they had been dealing with now for the better part of four hours.

Howe was suddenly beside himself with rage and indignation. How dare these rascals test the resolve of the greatest army in the world yet again so soon after having been trounced not once, but twice in just the last few weeks? Obviously, some people were unable of understanding and accepting the reality that they were outmanned, out-Generaled, and outclassed. What would it take to convince this army of rabble that they had no chance of winning this war?

"Colonel Levitt," Howe said sharply to one of the regimental commanders just to his right, "form your men immediately. We will attack these Americans and make them regret having tempted fate yet again. We will drive them from this field in panic and confusion, and end this pathetic little conflict once and for all!"

"Yes, sir" the colonel replied, not used to receiving orders directly from the Commanding General of the entire army. The colonel, a somewhat portly man by almost any measure, immediately urged his horse to a gallop with a speed that he had probably not displayed in many years. In a matter of minutes, the colonel's regiment as well as several other regiments had formed, and were preparing to move forward against the seemingly unstoppable Americans who continued to drive at their position.

Meanwhile, the Americans continued to appear in ever increasing numbers through the morning fog. Even worse, General Howe noted that the enemy was threatening to overlap the flanks of the British defensive position, thereby making their situation untenable. For the first time in the entire war, General William Howe was faced with the reality that, in order to save his army, he might need to retreat in the face of an enemy attack.

The British soldiers that had been organized by the portly colonel were given the order to advance, and so they did, directly into the American onslaught. At first the Rebels were somewhat stunned by the first organized resistance they had faced in almost two miles of pursuit of the British. The rolling attack in the center was stopped almost in its tracks as the Americans took the time to organize themselves into lines of battle in order to return the volleys of musket fire that they were receiving from the enemy.

However, it soon became apparent that it was a simple case of too little too late, as the attacking Americans continued to move against the British flanks, and additional men arrived to renew the assault on the center of the British position. Slowly but surely, the British line began to give ground, finally becoming an organized but hasty retreat.

General Howe, scarcely able to believe what he was seeing, realized that there was nothing to be gained by attempting to rally these men, and decided it was time for a general retreat.

But just as this realization had sunk into the mind of General Howe, he sensed a shift in the momentum of the battle taking place directly in front of him. At first it seemed as if the volume of fire coming from the enemy had increased, and Howe feared that additional enemy units had arrived to add their weight to the already devastating attack on his men. Then, inexplicably, Howe watched in amazement as the Americans made an about face away from his position and appeared to actually be firing in the opposite direction! Had a force of British soldiers miraculously circled around behind the Americans and attacked them from the rear?

General Howe didn't know the answer to that question nor, quite frankly, did he care. All he knew was that the pressure that had threatened to break the back of his army had suddenly been relieved, and he intended to take advantage it. He immediately called for the portly colonel who, for some unknown reason, had stayed close to his Commanding General as opposed to leading his men into battle.

"Colonel Levitt, with all haste, halt the retreat of our men and face them about! We must attack the enemy while we have this opportunity. Move, Colonel! The time is now!"

Brigadier General William Maxwell
9:10 AM - October 4, 1777
The Chew House
Germantown, Pennsylvania

The battlefield had become strangely quiet, at least in comparison to the ear-splitting volume that had existed until just a few minutes ago. Brigadier General William Maxwell and his Light Infantry found themselves in a spot in which the battle had temporarily lulled, the attack of the Americans apparently losing pace with the retreat of the British. Maxwell had therefore taken the opportunity to regroup and reorganize his men who until this point had been held in reserve. This had not sat very well with soldiers accustomed to being at the point of the attack.

Although the men were disgruntled at their lack of ability to take part in the battle up to this point, they were exhilarated by the success that had been achieved thus far by the rest of the army. Maxwell recognized that the day's efforts were almost certainly far from being over, and thought it might be a good idea to give his men a brief rest. The brigade having reformed, moved to a small area beneath a group of trees located 100 yards or so from the mansion the locals called Cliveden.

General Maxwell moved to the center of his troops and prepared to address them, letting them know that they would be staying here for a few minutes before they would move to participate in the attack on the main British defensive line approximately two miles away. Maxwell knew that his Light Infantry would be needed in any final attack, and he could ill afford to have them remain dormant for too long. It was just as well. These men were in no mood to sit back and watch the rest of the Continental Army defeat the British – they required no prodding from anyone to get into the action.

As General Maxwell faced his men and began to speak, a sudden blast of musket fire erupted just behind him from the direction of The Chew House. All heads turned immediately in that direction, watching in disbelief as a column of American soldiers passing beneath the shadow of the house seemed to drop in their tracks almost in unison.

Men began to shout and retreat from the mansion, pointing toward the upper windows of the house as an indication of danger.

To General Maxwell, the message was immediately clear – the enemy had occupied the house and were using it as a stronghold from which to fire upon the passing American army. All previous plans for a brief rest before rejoining the battle were forgotten, and Maxwell's comments to his men took on a very different sense of urgency.

"Men, prepare to form for an attack!" he shouted above the sounds of the sudden musket fire. "Regimental commanders, front and center!"

Immediately, several officers moved to their commander, as the men pulled themselves wearily off of the ground where they had dropped themselves just moments ago. The movements of the men, officers and enlisted alike, showed no panic or fear, but were rather like the actions of a group of men who were confident in their assignments and abilities. The Light Infantry was becoming, much like a large part of the Continental Army, a group of veterans.

Officers began moving among the soldiers, offering words of encouragement, extending a helping hand at times to assist a man in getting to his feet. Comments could be heard throughout the brigade, a number of men making jokes about the luxurious length of their rest period, others remarking sarcastically that it was about time that they were being asked to move out. Still others complained about the fact that the main attack was up ahead, and they were being forced to stay behind to "swat at a wasp's nest", as one soldier put it. The officers heard these comments with a grim pride. Everyone knew that if soldiers were either joking or complaining, all was well - it was silence that you feared.

In just a few minutes, the regimental commanders had returned to their units and began organizing the men into a line of battle. Maxwell noted that at least one other unit off to their left had begun the same type of preparations, and he was relieved that his men would at least not be making the attack on their own. At this point, no one had any clear idea about the number of enemy troops they would be facing in the house, but a larger attacking force was almost always better than a smaller one.

The men had loaded their weapons and dropped what little excess gear they might have been carrying. The jokes and complaints had been replaced with faces of grim determination, as everyone understood the gravity of the situation. Between the brigade and the house was an open area of perhaps 100 yards in all directions, affording the defending enemy soldiers occupying the stronghold a clear line of fire on any troops who chose to advance toward them. Depending on the size of the force they were facing, the Americans were either dealing with an uncomfortable reception from the British, or an almost suicidal attack. Everyone chose in their minds to bet on the former rather than the latter.

Maxwell addressed the men with some brief instructions. Clearly, the plan was intended to be simple and direct.

"Gentlemen, the brigade will be fanning out and attacking on a front that mirrors the front façade of the house in front of us," Maxwell said, pointing behind him to the object of their assault. "The two regiments on the left and the two regiments on the right have been tasked with providing a covering fire from the flanks. Meanwhile, the two regiments in the center will advance directly on the main doors at the middle of the house."

Many of the men nodded in understanding, appreciating the lack of complexity to the plan. Many of these men had been in the army long enough to know that when officers decided to get fancy in situations like this, it was the soldiers who tended to pay the price.

"Once the center regiments have breached the main doors," continued Maxwell, "we will secure the first floor of the house, allowing the other four supporting regiments to enter as well. Those regiments will pass through the first floor, and proceed to secure the upper floors."

"Begging your pardon, General," one scruffy looking sergeant spoke up, "exactly how do you figure we're going to – what did you call it, sir? – 'breach' those doors? Them doors look to be mighty thick and strong and able to hold up to a whole bunch of breachin'."

A ripple of laughter rolled through the Brigade, but the brief levity didn't detract from the relevance of the sergeant's question. It wasn't a matter of whether or not these men were willing to make this attack – they were. The question was what they would do if and when they reached their destination.

General Maxwell realized that every eye in the Brigade was looking directly at him, waiting for an intelligent response to the question. After all, didn't Generals know everything?

Just as Maxwell was about to admit that the man had a good point for which he had no good response, his attention was drawn to the sound of dozens of pounding hooves coming down the road just off to their right. The timing was so perfect, it was almost as if Maxwell had orchestrated the scene. Clattering to a noisy halt no more than 50 yards from where Maxwell and his men were standing was General Henry

Knox and several pieces of artillery.

"Those, gentlemen," Maxwell stated firmly, pointing to the cannon, "are the keys to the front door. Why, you men didn't think I expected you to knock those doors down with your thick skulls, now did you?"

The men roared in laughter, fueled by a combination of their General's remarks, as well as an outpouring of relief at the reinforcements that had just now arrived.

In addition to General Knox and his artillery, an unusually tall and physically imposing officer had also made his appearance on the scene. General George Washington had arrived to take command of the situation.

GENERAL GEORGE WASHINGTON
9:20 AM - OCTOBER 4, 1777
THE CHEW HOUSE
GERMANTOWN, PENNSYLVANIA

The large mansion appeared almost suddenly out of the morning fog that was slowly and stubbornly beginning to dissipate as the sun grew warmer. General George Washington was both an intelligent man as well as an experienced soldier, and he immediately recognized the threat posed by this potential citadel which had now been placed smack in the middle of his advancing army.

Washington was joined by Colonel Timothy Pickering, one of his staff officers who had just returned from delivering a message to one of the units advancing beyond their current position. Colonel Pickering was flushed and breathing heavily, having received a rather warm and unexpected reception from the enemy occupants of the Chew House as he rode back to report to Washington. This reception had been in the form of dozens of musket balls flying dangerously close to him and his horse.

"Colonel Pickering," Washington observed, "you appear to have caught the eye of some of our British friends."

"Yes, sir," Pickering replied, "I may have caught their eye, but I didn't catch their lead, only by the grace of God himself."

At that moment, General Henry Knox rode up to Washington looking flustered and anxious. Henry Knox was a well-respected general in the Continental Army, serving as the Chief of Artillery. Henry Knox was a former owner of a bookstore in Boston, and it was from books that he had acquired all of his military knowledge. Despite the fact that he had no formal military training, Knox had proven himself to be more than capable in the art of war. Prior to this current battle, Knox had distinguished himself by hauling 59 cannon over 300 miles through the frozen landscape of New York state and New England, eventually bringing these cannon to bear on the British in Boston. This single act of determination had compelled the British to retreat from the city. In addition, Knox was the man who had been charged with the responsibility of getting Washington's entire army safely across the Delaware River the previous Christmas, as well as getting them back across on their way to and from the stunning victory over the Hessians at Trenton, New Jersey.

"General Washington, I request permission to move my cannon into action against that house to our immediate front. I believe, sir, that the lessons of war dictate that we must attack and take that position before we can safely continue our attack on the main British force."

"General Knox," Colonel Pickering asked, " what lessons of war would there be that would apply to this particular situation? Why would we not simply bypass the house and leave its occupants to contemplate what life will be like in an American prison camp?"

"Colonel, we simply cannot leave what amounts to a fortress in our rear if we are to successfully conduct the remainder of this battle! We must remove it as a threat to our army!" Knox argued, becoming agitated at the fact that a mere Colonel would question his military wisdom.

"General Knox," Pickering continued doggedly, "this is not a fortress as you suggest. It is most likely a relatively small force of desperate enemy soldiers, who can be contained by dispatching one of our regiments to encircle the house at a safe distance. Such a tactic will succeed in bottling the enemy up in their fortress, as you say, and leave the rest of the army free to go about the business of winning this battle!"

The two men continued to exchange opinions, the discussion becoming more and more heated as neither man refused to yield to the wisdom of the other. Finally, General Washington stepped in.

"Gentlemen," Washington began, "you clearly both have excellent points of view, but the fact that they are in contrast to one another requires me to make a decision and proceed. I am afraid, Colonel Pickering, that in this case I must adhere to the guidance being provided by General Knox. General, prepare your cannon to bring their fire to bear on the house. Captain Spires," Washington said, turning to one of his junior aides, "if you would be so kind as to ride over to General Sullivan just off to our right and inform him that he is to prepare to attack the mansion upon my order after General Knox's artillery has created a situation such that an attack will be prudent."

As Captain Spires departed to issue the appropriate orders, Lieutenant William Smith rode forward and addressed General Washington.

"Sir, would it not be proper to first offer an opportunity for the enemy to surrender prior to our attack?" Smith stated. "As Colonel Pickering suggested, these may be desperate men willing to lay down their arms, thus precluding the need for us to mount a potentially costly attack on their position."

Washington considered the man's suggestion for a few moments, hesitating just long enough for Smith to press his point.

"General Washington," Lieutenant Smith continued, "it would be my honor to deliver a proposal of surrender to the enemy – with your permission, of course."

"Very well, Lieutenant," Washington concluded, "you may proceed in doing so. Take a drummer with you as a means of announcing your intentions, and insure that you have a white flag clearly visible to the enemy as you make your approach."

Lieutenant Smith broke into a grin, excited at the prospect of engaging in a significant, albeit dangerous mission. As a staff officer, Smith sometimes considered his duties to be mundane and routine, but this situation offered him the chance to prove himself as a soldier. He spurred his horse with enthusiasm, and rode off to carry out his orders.

Colonel Pickering looked sadly in the direction of the departing officer, shaking his head in dismay.

"What is it, Colonel?" General Washington asked.

"Sir, I have no doubt that an offer of surrender is the correct thing to do," Pickering said. "But I fear for the life of that brave young man, General. The soldiers inside that house are scared and desperate, and have a limited ability to see what is happening around them. They may choose to shoot first without considering the sincerity of our proposal."

Washington gazed thoughtfully into the fog, and briefly considered recalling Lieutenant Smith from his assignment. Colonel Pickering's comments made good sense, and the army could ill afford to lose officers of the character of William Smith. But in the end, it was Washington's sense of fairness – even in a business as evil as war – that won the day in the General's mind and conscience.

"We shall watch and see, Colonel," Washington replied slowly. "We shall watch and see – and we shall pray that God Almighty keeps his hand on that young man's shoulder."

—

Lieutenant Smith had appropriated a flag staff from one of the nearby regiments, and had attached a large portion of a white sheet he had discovered hanging in the backyard of a nearby house. Smith had also found a young drummer boy who had eagerly agreed to accompany him as he approached the mansion. Smith had instructed the boy to stay directly behind him, using his own body to shield the boy from any potential harm that might come their way.

The drummer had begun playing a steady beat which indicated a request for a parlay with the enemy, and Smith had raised his white flag high above his head as they approached within fifty yards of the house. Suddenly, a flurry of shots rang out from the house, and a dozen bullets flew all around the two figures, one of them striking Lieutenant Smith just above the knee. The brutal force of the bullet fired from such a close distance shattered Smith's leg, and he collapsed to the ground crying out in agony.

Immediately, several American soldiers ran out from the stone wall behind which they had taken cover, quickly reaching the Lieutenant and the drummer boy. One of the soldiers scooped up the boy in his arms, returning to safety behind the wall. Two other men, now under fire from the mansion, hoisted Lieutenant Smith painfully off of the ground, and also returned to where they had started.

General Washington and his staff watched in horror as the scene unfolded before them. Pickering had been right – either out of desperation or lack of understanding, the British soldiers had fired on the flag of truce being offered, fearfully wounding a brave young man in the process.

Lieutenant Smith had quickly been carried to the backyard of a house that offered protection from any additional enemy bullets. Unfortunately, Smith was beyond the point of needing protection, as blood had continued to pour from his wounded leg at an astonishing rate. Even before General Washington was able to arrive, Lieutenant William Smith had uttered his last words on this earth. He continued to repeat over and over that he had done his duty for his country, the words becoming ever softer until he finally died.

Brigadier General William Maxwell
9:45 AM - October 4, 1777
The Chew House
Germantown, Pennsylvania

The four American cannon that had opened fire on the British-held mansion consisted of two 3-pounders and two 6-pounders. They might as well have been throwing rocks at the house. The builders of the house had clearly had a penchant for quality construction, and no expense had been spared in the selection of materials for the structure. The walls were three feet thick and made of stone, and the cannonballs fired by Henry Knox's artillery literally bounced off of these walls, doing little more damage than knocking off bits of the house here and there.

General Maxwell watched in dismay as the fortress continued to maintain its ominous power, and it gradually became apparent to him that his men would have to conduct their attack under the most dangerous of conditions. He had experienced some initial optimism when one of the first few cannonballs fired had burst open the large front doors of the house, the spot that Maxwell felt was the potential key to a successful attack. However, the enemy had quickly barricaded the opening and placed a significant number of troops at that spot, making any assault targeted at that location almost as risky as before.

Despite his better judgment, Maxwell knew that he was bound to attack The Chew House. The orders he had received from General Washington via the courier had clearly indicated that the Commanding General expected nothing less. He had been instructed to allow the artillery to do whatever damage it could, thus increasing the likelihood of a successful attack. At that point, he was to use his best judgment with respect to the timing of his assault.

In the meantime, Maxwell's men had formed a firing line a short distance from the house, and they were keeping up a consistent rain of lead on the enemy. But again, the house afforded such excellent protection for the British that the Americans might just as well have saved their ammunition.

Maxwell had ordered a meeting of his regimental commanders in order to deliver his directions for their attack. These men had arrived quickly, aware of the significance of the orders they were about to receive.

"Gentlemen, let us begin by acknowledging the obvious – General Knox and his artillery have been about as much use as teats on a bull," Maxwell began abruptly. The comment had the desired effect of initially surprising his commanders, and then creating a roar of laughter that could be heard in all directions.

The nervous soldiers located within earshot, aware of the impending attack they would almost certainly be ordered to make, noted that their senior officers were apparently sharing something funny. The result was somewhat of a calming influence on the men – after all, how bad could things really be if the commanders were laughing it up?

"Unfortunately for us," Maxwell continued, now deadly serious, "we will be forced to attack an enemy position that has in no way been weakened, despite the genuine best efforts of our comrades. Our success will be based on two things – first, we must never falter in our movements forward. If we attempt to retreat in the middle of our attack, we will be subjected to a galling fire from the windows of the house while we muddle back and forth in the open ground. And second, we must be bold. That means that all men will take part in the attack, leaving no one in reserve. And everyone will *quickly* close the distance between ourselves and the house, thereby decreasing the amount of time that we are in the open. Is that clear?"

The group issued a chorus of "Yes, sirs", their eyes fixed on Maxwell, their concentration and attention absolute.

"As before," Maxwell continued, "our focus will be on the front entrance to the house, with the units on the flanks attempting to gain access through the first floor windows. I realize these windows have heavy shutters, but I suspect that some insistent coaxing from the butts of our muskets may encourage these shutters to give way."

Maxwell paused and swept his gaze across this group of officers he had come to know and trust. His eyes briefly locked on every man, an attempt to communicate his confidence in their individual abilities to lead their men.

"Very well, then. Return to your units and prepare for the attack that will commence at exactly 11:00," Maxwell concluded. "And may God be with you."

—

With a mighty roar ushered forth from the throats of hundreds of men, the Americans surged forward from dozens of positions in the direction of The Chew House. Immediately, the British met them with a hail of musket balls, as every weapon in the mansion that could be brought to bear on the attacking soldiers was discharged. Dozens of men collapsed painfully to the ground, as a number of projectiles found their intended targets.

This initial volley was followed by a strange silence as the occupants of The Chew House worked feverishly to reload their weapons. This pause allowed the attackers to cover a good portion of the distance to the house, as a surge of confidence swept through the Americans. Perhaps this attack would not be as bad as they had imagined.

A dozen or more Americans were able to reach the front doors and actually set foot just inside the entrance, but these men were quickly and brutally bayoneted by the British soldiers tasked with the defense of that location. One American soldier leveled his musket and fired a shot directly into the face of a British soldier moving toward him. The British soldier dropped his musket and grabbed his face, as two of his comrades directly behind him were showered with blood and brains. Almost simultaneously, the American who had fired the shot received bayonet thrusts into each of his sides as well as his chest. The man crumpled to the ground in a bloody heap as his attackers withdrew their bayonets from his body and moved toward another potential victim, replaying the scene again and again.

As another twenty or so Americans attempted to enter the house in support of the first wave, they were met by a volley of musket fire delivered by a group of enemy soldiers that had just arrived at the entrance, having been ordered from the second floor to reinforce their comrades. This volley swept away the second wave of the attack, leaving the front doors at least temporarily clear.

That is to say, clear of anything that even vaguely resembled a living human being. In a rough semicircle approximately ten yards from the front door was a pile of bloody bodies, which had until just recently been the noble frames of American soldiers. These soldiers had been reduced to forms that were either splayed grossly in a variety of contortions of death, or those which were pathetically writhing and moaning in wounded agony.

Meanwhile, other groups of attackers were attempting to breach the first floor windows as they had been ordered, but these efforts were yielding no better results than the failed attacks on the front entrance. In addition to the shutters, the windows were also reinforced by metal bars. Even more discouragingly, enemy soldiers guarding these windows took every opportunity to briefly open the shutters, shoot or bayonet any American soldiers close by, and quickly close the shutters. Finally, enemy soldiers on the upper floors of the house continued to fire down upon the attackers, many of whom had been forced to flatten themselves against the house in a desperate attempt to stay out of the sights of these marksmen from above.

—

General Maxwell watched the attack from a short distance away, constantly being urged by his staff officers to move back from the house. Although most of the firing coming from the Chew House was directed at the attacking soldiers, an occasional bullet whistled over the group of officers surrounding Maxwell. While many of the men flinched noticeably from time to time as these bullets flew by, Maxwell refused to give the enemy this satisfaction.

"Gentlemen, this strategy is clearly not working," Maxwell observed, stating the obvious. "We are having no success in either battering the house, nor in attempting to breach its entrances with concentrated attacks of our soldiers. And we are paying a horrific price."

The ground all around The Chew House bore grim testimony to the accuracy of Maxwell's comments. One could scarcely move more than a few feet in any direction within forty yards of the house without encountering a dead or dying soldier. As the distance to the house became less, so did the distance between the bodies of the Americans, in some cases so much so that the bodies were actually piled on top of one another. It was a level of slaughter that had rarely, if ever, been seen before in this war.

Major John White, a member of General Sullivan's staff, came riding up to the group of officers gathered around General Maxwell.

"General Maxwell!" White stated breathlessly, "I've been given orders by General Sullivan to provide troops to assist in your assault on the house."

"I'm grateful to General Sullivan for the offer," Maxwell replied, "but we were just discussing the ineffectiveness of our attack. I fear the addition of more troops may provide little to the effort, and only result in a greater loss of life than we have already incurred. Perhaps a change in tactics may prove to be the better course of action."

"With your permission, sir," Major White suggested, "I believe that we may be able to burn the enemy out of their position. If we can get the doors and windows to catch fire, the resulting smoke may cause panic and confusion amongst the occupants, while giving our men a chance to advance more safely through the screen it would provide."

General Maxwell nodded slowly, considering the idea proposed by White. Despite the fact that the house was mainly built of stone, the plan might work if enough of the windows and doors could be set aflame. If nothing else, it offered something besides the senseless carnage to which his men were now being subjected.

"There is a rather large wagon loaded with hay that I saw in one of the barns just a short distance back," White continued. "I believe that a few men may be able to push the wagon up to one of the side doors of the house where the firing is not so concentrated. Meanwhile, I'll organize several other men to approach the house from various directions at the same time with the intention of setting the window shutters on fire."

"Very well, Major," Maxwell agreed, coming to a decision, "you may proceed as you described. Please exercise caution – we have already lost too many good men."

Major John White saluted, spurred his horse, and rode off to put his plan into action.

—

Unfortunately, while the idea of burning the enemy out of their fortress was a completely different approach to the situation, it was to be no more successful than the initial attack launched by Maxwell's troops.

There was, in fact, a wagon loaded with hay in a nearby barn, and several soldiers were actually able to get it to one of the side doors of the house. However, when it was set on fire, it burned itself up harmlessly, never spreading to any part of the house. Several other attempts proved equally fruitless, as the soldiers approaching the house were either driven back by British musket fire, or were simply unable to coax the massive house to be set ablaze.

The most tragic of the attempts was made by the young Major White himself. White was able to make his way to one of the windows on the side of the house carrying a lighted torch. As he was attempting to apply the flame to the house, a British soldier thrust his bayonet through a gap in the shutter at the American officer. The bayonet drove into White's mouth, exiting out of the back of his throat. When his body was found at the conclusion of the battle, White was lying face down in a large pool of black congealed blood, the now unlit torch just a few inches from his outstretched hand.

Lieutenant Jacob Landes
10:00 AM - October 4, 1777
Market Square
Germantown, Pennsylvania

The American advance on the main British line located at Market Square had continued to pick up momentum as the morning had worn on, and Lieutenants Jacob Landes and Michael Sweeney suddenly found themselves in plain sight of the main force of enemy troops. The British had taken up positions on Church Lane to the Americans left as well as School House Lane on their right. Their position was not overwhelmingly formidable in that the British had not erected significant defensive works. However, both young officers were forced to acknowledge that the prospect of conducting a frontal assault against a sizable force of experienced enemy troops was not a particularly pleasant situation.

Nevertheless, the American advance had taken on a life of its own, the need for orders from the officers to continue to move forward long gone. The men sensed that they were on the verge of accomplishing something truly magnificent, and every man had a gleam of violence and expectation in his eyes.

A short distance back from their current position, Jacob had received a minor wound as a musketball had grazed his left arm just above the elbow. He had stopped just long enough to wrap a handkerchief around his arm to stop the bleeding, but it had gradually become a distraction to Jacob as it had begun to throb with pain. As a result, Jacob had failed to notice that a part of his unit was beginning to drift off to the left, as the combination of fog and smoke on the battlefield continued to hamper efforts at coordinating the attack.

"Jacob, over here!" Michael Sweeney shouted from a location about thirty yards to the right of where Jacob was now standing. "Bring your men back to the right, Jacob! Keep the unit together!"

Jacob's face flushed with embarrassment and anger at himself for having allowed the pain to temporarily take his focus from the task at hand. He quickly issued the necessary orders to his men, who made an immediate adjustment to come back in line with the rest of the 4th Pennsylvania. A minute later, Jacob found himself standing next to Michael who was gazing at his friend with a concerned look on his face.

"Jacob, are you all right?" Michael asked, gesturing to the makeshift bandage on Jacob's arm.

"Yes, of course," Jacob answered quickly. "Just a scratch, really – although it absolutely hurts like hell."

"Let's have a quick look," Michael suggested as he reached out for Jacob's arm. "You can't be too careful with these wounds that seem small at first. Remember Harvey Smullen thought that the wound to his knee at Brandywine Creek was just a scratch…" Michael's voice trailed off without completing his comment.

There was no need to. Harvey Smullen, a twenty year old from Skippack Township, had been able to run as fast as greased lightening. Anytime the various units engaged in contests requiring speed, Harvey was always the man nominated to compete from the 4th Pennsylvania. Near the end of the fighting on September 11th on Birmingham Hill, Harvey had been little more than grazed by a bullet, and had continued to fight until the end of the battle. However, within a couple of days the relatively minor wound had become infected, and within a week the army surgeons had been forced to amputate his leg just below the hip. But the decision to amputate had been made too late, the infection having already made its way from the wounded leg and into his body. Harvey had spent several days enduring incredible pain before finally dying alone in the middle of one night, lying on the floor of a barn.

As Michael quickly removed the handkerchief and examined the wound, his eyes became as wide as saucers as he uttered a hushed, "My God!"

"What is it, Michael? What's wrong?" Jacob asked, suddenly alarmed by his friend's reaction.

"My God!" Michael repeated, lifting his gaze up to meet that of Jacob. "You should be ashamed of yourself for even referring to this as a wound," Michael said, a wide smile suddenly splitting his handsome face. "Why, I've gotten hurt worse than this pulling out picker bushes in my Grandmother's garden!"

Jacob laughed out loud, a combination of the humor of his friend's jibe and the relief of realizing that he was not badly wounded at all. Michael joined in with him, neither men recognizing the incongruity of their laughter in the midst of their situation.

"Why you rotten scoundrel," Jacob almost choked, trying to contain himself. "You had me there for just a second. I thought you were going to tell me…"

Michael's laughter was abruptly cut off as a musketball smacked into his right side with a dull thud, knocking the wind from his body. His face contorted in pain, and Michael fell into the arms of his friend.

"Michael!" Jacob exclaimed, as he suddenly found himself bearing the weight of his friend. Slowly, Jacob lowered him to the ground, careful to lie him on his side opposite from where the musketball had hit.

"Jesus, Jacob, it hurts," Michael hissed through clenched teeth. "Can you tell how bad the wound is?"

Not wanting to look for fear of what he might see, Jacob hesitated pulling his eyes away from his friend's face. Finally, he looked down at Michael's side and was immediately appalled at what he saw. While the point at which the musketball had hit Michael consisted of just a small wound, the bullet had exited the body leaving a gaping hole that was literally gushing blood onto the ground. Jacob realized that unless he did something right away, his friend was going to bleed to death in the next few minutes.

Two men from the 4th Pennsylvania had arrived at Jacob's side, having seen the young officer go down. One of them was Corporal Stanton, the soldier who had so thoughtfully inquired as to the health of Jacob's father just before the start of the melee at Paoli on that terrible night. Stanton had shown himself to be a first rate man on the battlefield, demonstrating a combination of complete calm during a frantic situation along with a complete ruthlessness when confronting the enemy. However, at this point Stanton was about to exhibit yet another skill.

"Lieutenant," Stanton said, addressing Jacob, "with your permission, sir, why don't you move over just a bit and allow me to tend to Mr. Sweeney. I have a bit of experience with this."

Jacob looked at Corporal Stanton, undecided on whether or not to turn over the life of his friend into the hands of a man whose knowledge in this area was a complete unknown.

"Sir," Stanton continued quietly, "I grew up on a farm. I've been tending to sick and wounded animals since I was just a little kid. I'm sure I can handle the scratch here on Lieutenant Sweeney without too much of a fuss."

The calmness of Stanton's tone indicated a quiet confidence that reassured Jacob and, more importantly, Michael. The two friends met one another's gaze for a brief moment, during which Michael gave an almost imperceptible nod of his head.

"Alright then, Corporal Stanton – what do you need from me?" Jacob asked, Stanton having already moved into position directly next to Michael. Stanton had quickly removed several strips of white cloth from inside of his coat, and was carefully laying them across Michael's body in preparation for their eventual use.

"I don't need nuthin' right here, sir," Stanton stated matter of factly, his eyes never leaving his work. "But if it's not too much trouble, Lieutenant, I wouldn't mind if you got back into the battle and led the men. We've been kickin' the hell out of these Redcoats all day, and I don't suppose it would be proper to ease up just yet."

Stanton was right. There was nothing more that Jacob could do for his friend; certainly nothing more than the clearly capable Stanton was already doing. It was time once again to force emotion to the back of his mind and deal with the urgency of the moment. Jacob stood up and looked around the battlefield in order to assess the situation at hand.

—

Unfortunately, the situation had changed rather significantly in just the last few minutes. Whereas the entire American attack had been moving at a steady rate in the direction of the main British lines, Jacob now noted with concern that not only had that advance slowed off to their left, but it appeared to be ceasing altogether. What had changed so suddenly?

As that question crossed Jacob's mind, a volley of musket fire suddenly roared in the direction of the 4th Pennsylvania. However, this volley wasn't coming from the British lines to their front, but rather from *behind* the American advance! Somehow, it appeared that a group of enemy soldiers had been able to get behind the Americans, and was now threatening to catch them in a crossfire from both front and rear.

Jacob realized that action needed to be taken immediately, or they would risk being surrounded and annihilated. At that moment Lieutenant Colonel William Butler, the Commanding Officer of the 4th Pennsylvania, began shouting orders to face about and confront the enemy in the rear. Despite the fact that it would completely halt their attack on Market Square, Jacob knew that this was the right decision, as the troops from behind posed the greatest threat.

Jacob proceeded to add his own shouts to those of his commanding officer as well as other officers attempting to carry out the order. Reluctantly, hesitant to abandon what looked to be almost certain victory, some of the Americans turned to the rear and formed their lines in a somewhat disorganized manner. In fairness to these men, having to complete such a maneuver while being fired upon from two sides was no easy feat, and any group of soldiers in the world would have been hard pressed to accomplish it without the utmost of discipline and bravery. Meanwhile, other units either didn't hear the command to turn about, or simply refused to do so, and these men continued their original attack on the main British lines. The result was a complete breakdown of coordination, and a total loss of the momentum the Americans had enjoyed until just a moment before.

To make matters worse, if that were even possible, a number of the men began shouting to their comrades that they had either run out of ammunition, or were about to do so. These shouts were echoed by others, who indicated a similar situation for themselves. In a matter of just a few minutes, what appeared to be an American victory had suddenly become very dangerous for the Continental Army. Unless they were able to extricate themselves from their current position – and quickly – they would not only lose momentum, but they might very well lose the battle.

As Jacob and the other members of the 4th Pennsylvania struggled to maintain some form of organization in the midst of the chaos, any options were taken out of their hands all at once. The main British line at Market Square, now just over 100 yards *behind* the unit as a result of their about face, erupted in a loud roar as hundreds of British troops stormed from behind their flimsy fortifications and attacked the Americans.

The opportunity was gone. There would be no breakthrough and defeat of the British army on this day. The task now became one of proudly and safely withdrawing from the battlefield, such that the 4th Pennsylvania – and the rest of the Continental Army – could survive to fight another day on another battlefield.

In the end, that was the true key to ultimately winning the war for this army. While a victory on the battlefield today would obviously have been ideal, it was not a requirement. All that was required to maintain sight of ultimate victory was keeping the army intact and able to continue to carry on this terrible struggle.

LIEUTENANT COLONEL THOMAS MUSGRAVE
10:30 AM - OCTOBER 4, 1777
THE CHEW HOUSE
GERMANTOWN, PENNSYLVANIA

The inside of the Chew House was like a scene from Hell. The smoke was so thick that a man was unable to see from one side of a room to the other. The combination of musket fire from inside the house and cannon and musket fire from all around the house made it impossible to be heard from even a foot away without having to shout.

Several cannonballs had found their way through the front door or through one of the many windows. At the very least, these projectiles had succeeded in knocking huge holes in the interior walls and spraying chips of stone throughout a room at terrifying velocity. In the worst cases, the cannonballs had found their intended targets in the form of human frames with devastating result. One cannonball in particular had ricocheted off of several walls before finally coming to rest imbedded in the ceiling. Throughout the journey of this horrible piece of metal, it had mangled the right leg of a Private, laid open the entrails of a rather elderly Sergeant, and finally decapitated a Captain who had been sitting at the main dining room table tending to a slight wound on his hand.

Colonel Thomas Musgrave had been moving continuously throughout the mansion for the last few hours, attempting to stay aware of the situations that existed at various parts of the house. The fact that there were several floors, literally dozens of rooms, heavy smoke, and significant confusion made this task somewhat challenging. Despite these obstacles, Musgrave was cautiously confident that his men were holding up fairly well, despite the fact that the Americans had thrown everything they had at this position. On more than one occasion Musgrave had thanked God for the clearly gifted craftsmen that had constructed such a sturdy structure.

As Colonel Musgrave was descending the main stairway onto the first floor for what was possibly the twentieth time, he was met by Captain Hains, the officer in charge of those men assigned to defend this section of the house. Musgrave was mildly surprised to realize that he was genuinely pleased to see that the young Captain was still unhurt and carrying out his duties with the same cool confidence that he had displayed from the start.

"Sir," Hains shouted as he came up next to Musgrave, "the Americans have continued with their attempts to burn us out of our position. However, I'm pleased to report that all of these attempts have been unsuccessful and, in most cases - " at this point a cruel smile formed on the lips of the young man – "rather costly to the enemy."

"What is the condition of your men, Captain," Musgrave asked, choosing to ignore the rather heartless tone of the man's comments.

"Sir, the enemy has ceased concentrating their cannon and musket fire on the first floor, for fear of hitting their own men. As a result, other than the occasional attempt to break through a window or burn down a door, the men have been holding up rather well."

"Very well, Captain," Musgrave responded. "I would like to get a view of the front of the house in order to ascertain the results of the enemy's attacks. Is there a position that is more secure than another from which I can get such a view?"

"Yes, sir. That window over there," Hains said as he pointed toward a window on the right side of the room. "It is somewhat more recessed than the others. If the Colonel were to exercise caution and stand off to one side, I'm quite confident that he would be able to see the entire area in the front of the house."

"Thank you, Captain, I shall do so," Musgrave concluded as he moved quickly across the room to the suggested location.

Cautiously, Musgrave opened the shutter of the window ever so slightly, being careful not to fully frame himself in the opening. Although he hated the fact that he was acting in a fashion that bordered on cowardly, he hated even more the prospect of an American musketball driving itself into his body. Currently there was a lull in the fighting. The relatively quiet morning was only occasionally punctuated by a few random musket shots being taken at either real or imagined targets of opportunity within or around the mansion.

Musgrave's initial scan of the ground in front of the Chew House shocked him, despite the fact that he was a veteran of numerous battles. From the front doors of the mansion stretching back in a fan-like arrangement perhaps sixty or seventy yards, the ground was completely carpeted with the bodies of American soldiers. The concentration was so thick, in fact, that Musgrave morbidly noted that he could have walked on top of the bodies for at least thirty yards without ever having to set foot on the ground.

Most disturbing were the soldiers lying on the ground that were clearly still alive, but unable to propel themselves back to the safety of their own lines. Their pathetic moans and cries could be heard throughout the immediate area, begging for everything from a drink of water to the assistance of a friend. An American soldier of about thirty years old or so was lying just a few feet from the window at which Musgrave was standing. The man had been struck by at least one, maybe two musket balls in the gut, and was clearly in terrible pain. In a soft, pleading voice he was begging over and over again for one of the British soldiers to shoot him and put him out of his misery. Musgrave briefly entertained the prospect of complying with the wishes of the dying man, but realized that such an action could easily be perceived as an atrocity.

This was the dirty little secret about war, Musgrave knew. *Everything* about war was an atrocity. The act of focusing all of your energies to the purpose of killing another man had no glory or honor associated with it. It was barbaric and heartless in every way, and the only thing that constituted one thing as an atrocity and another as a noble gesture was the perspective of the observer.

Captain Hains had arrived at the side of Colonel Musgrave, and was treated to the same view as his commanding officer. Musgrave noted with no small amount of concern that the young Captain appeared completely unmoved by the horror that met his gaze, and he appeared to have an almost clinical perspective on the scene.

"It appears our American friends have learned yet another lesson at the hands of Her Majesty's men, wouldn't you agree, sir?" Hains asked his commander. "I seriously doubt that these cowardly ruffians will attempt to assault our position any further."

Musgrave realized that Hains was correct about additional attacks, as many of the American soldiers that were formed into firing lines around the house were beginning to withdraw from their positions and disappear into the diminishing fog. It appeared that he and his men would live to fight another day. Despite this revelation and its accompanying relief, Musgrave was surprised to find that he was experiencing a dull, burning anger in response to Captain Hains' cavalier comments.

"They are not 'ruffians', Captain," Musgrave hissed between

clenched teeth, as he turned to face the young man, "and they are certainly not cowardly. They are soldiers who are every bit deserving of your respect as your own brave men. What 'ruffians' would attack under such circumstances, eh Captain?"

Hains' emotionless expression had changed to one of surprise and embarrassment, as he realized that many of the enlisted man standing close by could clearly hear the conversation occurring between the two officers. But Musgrave's anger had taken him beyond the point of concern for appropriateness and protocols.

"Those men out there made their attacks fully aware of the almost certain consequences they would face. They have given their lives in pursuit of something that is, at least in their mind, worth dying for. Is that your definition of a 'ruffian', Captain?" Musgrave asked, the volume of his voice continuing to rise as more and more men turned their heads in the direction of the reprimand that was being given out by their commanding officer.

Musgrave realized that he had caused a scene at the expense of Hains, and decided that the young man had hopefully been taught a lesson. He lowered his voice to just barely above a whisper, and leaned toward the Captain until their faces were just inches apart.

"I fervently wish that our soldiers will act with such 'cowardice' when faced with a similar situation in the future."

Musgrave paused and took a deep breath, further composing himself.

"You are a fine young officer, Captain Hains, and you have displayed a level of competence and bravery for which you should be proud. But never – never, Captain – underestimate the resolve and bravery of those men out there," Musgrave stated, pointing in the direction of the American lines.

Lieutenant Colonel Thomas Musgrave moved away from the window, and went about the task of preparing to remove his command from their stronghold.

GENERAL ANTHONY WAYNE
11:00 AM - OCTOBER 4, 1777
MARKET SQUARE
GERMANTOWN, PENNSYLVANIA

General Anthony Wayne refused to believe what was taking place around him. The battle had been going superbly, with the Americans continuing to apply pressure on every part of the British line. It seemed to Wayne that it must only be a matter of time before the entire British line would collapse, flying headlong back to the temporary safety of Philadelphia. But temporary it would be, as the Continental Army would regroup, resupply, and launch the next ferocious attack necessary to regain control of the colonial capital.

But all of these possibilities were never to be realized, as Wayne watched his men begin to withdraw away from the main British line. Granted, the withdraw was a controlled one, but it was a withdraw nonetheless.

It had all begun to unravel just a few minutes before. General Wayne had been proudly atop his horse issuing orders at the top of his lungs for his men to advance and drive the enemy from the field. In one brief moment, several musket balls had struck his horse, causing the animal to shriek in pain and collapse to the ground dead. Wayne had luckily been thrown away from the horse, and had avoided being crushed by the weight of the creature. But Wayne now lacked the mobility that had allowed him to move throughout his command, as well as the advantage of being slightly above the fray and able to gain a better vantage point on the situation.

Within minutes of that loss, Wayne's men had been fired on from the rear by a unit just coming up through the fog. At first General Wayne, like everyone else on the battlefield, had assumed that a British force had succeeded in maneuvering into position behind the Americans. Not only would this threaten their rear, but also their ability to withdraw from the battlefield should the situation require it. This had immediately resulted in a halt in the main American attack on Market Square, and had required

Wayne's men to face about and deal with this new threat.

However, as Wayne's men re-formed and prepared to return a volley of musket fire in the direction of their tormentors in the rear, several of Wayne's men realized that their attackers were none other than members of General Stephen's Brigade of General Greene's Division – their own Continental Army!

General Nathaniel Greene had been in command of one of the four columns that had made the initial advance from the north toward Germantown. Greene's nearly 6,000 men had traveled down the Limekiln Pike and were ordered to move into position on the left center of the American attack. Although their advance had progressed fairly well, they had gotten somewhat of a late start, and had been delayed on at least one other occasion after beginning their march. The result was that the rest of the Continental Army, which should have been to the immediate *right* of General Greene, was actually to the *right front* of Greene, over a half mile ahead. This had caused Greene and his commanders to completely lose track of the rest of the army due in part to the speed of the advance, the morning fog, and the general confusion that invariably existed on the battlefield.

General Greene had posted General Stephen and his brigade to form the right flank of his advance, with orders to maintain contact with the rest of General Greene's command at all times. However, General Stephen had allowed his men to veer further off to the right, getting lost in a small woods and losing complete contact with the main force. As Stephen continued to move further and further to the right, he had eventually placed himself directly *behind* the rest of the attacking American army commanded by General Wayne, as opposed to being to the immediate *left* of Wayne. The result was the catastrophe that was just now beginning to unfold.

Luckily, the men of the two American units recognized almost immediately that they were facing members of their own army, and only a single volley along with some additional sporadic shots had been exchanged between the two units. However, the real damage was the loss in momentum of the main American attack.

General Wayne moved quickly in the direction of Stephen's Brigade to his rear, his face red with rage. Of all the stupidity! What could Stephen have been thinking? Did the man have no ability to direct the simple movements of his men?

As General Wayne came upon Stephen's Brigade, he shouted angrily at the men, "Where, in the name of God, is General Stephen? Where is that man?"

A small group of four men appeared on horseback, consisting of General Stephen and his staff. General Stephen rode in the front, as his three staff officers maintained a slight distance to the rear. General Wayne noted that these staff officers rode with their eyes toward the ground, refusing to meet the furious gaze he was casting in their direction. On the other hand, General Stephen appeared to be quite relaxed, almost nonchalant. The infantry moved to the side to allow their General to ride forward.

"Anthony, my good man," General Stephen addressed Wayne, "you appear to have lost your horse. Rather unfortunate, I would say."

"Rather unfortunate!" Wayne nearly shouted. "You have fired into the rear of a group of friendly soldiers; you have caused my men to cease their advance on the enemy's main line; you have quite possibly engaged in actions that may cause us to lose this battle; and you dwell on the unfortunate nature of the loss of my horse?"

General Stephen's expression changed gradually from one of cool detachment, to one of surprise, to one of smoldering anger.

"What are you suggesting, Wayne?" General Stephen demanded of the enraged man standing on the ground before him. "Neither I nor any of my men have done anything wrong. It was confusing as we moved forward, and it was difficult to stay – "

With that, General Stephen issued forth a huge belch, and swayed dangerously atop his mount. With great difficulty, he steadied himself and refocused his gaze down upon General Wayne.

Wayne's eyes widened in recognition as he looked up at his fellow General. "Why, you son of a bitch!" Wayne said. "You're drunk out of your mind!"

"Drunk? Why you insolent bastard!" Stephen bellowed. "I'll have you brought up on charges for making such accusations! Gentlemen," Stephen said, facing in the direction of his staff, "I order you to make note of the time and date that these statements were made by General Wayne. I will not have my honor questioned by any man!"

As General Wayne tore his gaze away from Stephen to look back at the staff officers in the rear, he noted that not a single one of them had made a move to comply with the order that had been issued by their General. In fact, while two of the officers had sat astride their horses with their eyes continuing to examine the ground, the third man had actually turned his horse and started riding slowly away.

"Major Fillman," General Stephen shouted at the retreating officer, "where the hell do you think you're going? I gave you an order, man! Stand fast or I'll have you shot for desertion!"

General Stephen began to fumble at his beltline where he apparently believed he would find a pistol. But there was none there, and as he continued to mumble to himself and grasp at his midsection his actions became almost comical. In fact, a number of the troops close by were forced to turn away for fear of their Commanding Officer seeing them laugh at his expense. All of this only served to further enrage Stephen, until he finally abandoned his unsuccessful search for a weapon and turned his attention towards one of the remaining staff officers.

"Captain Byning, I order you to shoot Major Fillman if he does not cease his cowardly actions immediately! Do you hear me, Captain?" Stephen nearly shrieked, becoming completely unglued. "If he continues to ride away, I order you to take your pistol out, and…"

"Captain, you will do nothing of the sort," General Wayne interrupted calmly, addressing the suddenly relieved staff officer. "General Stephen, do you really wish to add murder to the already lengthy list of charges you will certainly be facing following this engagement?"

General Stephen's expression had quickly changed from one of rage to that of a man who had just been slapped unceremoniously across the face. He opened his mouth to answer, but his alcohol-soaked brain could find no suitable response to the situation.

"Remove yourself from the Field, General," Wayne said scornfully to the now completely deflated man. "Captain, inform whomever is your next senior officer that he is now in charge of your Brigade, and send a messenger to locate General Greene and inform him of what has transpired here."

General Wayne paused briefly, not quite prepared to totally humiliate Stephen, even in spite of what he had done. He was, after all, a fellow General of the American Army.

"When I say 'inform General Greene of what has transpired here'," Wayne amended to the Captain, "I am referring to what has happened here on the battlefield – not to what has just happened here between General Stephen and myself. That is none of your concern, and is my responsibility to address that at the appropriate time. Do you understand, Captain?"

"Completely, sir," the young Captain responded, more than happy to be off the hook for having what he knew would have been a most uncomfortable interaction with a senior officer. Quickly, Captain Byning rode off in search of the commander officer, and away from the most bizarre experience he had ever had during his brief time in the Army.

Brigadier General Francis Nash
11:15 AM - October 4, 1777
Germantown, Pennsylvania

As he continued to ride toward the sound of cannon and musket fire, it became obvious to Brigadier General Francis Nash that something about the battle had changed significantly in the last few minutes. Not only had the volume of fire decreased, but the sound of the battle now seemed to be coming *towards* them as opposed to away from them as it had seemed earlier.

"Lieutenant Bartle!" Nash shouted above the noise, summoning his most junior staff officer. Bartle quickly arrived at Nash's side, eager as always to do the bidding of his commanding general.

"Lieutenant, I need you to ride with all possible speed ahead of us into the fog in order to locate General Wayne and ascertain the nature of the situation he is facing," Nash directed the man. "I have no desire to ride headlong into a situation about which I know nothing. Do you understand your orders, Lieutenant?"

"Completely, sir," the officer responded, and with a flourish was off into the stubbornly receding Pennsylvania fog. Within a matter of just a few seconds he was lost to Nash's view, and the General prayed for the man's safety. A battlefield was a place where anything could happen in a moment, and Nash truly hoped that there were many more moments left in the life of young Lieutenant Bartle. He seemed to be not much more than a boy when compared to the nearly 35 years that General Nash had been alive.

Because he was momentarily lost in his thoughts, General Nash failed to notice the arrival of Major James Witherspoon at his side. Witherspoon, having dismounted and walked up to address his Commander, was obliged to clear his throat in order to get the attention of the General.

"Begging your pardon, General Nash," Witherspoon began, "but may I have a word, sir?"

"Of course, Major," Nash responded, suddenly jolted out of his state of reflection. "What is it?" he asked looking down from his mount at Witherspoon.

"Sir, the unit commanders have requested permission to shift from column to line of battle. Apparently, they're concerned that the sound of the battle appears to be coming towards us, and they would prefer to not be caught flatfooted if you will, sir."

General Nash considered the request, having contemplated that exact maneuver himself just a minute or two ago. The question was, how far away was General Wayne, and to what degree did he need the support of Nash's unit? If Nash were to bring his North Carolinians on line too quickly, it would reduce their advance to a virtual crawl, thus taking additional time to close the distance between himself and Wayne. However, if he were to wait too long to deploy his men into a battle line, he risked the enemy appearing out of the fog and attacking his unit when they were completely unprepared. It was the classic case of determining how much to risk one's own men in order to assist others.

"General," Witherspoon nearly shouted in order to be heard, "the men are strung out for several hundred yards to the rear, and they..."

Nash was no longer able to make out what Major Witherspoon was saying, as the din of the battle seemed to increase and continue to move in their direction. In addition, for the first time the men began to notice an occasional whir of flying metal through the air, a clear indication that the battle was not far away. Nash motioned for his staff officer to move closer to his side in order to be heard, and Witherspoon moved next to Nash's horse such that the two were nearly touching one another.

"General," Witherspoon shouted, "if I may be so bold, sir, perhaps we should be bringing the men into line in order to prepare them – "

At that moment, a British cannonball came bounding through the fog directly at General Nash and Major Witherspoon. The ball plowed into the grouping of Major Witherspoon, General Nash, and General Nash's horse with terrifying results.

Major Witherspoon's skull was nearly shattered by the impact of the cannonball, as his head was crushed into an indistinguishable mass. His body was propelled several yards to the rear, coming to rest in a bloody, pathetic heap on the ground. While James Witherspoon's chest continued to rise and fall indicating that he was still alive, there was no way that any man could sustain such heinous injuries and still survive. When several soldiers arrived at his side just seconds later, they noted that the Major's breathing had already become ragged and sporadic – there would be no need for medical assistance in this case. Within just a few minutes, Major John Witherspoon had officially given his life in the service of his country.

Meanwhile, having caused the death of one man, that same cannonball had also impacted the thigh of General Francis Nash sitting astride his horse. The result was predictably devastating, as Nash was knocked from his horse landing on the ground in an unceremonious manner. Nash was momentarily stunned, having banged his head while also having the wind knocked out of him. He was able to raise himself up on his elbows as he shook his head in an attempt to clear away the thick cobwebs. Another of Nash's staff officers, Captain Stiles, was sitting nearby on his horse. He quickly dismounted and rushed to his General's side.

"General Nash, are you all right, sir?" the officer asked anxiously. The man looked to his left, his eyes falling on the mangled body of James Witherspoon, and he promptly stepped away to the side of the road and vomited into the grass.

"Come now, Captain, my appearance cannot really be that offensive, now can it?" Nash lightly chided Stiles. "Now pull yourself together, man, you need to issue orders to my commanders at once."

Stiles rose a bit unsteadily to his feet, coming back to the side of General Nash. While the man was clearly shaken, he was still in control of himself and capable of doing his duty.

"General, your leg is bleeding quite badly," Stiles noted. "I shall find a surgeon immediately, sir, before it gets any worse."

"No, Captain Stiles, you will do nothing of the kind," Nash responded in a surprisingly firm voice. "You will report to each of the unit commanders that they are to bring their men into battle line in the predetermined order, and begin moving in the direction of the musket fire to our front. Tell them to be watchful for our own units retreating through the fog, and be careful not to inadvertently open fire."

"Our units retreating, sir?" Stiles asked incredulously. "But we've been advancing throughout the morning and driving the enemy back!"

"Captain Stiles, please deliver my orders exactly as I have instructed – is that absolutely clear, Captain?"

"Yes, sir," Stiles responded just a bit shocked, "line of battle, be aware of retreating American soldiers, sir."

"There you are, Captain – now move along quickly," Nash ordered.

Several soldiers had arrived by Nash's side in the last minute or two, and one of them took the place of the departing Captain Stiles. He gazed knowingly at Nash's leg, then looked him in the eye.

"General, I ain't no Surgeon, but if you'll permit me I'm thinkin' we might want to wrap that there leg in something before you bleed to death, sir."

For the first time, Francis Nash realized that he had been wounded, and he allowed himself a look at his leg. What he saw caused his head to momentarily begin spinning, as he watched the blood literally spurting from the main artery in his thigh. Pulling his gaze away from the wound, Nash was further horrified to see the remains of what had been his beloved horse just a minute ago. The fateful cannonball had completely ripped open the belly of the majestic animal, and its entrails had been splattered for several feet. Nash knew that the horse did not have long to live, and prayed that one of his men would mercifully cut short the remaining painful minutes of the animal's life.

"Very well, Corporal, do what you can," Nash said to the soldier by his side, and the man immediately began to pull several cloth strips from his pockets and wrap them around the General's leg. While the result was anything but perfect, at the very least the artery stopped shooting blood into the air. However, the strips of cloth became saturated as quickly as they could be placed onto the wound.

Out of the fog to his rear, General Nash could hear the approach of his North Carolina brigade. As they appeared, he was pleased to see that they had in fact come into battle line, and were moving in a disciplined manner in the direction he had ordered.

Nash realized that the appearance of their commanding general lying badly wounded on the ground would have a negative effect on the morale of the men, a result that could simply not be tolerated as they moved into battle. Quickly, Nash removed his coat and placed it over his wounded leg just as the first line of troops came abreast of him. The line wavered noticeably as they observed their commander lying on the ground, but Nash quickly allayed their concerns.

"Never mind me," Nash instructed, "I have had a devil of a tumble – rush on my boys, rush on the enemy – I'll be after you presently."

The soldiers, reassured that Nash would be up and about in no time, pushed on into the fog. While the nature of what awaited them just ahead was unknown, at least they were assured that their general would be fine.

GENERAL WILLIAM HOWE
11:15 AM - OCTOBER 4, 1777
MARKET SQUARE
GERMANTOWN, PENNSYLVANIA

There are times on a battlefield when it feels as if the hand of God Almighty Himself reaches down and guides the course of the fight, making all of the preparation, execution, and bravery of Man simply a footnote to the whims of a Supreme Being. This was one such time.

General William Howe had literally been on the verge of ordering a general retreat from the army's main line located here at Market Square. The Americans had the advantages of momentum and numbers as regiment after regiment seemed to appear out of nowhere and attack the British. Even a counterattack by one of the most veteran units in the British army had done nothing but temporarily slow the onslaught.

It was at that point that God had chosen to enter the fray, at least from the perspective of General Howe. The main attack concentrating on the center of the British line had simply ceased to advance, and had even appeared to turn to their rear. From where Howe was standing, he could see no reason for such odd and damaging behavior, and he made a mental note to eventually ascertain the reason for these actions. But right now, all Howe knew was that his army was out of immediate danger of having to retreat, at least for the time being. The question was, would the Americans be able to regroup and renew their attack? If that was the case, Howe suspected that his men would be unable to hold their currently tenuous position.

But God was not finished shining His countenance down on the British this day. The Almighty sent a messenger directly to General William Howe, albeit in the rather earthly and unmilitary form of Colonel Charles Levitt. At first, Howe was furious to see the Colonel approaching him on horseback, having previously ordered the man to halt the retreat and form another counterattack. But Levitt's expression as he arrived at Howe's side was one of beaming confidence, a stark contrast to the fearful look with which he had departed just a few minutes ago.

"General Howe," Levitt said as he arrived, "I wish to report that I have been successful at forming a number of regiments who are now prepared to counterattack the Americans upon your orders, sir."

"Very well, Colonel – do so immediately, as I believe the time for us to strike is now," Howe responded impatiently.

"Time indeed, sir," Levitt said, with a broad smile that actually bordered on being unprofessional considering the circumstances.

"Damn it, man, wipe that ridiculous smile off of your face. You are about to lead an attack against an enemy that is numerically superior to ours, and you're looking like a child on Christmas morning."

"Ay sir," replied Colonel Levitt, continuing to smile in spite of himself, "and Christmas morning it may be, that we have been given the gift of an enemy without ammunition!"

"What do you mean, Colonel?"

"Sir, a number of our soldiers deployed forward as skirmishers have reported that they can hear the Americans calling out to one another in the fog, stating that they have either little ammunition, or no ammunition at all," Levitt reported. "They can hear the American officers cursing at their men telling them to keep their mouths shut before the enemy hears them – but it would appear to be a bit late for that, sir."

Howe, in spite of his perpetually stellar military bearing, was forced to allow himself a slight grin of his own, which he was careful to hide from the uncomfortably enthusiastic Colonel.

"How many regiments have you formed as a reserve behind your attacking units," Howe asked.

"Two, sir, with a third remaining behind to hold the center of our position," Levitt explained.

"Very well, Colonel, here are your new orders. There will be no reserves remaining behind, and you will deploy every man in a single battle line to counterattack the enemy. Is that clear, Colonel? The three regiments you have formed in reserve are to be incorporated into the main assault."

Colonel Levitt, momentarily taken aback by the audacity of the order, simply sat on his horse and stared at General Howe, his childish grin erased from his face. But the man quickly regained his composure pulling himself to rigid attention, and crisply addressed his Commanding General.

"Yes, sir," Levitt replied in a serious and determined voice. "I will see to it immediately, sir. I will begin the attack within ten minutes."

"You will begin the attack within *five* minutes, Colonel," Howe ordered sternly, fixing the rotund man with an icy stare.

It was all the Colonel could do to spur his horse, and mutely depart back toward his gathering troops.

—

When it began exactly five minutes and fifteen seconds later, the British attack was ferocious and unstoppable. In addition to the regiments that Colonel Levitt had formed, he had also been able to concentrate the fire of several cannon in support of the assault. The result was a wave of metal and men directed at the Americans, many of whom had truly lost the ability to respond with fire of their own. The long day of fighting combined with the surprising speed of their advance had created a situation for the Americans in which they had run out of ammunition, and outpaced any possibility of being resupplied.

To their credit, the Americans refused to retreat in any manner that was not stubborn and organized. Considering the fact that they were exhausted, out of ammunition, and facing a violent and coordinated counterattack, their withdrawal was amazingly disciplined.

General William Howe observed the attack and the withdraw of the Americans with a mixture of relief and an uncomfortable feeling of grudging respect. Perhaps these Americans weren't the total rabble that he had classified them to be, Howe mused. They had confronted the cream of the British army in a direct, coordinated attack, and had driven them backwards for a distance of over two miles. All of this after having suffered a major defeat just a few days earlier at Brandywine creek, as well as the humiliating occurrence at Paoli.

Howe angrily shook his head as he roused himself from his contemplation. What was he thinking? Of course they were rabble! To believe otherwise would be the first step to acknowledging the legitimacy of their struggle. At one point in the past, William Howe had actually harbored a bit of sympathy for the American Cause, but that was at a time when he was back in England and watching the events in America with a detached curiosity that bordered on amusement. But the moment he had accepted command of all British forces in America, that curiosity and amusement had been quickly replaced with a sense of duty that precluded even a shred of sympathy for those who threatened his ability to accomplish his assigned mission.

William Howe considered himself to be somewhat of an enlightened man, capable of understanding the complexities of a situation. This quality made him different in many respects from most officers in the British army who tended to see the world from a black and white perspective. It was for this reason that Howe could appreciate what the Americans were attempting to do with their insurrection against the British Crown. But the difference between appreciation and acceptance was a wide chasm in William Howe's mind, and the occasional exhibition of discipline and bravery by these Americans was grossly inadequate to even begin to bridge that gap.

GENERAL GEORGE WASHINGTON
1:45 PM - OCTOBER 4, 1777
GERMANTOWN, PENNSYLVANIA

The euphoric feeling that seemed to always accompany the fight was beginning to dissipate as General George Washington sat astride his horse and observed the events around him. While the tide of victory seemed to be flowing in the right direction for the Continental Army just a short time ago, it now appeared to have all been an illusion. The Gods of War had played a cruel joke on the Americans, convincing them that today would be their day, but then snatching that reality from them at the last moment.

Despite this fact, Washington felt a grim sense of satisfaction at what his men had accomplished. They had met the British Army in direct combat, driving them back for miles before unpredictable mistakes had denied them the victory that they so clearly deserved. Even now, as the enemy had regained their senses and launched a full counterattack, the Continental Army was withdrawing slowly and stubbornly, maintaining every semblance of military discipline as they did so.

General Henry Knox, Washington's Chief of Artillery, rode up to the Commanding General, hesitant to disturb his commander who was obviously lost in his own thoughts at the moment. Knox was also conscious of the fact that the Continental Army had chosen to repeatedly assault the Chew House based on his advice to Washington. Knox – as well as General Washington – could now see that this course of action had certainly lost the momentum of the American attack, and quite possibly had cost them the battle. Knox was unsure as to the nature of the reception he would receive from Washington, the first time they would speak since all of this had become clear.

"General Washington," Knox said, clearing his throat, "our division commanders are requesting permission to order a general withdrawal from the battlefield. What are your orders, sir?"

Washington turned in his saddle to face Knox, a look of profound sorrow on his face. Although the war had only been raging for two years, it appeared just now to Knox that General Washington had aged a lifetime during that short period.

"Order the commanders to withdraw from Germantown," General Washington stated heavily. "Instruct them to deploy rear guards to harass any enemy that choose to pursue us, and direct their men to use the Skippack Pike as their route of movement. We will be relocating the army back to our position at Pennypacker Mills."

"Yes, sir," Knox replied, saluting Washington. "I will see to it immediately, sir."

Knox turned his horse away from Washington, preparing to ride off in the fulfillment of his duties. However, he suddenly turned back to Washington and addressed the General.

"Sir, if I may?"

Washington looked up at the portly Chief of Artillery, realizing that Knox had something to say. Washington wordlessly nodded his head, indicating his assent for his subordinate to speak.

"General Washington, I endeavor at all times to provide my utmost service to this army and this country. It was with that intent that I gave you my advice regarding the fortress we encountered. Had I known, sir, that – "

"General Knox," Washington interrupted, his gaze now fixed firmly on the man, "I assume you realize that I, and not you, are the Commanding General of this army."

Knox physically recoiled, almost as if he had been struck in the face.

"Of course, General Washington – I am fully aware of that, sir."

"Then, General Knox, you are also aware that responsibility for any decisions that are made is mine and mine alone. I consulted you for your opinion, General, and you gave me that. I found that opinion to be founded on a strong knowledge of warfare, experience in battle, and an uncompromising strength of character. As a result, I took that advice."

General Washington paused just long enough to give emphasis to his final words.

"Were I to find myself in a similar situation in the future in which I would require your opinions – and I am quite certain that I shall – I will most likely follow whatever advice it is that you suggest. Is that understood, General Knox?"

General Henry Knox felt an overwhelming wave of relief course through his body, as he realized that he had not lost the confidence of the man whose approval mattered more to him than anything in his life. Knox allowed himself a slight smile as an acknowledgment of the respect that he had just been afforded.

"General Washington," Knox replied simply, "I shall see to your orders now, sir."

—

Although it was a disciplined and deliberate withdrawal, it was also a dreadfully exhausting one. The Americans had marched a significant distance during the night and morning hours of October 3rd and 4th, had engaged in combat for over five hours, and had now been ordered to retreat back up virtually the same route they had traveled approximately 24 hours earlier. Even those soldiers that had escaped unscathed from the battle labored to place one foot in front of the other, while those that had suffered wounds and other injuries endured unimaginable agony during the journey.

General Washington had remained in Germantown long enough to insure that an official rearguard under General Wayne had been assigned and placed appropriately. Although the British attempted to pursue the retreating Americans, it was little more than a half-hearted gesture. The British had had quite enough themselves.

Washington rode north with his staff along the lines of the Continental Army, offering encouragement and hope along the way. He was pleased to see that he received an enthusiastic reception from each and every unit that he passed, soldiers shouting their desire to meet the British again and this time whip them convincingly. Washington understood that these statements of bravado were part of a catharsis through which these men needed to go, but he had to admit that they had a strangely healing effect on his own wounded pride.

Washington's normally small staff was even smaller, several of them having been dispatched north to prepare for the arrival of the army. There were literally hundreds of details that needed to be addressed, and these men had time and again demonstrated their amazing abilities in this area. The fact that the Continental Army was in a constant state of being undersupplied made the results achieved by his staff all the more impressive. Washington made a mental note to renew his efforts to procure additional supplies for his army, a struggle that he had been fighting the entire time he had served as Commanding General.

It would soon be time for the army to enter their winter quarters. When and where this would occur had yet to be determined, in part due to the fact that the British might yet attempt an attack on whatever position the Americans chose to occupy in the next few days. It was for this exact reason that Washington was driving his men to make this exhaustive march. It was simply not sufficient to put a mile or two between themselves and the enemy. Washington would not feel safe until he had created a wide buffer between his army and the British; a buffer into which he could place patrols; a buffer which would allow his men time to prepare for any assault launched against them.

So for now the tired men continued to march, driven forward by a pride they had in themselves, and a trust they had in their Commanding General. As Washington paused briefly by the side of the Skippack Pike watching his soldiers trudge past, he made a silent promise to never let either of these die.

LIEUTENANT JACOB LANDES
OCTOBER 7, 1777
TOWAMENCIN TOWNSHIP, PENNSYLVANIA

The Continental Army had established their latest camp along a lazy, meandering creek that ran directly through the property of Joseph Wampole, a Pennsylvania Dutch farmer who had grudgingly allowed the men to use his land. The amount of filth, trash, and disruption caused by such a large group of men inhabiting such a small area had quickly caused Mr. Wampole to regret his decision, regardless of the worthiness of the cause these men were pursuing ostensibly on his behalf.

In the opinion of Lieutenant Jacob Landes, General Washington could not have chosen a better location. The Wampole farm was less than a six mile ride from his family's home in Salford Township, and Jacob was actually well acquainted with the four children who still lived and worked on the farm. The proximity to his home had allowed Jacob to already visit his family once, and he had no doubt that there would be other opportunities in the near future.

In point of fact, Jacob's family visit had not exactly been a social call. General Washington was deeply concerned that the British might consider pursuing the tired American army and attempt to defeat them once and for all with a final, swift attack on their position. As a result, Washington had ordered patrols to be dispatched in every direction as a means of providing information on the whereabouts of the enemy. While none of these patrols had yielded any contact with the enemy, at least one had allowed Lieutenant Jacob Landes to enjoy a brief visit and lunch with his family.

Jacob, now seated by a smoldering campfire just outside of the tent he shared with three other junior officers, couldn't help but smile when he recalled the sense of pride he had felt when he and four of his men had ridden up to his family's house.

—

"Ma! Ma! Come quick! Some soldiers are ridin' up to the house!"

shouted young Caleb Landes. Caleb had been brushing down one of the horses just outside of the barn when he had spotted the five soldiers trotting down the road in his direction.

Almost immediately, every member of the household dropped what they were doing and came running outside to verify the report being delivered by the youngest member of the Landes family. One look down the road was enough to show that Caleb was, in fact, correct. But it took a harder look from everyone to fully comprehend the significance of what they were seeing. These weren't just any five soldiers coming down the road – these were soldiers being led by their very own brother, Lieutenant Jacob Landes!

Jacob did his absolute best to maintain his professionalism in front of the four enlisted men that were accompanying him on the patrol, but his brothers and sisters had no such semblance of formality. They nearly dragged Jacob off of his horse and smothered him with the affection they all so desperately needed to feel.

As it turned out, there was no need for Jacob to put on a show for his men, as they all sat astride their horses with grins that nearly split their faces in half. For that brief moment, these men were back with their families as well, vicariously enjoying this moment of pure love and connection through the young officer they had come to admire and respect in such a short period of time.

But that sense of satisfaction on the part of the four men wasn't enough for the Landes clan. This was a family that had grown up with the staunch belief that if you were a friend of *anyone* in the family, then you were a *part* of the family. There were no questions asked, and no need to prove anything. If you were good enough for my brother, then you were good enough for the rest of us.

With that foundational principle firmly in place, the Landes family immediately sensed that these four soldiers that had arrived with their brother were special to him. And the only course of action was obvious – they, too, were dragged from their horses and showered with a welcoming affection fit for royalty. In that moment, the four soldiers suddenly understood how young Jacob Landes was capable of caring for his men as deeply as he did. A man that had been raised in an environment of such genuine closeness was capable of possessing a virtually bottomless well of positive emotion.

Of course, a veritable feast was quickly prepared for the five soldiers, who consumed it with an enthusiasm that betrayed the pathetic nature of their typical fare in camp. In addition, they were each provided with a basket that contained enough food for at least two more meals, provided they were to keep the treasure to themselves. Naturally, none of the five would eventually do such a thing, choosing rather to share it with their less fortunate comrades back at the Wampole farm.

The conversation was animated, and continuously punctuated with boisterous laughter. While some time was spent discussing the war, it was intuitively understood by all that this was not the preferred topic. The true purpose of this visit was to escape from that often horrid reality, if only for a short while.

The visit had been brief, but the greatest moments in a person's life are rarely measured in minutes and seconds, but rather by their impact. Jacob had been re-grounded to those fundamental priorities that had made him into the man he was. The Landes family had been reassured that while their eldest son had gone away, it would never be for good. And the four men that had arrived with Jacob were reassured that the sacrifice they were making in terms of time away from their own families was, after all, worth it.

—

Jacob shook himself away from the memory of his recent visit home, and back to the situation at hand. He realized that most of the men around him had begun to move away from their encampments, all heading in the same general direction. Jacob suddenly remembered that all officers and enlisted men not on guard duty or patrol had been ordered to muster at the far northeastern corner of the camp at noon. No other details had been given, but the solemn nature of the communication had made it clear that the purpose of the gathering was not to be enjoyable.

Jacob pulled himself to his feet, and began following the other men. After a hundred yards or so, Jacob could see that the men were gradually forming around a gigantic oak tree set in the corner of the Wampole farm. As Jacob drew closer, he could clearly see that a rope with a noose formed at its end had been tied to one of the lower boughs of the giant tree. The mystery around the purpose of the formation was now clear. But the question remained: who was to be the unfortunate soul that would soon find himself dangling at the working end of the rope? Was it a young man who had deserted the army in the face of the enemy? Was it a soldier that had raped or murdered a local civilian? Was it someone who had committed the relatively insignificant crime of foraging supplies from the wrong farmer?

Jacob quickly moved to the front of his Pennsylvanians and began organizing his men into some semblance of a military formation. For all of their bravery and impressive performance on the battlefield, his men still chomped at the bit when ordered to conduct themselves in formal military manner – it was simply not in their nature to do so, at least not yet. But given a minute or two and the copious cursing of the senior enlisted men, the 4th Pennsylvania was soon standing tall and proud amongst the many other units of the Continental Army who anxiously awaited the answer to everyone's question: who was the unlucky bastard today?

The steady beat of a drum could be heard in the distance, and all the orders and cursing in the world couldn't prevent nearly every man from craning his neck in the direction of the sound. Even Jacob found himself unable to resist the temptation of sneaking a glance in the direction of the drum.

At first little could be discerned, as all that was visible was a small group of men trudging purposefully toward the formation. As the group got closer, it became apparent that several guards had been formed in a circle around someone marching in their middle, but the identity of that individual was still unknown. Eventually the group made its way to the center of the formation, and the guards parted in order to reveal their ultimate victim. A collective gasp escaped from thousands of men, as their eyes gazed on the object of their conjecture.

A young man, perhaps no more than his mid-twenties, walked calmly in the direction of the oak tree just a few paces away. The source of the surprise from the soldiers was due to the fact that this young man was wearing the uniform of a British officer!

The young British officer, flanked on either side by an armed American soldier, looked neither to the left nor to the right as the trio made their way to the base of the oak tree. His face might have been set in stone, so steady and severe was his countenance. Despite what this man might have been feeling inside, his appearance gave away not the slightest hint of fear. Despite the fact that his hands were tied firmly behind his back, he still managed to carry himself with an air of authority that nearly prompted many of the enlisted men in ranks to render him a well-deserved salute.

An American colonel was standing just off to the side of the noose, which was hanging eight or nine feet from the ground. Directly under the noose was a small table, predictably for the condemned man to stand on just prior to his ultimate demise. In his right hand the colonel was holding a set of orders, which every man knew contained the final answer to the mystery of who this man was, and what he had done to deserve such a cruel fate.

Once again the lone drummer took up his tight staccato beat, as the young British officer stepped onto the small table at the behest of the two armed escorts. One of the escorts then joined him on the table as the noose was fitted around his neck and briskly tightened to fit snugly. Just as before, the young man showed no fear – in fact, he continued to show no emotion at all, despite the fact that he was obviously nearing the moment of his death.

The American colonel moved to the front and center of the formation of troops, and cleared his throat loudly as he unwrapped the set of orders he was about to read. Despite his best efforts, the colonel was clearly uncomfortable with what he was about to do, and those that were closest could see a visible shaking of the man's hands as he began to speak.

"Be it known to all members of the Continental Army of the United States, that this man before you now; known as Lieutenant Corbin Wallingford of His Majesty's British Army – also known as Lieutenant Corbin Wallingford, formerly of the Continental Army – "

The colonel was forced to stop speaking as the astonished murmur that went up throughout the assembled men was loud enough to drown out his voice. With that first sentence, the mystery of the identity of the condemned man had been solved. But there was more to hear – what had this man done that warranted his hanging? The act of changing from the American to the British side was a relatively common event, albeit a disturbing one. Why had this man been singled out to pay the ultimate price for that decision?

The colonel, gradually gaining control of his emotions, cast a disapproving glance throughout the ranks that surrounded him. The soldiers took their cue, and quickly became silent.

" - shall be hanged until dead by the order of the Commanding General for committing the following acts of treason:

"On or about the 7th of July in the year of our Lord 1777, Lieutenant Wallingford, at the time serving as an officer in the British Army, did betray the identity of one Lieutenant Samuel Colburn, an officer and scout of the Continental Army, to the enemy. This was an act of cowardice and treason that resulted in the hanging death of Lieutenant Colburn, and was in direct violation of the accepted conduct and ethics of war."

Once again, the volume of response from the men compelled the colonel to pause briefly before he continued his reading of the charges.

"Furthermore, on the evening of the 20th of September in the year of our Lord 1777, Lieutenant Wallingford, again serving as an officer in the British Army, did serve as a guide to the enemy in leading the cowardly ambush on the American troops camped near Paoli. Lieutenant Wallingford willfully utilized his knowledge of the surrounding area to propagate an attack on the troops at that location, which resulted in the brutal massacre of over 50 American soldiers."

This revelation prompted absolute silence from the troops. The sheer treachery of this act left even the most talkative soldier completely speechless, as the magnitude of this man's actions became clear to everyone. Even the softest heart was instantly hardened, as men silently recalled the names and faces of those who would never again sit around the campfire, their lives brutally snuffed out on that fateful night. The fact that the event had occurred just a few weeks before made these memories that much more painful.

"As a result of the treachery that Lieutenant Wallingford has willingly displayed toward these men, this army, and this country, and the deaths that can be lain directly at his feet, I hereby order Lieutenant Corbin Wallingford to be hanged by the neck until dead. Signed, George Washington, Commanding General, the Continental Army of the United States of America."

The colonel folded the orders, looked toward the condemned man, and gave an almost imperceptible nod to the two escorts. It was clear that Wallingford was to be shown no mercy in the form of a blindfold, and was not to be given the general courtesy of making any last remarks. This execution was to be quick and brutal. With that, the two men grasped either end of the table upon which Lieutenant Wallingford was standing, and yanked it firmly from beneath him.

The moment suddenly took on that quality of seeming to move in slow motion, as the man dropped the few feet toward the ground before the slack of the rope had been expended. With a slight jerk, the body bounced upwards a short distance before finally settling into place. The man's face took on a grisly appearance, as the eyes nearly bulged out of the head, and the tongue protruded grotesquely out of the gaping mouth. Despite the earlier calm resolve of Lieutenant Wallingford, the creature that now dangled at the end of the rope had lost all semblance of dignity and humanity. The legs began kicking uncontrollably in a vain attempt to attach themselves to something firm. An awful stench emanated from the body as the dying man's bowels involuntarily released themselves.

Many of the men were unable to watch the scene taking place before them and turned away. Others, equally appalled at what they were observing, were simply unable to do the same, taken by some macabre sense of fascination.

Finally – mercifully – after perhaps two minutes had elapsed, the body had ceased its death throes and had come to a final resting position. The body twirled back and forth at the end of the rope, allowing the men standing in every direction the opportunity to see the now bloated, purple mask that had until recently been the handsome face of a young man.

—

From a distance of perhaps a hundred yards, General George Washington sat astride his horse and observed the results of his orders. Many officers had applauded the General for his stern discipline, congratulating Washington that he was doing, as one officer had stated, "what a good Commanding General must do." To Washington, this was perhaps one of the worst orders he had ever been forced to give. He despised himself for writing the orders, yet he knew it was what had to be done. This revelation was of no consolation as he watched the tragedy unfold before him.

At least Washington had spared those still naively innocent of the horrors of war from having to endure the scene. Three young children, probably no more than ten or eleven years old at the most, had come from a nearby farmhouse to see what all the stir was about. General Washington had prudently placed himself and his horse in such a position that it had blocked the view of the youngsters, thus sparing them from almost certain nightmares. They had complained at first, but Washington's stern gaze cast down upon them from high upon his mount had quickly silenced the children. They had turned away sullenly, and plodded silently back to their home.

—

Thus ended a tragic chapter of the war – a war that had started out as nothing more than an insurrection by a small number of disgruntled men and women. And while it had since grown to have international implications, it was still truly defined by the individual scenes that had just been played out on a small farm in rural Pennsylvania. This scene was either an example of heroism or treachery, depending on which side of the battle lines you stood.

BRIGADIER GENERAL FRANCIS NASH
OCTOBER 8, 1777
TOWAMENCIN TOWNSHIP, PENNSYLVANIA

The conditions that had been arranged for the wounded and dying men was as good as could be expected. After all, it was simply a small house that had been transformed into a hospital, a term that could only be used in the most generous sense. The few actual doctors that were available had long since passed the point of exhaustion, as their skills had been in constant demand for over four straight days since the beginning of the battle at Germantown. In addition to these surgeons there were a number of volunteers, many of them women, who moved throughout the soldiers providing whatever means of physical comfort they could with the meager resources that were available.

The previous occupants of the house, the Gotwals family, had moved out almost immediately upon the arrival of the army. While the family was willing to make the significant sacrifice of turning over their home for use as a hospital, they simply didn't have the stomach for experiencing what that actually meant. Few people did.

Now that several days had passed since the battle, the doctors had begun the process of separating the men into more manageable groups. Those that were well on their way to recovery were either placed outside on the lawn, or were sent back to their units where they could complete their convalescence. Those that still required continued attention and assistance were kept on the main floor of the house, where they were closest to the food, water, and medical supplies. For those men that occupied the rooms on the upper floor, their surroundings were almost certainly the last thing they would ever see. These rooms were filled primarily with either head or stomach wounds, or men who had begun to succumb to the infections that had developed in their bodies, a plague that continued to puzzle and frustrate even the most skilled physicians.

—

In the largest bedroom on the second floor, Brigadier General Francis

Nash was lying in extreme discomfort, a fact he believed he had kept from those that tended to his wounds. Unknown to him was the fact that the doctors and volunteers had seen more than their share of men bravely and quietly dealing with their pain – they were all well aware of what Nash was going through. And while everyone was doing everything that could possibly be done for the young general, it did little to ease the physical burden on Nash, or the psychological burden on his caretakers.

All of the furniture had been taken out of the room in order to allow more men to fit into what was still a confined space. As a rather poor replacement for the comfort of a bed, the men had been placed on piles of hay which were then covered by a single thin sheet. Francis Nash was currently resting on his fourth bed of hay, the first three having been replaced after they had been completely soaked through with his blood.

Lying next to Nash was a young lieutenant with whom he had been having a sporadic conversation over the last few hours. The lieutenant had previously been lapsing in and out of consciousness, but he appeared to be taking a turn for the better. The interactions between the two men had become more frequent, and the lieutenant was becoming visibly stronger. Nash could tell this through the tone of the man's voice, as well as the clarity that had returned to his eyes. As a result, Nash was not surprised when one of the female volunteers – who was obviously enamored with the handsome lieutenant – had come into the room and informed the man that he was about to be moved down to the first floor of the house. It was bittersweet news to Nash. He was obviously happy for the man, as this was a clear indication that his prognosis had dramatically improved in the opinions of the doctors. But it saddened Nash in that he would miss the company he was just starting to enjoy. None of the other men in the room around him were in any condition to carry on anything that even closely resembled a lucid conversation. In addition, it forced Nash to confront the reality that this was a room from which he himself would never depart.

"Well, Lieutenant, it appears as if you and I will have to continue our conversation at a later date," Nash commented, making every effort to conceal his disappointment. He had no desire to make the young man feel guilty about the fact that at least one of them was leaving in a condition other than having a sheet draped permanently over them.

"Yes sir, it appears so," replied the lieutenant. "It has been an honor to have had the opportunity to get to know such a fine officer as yourself. While I've obviously never had the privilege of speaking with you before, I know many of the men in your command. They have always spoken highly of you not only as a general, but as a truly considerate person, if I may say so, sir."

"You most certainly may say so, Lieutenant, although I fear there have been times when my orders were not received by my men with quite the popularity as your kind comments may suggest. After all, the job of a General is to win battles, not popularity contests."

Nash immediately regretted making the comment, fearing it might be perceived by the young man as a reprimand. He meant it in no such way; he was merely attempting to divert the compliment away from himself. Nash had never been particularly adept at graciously receiving praise, whether it came from the Commanding General or from the lowest Private in his command. This fact had always been a source of amusement to those around him, as men had watched the general squirm in a most uncomfortable manner when placed in that situation – a situation which had, in fact, occurred on quite a number of occasions.

But the lieutenant was unaware of this history, and forged ahead without the slightest hesitation.

"Yes sir, that may be true. But you have been one of the members of this army almost from the very start. Because of generals like you – because of men like you – we are becoming a fighting force that the British cannot simply brush to the side and continue to pursue their own treacherous goals. I cannot profess to be a soldier of great experience, sir, but even I can sense that we as an army are at a crossroads."

Nash raised himself up painfully on his elbows and looked directly at the young man.

"A crossroads? In what sense do you mean, Lieutenant?"

"Sir, if we continue to have the leadership that is required, our resolve will only grow. If our resolve continues to grow, then so will our abilities to fight and win this war. You, sir, are the foundation of that leadership."

For perhaps the first time in his military career, Brigadier General Francis Nash was completely comfortable with the gracious comments that were being made about him. He was comfortable with these comments because he knew, without any doubt, that they were being made with absolute sincerity by this young, inexperienced officer. And he also knew, without a doubt, that the comments were accurate. He realized, with a startling suddenness, that this fact made him completely at peace with what the very near future held for him.

"Lieutenant," Nash joked weakly, "if I didn't know better, I would assume that you were bucking for a promotion." But the mild humor did nothing to prevent the tears from forming in his eyes.

"Promotion! Good Lord, no sir! When I first joined this army a few weeks ago, my best friend, Lieutenant Jacob Landes told me that I had no business wearing a uniform! I realize now that he only said that as a means of motivating me to be a better soldier. I truly hope that transformation has taken place to at least a small degree."

Nash could feel his strength continuing to leave him, as the simple act of sitting upright was becoming difficult. His body told him it was time to lay back down, but his mind refused to comply.

"Your friend is a wise man, Lieutenant," Nash said. "I would suggest you keep him close by in the future. And that future, Lieutenant, belongs to you and your friend, and other soldiers like you. I appreciate your acknowledgment of what I have attempted to do for our country, as so many others have done as well. But now, it is your turn. I have given all that I can, and I only hope that it has been enough. It is up to young officers and men like you to continue the struggle for our freedom."

The young lieutenant appeared suddenly startled, as the reality of what Nash was saying hit home. He moved over and sat next to Nash on the floor.

"General Nash, please don't speak that way, sir! There is more for you to do, and in a few days you'll be able to do it. Men like you cannot simply be replaced by someone who simply walks up and – "

"Lieutenant, please. Don't you know better than to argue with a General?" Nash said with a smile. "I have no fear of what lies ahead for me. I face whatever the good Lord has planned with a light heart, and a great confidence. And you, Lieutenant, have helped me to realize that."

Nash allowed himself to lay back down on his bed of hay, soaked through yet again with his life blood. But he maintained his gaze on the young man.

"Lieutenant, I have had the pleasure of getting to know you without ever having the decency of asking your name."

The young man, now blinking back tears of his own, took a deep breath and addressed the man lying on his deathbed in front of him. His voice took on a tone of strength and resolve as he addressed Nash.

"My name, sir, is Michael Sweeney. Lieutenant Michael Sweeney of the Continental Army of the United States."

—

Lieutenant Michael Sweeney from Pennsylvania would never continue his conversation with Brigadier General Francis Nash from North Carolina. Later that day, General Nash would die in the bedroom of the Gotwals house, having painfully bled to death over a period of four days.

On October 9, 1777, Francis Nash, along with several other American officers killed at the Battle of Germantown, was laid to rest at the Towamencin Mennonite Meetinghouse Cemetery in Towamencin Township, Pennsylvania. The funeral service was attended by hundreds of officers and men from Nash's unit, as well as many other brigades outside of his own. Apparently, Francis Nash had earned the respect and admiration of more men than he would ever know.

One of Nash's closest friends, whom Nash had served with since the beginning of the war, was asked to make a few comments about his fallen comrade. In a speech filled with tears and pathetic attempts to remain firm, General Nash's friend described the years of service, and the many fine deeds which could be attributed to the young general. He concluded by stating in a voice choked with emotion, "Francis Nash was one of the most enlightened, liberal, and magnanimous gentlemen that ever sacrificed his life for his country."

There was a distinct scarcity of dry eyes in the crowd; and not a single man would even think to dispute the statements made about this general from North Carolina.

GENERAL GEORGE WASHINGTON
OCTOBER 9, 1777
TOWAMENCIN TOWNSHIP, PENNSYLVANIA

George Washington was unable to remember a time at which he felt so completely exhausted. Despite the fact that his army had been encamped for the better part of a week, Washington had found it nearly impossible to get anything even closely resembling a prolonged period of rest and recuperation.

At least, Washington mused to himself, when you were in the thick of a battle, you could focus on dealing with that one thing in front of you. However, when the army was in camp the Commanding General was tasked with balancing the priorities of the army, the government, and the local population. At least the army was forced to follow the orders he gave, he acknowledged with grim amusement. The other two, not nearly so much.

Despite the fact that Washington had placed his army a good distance from the current location of the British and had established a rather rigorous system of patrols in a wide arc around his camp, he still knew that he was never truly safe from an attack. He also realized that his current location was not the ideal spot to set up anything permanent in the way of defenses, and that he would eventually need to relocate his army to a spot that afforded a distant view of what might be approaching. In addition, this future semi-permanent winter headquarters must offer topography that was conducive to entrenching a somewhat battered and tired fighting force.

To that end, Washington had dispatched several of his engineering officers to locate such a position, and provide Washington with a detailed overview of the potential strengths and weaknesses of moving the army there. While the engineers had already come back to the general with several possibilities, the location that appeared to hold the most promise was a nearby area the locals referred to as Valley Forge.

—

The sun had set several minutes before, as the darkness of the approaching evening spread itself over the camp. Numerous fires had started to appear, as the men began to prepare themselves to deal with the constantly lowering nighttime temperatures of the Pennsylvania autumn. While winter was still a number of weeks away, if one listened carefully you could clearly hear its stealthy, chilling approach. And while the cold weather generally provided a break from the fighting as both armies pulled in their claws, another enemy quickly took its place. Disease, starvation, and exposure could exact a toll on an army that far outweighed the violence imposed by the cannon and muskets of one's enemy.

Washington had been enjoying a rare moment of solitude sitting by a small campfire that had been prepared for him by his staff. So lost in thought had the general been, that he had failed to notice the approach of his Military Secretary, Colonel Robert Harrison.

"Begging the General's pardon," Colonel Harrison began respectfully, "you may wish to know, sir, that your dinner is waiting for you in your tent. As the General has not eaten since early this morning, I thought you might be hungry, sir."

The sudden rumbling in his stomach caused by that overlooked revelation confirmed that he was, indeed, ready to partake in whatever food might be available. The quality of that food was often poor to say the least, and it pained Washington to realize that if the Commanding General's food was bad, he could only imagine the disgusting fare that would be provided to the average soldier.

"Thank you, Colonel, I shall eat in just a few minutes," Washington responded. "But first, would you join me by the fire?"

Colonel Harrison had been asked to share the company of the Commanding General on any number of occasions. After all, the nature of his duties as Military Secretary made it necessary for Washington to often dictate orders to Harrison. But Harrison sensed that this most recent request had less of a ring of formality, and he was pleased that he was being invited to simply provide company to the general. Even after all this time, Harrison continued to be in awe of the man sitting before him, as he knew many others were as well.

Harrison chose to sit on a small camp stool located on the opposite side of the small fire, a position which maintained the respectful distance commensurate with his role as a subordinate. He settled himself as comfortably as he could, preparing for the lengths of silence that often defined an audience with George Washington. The General tended to think things through before he spoke, a habit which often resulted in extended gaps in the conversation. Those unfamiliar with Washington's communication style sometimes found this to be awkward and uncomfortable. Harrison had long since become accustomed to his Commander's quirk, and had even found himself engaging in similar behavior. After all, the purest form of flattery is imitation.

"Colonel," Washington began after a minute or two, "this army has endured as much suffering and humiliation as any army in history. They have been routed and bayoneted by the enemy. They have witnessed their own government virtually turn its back on them with respect to supplies, arms, and the meager compensation they so richly deserve. They have even had the people of the very country they are fighting to establish turn against them and aid the enemy."

Washington's eyes had never left the fire, and Harrison knew that the General was talking as much to himself as he was to his companion. The Secretary remained silent, his gaze also fixed on the flames in front of him.

"We have fought three major engagements in the short span of just the last few weeks. Three engagements against an enemy that, by all military logic, should have wiped us off the face of the earth!"

Harrison looked up with surprise at the General. Although what he was saying was absolutely the truth, Harrison had never actually heard Washington acknowledge that reality. While others had referred to the superiority of the British, Washington had maintained a constant, almost stubborn façade that reflected the belief and confidence he had in his men. It was one of the many traits that caused soldiers to be willing to follow this man, even against seemingly impossible odds.

"And yet, sir, your army remains camped all around you as we speak. They are as ready as they have ever been to continue this war," Harrison said with just a trace of defensiveness in his voice. After all, he was part of this army as well.

"That is exactly my point, Robert," Washington said forcefully, referring to his Secretary by his first name for perhaps the only time in their relationship. "What motivates these men? What keeps them away from their families for months, sometimes years at a time? Eating food that is nearly impossible to ingest! Suffering indignities that are nearly impossible to endure! Fighting for a cause that is nearly impossible to define!"

Washington's shoulders slumped, the quintessential figure of a man who was physically and emotionally exhausted. When he continued to speak, it was in the quiet, tired voice of a man who needed to sleep.

"My mind tells me that we have no chance of winning this war. My experience and logic insist that this is true. But my heart and soul is certain not only that we *can* win this war, but that we *must* win this war. I have been witness to - these last few weeks - a glimpse of freedom. The battles we fought along the Brandywine Creek, at Paoli, and at Germantown have shown me what is possible for this army and for this country."

Washington looked into the eyes of the man sitting across from him, and saw a fire reflected there that had nothing to do with the flames at their feet. Washington smiled with satisfaction, knowing that there was at least one other man that shared his certain vision.

"Let us retire to get some rest, Colonel Harrison. Tomorrow begins the next chapter in what will eventually be a truly memorable history. But there is much work to be done before that time."

"Indeed, sir," Harrison replied simply as he stood up, turned, and disappeared into the gathering darkness.

© Black Rose Writing

CPSIA information can be obtained at www.ICGtesting.com
Printed in the USA
LVOW121810290812

296537LV00005B/99/P